The Alpha Chronicles

By

Joe Nobody

ISBN 978-0615844930

Edited by:
E. T. Ivester

Contributors:

D. A. L. H.
D. Allen

www.HoldingYourGround.com

Published by

www.PrepperPress.com

This is a work of fiction. Characters and events are products of the author's imagination, and no relationship to any living person is implied. The locations, facilities, and geographical references are set in a fictional environment.

Other Books by Joe Nobody:

- **Holding Your Ground: Preparing for Defense if it All Falls Apart**
- **The TEOTWAWKI Tuxedo: Formal Survival Attire**
- **Without Rule of Law: Advanced Skill to Help You Survive**
- **Holding Their Own: A Story of Survival**
- **Holding Their Own II: The Independents**
- **Holding Their Own III: Pedestals of Ash**
- **Holding Their Own IV: The Ascent**
- **The Home Schooled Shootist: Training to Fight with a Carbine**
- **Apocalypse Drift**

Fort Bliss
El Paso
Fort
Stockdale
Midland Station
Alpha
Beltran Ranch
Meraton
Preston

Prologue

Nine years before the collapse...

A shudder traveled through the airframe, a sure prediction of the pain to come. Despite 90 pounds of kit, ammunition, and weaponry, Bishop felt his backside lift off the inflexible, aluminum bench, the ascent partially restrained by the straps crisscrossing his chest. Gravity regained control as the wings found air, promptly slamming him back down with spine-compressing force. *That wasn't as bad as the last two*, he thought. *Things are looking up.*

Across the aisle, Spider began rubbing his jaw, a grimace on his face. "I think that one knocked a filling loose," he shouted over the steady drone of the engines.

"Bullshit," Bishop grinned, "You don't *have* any teeth."

His friend never managed a comeback - the effort interrupted by another shudder, freefall, and kinetic re-acquaintance with the bench. Spider remained silent, evidently deciding it wasn't worth the effort.

The ancient, rattletrap Lockheed L-100 cargo plane had achieved wheels-up three hours ago, the two South African pilots' sobriety as questionable as the airworthiness of the craft. Somehow, the four-fan trashcan had managed to stay airborne – so far.

They were four days behind schedule, and Bishop wondered if that hadn't affected the decision to fly. Wave after wave of monsoon thunderheads were pounding Central Africa, the weather unconcerned with the urgency of their mission. A short time ago, a gap appeared – a break in the pattern that management deemed wide enough to attempt flight. The order to mount up given, the 11-man team had boarded the plane, most of them happy to just be doing *something*.

Now, Bishop was questioning the wisdom of the decision. While he had been as bored as anyone at the remote airfield, becoming a bloody splat on some remote jungle floor didn't seem like the better option. Shudder... freefall... pain.

He didn't like the helpless feeling. The dark, coffin-like interior of the cargo hold was cramped, windowless, and smelled of old oil and nervous sweat. Fighting down a welling sense of claustrophobia, he forced his mind to review the pre-mission briefing held seven days ago.

The Colonel had begun by addressing a large team of personnel, hastily gathered at the HBR security center in Houston. Providing the background first, he informed the group that HBR had contracted to explore for oil and natural gas in central Africa. The company had shipped newly developed, top secret, seismic technology for the job. A screw-up in scheduling allowed the equipment to arrive in country before the Colonel's security forces, and the extremely valuable machinery had disappeared.

Three days later, word had spread throughout the energy community that the hijacked merchandise was for sale to the highest bidder. HBR had spent hundreds of millions of dollars on research and development of the new toys, and desperately wanted the property back.

"There's no local government functioning in the area," briefed the Colonel. "The region has been in absolute chaos for 25 years. Coups, civil war, corruption, and organized crime have dominated the local politics. A man named Ditto Ombomtu has surfaced as the ringleader. Mr. Ombomtu is quite the colorful figure."

The Colonel lifted a sheet of paper from the conference table and began reading. "International wire fraud, embezzlement, prostitution, blackmail, narcotics, kidnapping, slavery, extortion - the list goes on and on. Clearly, our friend Ditto is an active local businessman. He is wanted by our FBI, Interpol, and numerous other law enforcement agencies around the globe."

During the Colonel's pause, Bishop lifted his hand for a question. The Colonel acknowledged the gesture with a nod. "Sir, does the charge of international wire fraud mean this is the guy filling up my inbox with all of those emails claiming to be from the Nigerian Central Bank, or an African prince or whatever?"

The Colonel grinned at Bishop's question, "Why yes, it does, Bishop. I see here on this report that Mr. Ombomtu runs one of the largest internet spamming sites in the world. I'm sure we've all received solicitations from this man."

"I want the kill shot, sir," Bishop retorted, his tone indicating the request was only partially tongue-in-cheek.

The roomful of operators erupted in laughter, which was quickly followed by others competing for the privilege of ensuring Mr. Ombomtu's demise, some of the men being very creative how the criminal should die.

The Colonel was a wise and experienced leader, allowing the interruption and follow-on banter to continue for a short period before clearing his throat. The room immediately fell silent.

"While I know you weren't completely serious, Bishop, I want to make it clear that there will be *no* kill shot. HBR needs Mr. Ombomtu alive and talking. He's probably the only person who knows where our equipment is located, and management wants that technology back. Your mission is a snatch-and-grab only. Do I make myself understood?"

Every man acknowledged with a crisp, "Yes, sir."

The Colonel surveyed the room, making eye contact with each individual. "The reason why I'm sending so many men on this mission is because we need this man alive and chirping like a bird. Unless you come across our goods, bring him back breathing. I'll take care of his debriefing, *personally*. I promise everyone here that Mr. Ombomtu *will not* enjoy my interview."

Shudder... freefall... pain. Bishop shivered, recalling the Colonel's tone of voice. He wouldn't want to be in Mr. Ombomtu's skin if the team took him alive.

Movement at the front of the plane drew Bishop's attention. Sitting directly behind the pilots, he observed the team's leader speaking with the aviators in the cockpit. Word quickly passed down the line – 10 minutes.

The man running the show was a large British chap who everyone called Stoke - the name derived from the fellow's unwavering loyalty to the Stoke City football club back home in England. Ex-British Special Air Services and HBR's expert on the Dark Continent, Stoke was both well-liked and respected by everyone at the company. There were even rumors that he would take the Colonel's position, should the current head honcho ever decide to retire.

The plane began executing a gut-scrambling descent through a narrowing gap, the reforming monsoon closing in rapidly on all sides. Every man aboard believed he was going to die. When the plane finally came to rest on terra-firma, Bishop disembarked on shaky legs and immediately turned to study the undercarriage.

"What's the matter?" Spider asked.

"I can't believe this bitch still has wheels after that landing. I think the captain should change his name to Hop-along Cassidy," Bishop replied, shaking his head.

The cloudburst resumed exactly three minutes after boots were on the ground.

Within an hour of their arrival, the absolute best technology available to the modern light-fighter was rendered ineffective by the jungle, at least in regards to foul weather gear. Synthetic wicking materials were overwhelmed first, quickly followed by rivulets of rain discovering every conceivable nook, seam, and opening in the team's ponchos, load vests, and packs. Waterproof boots quickly became buckets, filled from the top by the constant flow of rain seeping in from the top. Before they could even form up to move out, the operators fell victim to a two-dimensional soak, outside from precipitation and inside by perspiration.

It wasn't long before the equipment began to fail as well. Fog-proof optics, watertight battery compartments, and all-weather electronics had evidently never been tested in environments such as the central African jungle, especially during monsoon season. About the only thing that functioned normally was the constant stream of creative cursing spouted by the frustrated team. The eruption of vile language mimicked the dialect of the rain – steady and unrelenting.

Two days later, tucked in a shadowy nook of heavy foliage and shrouded by drooping ferns, only the whites of Bishop's eyes were visible. The carefully applied layer of brown and green camouflage face paint was redundant now, completely covered by 48 hours' worth of mud and grime. The soaked brim of his bush hat sagged from the weight of precipitation, a condition due to Bishop's sweat and the never-ending inundation from the sky.

He was studying what was essentially a trail - a path that had transformed into a muddy creek. In its current, semi-submerged state, it was practically impossible to determine if the route was used by two or four-legged animals. The operator was only interested in the former.

Bishop was as miserable as he could ever remember. Every inch of his body hurt, itched, ached, or had been chaffed raw from the constant exposure to water and salt. His feet and hands were crinkly like a kid playing in the bathtub for too long. His skin was peeling off in large chunks, leaving red, irritated flesh beneath. Even breathing was difficult, every inhalation of the heavy air requiring twice the normal effort.

Sensing his partner's presence behind him and convinced the trail was unoccupied, Bishop turned to Spider and whispered, "I'm thinking of a number."

Spider's brow furled, the movement of skin causing small flecks of filth to run down his cheeks. "What the fuck are you talking about?"

"I'm thinking of a number. Guess what it is."

"Now how the fuck should I know what number you're thinking of? Do I look clairvoyant or some shit?"

Bishop grunted and shook his head. "You shouldn't use words like that, Spider. It'll ruin your carefully crafted warrior image."

"How 'bout I enhance my image by issuing you a fully crafted ass whooping when we get back to civilization and dry clothes?"

Bishop ignored the threat and continued. "The number 100 keeps flashing through my head. One hundred degrees. One hundred percent humidity. One hundred percent fucked up place to be, and I'm one hundred percent sure this is the right trail."

Spider's eyes widened, and then he moved to spy over Bishop's shoulder at the muddy path beyond. After a minute of study, he turned and inquired, "What's so different about this one compared to the last three? They all look the same to me."

Bishop extended his shotgun, the condom tipped barrel slowly lowering a stem so both men could see the trail. "Look there... at the edge... six inches from the rock. Do you see that oddly shaped impression?"

Spider studied the area for a moment and finally nodded. "So?

That could be anything. I don't get it."

Bishop scanned up and down the trail, making sure the route was still unoccupied. Using slow, deliberate body movements, he stood and ventured closer to the track. He removed the shotgun's sling from his shoulder and grasped the weapon by the barrel, holding the stock above the muddy indention. The hole was a perfect fit for the butt of a weapon. He smiled at a surprised Spider before returning to his concealment.

"That don't mean shit. That hole could've been made by anything."

"Go look *in* the hole."

Spider threw his friend a questioning glance, which was quickly answered by Bishop pointing with his head and mouthing the words, "Go on."

Spider moved to Bishop's side and then crawled a few feet through the mud to study the impression. When he was close enough, he could see the rainbow colors of an oil slick residing on the surface of the puddled water inside.

Sliding back to their hide, Spider glared at Bishop and hissed, "So?"

Bishop rolled his eyes, his partner's stubbornness grating on his nerves. He took the stock of his shotgun and pushed the butt into the ground between the two men. Reaching to a nearby palm, he pulled the branch downward until the water beading on the surface ran into the newly created impression. A clearly visible oil slick appeared on the surface.

Spider's eyes grew wide with disbelief. "What the fuck," he whispered.

"Anybody who carries a weapon in this weather has to coat it with a gallon of oil. Hell, we're practically giving our own blasters a lube-bath every few hours. Besides, picture yourself trudging down that path."

Bishop paused and pointed to the slowly flowing water. Using the scattergun's barrel, he indicated a disturbance on the surface. "There's probably a big rock or submerged branch causing that ripple. If you were wandering along, carrying your rifle and tripped right there, that imprint is right where you would have used the weapon to prevent your fall. A rifle-cane. Now, de-fuck that pessimistic bullshit, and let's get back and tell the others – I'm sure."

Spider checked the scene one more time and shook his head before turning to follow his friend back to their camp.

The two scouts approached carefully, signaling the sentry that they were friendlies. After clearing a small rise in the jungle floor, Bishop and Spider entered the temporary bivouac.

A small cluster of HBR personnel huddled under a makeshift tarp, the mud-splattered group making a futile attempt to stay dry. There wasn't any fire, a consequence of every burnable molecule of fuel for 100 miles being soaked to the core. The men were using the brief rest to clean equipment, partake of the gourmet MRE, and wring out wet socks - anything to make their soggy existence more palatable.

"Welcome back to the Four Seasons South, lads. What have you got for me?" Stoke greeted.

Bishop took a knee, unfolded a plastic map of the area, and pointed. "We found their trail here, sir. I'm sure armed men passed through the area no more than an hour ago. I believe they are headed up the mountain. The trail ran at 340 degrees magnetic for as far as we could see."

Stoke rubbed his chin and nodded. "Makes sense, doesn't it? Didn't our satellite photos show an abandoned village on this side of the mountain?"

Spider cleared his throat and asked, "Do you think they've hidden the equipment at the village, Stoke?"

"No lad, I think HBR's precious trinkets are probably well on their way to some coastal port by now. They'll be shipped to a facility where a clever fellow in a lab coat can reverse-engineer our technology. There's no way we'll get it back unless we find the mastermind of the heist."

Bishop folded his map and tucked it into his chest rig. "Stoke, what are the chances this Mr. Ombomtu will give up without a fight? I mean, it's not as if the guy is leading a revolution or working for a government. He's just a greedy businessman from what I can tell."

Stoke looked Bishop in the eye and then smiled. "Private enterprises are the worst ones, Bishop. I'd much prefer to tangle with rebels or rogue military units – they're only motivated by honor or loyalty to a cause. Now a corporation…well…that's bad news. A company is always the worst enemy to fight. To them, it's not personal; it's simply business. Removing emotion from the leadership of any conflict makes it bloodier."

Bishop was skeptical. "Really? I would have thought religious fanatics would be the worst. Hell, I would have guessed corporations would be the pussies on the grand scale of thug nasty."

Shaking his head, Stoke rested his hand on Bishop's shoulder. "Think about lawsuits and hostile takeovers, lad. Brutal… absolutely brutal. I've read stories about businesses bankrupting themselves, fighting to the death. Money without a conscience is the root of all evil."

Stoke turned and began rousting the men. "Time to hutch up now, you blokes. We have a job to do, and I'm filly with being damp. Move along now, lads. This isn't Her Majesty's Royal Gardening Society."

Groans, muttered curses, and assorted griping ensued. Spider decided to help and added, "Come on, you lazy fucks. People back home pay a butt-full of money for a trip to the waterpark. Hell, we've not only got water, but mud and 20 varieties of poisonous snakes, too! This op's like a vacation to a health spa and zoo combined. Shit, we're even blessed with foot-long centipedes."

Spider's logic met with some verbal feedback, including one operator grabbing his crotch and taunting, "Hey, Spider! I've got yer foot-long… right HERE!"

Stoke ordered the column to move out, Bishop taking his place at the front, off-center to the right, and 100 feet in front of the main body of contractors. Sensing, more than seeing, he knew Spider would keep even with him, but to the left. The formation moved forward like a pitchfork missing its middle prong.

The unit hadn't traveled more than 50 steps when the rain suddenly stopped. Bishop didn't realize it at first, the runoff cascading down through the canopy above for several more minutes. Shortly after, the sun shone brightly, lighting the jungle floor through small peepholes of light in the dense vegetation above.

The men's initial reaction to the change in weather was positive - for about an hour. After days of precipitation, the subtropical sun turned the super-saturated terrain into a steam bath of misery. Waves of moist heat rose from the jungle surface, unwelcome by men burdened by heavy, saturated clothing and humping packs often weighing in excess of 100 pounds.

The suffering was made worse by their destination, the now-abandoned village requiring a climb of 4,000 feet along the incline of some unnamed mountain. Bishop could think of several names for the hill that was causing his legs to cramp, most of the labels unfit to be printed on any map.

With his shotgun in his left hand and a razor sharp machete swinging from his right, he cut his way through some of the thickest undergrowth he'd ever seen. "This is no place for a boy from West Texas," he mumbled to himself.

Bishop peered out from under the jungle foliage at a completely altered landscape. The dense, triple-canopy above had begun thinning as the column gradually worked its way up an ever-steeper incline. As the altitude increased, Bishop noted two distinctive changes. The first was the undergrowth; most of the diminishing plant life now tinted an earthy brown rather than the viscoid entanglement of emerald-green they had struggled through for miles. The second variation was an increased difficulty in catching his breath, the thinner air containing less oxygen.

As if some mighty God had drawn a line on the side of the mountain and dared the vegetation to cross his mark, the jungle suddenly ceased. The tropical bush was replaced by waist-high, mud-colored grass covering the mountain's slope.

Any drastic change in surroundings dictated a stop. Knowing it would be a few minutes before the main group caught up to his position, Bishop took the opportunity to drop his pack. The relief experienced after removing the heavy kit was practically orgasmic.

Since combat in a jungle environment is often close up and personal, Bishop had selected a 12-gauge, automatic shotgun for the mission. The weapon was devastating within 75 yards, but lost effectiveness at long distance encounters. Scanning the open, prairie-like landscape in front of him, he expected Stoke to reassign him from a scouting role back to the main formation. Wide-open spaces required the point man to have a longer-range weapon. Still, he had packed a few dozen slugs, and they would extend his capabilities if it came to a fight. He decided to use the time to replace the seven rounds of buckshot with a mixed load, every other shell being a one ounce, solid plug of lead. The operators called the process "candy striping."

Just as he finished reloading, the main body arrived. Stoke took a knee beside Bishop and scanned the open grasslands. "Any movement?"

"No, sir. I've not seen any sign of life other than a few birds."

Nodding, the Brit turned to the men and announced, "We'll hold up here until dark. You've got two hours. Make the best of it. Red, you've got the first watch."

No one wasted any time dropping packs and removing chest rigs and harnesses. While the team had to stay in thick bush to provide cover, occasional patches of sunlight penetrated the canopy overhead. Bishop had to laugh as he walked by one such island of solar warmth. Four pairs of white, prune-wrinkled feet protruded into the pool of brightness, the smarter men knowing healthy feet improved their chances of surviving. Bishop wasted no time in joining the foot-drying party.

There was a half moon rising over the African landscape when the scouts moved out. Bishop lagged back, joining the main group, glad to be rid of the responsibility associated with walking point. It was a stressful job in so many ways. Besides being the first guy available for target practice, the scouts were responsible for detecting tripwires, ambushes, and other threats. A higher level of focus and concentration was required to do the job properly, that stress exponentially increasing a man's mental and physical fatigue.

In the open ground, the two scouts stepped about 150 meters in front of the main cluster of men. While every operator was equipped with night vision, the two point men worked their devices hard, scanning not only the ground immediately in their path, but checking all access points to the formation.

Each shooter was equipped with glow-in-the dark Velcro panels. These small patches could be placed anywhere on a contractor's load vest or hat. While the night was bright enough for the main body of men to stay together, the scouts utilized the patches so visual contact could be maintained.

As the group progressed down a gentle slope, Bishop could see both of the glowing green patches off in the distance. The ghost-like visual of two seemingly suspended, green dots was enhanced by a spooky bobbing motion as the point men tread. If the ghoulish specks disappeared, the main group would stop - a signal that something was amiss up ahead. If a scout heard or saw a potential threat, his first move was typically to go prone and thus the patches' phosphorescence would vanish. He could also cover the glowing cloth with his hands, a signal informing the men behind to be alert.

Three hours later, the point men both disappeared at the same time, but the action was anticipated. According to the maps and satellite photos, they had arrived at the abandoned village. Stoke gave the hand signals, and the team flattened out to form a skirmish line. The boss then trotted off to the nearest scout to have a look for himself.

Bishop took a knee and waited, the adrenaline of pending action competing with the exhaustion of a long, physically demanding mission. The man to Bishop's right whispered the order to "Move to the ridge," which Bishop then repeated to the next in line.

A small rise bordered one side of a cluster of mud huts, partially intact fences, and worn dirt paths. Most of the thatch roofing was missing from the skeleton of support poles rising into the night sky. The place smelled of damp earth, burnt wood, and something even more unexpected… cordite.

Scanning the area with his night vision, it quickly dawned on Bishop that a battle of some sort had taken place here. The green and black image displayed through the scope didn't provide as much depth perception as normal vision, but the evidence was clear – this place had suffered either an artillery shelling or a mortar attack. Bishop guessed it was the latter.

Circular indentions about four meters in diameter were detectable through the compound, the rows of blast rings running in almost perfectly straight lines. While the impact zones weren't exactly craters, the vegetation was less dense inside the affected areas. If a structure's foundation was within a ring, it showed damage. Whoever had attacked this place had showered quite a bit of ordnance into a relatively small area.

The battle damage wasn't a huge surprise. This part of Africa had known little but conflict and war for decades, and it was likely that any town or city would have experienced some level of violence.

"Fifteen meter spread, straight line for one pass," sounded the command from Bishop's right. He again relayed the whispered instructions down the line.

When Stoke stood and began walking into the center of the village, the rest of the team joined him, forming a line with weapons at the ready, and heads pivoting right and left.

The place was completely empty – no sign of current, or even recent occupation.

The team regrouped at the far edge of the settlement, Stoke clearly not happy that their search wasn't over. The leader unfolded a map on the bare earth, the red lens of his flashlight providing illumination. "Now where the hell would they be going? We are 20 miles from anything remotely resembling civilization. Even if his intent were one of these paltry hamlets, there's a lot easier route than the one we've been on."

Bishop studied the map and pointed, "Aren't there any structures or homes around this big lake? Back home, people always settle around water."

Stoke pulled a handful of reconnaissance photos from his satchel, flipping through several before locating the shoreline. One by one, he studied the images, eventually looking up and shaking his head. "There's one small structure here at the dam. It appears to be some sort of control building or maintenance shed. The lake was created 11 years ago by a United Nations project to keep the valley below us from flooding. The UN hoped to foster more agriculture in the region that had been prone to high water each monsoon season. According to one report I read, the project has been pretty successful both in the output of crops and relocation of displaced persons."

Bishop checked the photo Stoke was holding, trying to get an image of the place in his mind. "Sir, do you think our target headed to that lake?"

Before Stoke could answer, one of the outward facing sentries hissed, "Movement… grass… west side of the path."

Only a blink of time passed before the contractors were moving, each man taking a position and reading his weapon. Like a well-drilled sports team, each operator seemed to instinctively sense where he should go. Bishop scurried three steps to a fallen tree, probably a victim of the mortar attack from not so long ago. Going prone behind the cover, his first instinct was to survey the area to verify someone was behind him. The semi-circular perimeter appeared intact.

Scanning to his immediate front with the night vision was the next step. Once he was convinced the threat wasn't danger-close, he mounted the device in front of the red-dot optic that topped the shotgun. The dot's tube blocked part of the NVD's field of view, but Bishop could still affectively aim and scout using the light amplification technology.

The main trail twisting from the village to the lake passed immediately in front of Bishop's position. The worn path was bordered by waist-high brown grass and the occasional shrub or short tree. *That grass is going to be a problem*, he thought. *It will conceal any threats until they are within a few feet. They can see me, but I can't see them.*

Stoke had taken cover behind the trunk of Bishop's tree. Only ten feet away, Bishop took a chance and whispered, "This isn't good, Stoke. This isn't the place for a fight. Can we pull back into the village?"

"You're bloody right about that, lad. Pass the word, we're falling back."

Before anyone could move, another contractor warned, "Movement… grass… east side of the path."

The news complicated things, as it appeared there were at least two separate threats, each approaching from a different direction.

"Bishop, you and Spider cover our withdrawal – see you in a minute, lads."

Nine of the contractors rose in unison, the group falling back toward the main cluster of huts and fences. Bishop and Spider remained behind, each man's head and barrel pivoting, looking for work.

Without warning, a long burst of automatic fire exploded from the grass, the rounds snapping well over the contractor's heads. Several throats erupted in battle cries, and then a cluster of shadows appeared at the edge of the grass. They charged, screaming, firing, and rushing directly at Bishop's position.

The safety came off the shotgun without thought. Bishop's training kicked in, his immediate reaction to pull the trigger held in check until the red dot of his optic centered on the lead man. The scattergun roared, the stock recoiling hard against Bishop's shoulder. The weapon's kick moved the barrel to the right, and Bishop didn't fight it. Another outline of a man appeared behind the dot, and 10 pellets of double-ought buckshot departed the weapon's barrel at 1375 feet per second.

Spider's weapon began barking close by, but Bishop sensed it wasn't firing at his targets. Someone was trying to flank their position.

A huge ball of white and red flame exited Bishop's barrel with every shot, the affect providing the attackers with an excellent point of aim. Hunks of tree bark and small geysers of soil warned Bishop that the fire directed at him was becoming more accurate - but there wasn't time to move. He pumped round after round at the approaching threats, his aim drawn by the optic's view - flashing muzzles and black on green images advancing toward his position.

His shotgun held seven rounds plus the one in the chamber. In what seemed like a matter of only a few seconds, the weapon locked back empty. Bishop reached for his side arm, but sensed an attacker only a few steps away.

He could make out individual features of the threat, specifically the barrel of the AK47 battle rifle coming to bear. Bishop rolled hard left, his hand trying to grasp the grip of the pistol at his waist. A stream of deadly lead-pills slapped the ground where his body had been a split second before.

The .45 Colt automatic pistol cleared its holster on Bishop's second roll, the safety flipped off as he extended the weapon toward the attacker. There wasn't any need for either man to use sites or aim, they were that close.

Both men rushed their shots, both projectiles whizzing harmlessly off into the air of the high plains. Bishop fired a second round and then a third, but his opponent remained standing. Bishop made it to his knees, readying to leap at the foe and puzzled by the seemingly ineffectiveness of his pistol. *Body armor*, rushed into his mind, *the guy must be wearing armor*.

Right as Bishop coiled to leap at his foe, the opponent fell straight over like a stiff plank of wood - the body generating a solid thud as it hit the earth. Shotgun shells began flying from the bandolier into the tube of Bishop's weapon, the reload slowed by the darkness, shaking hands, and a concerted effort to keep an eye on the grass.

"You okay?" gasped a winded Spider.

"I'm good… you?"

"Yeah… but damn that was close. I had five of the fuckers doing the Chinese wave attack over here."

"Five? Is that all? Where the fuck were you? I had at least twice that many and was wondering if you'd decided on a nap or some shit. Thanks for the help, buddy."

"Bullshit on that! I call bullshit! Twice that many, my ass. What did you have… two?"

The sound of boots stopped the exchange, three members of their team rushing up to help. "'Bout fucking time you guys decided to join in," Spider snapped. "Were you ladies enjoying a nice picnic back there?"

"Fuck you, Spider. We figured you guys were fighting a couple of stray dogs or maybe shooting at each other by accident."

Stoke and the rest of the men joined up just as the low groans of a wounded man drifted through the air. When they were confident the attack was over, Stoke positioned some men for security and then began to circuit the battlefield, shining his red flashlight on the bodies that littered the plain. Bishop accompanied the Brit, partly out of morbid curiosity, partly to provide security.

Starting with the victim of Bishop's pistol, Stoke kicked the AK clear and then rolled the body over with his boot. The crimson beam sought the downed man's hands first, Stoke being weary of the combatant playing possum and perhaps gripping a hand grenade or sidearm. After finding empty hands, the ray of light traveled up the causality's chest where two large purple circles of blood indicated the fellow was no longer a threat. When the light reached the face, Bishop inhaled sharply.

The dead attacker was just a kid, no more than 13 or 14 years old. Bishop turned away, his stomach convulsing in painful spasms. Trying not to vomit, he lurched a few steps, half bent at the waist and stumbling badly. Spider moved to his friend's side and in a firm voice instructed, "Steady there, partner.... Drink some water.... Go on."

Reaching for the tube connected to Bishop's camelback, Spider helped with the mouthpiece while steadying his buddy's wobbly legs. After gulping down a couple of swallows, Spider escorted Bishop to the fallen tree and helped him sit down.

"They're all kids," a voice sounded in the distance. "What the fuck is going on here, Stoke?"

Before the leader could respond, one of the sentries yelled, "Shit!" A commotion followed, the sounds of someone grunting, a solid thud, and then "Got him!"

All eyes and a few rifle barrels sought the source of the disturbance, the high blades of grass rustling violently. One of the contractors emerged, half dragging and half carrying a struggling man. Once clear of the vegetation, the large HBR shooter unceremoniously lobbed his cargo into the middle of the gathered contractors. "I found this fucker hiding in the grass over there. He ain't no kid."

Flashlight beams illuminated a middle-aged man, his frightened eyes darting around while his hand attempted to shade his eyes. The captive was dressed in a dirty, mud smeared, white dress shirt, khaki slacks and a pair of expensive looking dress shoes. He didn't appear to be carrying any weapons.

Stoke tilted his head, studying the terrified prisoner. "He's not our Mr. Ombomtu, that's for sure."

Seemingly dismissing the captive as worthless, Stoke half turned away and issued an order to a nearby contractor. "Red, go ahead and kill him. He's not the guy we're after. And besides that, he makes me sick, using a bunch of kids as a shield, relegating them to a suicide mission. Make it quick."

Red cycled his M4, raising the weapon to his shoulder. The captured man screamed, "No! Wait! I know where Ditto is."

Stoke reached out and touched Red's rifle, gently pushing the now centered barrel downward. Pivoting abruptly, he took a menacing step and then towered over the terrified man. "Don't fuck around with me…talk or die."

"Di... Di... Ditto is at the lake," the prisoner stuttered in heavily accented English.

"How many men does he have with him?"

"I'm... I'm not sure. You've killed some of his army tonight."

Bishop jumped up from the log, his eyes full of fury. He grabbed the prisoner by the hair and dragged the protesting man to the closest causality. "That's not a fucking soldier, asshole. That's a child. Is that what you call an army?"

Realizing everyone was staring, Bishop shoved the captive to the ground, spit on his back, and then returned to his perch on the log.

Stoke didn't waste the moment. He bent over the whimpering prisoner and whispered, "You'd better start talking, lad, and talking really fast. I'm not going to be able to control my men much longer."

The guy looked up at Stoke and then chanced a glance at Bishop. Bishop met the fellow's gaze with a stare of pure hatred. Never diverting his eyes, Bishop reached to his chest rig and pulled his fighting knife from its scabbard, the moonlight and red torches reflecting an evil hue around the blade.

"Ditto has many more fighters with him. These are his soldiers. Orphans…vagabonds…all his fighters are young like these. All the older men are dead from past wars."

Stoke pressed, "I thought Ditto was a businessman. Are you saying he's involved with the government or military? What do you mean by, 'his soldiers?'"

The man was clearly confused by the question. "I... I... I'm not sure what the word is. These soldiers work for Ditto. He pays them, like me. Some of his army carries rifles, some work on computers, some in the warehouses. Ditto is a very powerful man with lots of army men."

Stoke sighed, obviously frustrated by the language barrier and the potential for the mission to cross unintended boundaries. He stepped closer to Bishop and commented, "Getting our property back from a local businessman is one thing. But we have to be sure we're not crossing swords with the government or the military. This mission isn't authorized for that, and I'm sure HBR doesn't want headlines insinuating the company is executing a coup or whatever else the bloody press wants to spin."

Bishop nodded toward the cluster of dead attackers. "No army that I know of recruits teenagers, Stoke. They have to be part of Ditto's security force or private employees."

"You're wrong about that, Bishop. Many military organizations in this part of the world use child soldiers. It's more common than anyone from the West likes to admit."

Bishop digested his leader's words for a bit, the look of disgust still painted on his face.

Stoke patted him on the shoulder and added, "I know you're upset about this, lad. Killing is bad enough, let alone having to kill someone so young. Let me assure you...those 'children' would have shot you dead without a second thought. They would have stripped your carcass clean and left it for the dogs to eat. Child warriors have no conscience... no sense of life or death. In some ways that makes them very affective."

Bishop nodded his thanks to Stoke for the words. While he still wasn't over the shock, he pulled himself together enough to consider the mission. "You didn't ask, sir, but I think we need to go to the lake and get this bullshit over with. Every minute we spend in this shithole makes things worse. That's my unsolicited input, sir."

The team leader nodded and turned to face the prisoner again.

"How did you know we were here?"

"I don't know. Ditto has very many friends in very many places. A runner brought news this morning that 11 men had landed in the jungle and were hunting Ditto. He has sent for more soldiers. They will be here tomorrow."

A sigh of exasperation escaped Stoke's throat. The Brit stood, rubbing his chin, clearly in thought. Speaking to no one in particular, "So we're expected then. Perhaps not such a bad thing, eh, lads?"

After a period of silence, Stoke cleared his throat, a habit that signaled he had reached a decision. He motioned to the closest man watching the prisoner and instructed, "Tie him up… loose enough so he can get away in a few hours. Leave him one bottle of water. We'll retrieve him on our way back if he's still here."

The column of contractors vacated the settlement, moving toward the dam and leaving an unhappy, bound captive behind. The villagers had evidently traveled to the shores of the mountain lake on a regular basis, as the path was well worn and quite wide. As soon as they were out of visual range of the hamlet, Stoke, Bishop, and Spider dropped out of the formation and cut off into the grasslands.

It was just over two miles to the earthen dam, the anticipated ambush hitting the main column of contractors about halfway between the village and the lake. Stoke and his two escorts traveled three hundred meters away, keeping on a parallel line with their comrades back on the trail.

The contractors had easily detected the amateurish trap created by the child-army. Normally, they would have rolled up the flank of the hidden attackers in a matter of minutes. On this early African morning, however, their plan had been to make it seem like they had fallen into the snare.

Three of the largest casualties from the settlement's skirmish were dressed in spare clothing provided by the HBR operators, the bodies carried along with the main group of men. Stoke had ordered the morbid feint just in case the grass contained curious eyes that were accounting for the living interlopers.

When the AKs started spitting lead at the ambush site, those three corpses had been recycled, abandoned to create a ruse that the attackers' trap had been effective.

The eight remaining "living contractors" had instructions to keep their foes busy. If at all possible, they were to pressure the child-soldiers into calling for reinforcements.

While the contractors played a dangerous game at the ambush site, Stoke and his two comrades continued toward the dam's control house. The plan was simple enough – pull as many of Ditto's men away as possible while giving him a level of comfort that his enemy still remained some distance off. Stoke hoped the aggressors were as exhausted as his own men.

Bishop was walking point when the smell of water alerted his senses. A few meters later, the crest of a small knoll brought the lake into view. The dam had been constructed across a narrow gap that nature had cut through the surrounding cliffs. The gorge below the dam's spillway wasn't especially wide, but looked to be about 150 feet deep and ran for as far as they could see into the distant plains below.

Monsoon rains that drained from the mountains to the foothills before flooding the savannah would have been channeled through here before the dam was constructed. It was easy to visualize the torrent rushing through the narrow gap on its journey to smother the flatlands below.

Given the recent weeks of nonstop deluges, the lake nearly topped the dam, moonlight glistening on its undisturbed surface. Two huge spillways at the bottom of the chasm roared with the sound of high-pressure water being allowed to escape downstream. From their angle, Bishop estimated that the two flood control gates were opened to one-quarter capacity – enough water to form a medium sized river surging toward the valley below.

At the edge of the lake was a concrete block structure about the size of a modest American home. A circle of light surrounded the facility, courtesy of an overhead, florescent fixture mounted high on a utility pole. The hum of a generator sounded in the distance, the engine barely audible above the crash of the water rushing from the bottom of the dam. The three contractors identified four sentries almost immediately, their attention drawn to the distant popping noises being generated from the firefight occurring just over a mile away.

Stoke tapped Bishop on the shoulder and pointed to a nearby bush. A quick scan with the night vision identified another guard hiding in the foliage. That made five, and all three spies were positive there were more.

Ditto may have been a successful business-crook, but he wasn't skilled in the tactical arts. Once Stoke identified the sentry hiding in the scrub, it was simple to find the other three, all using similar vegetation for concealment. An amateurish mistake.

Stoke glanced at his team and waved the two men in close. He whispered, "Lads, I know I don't have to say this, but you both know *I do* have to say it – we're in stealth mode as of now." The other two men signaled their acknowledgement.

Spider immediately dropped his pack and began digging out the components to assemble his bow. Stoke produced a long, canister shaped object and screwed it onto the end of his barrel. Bishop pulled a similar device from his pack and attached it to the muzzle of his pistol.

While Spider rummaged for arrows, Stoke and Bishop rearranged magazines for their weapons, each man loading special sub-sonic rounds for his respective firearm. The change was necessary to maximize the effect of the noise cancellation devices, or CANS.

Bishop unloaded the lethal rounds from his shotgun, replacing the deadly lead-filled shells with special purpose rounds that amounted to small sandbag pellets. These non-lethal projectiles would disable a man for a few moments with a properly placed shot – normally to the chest. It had been determined in the planning phase that Bishop was the primary takedown man - should Mr. Ditto decide to resist. Remembering a line from a science fiction television show, Bishop looked up at Spider and whispered, "Resistance is futile."

The changeover to stealth mode wasn't without sacrifice. The lethality of each of the three men was now greatly reduced by either range, kinetic energy, or rate of fire. It was a compromise unstated, but one the trio fully understood.

In a perfect situation, Stoke would have ordered their target observed for many hours, the knowledge of sentry placement, shift changes, and the general habits of the opposition increasing the odds of success. This morning, there simply wasn't time. The sun would be rising in three hours, daylight providing an advantage to the defenders. Reinforcements were thought to be on their way, and every minute that passed increased the chances that HBR's equipment would no longer be within reach. In addition, the game of cat and mouse being played by the rest of their team at the ambush site couldn't go on forever. It was time to roll the dice.

The sentry closest to the three contractors had to be eliminated first, his position denying a route that would provide the attackers the best angle. "There's some good news, lads," Stoke announced. "The crash of that waterfall will muffle the noise of our weapons – somewhat."

Stoke shouldered his rifle and looked at his teammates, "Ready?"

Each man nodded his status, and Stoke's gaze returned to his optic. Three "thumps," not unlike someone slapping a pillow with an open hand, sounded from the shots. Bishop watched the dark outline of the sentry start to rise and then slump over flat on the ground. Before the body came to rest, the three HBR employees were moving.

Bent at the waist and running hard, the men stayed together until they reached the hide formally occupied by the now deceased sentry. After verifying their first target was no longer capable of sounding the alarm, it was Spider's turn to test his marksmanship.

Lying on his side in the grass, Spider raised the complex-looking, compound bow to his shoulder. The carbon fiber frame and hi-tech cord were further enhanced by a red dot optic similar to the one used on Bishop's shotgun. It took a few moments to acquire a point of aim, and then a solid "thack" sounded as the arrow disappeared into the night. Another guard fell, Spider's steel-tipped projectile finding its mark right behind the unfortunate fellow's ear.

The fall of the second sentry completely exposed the lakeside approach to the remaining guards, all of whom were focusing their attention in the direction of the trail and the distant sounds of the firefight beyond.

Within four minutes, the dam's control house was completely unguarded.

The entrance consisted of a single metal door slightly recessed in the block wall. Faded, peeling green paint and a rusty knob indicated the facility hadn't been a top maintenance priority of any local authorities.

Spider and Bishop bookended the opening, the two men's hustling approach abruptly challenged by their shoulders slamming into the wall. Stoke calmly approached and whispered, "Alrighty, lads. Let's hope the master's asleep, dreaming fitfully of his soon to be received, ill-gotten gains."

The door was unlocked, and since Bishop was armed with the primary nonlethal weapon, he went first. Swinging around the doorframe in a crouched position, the contractor swept the lighted reception area with the shotgun, ready to pull the trigger on anything that moved.

The HBR team was greeted by two metal desks, a pair of inexpensive office chairs, and a water cooler devoid of the large plastic bottle that would normally rest on its crown. Bishop moved inside the room, making a hole for his teammates to follow. Within seconds, the lobby was cleared.

Without a sound, the three men proceeded down a hallway lined with bare walls and three wooden doors. Boots stepped heel to toe, Bishop's shotgun sweeping left and right, the motion matching the movement of his pivoting head.

When the team approached the first doorway, Spider rushed past, quickly taking a knee and covering the remaining length of the hall. Bishop positioned himself opposite of the entrance, as Stoke reached for the brass door handle. It was locked. Both Bishop and his team leader sized up the portal, the two men concluding that the flimsy frame and lock would be no match for a well-placed war boot. The breech should be easy, but the noise generated would announce their presence to anyone in the building. "Next," mouthed Stoke.

Bishop had to agree with his boss. Surprise was a huge advantage, especially when the mission called for taking someone alive. If their target wasn't in the next room, they could always come back and kick in the door.

The next office was empty, a storage area for manuals, moldy smelling, cardboard boxes, miscellaneous office supplies, and discarded tools.

As the squad moved to the last option, the door at the end of the hall surged open, a large man in disheveled clothing filling the threshold while rubbing the sleep from his eyes. His arrival surprised the team as much as the presence of the team shocked him.

Bishop recognized the man instantly from the file photographs, centered the shot and pulled the trigger. Ditto Ombomtu possessed quick reactions and was extremely lucky. As the enormous blast of the shotgun filled the tiny space of the hallway, Ditto managed to step back and spin at the same instant. The sandbag projectile brushed the man's shirt, punching a quarter-sized hole in the plaster after missing the target.

Ditto's natural reaction was to slam the door, and just that quickly he was out of sight. "Fuck!" hissed Bishop, as Spider and Stoke made for the walls on each side of the entrance. Bishop had just caught up with his friends when the door beside them splintered out fountains of wood chips from several rifle rounds fired from the other side. Ditto was announcing that he was officially armed and dangerous.

Before the wood-dust from the abused entrance had begun to fall, Stoke commanded, "Banger… hurry!"

Spider reached into a pouch on his chest rig and pulled out a flash-bang grenade, extracting the pin on the device and tossing it over to Stoke. The 3.5-second timer began its countdown as soon as Spider's thumb released the spoon. Slightly longer than a can of tomato soup, the cylindrical device was designed to emit a super-bright light and debilitating pressure wave of sound. The intent was to leave anyone in the vicinity of the explosion unable to resist, stumbling around blind, deaf, and confused.

While the device was still airborne, Stoke reached for the doorknob and pushed in. In a sub-second span of time, the Brit caught the "hot potato" and tossed it into the opening. All three contractors half-turned away, covering their ears and squinting their eyes closed.

The concussion of the blast rattled the building and the contractors' chests. Stoke didn't waste any time, throwing the door open and ducking low as Bishop swung around the frame, scanning with his scattergun.

This room appeared to be another office - littered with scattered papers, an overturned chair, and a thick blanket of smoke. Bishop noticed a cot in the corner, rumpled quilts, and a single white pillow, evidence of where Ditto had been catching his beauty rest. Their target was nowhere to be found.

There was only one other way out, a single exit adorned with a distressed metal sign reading "Machinery Room." Bishop and Spider both moved for the door.

"Careful now, lads," Stoke warned. "Our friend isn't just a desk jockey and clearly isn't afraid to fight. Let's make our next move a smart one."

Stoke shifted to the wall and slowly twisted the knob, slightly surprised the lock was not engaged. He pushed gently, and the door opened inward. Without exposing himself, Stoke called out, "Ditto Ombomtu, we only want the HBR equipment you stole. Give us our property back, and we'll be on our way."

For a moment, the contractors didn't believe they were going to receive an answer. Bishop and Spider maintained eye contract with Stoke, waiting on his command to enter the room. Eventually, a raspy voice retorted, "The equipment I *found* has already been sold. You've wasted your time and many lives for nothing."

Stoke actually smiled before responding. "I see. If what you say is true, then there's no reason for us to take you alive then, is there? We should just kill you for revenge and be on our way."

The words that came from the machinery room chilled the three contractors to the bone. "If you kill me, tens of thousands of others will die. Step into this room, and I'll show you why."

For the first time during the entire ordeal, Bishop saw indecision cross Stoke's face. While his boss said nothing aloud, the dissonance of thoughts streaming though the man's head was obvious. *Was it a trap? What the hell was the cornered man talking about?*

Ditto either liked his position or didn't have patience for the status quo. "Come on in. I won't shoot you."

Shrugging his shoulders, Stoke stepped carefully into the

doorway, ready to dive out of the way. Nothing happened, so he continued a few steps further inside. Spider and Bishop followed immediately behind.

What the contractor saw was a slice of Ditto's face peeking from behind a large steel and bronze console decorated with rows of lights, buttons, meters and switches. The entire room was lined with pipes, large valves, and other assorted machinery, obviously used to control and maintain the nearby dam.

"This instrument is used to control the spillway below," Ditto said calmly. "The lake is full from the recent rains. If I open the gates all of the way, the dam will fail. The flashflood of water will kill thousands of innocents down in the valley. Leave this place.... Leave now, or the blood of thousands will be on your hands."

Stoke actually managed a convincing laugh and then became serious. "I don't think so, Ditto. I think my men can kill you before you hit that button. Even if we are a little slow, we'll just kick your dead body out of the way and close the gates before too much damage is done."

Ditto peered around the machine, a genuine grin painted on his face. Without a word, the man held up a hand grenade being squeezed tightly in his right hand. "I don't think so," he touted. "If my grip leaves this device, the explosion will destroy the control panel. A wall of water will rage down the valley, and you'll face the wrath of those who want your heads to balance the scales of justice."

Stoke looked at the floor and pretended disgust. "Ditto, you know that's not going to work. Even if I believed you, I can just pull back my men and wait you out. You're bound to run out of food sometime. You've got to leave eventually. We'll just surround this place and wait out the siege."

It was Ditto's turn to laugh. "You take me for a fool. I have hundreds of men on their way here. They will kill you on sight. You should be running right now before they get here and skin you alive."

"They will die, Ditto. Just like all the men you sent before. Why don't you be a smart lad and just tell me where our machinery is? That's the only way out, Ditto."

"It seems we are at an impasse," was the response from behind the console. “Perhaps I can offer an alternative that would be agreeable to all parties.”

“*Always the businessman*,” Bishop thought.

“Go ahead. I’m listening, Ditto.”

“While I have sold the recovered equipment to my Russian colleagues, I have not delivered the merchandise as of yet. It is possible that I could cancel their order and accept equal payment from your firm. A sum of 50 million dollars US, wired into one of my accounts, would ensure I provided an address where the equipment could be found.”

The offer actually relaxed Bishop. Aiming a weapon at a man whose finger hovered over a trigger of mass destruction was wearing his nerves thin. The hope of a non-catastrophic solution lessened the tension in his shoulders.

Strokes’ response eased Bishop’s frayed nerves a bit more. “Ditto, $50,000,000 seems like quite a lot for a ‘finder’s fee.’ An arrangement like that is above my level of authority. I’ll have to contact my people before I can agree to anything.”

“Take your time.... I’m not going anywhere... but not too much time. My soldiers will be arriving soon.”

Stoke whispered to his men, “Watch him. Don’t do anything unless he tries to leave this room. I’m going to contact Houston on the satellite phone and see what they want us to do.”

Without waiting on a response, Stoke left the room.

Twenty minutes later, the team leader reappeared in the machinery chamber. Without any word to his two men, Stoke began speaking. “Ditto, I have agreement from Houston for your proposal. I’ll need the routing information and account number for the bank where you want the funds transferred.”

Stoke then shocked Bishop. The team leader half turned and whispered, “Take him out. Do your best and try and knock him down.”

Bishop was stunned, his lips trying to mouth words of protest, but his tongue unable to form any sounds. Stoke grabbed Bishop’s shoulder and said, "Do your best, lad. Don't forget to get out of the way of the grenade."

Ditto began rattling off numbers, but Stoke interrupted him. "Ditto! Ditto! Wait. I'm not going to send 50 million dollars racing off into cyberspace based on my memory. Write the damn numbers down so there's no mistake."

Conflicting thoughts were racing through Bishop's head a mile a minute, his logic reeling from the implications of Houston's decision. Somehow, he focused enough to return his cheek to the stock of the shotgun and his finger to the trigger.

Ditto paused and then responded, "Pardon my lack of preparation Mr. HBR man, but I seem to have left my paper and pencil in my *other* office."

"I'll get you what you need. Hold on one second."

Returning quickly, Stoke leaned his weapon against the doorframe and slowly stepped towards Ditto with his hands held high. He held a scrap of paper and a pen in one hand. When he was within reach of the bureau, Stoke carefully set the items on the surface and then began backing up.

Ditto's eyes never left the team leader, a bare shadow of the man nervously watching from his cover.

Bishop was ready. Despite his shaking hands and churning stomach, the red dot of the shotgun's optic never moved from the bridge of Ditto's nose. When Ditto reached for the pen and paper, Bishop squeezed the trigger.

The single ounce of plastic-encased sand exited the muzzle traveling at over 1300 feet per second. After leaving the tight confines of the shotgun's barrel, the un-aerodynamic projectile wobbled slightly but held its course, striking Ditto directly in the mouth.

Only small snapshots of time entered Bishop's mind after his shot. Ditto's head snapping backwards... blood and bits of flesh showering into the air... the hand holding the grenade instinctively moving to the pain tearing through his face... the explosive device coming loose and drifting through the air.

Spider had already lifted his boot to step when the metal case of the grenade pinged with impact on the concrete floor. Bishop watched his friend casually take two more, big steps and scoop up the ticking bomb. With a single motion, the contractor flung the volatile, incendiary device toward the far corner of the room.

It dawned on Bishop that he was still on one knee, and he twisted to dive for cover. There was just enough time to sense the cold surface of the concrete against his cheek before the room was filled with the violent shock wave of the grenade. Shrapnel whizzed through the air, the screaming slices of metal mimicking the sound of giant, angry bees. Pipes, walls, and machinery sounded with the impact of the deadly hunks of steel... pings, thuds, and rattles all around.

Stoke was up first, immediately moving for Ditto and the control panel. Bishop followed next, rising to his feet before Spider could recover from his less than acrobatic dive.

Bishop didn't care anymore about the machinery, HBR's investment, or Ditto. As he half stumbled through the fog of cordite smoke, his eyes were fixed on the handle that controlled the floodgates. It took a moment to figure out the controls. There were meters, slide levers, and several warning lights. Bishop finally found the gauge that was labeled "Gate 1 Capacity," and then its twin, "Gate 2."

Both indicators read 30%.

Bishop exhaled, closing his eyes and tilting his head skyward. The respite was short-lived as Spider began pumping him for information. "Did this fucker open them? Is the dam going to hold?"

"They're fine," replied Bishop. "No flood. He didn't even touch the controls."

Stoke spoke up from behind the control panel where he was bent over a groaning Ditto. "Come help me with our new friend, lads. He's a little too unstable to walk on his own. Does anyone know a good local dentist?"

The hotel balcony was on the third floor and provided an excellent view of the pedestrian traffic plying the sidewalks below. Bishop sat with his bare feet soaking up the sunshine while he sipped a glass of real lemonade – the casual tourist, people-watching from his roost.

He was seriously considering another nap when three knocks sounded at the door. Cursing the interruption, he rose slowly and gingerly strode to the entry. Peering through the peephole, he immediately recognized Spider's face behind the middle finger flipping an obscene gesture.

Bishop couldn't resist. "Who is it?" he sang.

"You know damn well who it is, let me in."

"I'm busy."

"Bullshit... quit fucking around and open up."

"I've got two young ladies visiting right now, and they're very modest around strangers."

Spider paused as if he were actually considering the truth of Bishop's claim. After some minor deliberation, he presumed the story was a stunt and began cursing at his friend.

Bishop let his buddy generate a small head of steam before undoing the deadbolt and opening the door. He grunted when Spider stuck just his head inside, looking around to insure there weren't any women.

"You fucker... always a clown... one of these days that shit is going to come back and bite your ass."

"Did you stop by to tutor me on the finer arts of social interaction?"

"No, asshole, I stopped by to tell you to pack up. The Colonel and his crew recovered the equipment and we're flying out of this shithole in four hours. The truck is going to pick us up out front. Be there or be square."

Bishop nodded, a deep grimace crossing his face.

Spider detected his friend's mood and probed. "What's wrong, Bishop? You've got that look in your eye."

"I don't know, Spider. I'm considering resigning. I'm not sure I want to work for someone who puts money ahead of human life."

Spider's head sunk, his chin resting on his chest. "I know, I've been thinking the same thing. Management's decision to take that chance up at the dam versus paying some money has been bothering me, too. That whole thing could have ended in a huge cluster fuck."

Stoke appeared in the doorway, his hand raised to knock on the still open door. "Oh hello, Spider. I was just coming by to give Bishop the word. Is everything all right?"

"Yes, sir. Everything is fine. Spider and I were just discussing our future."

Stoke entered the room, closing the door behind him. He looked to each man, a fatherly expression on his face. "Now let me guess, lads. You're both feeling blue about the gamble we took up at the lake. You're both wondering if you want to work for such greedy bastards that would make a decision like that. Am I right?"

Spider nodded without making eye contact with the older man. Bishop remained silent.

"I'm not going to lecture either of you. You're both grown men and in control of your own destiny. I do, however, want to ask you both a simple question. Can either of you name me one potential employer who doesn't do the same thing? When a bank repossesses a farm, aren't they in effect putting money ahead of people? When a factory furloughs workers, isn't that the same commercial sin of placing the corporate bottom line ahead of the needs of individual workers? What corporation would you go to work for with completely noble intentions? I know, you can go find a job for a tobacco company – there's an employer who doesn't put money ahead of life."

Stoke looked at both men, making sure his point was making it through. His tone softening, he continued. "I don't know of any employer who doesn't give money a high priority in any risk assessment. The problem might not be that of a weapon killing someone. The issue may involve closing a plant or reducing redundant staff and sending them off to the unemployment line. It's all part of life, gentlemen. If HBR had paid our friend Ditto those funds, who knows how many of your American mates they would've had to let go? Who can tell how many families would have suffered because of paying a criminal huge sums of money? Besides that, an "entrepreneur" who is willing to fuck the Russians after they paid for our merchandise might not be the most reputable business partner either."

Bishop and Spider looked up at the older, wiser man, both of their faces indicating they were absorbing his message.

Stoke placed one hand on each contractor's shoulder and continued, "Just think about it, lads. Give it few good mental cycles before you do anything rash. HBR is as good a master as it gets. They're not perfect, but they get it right most times."

Bands of color brought my eyes
From desert floor ‘cross cobalt skies.
Ahead stood stark, against the blue
A tree, smit by nature, grew.
Still green in spots from life persistent
Lightening had split the wood dehiscent.
Strong it stood as it long would
By God’s great hand,
Held straight to stand.
My eyes moved on and found their rest
Upon a wondrous eagle’s nest.
What else could this great land present,
To such a soul that must lament?
Looking deeply, inward most,
My view came upon The Host;
The Holy Spirit dwelled within
This heart, this land, this gracious wind.
And in my heart there came a peace
That only rests within the beasts.
To see the feathered eagle’s wings
Unfurl against the cobalt sky
And with it draw my eye once more
‘Cross bands of color to the desert floor-
Lament no more.

DALH 2013

Chapter 1

January 8, 2016
Alpha, Texas

Diana blinked her eyes, wondering if she had been dreaming or had really heard the noise. Confused by her rapid transition from REM sleep, she wasn't entirely sure where she was or why she was there. Something about a whistle. Something about that was important.

Her neck was stiff, one arm was asleep, and she was still wearing yesterday's clothes. Commanding her body to shift for relief, the stack of papers on her chest fell to the floor and scattered. It all instantly came back - she had been reviewing the endless volume of paperwork when exhaustion had overcome her determination to clean out her inbox.

Sitting up on the office couch, she rubbed her eyes and threw a disgusted look at the chaotic mass of forms, requests, and status reports strewn about the floor. *No rest for the wicked*, she thought.

As she bent to rearrange the clutter, the distant whistle sounded again. The signal caused her head to snap up, energy suddenly surging through her veins. The whistle was a call for help... an emergency... a rudimentary alarm system for a community that didn't possess working telephones.

Half-stumbling toward the office door, she was relieved to discover Nick snoring away on the reception area's couch. With only a minor pang of guilt about waking someone who needed rest as much as she, Diana gently called out, "Nick.... Nick.... Someone's blowing a whistle."

Being a professional military man instills many small, hardly noticeable habits in a person. Long-time soldiers learn to eat quickly, sleep anywhere, and store their personal items in a regimented, efficient way. One such attribute developed over many campaigns in hostile lands is the capability to awaken quickly – to transform from a deep slumber to alert and ready faster than most.

While the question of "Whistle?" was rolling off his tongue, Nick's legs were already sweeping off the sofa, heading for the carpeted floor. Before Diana could react, his right hand had touched the rifle leaning nearby while his left was reaching for socks and boots.

"I heard a whistle, twice I think. I'm sure of the second signal."

Nick was tying off his boot when the third screech of alarm reached the couple's ears.

"Something's very wrong," Diana announced as she pulled on her flats.

Two minutes later, the couple bounded down the church steps, unsure of what they were facing. While Nick and some of the men carried handheld radios for communication, the vast majority of Alpha's citizens did not. No telephone service meant no calling 9-1-1. It had become common practice for the townsfolk to use whistles when an emergency required quick response.

The handy, little noisemakers provided a first-rate solution. The flat desert terrain, coupled by the still Texas air, provided an excellent environment for their effective use. Plentiful, cheap, and easy to use, anyone of any age could call for help with a single, strong exhalation - the only shortcoming being that the responders didn't have any idea about the nature of the crisis. An elderly person may have fallen. Looters might be trying to break into a home. A child may have gone missing, or someone could be too sick to get out of bed.

The cause of tonight's alarm became obvious moments after the couple pushed through the church's front doors. A red glow on the horizon announced something was on fire, and it wasn't a trash barrel. A telltale whiff of smoke, scorching plastic, and toxic fumes provided a confirmation that whatever was burning, it wasn't inconsequential.

Nick glanced down at his rifle and chest rig, sure he wouldn't be needing the firepower, but not wanting to take the time to return the equipment to the church. He and Diana ran to the nearby golf cart and were soon speeding toward the firestorm.

On the way to the blaze, Nick pondered the cause of these random fires. Without the expertise and training of a professional investigator, there was really no way to be sure. Alpha's entire fire department had succumbed to the toxic cloud of gas released that fateful Sunday morning when the chemical plant exploded.

There had been a rash of small blazes after the power was restored. Appliances having electricity for the first time in months were no doubt the cause of some fires. Any electrical connection could short out. HVAC systems overheating and general wiring faults were probably as much to blame – but there was no way to be sure.

It was clear from several blocks away that they were approaching a full-fledged inferno. The red and yellow flames flashing skyward outlined the dark shadows of numerous onlookers. There were a half dozen men with garden hoses trying to spray water on the blaze, but they were completely outmatched. The heat was so intense the would-be firefighters couldn't get close enough for their weak streams of water to arch onto the flames.

Nick hopped out of the cart before it came to a complete stop, sprinting as close as possible to the firestorm to assess the situation. The clapboard-clad bungalow where the flames had begun was a total loss, already consumed by the roaring blaze. He prayed there wasn't anyone inside. The neighboring, downwind Victorian would reach the same state in a matter of minutes. A dense cloud of dark, black smoke already enveloped the structure, intermittent wisps of flame visible through the windows.

"Forget about that house!" Nick yelled at the hose-men. "Move next door. That one's gone, but we might keep the flames from spreading."

Diana was now behind him, quizzing several onlookers. "Where's our fire truck?"

"It's still inoperable. We haven't gotten around to having it repaired," replied one man.

Nick hustled to Diana's side and shouted over the noise, "Send someone to the fire station, and at least bring back some serious hose." He pointed to the fire hydrant in the middle of the block and continued. "Make sure and retrieve the tools to break that hydrant loose. If we can hook up the big hose there, we might be able to keep the blaze from spreading."

Diana nodded, "I'm on it," and then hustled off to organize some men.

Just as Nick turned to see how the small hoses were doing, a man raced toward Nick, grabbing him in a panic. "There are people in the second home. I just talked to the neighbors, and they're sure. At least two adults and one child."

"Are you sure? How can anyone be sure?"

"The neighbors and I have looked all around for them. I've circled the house twice and asked everyone. They have to be inside."

"Shit!"

Nick ran to the golf cart where he knew Diana kept a blanket. Being cold natured, she often wrapped herself in the spread while riding in the open-air vehicle at night. Rushing back with the quilted wool cover, he approached one of the men using a hose and yelled, "Soak me!"

"What?" responded the surprised man.

"I said, 'SOAK ME!' Spray me down with your hose. I'm going inside. Spray down the blanket, too!"

Shrugging his shoulders, the man turned the water on Nick and began drenching the big fellow from head to toe. While Nick was receiving his shower, Diana realized what he was going to do and scurried over.

"What are you doing? You're not going in that house, Nick!"

"There are people inside, and I have to try and get them out. I need an axe or crowbar or something heavy."

"I've got a big axe in my garage," offered the man operating the hose.

"Get it, please, and hurry."

Handing off his hose to Diana, the gent hustled off.

Nick, now dripping wet, pointed to the blanket lying on the ground and instructed, "Soak that, too. I'm going to use it as a cocoon."

Diana could tell there was no talking him out of it. Shaking her head in disgust, she redirected the water. While Diana worked the hose, Nick ran dripping back to the cart and began digging around in his chest rig. He found his goggles, gloves, and baklava mask, quickly pulling the gear on.

By the time he returned, the axe owner was back, and the blanket was ready.

Nick looked like some sort of robotic mass murderer as he approached the burning home. With the pickaxe on his shoulder, blanket hood, and only a goggle-covered, masked face visible, Diana wondered if he wouldn't scare the occupants to death before the fire could overwhelm them.

One kick from his size 14 boot made short work of the door, the breech greeted by a new column of dark, toxic smoke rolling from the top of the threshold. *Stay low*, he reminded himself. *Heat rises, and the poisonous air will go with it.*

The living room was dense with confused clouds of brown and black haze. Nick dropped to his knees, the blanket-shield making it difficult to crawl. He guessed the layout of the two-story home would position the master bedroom on the first floor, the child's room above.

Deciding to bend low at the waist rather than crawl, he could see flames spreading through the kitchen area and the back of the house. Despite his wrapping of wet cloth, the heat was intense. The rapidly spreading blaze suddenly illuminated the staircase, and Nick headed that way. His passage was blocked by a completely engulfed china cabinet that had collapsed across the hall, two of its legs weakened from incineration. Using the axe with one hand, he quickly splintered the blockage and then hopped over the smoldering remains.

He passed the door to the master bedroom on the way to the stairs. Peering inside, the smoke cleared just enough to make out the outline of at least one person lying in the bed. The curtains and part of the carpeting were already fueling the fiery beast, and visibility was degrading by the second.

Nick leaned the axe against the wall and moved to the bed. A man, probably in his early 30s, was lying in the hazy air, his mouth wide open as if grasping for breath. Nick pulled back the covers and watched for a moment, relieved when the fellow's chest shuddered with a weak inhalation.

Nick scooped up the man, effortlessly tossing the unresponsive body over his shoulder. His intent was to return to the front door, but the living room ceiling was now engulfed and sagging. Turning back, he realized the back door leading from the kitchen was an inferno and impassable.

Using his left hand while holding onto his limp cargo with his right, Nick swung the blade hard at the bedroom window. The glass gave way without any problem, the remaining shards removed with a few circles of the axe head.

Nick started to climb out with his survivor, but a thundering collapse sounded behind him. Realizing he wasn't going to be able to climb the stairs if he waited much longer, Nick lowered the rescued body out the window as far as he could and then flung it with a heave. The man landed with a thud, but Nick was sure the guy would prefer sore to dead.

Nick turned to find the firestorm had fully invaded the bedroom and was blocking his exit. The now open window was a magnet for the smoke, which blocked everything from view except the red-hot flames sprouting through the poisonous fog. Twisting low to the opening, he took two breaths of the cleanest air available and then held a final lung full.

Charging like a linebacker, Nick entered the inferno moving as if he were being chased by hell's hounds. It was only a few steps to the stairs, but those were some of the most frightening footfalls he could ever remember. Red embers filled the air, competing with hot whisks of fumes and boiling, angry spouts of flame. Foul, sulfuric-thick vapors swirled around his head, the venomous clouds riding the thermals generated by the incineration of tinder. By the time he reached the bottom step, his blanket was steaming, and he could sense the heat through the soles of his boots.

Taking the steps two at a time, Nick found himself in even denser haze. Going prone, he could barely detect four doors surrounding the small landing. Picking the closest one, he again held his breath and found the knob, feeling for the latch more from memory than being able to see in the dense, toxic fog.

The door yielded, but inside was a bathroom empty of inhabitants. As the smoke hadn't filled the room just yet, Nick took the opportunity to exchange the air in his lungs, the effort burning his throat and filling his mouth with a foul, metallic taste.

Nick bent low again to get a bearing on the next entryway. As he attempted to stand, he became dizzy for a moment. *I've got to get out of this hell*, he thought. *The fumes are getting to me.*

Heat wasn't helping Nick's body either. Even away from direct contact with the flames, the ambient temperature upstairs was approaching 150 degrees. Sweat streamed from every pore of his body, instantly evaporated by the super-heated atmosphere. He was being boiled alive.

He hit pay dirt inside the third room. Lying on the floor was a woman in a nightgown, her body acting as a shield while covering a small boy. Nick didn't check to see if either was breathing – there just wasn't time. Already his stomach was churning, and he had a headache unlike anything he'd ever felt. Throwing off the now dry, worthless blanket, he lifted the woman off the child and then managed to get both to his shoulders.

The trip out of the building was accomplished from memory without benefit of sight. Every cell of Nick's body screamed with protest as he lunged down the stairs. Pain racked his chest and head, his muscles protesting the lack of clean, usable oxygen. The heat was overwhelming. The loss of vision reminded Nick of swimming under water in the dark. The roar of flames and blinding smoke deprived him of sensory input; the only thing registering in his brain was pain and heat.

When he reached the bottom step, he didn't pause, but just kept moving. The flames had actually died down in the kitchen, and Nick moved that direction thinking of the back door. Without the rolling billows of smoke, moving to the rear of the home was like entering the dark world of a blackened forest, simmering ripples of heat radiating from every direction. Nick's mind conjured up visions of wolves with smoldering red eyes and fur of toxic fumes – the ferocious animals nipping at his heals with white-hot fangs. Like so many nightmares, he couldn't outrun the beasts while carrying his heavy cargo.

A vision of the back door suddenly appeared in front of him, the threshold to life and cool air just a few feet away - but the path was blocked. Part of the second floor had collapsed, heaps of smoldering boards and drywall hanging at odd angles.

Nick didn't care anymore - he couldn't. He wasn't going to die in this place. After all of the battles... all of the firefights... wounds and wars, there was no way he was going to burn alive. *Dig deep, you son of a bitch*, he thought. *Go down deep inside and live. Bring it all out and live. Leave any of it here - and die.*

One boot lashed out against the blockage...and then another. Despite the two bodies on his shoulders, he threw everything he had left into the strikes. Timbers cracked with the impact, embers swirled around his legs. Another landed... and then another... and then he arrived at the door. It was too late. Nick felt his knees buckling, the weight on his shoulders too much for his severely dehydrated frame. The poisonous smoke ached in his stomach, and his chest felt like it was in a vise.

Nick felt the hot floor on his knees, and realized his legs had given out. He sensed his upper body swaying and made a determined effort to fall backwards so his face wouldn't burn on the floor.

And then hands were reaching for him - many hands, seemingly coming from every direction. *They're angels*, he imagined. *Angels coming to pull me from the burning pits of Hades.*

The first sensation Nick noticed was of cold grass on the back of his neck. His next recognizable impression was the strong smell of rubber, competing with the odor of noxious smoke. The smoldering stench reminded his brain where he was, or at least where he'd been, and he attempted to sit up. Voices echoed in his ears... voices that he couldn't quite place, but knew he should recognize. Kevin! His son was here!

"Dad, stay right where you are. Just stay down."

Nick opened his eyes for a moment and initially believed himself to be blind. Only small, hazy pinpoints of light in a coal-black background filled his vision. At the same time, the taste of new rubber grew in his throat. A few blinks later, he realized he was looking up into the night sky, the stars slightly obscured from the smoking ember remains of the house nearby. Kevin's face appeared in his line of sight, the look of concern on the boy's face changing to an expression of sheer joy over seeing his father's eyes open.

The new rubber belonged to the Ambu bag covering his face, the breathing balloon steadily pumped by Diana. Nick's sudden spasm of coughing dictated the removal of the device.

After clearing what felt like several large hunks of steel wool from his chest, Nick managed to tilt his head slightly where he saw other people kneeling over the prone bodies of a woman and a small boy. Before he could ask any questions, Diana held a bottle of water to his lips while helping him lift his head.

"You scared the living shit out of me, mister," she hissed. "If you ever... *ever* do anything like that... I'll never speak to you again. God help me. I love you, Nick."

The big man managed a smile and then nodded toward the other patients.

"The father is going to be okay. The last two are breathing on their own, but still out. You saved three lives, Nick. You ever pull a stunt like that again and I'll...."

Diana's pending threat was interrupted by a collapsing wall of the nearby home. Hot cinder fireflies danced skyward, quickly doused by a thick stream of water arching through the night. Nick could make out three men struggling with a large hose, spewing volumes of water onto what little remained of the structure.

Twenty minutes later, Diana and Kevin assisted a weak, wobbly Nick on the golf cart. His jeans and t-shirt smelled so strongly of scorched ash, the Deacon forbid him to enter the sanctuary, instead forcing him to undress and then shower in one of the auxiliary buildings. Kevin refused to leave his father's side, closely observing his every move in case his dad became weak or dizzy again.

Two large containers of water and a double dose of aspirin later, Nick crawled into bed.

Early the next afternoon, a grumpy, aching, and slightly singed Nick finally joined the living. After brewing a cup of coffee and swallowing a couple of additional painkillers, the big, grouchy bear located Diana in her office. Three gentlemen occupied the visitors' chairs facing the deacon's desk.

Nick's foul mood was nothing compared to Diana's. The scowl on her face and tone of her voice warned the ex-Green Beret he was within range of a dangerous woman. He determined silence was the astute tactic of choice, even before he managed a seat on the couch.

"I want to know why the fire truck wasn't a higher priority. I think the townspeople deserve an explanation from all of us, and I think they deserve it immediately," Diana said in a serious tone.

"But… but Diana, we have so many projects going on, and our resources are tapped. The only fire engine we have left had its tank spiked to loot its fuel. No one has lubricated or maintained the equipment in months. The tires are flat, and the battery is dead. On top of all that, our welder – Alpha's own 'McGyver,' has been overwhelmed by the volume of work required of him. I don't know where we would be without his creative solutions, fixing machinery without the luxury of ordering parts over the internet. The fact is, Miss Brown, we just hadn't gotten around to repairing the engine as other priorities took precedence."

Diana sat her elbows on the desktop, both hands massaging her temples. "I know we're all doing our best, but we've got to organize and do better. Last night's fire could've turned into a complete disaster. We were lucky the wind was calm. We could have lost that whole side of town. Who knows how many bodies we would be burying this week if that had happened?"

"Deacon, everyone is working extra hard to get civilization back on track, but the priorities are difficult to determine and manage," pleaded one of the gentlemen. "We're working down our list, but people don't always agree which is the most important task. It's impossible to override the opinion of others when everyone is a volunteer, and there's no structure or hierarchy of authority."

Nodding at her visitors, Diana stood and moved around her desk – a signal the meeting was over. "Okay, gentlemen, thank you for stopping by. I'll not keep you any longer this afternoon. If anyone has any suggestions on how to improve our situation, please, please bring them to me."

The three elders pushed back their chairs and executed the proper social amenities. Hands were shaken, Nick was robustly thanked for his heroism, and his health was verified.

Returning to his perch on the couch, Nick studied Diana as she escorted the three men from her office, trying to determine her frame of mind. Obviously, the pressure and workload of running a small town was an extreme burden, but he detected something deeper was troubling her.

The deacon-turned-city-mayor returned, avoiding eye contact with Nick. She hurried past without a word, silently returning to her desk where she unfolded her laptop and focused on the display.

Nick let the tapping of Diana's keystrokes dominate the room, sipping his coffee and staring at nothing. After a few minutes, he decided Diana needed solitude and rose to leave.

"We've got to change something. This isn't working," sounded a cold voice from behind the computer.

Nick paused mid-step, unsure of Diana's meaning. "What isn't working? Us? The town? Your computer?"

Pivoting to face the woman he loved, Nick's face exposed more concern over the potential answer than he intended.

Diana reached up and closed the laptop's cover, her eyes locking with his. "Oh, don't be silly. I'm not talking about our relationship. Unless you've found some hero-groupie on the side, I'm as much in love with you as ever. I'm talking about the town… our society… how we're rebuilding Alpha."

A sigh escaped the big man's chest, his eyes mellowing. "You had me worried there for a sec. I thought you were still mad at me over last night."

Grunting, Diana waved him off. "Oh, I am, but not super-duper mad. That was a reckless stunt you pulled. It could've turned out badly. I've already lost my son and my father because of this mess – I'm running out of loved ones to donate to the cause."

Diana sauntered over to Nick's side of the room, extending her arms for an embrace. He welcomed the invitation, holding her close and relishing the moment. With her head against his chest, the deacon summed up her current municipal dilemma. "Everyone's heart is in the right place, but we've got to change how we're organized. There needs to be leadership, structure, and guidance."

"Go on."

Looking up, Diana continued. "The fire truck was listed as a critical project weeks ago. The reason why half the town almost burned down last night was that no one had the authority to follow up. No one pushed here and pulled there. Our volunteer force ultimately isn't accountable to the town."

"I don't know about that. It looked like those three gentlemen were answering to you just a bit ago. They all left here with their tails between their legs; at least it looked that way to me."

"That's just the problem, Nick. I'm not officially in charge of anything. I am just leadership by default. There are groups of people who are starting their own projects that the church elders and I don't even know about them. There's a vacuum of authority, and it's going to keep hurting everyone until it's filled."

Base Hospital
Fort Bliss, Texas

Terri's body couldn't tolerate the bedside chair any longer. Being close to five months pregnant, her back and shoulders eventually demanded that she locate a more suitable place to rest. The couch in Bishop's room was actually a luxury compared to both the hard-bottomed chair and her bunk back at the camper. She glanced longingly at the cushions.

The steady rhythm of the heart monitor provided a background of white noise. The constant tempo of the machine worked on the exhausted woman's mind, a hypnotic effect similar to a train's clickity-clack wooing the weary passenger to sleep. The contraption's beeping provided a secondary benefit as well; Terri could relax, comfortable in the knowledge that she would hear any change in Bishop's condition.

Despite her fatigued state, Terri's sleep had been troubled and restless the past few days. Beyond obvious concern for her husband, the uncertainty of life without him weighed upon her. The brutal treatment she had received at the hands of her kidnapper added more insomnia-baggage. Terri suffered.

She didn't look up at first when the door to Bishop's room opened. Nurses, the occasional doctor, or other medical professionals commonly plied the threshold, and she was too tired to care.

Something about the visitor's pace grabbed her attention, the movement from the corner of her eye slower than the typical rushed caregiver. A glance showed the Colonel struggling to open the door while walking with a cane.

She started to rise, but the recovering man waved her off with a grumpy, "I've got to learn to do this."

"As you wish, Colonel," she replied in a cold, monotone voice.

"How's he doing?"

"The same. He's not regained consciousness since being in surgery for nine hours. The doctors are unsure if he ever will. He's in God's hands now."

The Colonel shook his head and grimaced, not sure how to respond. After a pause, he switched his attention to Terri. "And you?"

"I'm fine. Thank you for asking," sounded a practiced response.

"Terri, don't bullshit me. I know you're not fine. No one could be *fine* after what you've been through. As a matter of fact, you're the real reason why I wanted to stop by. I can't help Bishop, but I hoped I might lend comfort to you."

Terri's eyes turned to ice. She tilted her head and stared hard at the older man. "Colonel, I'm not in a place to be comforted. Actually, I don't want to feel better. I'm enjoying my hatred... relishing in my acidic rage. I'm very content wallowing in a deep revulsion for my fellow man."

The Colonel lowered his head, chin practically resting on his chest. After a pause of contemplation, he stirred, making for an empty visitor's chair using deliberate, measured steps. Gingerly lowering himself onto the hard plastic seat, he raised his eyes and studied Terri for a moment. "I don't blame you. You've looked into the eye of the beast, and now you know him. It's an experience that will change you forever. How you react to that exposure will determine the quality of your life from this point forward."

"The beast? I'm not sure what you mean Colonel. I've just had a brush with power-hungry, self-centered men... human beings who possess an unquenchable thirst to achieve dominance over others and will stop at nothing to achieve status. You can call evil anything you want – it's still evil."

The Colonel shrugged at Terri's response. "Evil is too simple a term. Besides, I didn't come here to quibble over semantics. I came here because you and I now have something in common. A window was opened, and we both looked inside. We both have been repulsed by what we saw. It just so happens my glimpse into that portal occurred 25 years ago. Time and experience have allowed me to deal with it. I hoped I might help you to do the same."

Terri's demeanor changed with the Colonel's words. After a deep sigh, she said, "You'll have to forgive me, but I've got you pegged on the problem side of the ledger. You can see why, can't you? Bishop and I would've never gotten involved in this whole mess if not for your relationship with the previous president."

"Yes, I can see how easy it would be to connect those dots if I were in your place. Did Bishop explain why I had a relationship with the previous Commander in Chief?"

Terri shook her head, "No."

"Let's just say my reaction to staring the beast in the eye was to withdraw... to retreat." A harsh look crossed the man's eyes, his focus moving to the floor. "It might be more accurate to say I ran and hid."

A man like the Colonel admitting to running or hiding from anything renewed Terri's interest. While she didn't know the man sitting across from her all that well, Bishop had always painted a picture of an ultra-brave, incredibly tough individual - a man who had never sampled the stench of fear.

"The man my husband has described would never retreat, Colonel."

Grunting, he responded, "This enemy is all encompassing, young lady. It corrupts the stoutest of souls and weakens the most powerful of intellects. You can't defeat it, only limit its scope. Even then, that resistance isn't a matter of morals, muscles, or superior firepower. All of those things mean nothing when fighting my so-called beast."

Pausing for a moment to adjust his cane, the Colonel's gaze fell on Bishop lying in the bed. A shadow of pain crossed behind his eyes before he continued. "The person who holds the office of the president is the most powerful man on earth. That word 'powerful' is correct by so many definitions; military might, economic potential, social influence – it's really the king of the human-hill... the pinnacle of accomplishment for mankind. In the history of our species, there have been other, similar positions. Their titles might have been different - King, Emperor, Kahn... it really doesn't matter. When there is a single role for any human being that wields that much power, the beast raises its mighty head and lays waste."

"Power corrupts, Colonel. Is that where you're going with this?"

"No. Again, that concept is too single-dimensional for what really occurs. But, we can talk about this later. Right now, you look exhausted. Why don't you go lie down on that couch for an hour, and I'll keep watch over Bishop. I promise to wake you if he moves a muscle."

Terri looked at her husband lying beside her. She reached up and brushed his cheek. "Okay, Colonel. I'll take you up on that offer. Thank you. But be advised, I would like to continue this conversation after I've had some rest."

"Of course we can."

An hour later, Terri watched as the Colonel rose to leave, a new understanding of why her husband respected the man so much.

"Colonel, before you go, you said you could help me deal with this... this beast thing."

"It's very simple, really. You can either withdraw, as I did, or you can fight to limit the size of the beast – reduce its influence. It thrives on mass. If you reduce the size of the buffet, it can't grow."

The Colonel turned without further comment and made his way to the hall.

As her mind replayed the Colonel's words, she sensed something was different. The monitor sounded the same. Or did it?

Sighing loudly, she rolled her feet from the couch and took a step toward Bishop. Her eyes were mainly concerned about the monitor, but movement drew her attention. His eyes were open!

"Bishop! Bishop, it's Terri. Can you hear me, baby?"

The patient's throat moved, his Adam's apple bobbing as if he wanted to talk. Terri moved closer, her heart racing but afraid to breathe in case he said something.

"Bishop, can you look at me?"

Her husband's eyes fluttered for a moment and then closed. Terri watched, her hands clasped as if in prayer. Time passed, and she was about to turn away when Bishop's mouth moved... once... twice... and then he whispered hoarsely, "Water."

Terri was overwhelmed for a moment, before ransacking the room to fill her husband's request. The nightstand was void of liquids, and there weren't any cups to fill. A single tear slid down her cheek as she kissed Bishop's forehead and promised, "I'll get you something to drink. Just hold on, Bishop."

Hitting the call button hanging from the bed's rail, Terri paused and then headed out of the room. Her intention was to race to the nurses' station and get some water. She made it to the door where she smacked headlong into an RN on her way to answer the alarm.

"He's awake! He opened his eyes! He said the word 'Water,'" came bubbling from Terri's throat.

The nurse moved to check the patient, but Bishop did not respond. "Okay, tell me exactly what happened," the lady instructed a disappointed Terri.

Chapter 2

Alpha, Texas
January 10, 2016

Word of a wondrous land filled with neon lights, culinary delights, and a functioning economy spread quickly throughout West Texas even though the collapse of the US economy had left a gaping hole in the communication sector. Prior to the fall, Americans were constantly pelleted with updates and salacious gossip via Facebook and Twitter and internet news. Citizens had been spoiled by the ability to be "in the know" every second of every day. Living through the most newsworthy event of US history without the benefit of cable-delivered updates created a vacuum that demanded to be satisfied. And so the news of West Texas' move from simply surviving, to all out thriving passed through multiple venues, some sophisticated and deliberate, some accidental and "no tech." Despite the low population density and lack of phone service, information managed to get around.

Without television, internet, or newspapers, people's hunger for any sort of update was intense. Rumors, exaggerated claims, and false reports dominated most of the exchanges, but people didn't seem to care. Any story from the outside world, even if make-believe, seemed to provide a break from a life that had turned into a mundane existence.

Two ranch hands, each riding fence for neighboring spreads, stopped to exchange gossip. It took a while, but one finally convinced the other that he wasn't joking - Meraton had electricity, air conditioning, and frosty alcoholic beverages.

Another man stopped in to visit an elderly neighbor while on a hunt, the former anxious to see the excitement on his friend's face as he told the story of Alpha's streetlights glowing on the distant horizon.

The distribution of information wasn't always haphazard. Alpha and Meraton were each home to a single surviving HAM radio operator. Both men's equipment now glowed warm with energized tubes and charged circuits – all because of the wind. The capabilities afforded by the long-range communications reached far beyond an amateur broadcaster in Meraton being able to share updates with a comrade in Alpha. Signals were sent and received from all over the nation, and even a few voices from abroad were detected.

By whatever means, more and more people learned of the miracle of West Texas each day. Most were enamored with the story because of the sliver of hope it engendered. Desperate citizens who were barely hanging onto life possessed a deep thirst for a drink of optimism. Most people couldn't muster the wherewithal to pick up and travel to the fabled paradises of Meraton or Alpha. Unless their current existence was unsustainable, most of the survivors deemed the risk of relocation too high. But there were many who had run out of options – many who felt they had nothing to lose.

Some people called them refugees. Others preferred the term immigrants. The influx started as a trickle, quickly building into a steady stream of new arrivals. While their method of transport varied, the virtual parade of horse-drawn, ox-powered, and conventional cars and trucks was inspiring, and occasionally comical. Some people hiked great distances while others drove into town via what appeared to be freshly detailed luxury sedans. A few surviving over-the-road semi tractors were part of the mix, their owner-operators pulling in with trailers full of every conceivable cargo, including human beings.

The deluge of humanity was unexpected, but initially caused little concern. Alpha had plenty of available housing, the community having suffered the loss of 80% of its population to a poison gas cloud followed by months of anarchy and conflict. As more and more travelers arrived, Deacon Brown realized the need for some sort of organization and administration to handle the growth.

Most of the new arrivals were disoriented; many were hungry, and more than a few suffered serious medical conditions. The church's council of elders decided to set up greeters on each highway leading into town. The refugees would be directed to the courthouse where a welcoming committee would help everyone become acclimated. Housing was assigned, occupations and skills documented, and work assignments made. The town's population swelled by 10 the first day, 26 the next, and over 40 per day after that. Meraton, not having experienced the same loss of citizens as Alpha, didn't have any abandoned homes.

Pete asked that all new arrivals that wandered into their little village be directed to Alpha.

"Nick, we are going to need more than a deacon of a local church to run things. This is getting out of hand. I have no real authority. I wasn't elected to anything, and it won't be long before my decisions are openly challenged."

"Hold an election, Diana. Everyone here was raised on the democratic selection of leaders. Announce the formation of a government, and let everyone vote."

Diana set aside the stack of papers she was browsing, a look of frustration on her face. "You make it sound so easy."

Nick stood and stretched, his toned frame expanding as he worked the stiffness from his limbs. "It *is* easy. Make up some posters, get some ballots, and pick a date. Give anyone who wants to be the mayor one week to sign up. Set a date a week later for everyone to vote. Have a debate if somebody feels it necessary. There's nothing else to do around here at night anyway."

Diana shook her head, slightly annoyed at how simple her friend could make things sound. "And what? We'll elect a dictator? What about checks and balances? How do we establish justice? It's not that simple."

Nick moved behind the woman he loved and rubbed her shoulders. "I've had some pretty extensive training in how to organize resistance forces. Maybe I'm oversimplifying things, but this is not insurmountable."

After helping with the stress in her shoulders, Nick picked up a map of the town, the rendition created as part of the kit passed out to newcomers. Taking a pen and ruler, he divided Alpha into four sections. In the middle of town, the section with the highest population, he made a large circle.

Showing his artwork to Diana, he continued. "Each section of town can elect a councilman, or district representative. Those people sit on the council. Five districts equals an odd number of votes, so there's never a tie. Simple majority rules. The mayor can veto any vote. It takes four council votes to override the veto. Plain, simple and fair."

Diana scratched her chin, pondering Nick's suggestion.

He continued, "The mayor is responsible for enforcement of the council's rules or laws. Budgets, civic projects, and other efforts should be voted on by the majority. Once something is passed, then the mayor is in charge of executing."

Looking up and smiling, Diana acknowledged the simplicity of Nick's structure. "At worst, it's a place to start. I guess we can always modify it as we grow."

Nick nodded, "Even before the collapse, every city and state had unique methods of local governance. Organize something to kick start the process, and the people will modify it as we go."

Diana stood and hugged the big man. After the embrace was over, she pulled back with a sheepish look on her face. "Should I run for mayor?"

"Of course you should. I've been impressed by how effective you are as a leader. The people respect your judgment, and they naturally sense that you have their best interests in mind as you guide them. Also consider that in many aspects, you are already performing the job right now, without the help of five council representatives or the Good Housekeeping Seal of Approval from the citizenry."

Turning away, the former church leader hesitated. "But... but I make so many mistakes... so many bad calls."

Nick squeezed the woman's shoulders and said, "People don't expect anyone to be perfect, Diana. They will demand honesty and transparency to trust their leaders. They will want someone's heart to be in the right place. They need a real person to take charge – someone who is one of them. Not a plastic politician with a perfect smile who's in bed with some special interest. Alpha isn't Washington, and most of the folks who survived would tell you our old capital wasn't working very well anyway. As long as you serve the people and put them first, then you'll do well."

Base Hospital
Fort Bliss, Texas
January 10, 2016

Terri's sleep deficit worsened after Bishop's brief awakening. Next to her on the bedside table resided a full water beaker and several paper cups – ready at a moment's notice.

While she possessed a desperate longing for the couch and rest, her mind found the concept of being away from her husband unacceptable. She was absolutely convinced that Bishop would need her the moment she wasn't at his side.

Every hour that passed made the situation less tolerable. Reaching for Bishop's hand, she finally whispered, "Bishop, I've got to rest. I'll be over on the couch if you need me. I love you so very much, baby."

"Okay. Love you, too."

Terri's head snapped around, thinking someone else was in the room and was playing a very bad joke. After finding no one, she leaned close to her husband and whispered, "Bishop, would you like a drink of water before I lie down?"

"Yes, please. I'm very thirsty."

Terri's hands came together as if she was praying, her face flashing a genuine smile. She was so excited, she almost forgot the patient's request.

Quickly filling a cup, she coached, "Bishop, I need you to tilt your head forward and take a drink."

Touching the vessel to his lips, she almost squealed when his head made a partial motion forward. His lips opened, and he managed a swallow. Another followed… and then another.

"Bishop, how long have you been awake?"

"I'm not awake. You're dreaming."

It took Terri a moment to realize the joke. It really *was* Bishop… he really was in there.

"In my dream, you want more water. So tilt your head forward again."

He complied and managed several swallows. Terri pressed the call button again, hoping Bishop would manage to stay awake long enough to speak to the nurse. While she was waiting, his eyes fluttered and then opened, squinting at the brightness of the room.

Terri had never felt such relief as when he tilted his head slightly, and he looked her straight in the eye. She smiled lovingly at him, and he attempted to return the gesture.

The nurse entered the room and strode purposely to the bed. "Well, Mr. Bishop, welcome back to the world. My name is Lieutenant Haley. How are you feeling?"

"I've been better. Why is my throat so dry and sore? It really sucks," he crackled.

While she charted the patient's pulse and other vitals, LT Haley responded. "We had you on oxygen to help you breathe. It dries everything out, but it beats the alternative. Do you have any other pain?"

Back and forth the evaluation went, the nurse quizzing her patient and Bishop doing his best to answer. When she had finished, she asked, "Bishop, do you have any questions for me?"

"Yes, ma'am. Just how bad is it?"

"The bullet entered at an odd angle. I heard the surgeon comment that he'd never seen anything quite like it. The bullet penetrated your body immediately in front of your clavicle, the collarbone, the impact fragmenting the slug. Some part of the bullet nicked the subclavain vein an inch from your heart. You were very, very lucky. It was the small slice in the vein that almost got you a near fatal loss of blood via hemorrhage."

Bishop's groggy mind took a bit to digest everything the nurse had said. After a bit, he managed, "So, what you're saying is a headlong collision with 130 grains of lead isn't a good thing to do?"

Nurse Haley laughed and patted Bishop's arm. "Yes, that about sums it up. You're going to be sore for a while, young man. You won't have full use of your left side for several weeks."

Terri piped up, "But he's going to be all right? I mean... eventually?"

The nurse smiled, "I'm not qualified to answer that, but the doctor will be in this afternoon. That would be a better question for him."

Terri accepted the woman's answer with a grimace, but didn't press.

"You'll be very sleepy for a while, Bishop. You're on some serious pain medications. Don't fight it or worry about it. I'll be back in a few hours."

Terri watched as the nurse replaced the chart before leaving the room, and then enthusiastically gripped Bishop's hand. Bishop seemed content to just lie among the pillows and gaze at his wife. After a while, he squeezed her hand slightly and announced, "Terri, I'm getting sleepy again. Why don't you rest for a while too?"

Ten minutes later, Terri finally relaxed and entered a deep slumber, her head just touching Bishop's shoulder, her hand still clasping his.

West Texas
January 13, 2016

The rising moon provided more than enough light to silhouette the two riders, the outline of their horses and hats clear against the brightening night sky. The cowboys had chosen their perch well, atop a crest that surveyed two valleys, each filled with dark profiles of grazing cattle.

The herd was restless for such a calm evening – a state the two riders attributed to their presence and the impending roundup that would begin at sunrise. "Sure sounds like they're protesting tonight," commented one of the hands.

"I don't know man. There is an edge to their lowing. You don't think we've got a mountain lion around, do ya?"

"Naw, there's not been a big cat up this way for 15 years. We would have seen tracks or a carcass by now. They're just pissed 'cause we're going to make 'em walk in the morning."

"Thank heavens our watch is up in another hour, these early morning rounds are killing me."

The listener grunted, responding, "Oh stop yer whining. Next thing ya know you'll be wanting an air mattress under your bedroll."

Behind a short outcropping, some 250 yards away, the outline of the speaker was centered in the cross hairs of a 10-power scope, the optic mounted on a 30-06 bolt-action rifle. The man holding the long gun pulled his eye away and whispered to his partner. "I could knock those two off their horses from here – no sweat. Do you want me to take 'em out?"

"And what would you do with the nine others in the camp just over the ridge?"

"We could handle them too."

"Maybe... maybe not. Come on, let's head back to the trucks and see how the other guys are doing."

The man with the rifle was disappointed, the moonlight illuminating just enough of his face to show a scowl. The two men carefully worked their way down the slope, gingerly stepping around the chance lemon cactus and clusters of protruding, thorny ladyfinger.

"What's the prognosis?" the man without a rifle asked as they approached.

An older man's head appeared from under the raised hood of an old pickup, his face looking pale and ghost-like in the beam of a flashlight. "It's fucked. The engine is completely locked up and won't even turn over. No way it's hauling any beef tonight."

"Shit!"

The outburst startled the three steers in the bed of the vehicle. Hooves thumped on the truck's metal bed, the pressure of the weight of the livestock causing the cattle rails to groan.

"All right, all right. Let's get those three off the back of that truck so we can tow the damn thing out of here. Hurry, before those cowboys wander out this way, and we end up in a shootout. One of you go back and keep an eye on those riders."

Up on the ridge, one of the rider's heads tilted toward the north. "Did you hear something?"

"No, but I heard an owl just a couple of minutes ago."

"Naw, that wasn't it. I heard something like metal grinding on metal. Came from over that way."

"Are you sure?"

Pulling a pistol from his holster, the reaction made it clear to his partner that he was indeed sure. "You think we should go back and get the others?"

The question was a difficult one. Rustlers had been in the area, stealing several head a few weeks ago. If the two men retrieved their co-workers for nothing, the ribbing would be relentless. If they found armed poachers were the source of the noise, they might wish for reinforcements.

"I'm going to go check it out. You go back and get Mack and the boys. I'll be working my way up that narrow canyon, so don't shoot me by accident."

Carefully guiding his steed down the rocky slope, the cowboy finally reached the flat, hard-packed bottom. The creak of saddle leather broke the silence of the desert as he dismounted, quickly reaching down to remove his spurs and avoid the jingle bob of the rowels.

The moonlight cast odd shadows across the valley floor, dark pools of light combining with the black shapes of outcroppings to limit a man's field of vision while at the same time providing countless places to hide or spring a bushwhack. The ranch hand moved cautiously, pistol drawn and head pivoting right and left. The Glock .45 caliber felt good in his hand, the plastic, high capacity weapon his preferred sidearm – long ago replacing the less accurate, less capable six-shooter. He led the horse, the beast of burden, a potential necessity for a quick getaway or to give chase. As a last resort, a man *could* take cover behind his horse, but that was *only* as a last resort.

Three hundred yards further down the valley and obscured by a bend, the leader finished tying off the towrope, the thick cord of hemp now a lifeline for the disabled truck. After double-checking the knot, he peered toward the back in time to witness the last steer being motivated to back off the ramp and out of the bed.
Rapid footfalls caused his head to snap up, the man assigned to keep an eye on the cowboys rushing closer. "One of them is coming this way… I think they've heard us."

"How far away?"

"Three hundred yards, give or take. He dismounted, and then I lost him."

White teeth flashed in the moonlight, the smile gleaming wicked phosphorescent in the lunar radiance. Turning to the cab of the truck, he extracted a large satchel and began rummaging inside. Producing a bundle of tubes and a large spool of wire, he looked up and declared, "I'm going to buy us some time. Make sure these lazy shits have everything ready to go when I get back." Before the man could acknowledge, the boss was gone, swallowed up by the darkness.

The bundle of TNT was hustled 50 yards up the draw where a steep face of rock towered over the bottom landscape below. Some thousands of years ago a chunk of the cliff had buckled, the geographic event leaving several slabs and larger boulders that narrowed the passage. There wasn't time to scientifically place the packet of explosives, so he deposited them near the bottom of the vertical wall.

A long screwdriver was shoved in the spool after the wires were judiciously connected to the bundle. Playing out the thin electrical cable, the boss stepped backwards toward the waiting trucks.

The tailgate of the broken down jalopy was still open. The head honcho hopped up on the shelf of metal and then commanded, "Let's go now... real slow. I'll signal when I want you to stop."

With his feet dangling over the edge, the tow vehicle engaged, the initial jerk of the rope almost dumping the passenger off the gate. The slight convoy of trucks began to shuffle across the valley, wire spinning off the ever-dwindling spool.

The pursuing ranch hand proceeded cautiously until he recognized engine noise. The drone was coming from around the next bend, or so he thought. He knew that the vertical rock walls could distort distance and sound. He was trying to choose between mounting up and chasing or waiting until help arrived.

The decision was made for him, the thundering of hoofs made by several riders removing any option and providing enormous relief for the lone rider. He mounted up and waved his hat, a signal that he hoped would be recognized as friendly.

The truck-boss whistled for the procession to stop and without waiting, jumped off the tailgate. Trailing the almost empty spool, he again dug in the satchel and produced a 6-volt battery that might be used on a motorcycle or outboard motor. He switched on his flashlight. Holding the torch in his mouth, he hooked the ground wire first. Looking back, he moved the hot cable toward the positive connection.

Mack and the rest of the men charged up, stopping beside their man. "I heard engine noises around that bend – I think they're pulling out," he reported.

"Let's go," the foreman commanded.

Spurs raked horseflesh, and the animals charged into the night. The group had ridden less than 30 yards when the cliff in front of them exploded in a blinding flash of white followed by a clap of thunder that would have embarrassed any storm. The horses reacted first, pulling up so quickly that their riders were almost thrown over their mount's heads. Others spun wildly to flee the detonation.

A rainstorm of rocks and dust was next. Two of the men were struck by softball-sized rocks dropping out of the sky, resulting in a broken arm and soon-to-be throbbing and bruised shoulder.

After retreating a few hundred feet, Mack immediately conducted a headcount, relieved to find all of his party intact, although badly shaken.

"Should we go back after them?" a hand questioned, his tone making it clear he wasn't in support of the idea.

"No," Mack answered. "They're long gone by now, and I imagine that blast collapsed the wall and blocked the pass. Besides, we're not in a position to fight high explosives. There might be more where that came from."

Alpha, Texas
January 13, 2016

A mild north wind produced a rare chill in the air, but the conditions weren't enough to keep the citizens of Alpha indoors. Almost relishing in the breeze, the residents of the normally blistering, arid climate seemed to enjoy the change in their routine weather and went about their business in rarely worn jackets and light coats.

For three days, Diana had been making the rounds, chatting to every person within earshot about organizing the town and conducting elections. After the first day, she had used the large copy machine in the church's basement to print off a few hundred single page flyers outlining a plan and her proposals. The documents were distributed quickly, her heart warmed by seeing small groups of people standing around and discussing the vote.

In general, the people of Alpha understood both the concept and the need of an organized society. Many shrugged off the idea of elections, making random comments like, "Why don't you just go ahead and do it Diana?" Others asked probing questions, and a few offered suggestions.

The warmth of the deacon's mood overwhelmed the colder air, the bounce in her step perkier than anyone could remember since the collapse. Each carrying a stack of poster-sized signs, Diana and four volunteers marched from the church's grounds toward the city's center armed with nails, hammers, and the carefully created notices of the election. The purpose in Miss Brown's stride was obvious to any observer.

Nick intercepted the squad a few blocks away, his curiosity overriding an already overbooked calendar of his own. "So, you're going to post official notice. How did the signs turn out?"

Holding up an example, Diana beamed with pride. "I'm so excited, Nick. The teenagers' Bible study group did a really nice job on these. We're going to open registration at the courthouse tomorrow and hold elections a week from today!"

Nick studied the poster, grinning at Diana's excitement and a major step forward for the town.

"This is huge, Diana - a really important time for our community. I'm so proud of you and the others."

A few hours later, the signs were displayed all over Alpha, and the population's excitement was stimulating. It wasn't an expectation of any post-election miracles, but more a feeling of community spirit and participation. Democracy was returning to West Texas, and for many, that was almost as important as electricity.

Meraton, Texas
January 14, 2016

Pete shadowed Betty throughout The Manor's garden, his role diminished to pack mule for a bag of fertilizer and its accompanying bottle of spray insecticide.

"Multi-tasking, Pete. If you want to talk to me, you're going to have to do it while I'm tending the grounds," she had declared. "I'm too busy right now to just sit and gab."

Watching the hotel's manager snip errant stems, Pete began, "I wanted to talk to you about the news that Alpha is holding elections. I got the word from the HAM operator, and I think it's an incredible idea."

Betty turned and exchanged her clippers for the bag in Pete's hand. Sprinkling a handful of granules on the soil, she responded, "I heard about it this morning from one of the guests. Word must be spreading pretty fast."

"I think everyone is excited. I believe we should do the same here in Meraton."

Betty stopped her activity, turning to face her friend. "Pete, is there something wrong? I thought you were happy being our unofficial mayor?"

"There's nothing wrong. It's just that Meraton deserves a real mayor – not the local bartender. As we continue to recover, image is going to be important. I don't think it looks good for the mayor to be serving moonshine. Besides, if we're going to continue to grow, we need to have an *official* mayor, not the unofficial kind."

Betty studied her friend's face, finally judging he wasn't being entirely truthful about nothing being wrong. That decided, she returned to her chores. "And who would run this town? You've been a key part of why things have run as smoothly as they have."

"That would be up to the voters. We could divide Meraton like they're doing in Alpha and elect a council. It's the right way to do things and will eliminate problems as we continue to expand."

Betty grunted, “Pete, I don’t know of any other person I want making the decisions for Meraton. There’s no one here who can handle that job as well as you can. I’ve got no problem with an election, as long as you run for the top spot.”

Pete waved her off, “Meraton had a mayor and city council long before I rode into this one-horse town. Things were just fine then. I am telling you, Betty… I don’t think it looks good for the guy managing the city to manage a honky-tonk, too.”

Betty stood and motioned Pete to follow. Ambling behind The Manor’s main building, Betty pointed to a freshly tilled area. “Do you see that, Pete? That’s my new garden. It’s not very attractive, or nice to look at, just a garden that will grow food. I’ll have squash, beans, tomatoes and even a watermelon or two if they take.”

“Looks nice, Betty. When did you manage to do all that?”

“I’ve been working on that particular plot of earth on and off for a few weeks now. Do you realize how sacrilegious that garden is?” Pete’s forehead knotted, not quite understanding where she was going.

Without waiting for his answer, she continued. “The Manor’s gardens were a tourist attraction for years. Many people around town still believe Meraton wouldn’t have survived if it weren’t for these gardens and the visitors who drove for hundreds of miles to see them – visitors who spent lots of money in our little community. For me to waste the land, fertilizer and time planting this section with regular old, everyday vegetables would have been insulting just a year ago. The act would have belittled these fancy gardens… *ruined our image*, so to speak. Now, no one even cares because they all understand I need the food to survive.”

Pete spread his hands, a gesture indicating he still didn’t understand.

“Having the town’s barkeep running the show may not be pretty. It may not hold up that reputation that was important before everything fell apart, just like my garden. But times have changed. The town needs you and others like you to survive, just like I need this garden. You’re not exotic like the rest of these plants, but you can get the job done, and that’s what is important now.”

Pete snorted, "So you're saying I'm not pretty, and I'm a vegetable?"

Betty didn't even flinch, instead stirring the fresh compost with her trowel. "Yup, that's exactly what I'm saying."

Pete waved his friend off and started to turn away when he paused and spun back around. "I'll run for mayor, but you have to run for the city council. Deal?"

Laughing, The Manor's manager shrugged her shoulders. "I guess two vegetables won't hurt. We can make a salad."

"We'll make a damned good salad."

"You've got to sit up," announced Nurse Haley. "We've got to get you on your feet."

"What? Are you serious?" protested Bishop. "I know news travels slowly these days, but in case you haven't heard, I was shot only a few days ago."

"I'm well aware of your time-line, Bishop. You should've been on your feet yesterday, but your doc had mercy. Come on. Now."

"I don't think this is a good idea just yet."

"If we can prove you're mobile, we can remove all of these tubes. You can eat regular food, and I might even be able to arrange a cup of coffee now and then."

"Coffee? Okay, let's get this over with."

Pulling back the covers and arranging IV tubes, the lieutenant motioned with her hands for Bishop to sit. Taking the arm on his good side, she gently helped the weakened man to rise.

After several cringes and grunts, Bishop finally managed the edge of the bed. He glared at the nurse and proclaimed, "That sucked."

“I know, but you did well. Stay upright for 15 minutes, and I’ll see what dietary has to say about a half cup of coffee. Tomorrow, I’m going to make you walk and pour your own java.”

Bishop’s voice carried astonishment, “Walk?”

“You heard me, trooper. The sooner we get you moving around, the faster you’ll heal. I want to see you completely up and at it in two days.”

Shaking his head, Bishop muttered, “I think I woke up in the wrong place. This must be the interrogation unit because I’m being subjected to torture. Somebody call Geneva. I think my Florence Nightingale has turned out to be Attila the Hun instead.”

Ignoring the snide remark, the nurse began jotting notes on the chart. Turning to leave, she glanced over her shoulder at Terri and instructed, “Don’t let him cheat on me. I’ll be back in a few minutes.”

“Yes, ma’am.”

Chapter 3

Midland Station, Texas
January 16, 2016

Cameron James Lewis noted the children's artwork taped to the walls as he passed through the hallway of the James Lewis Elementary School, a facility named after his father. The presence of such non-essential decorations actually comforted the executive's mind, a subtle message buried in the swirling colors and stick-figure drawings that there was a future for his species, town, and company.

He paused to examine some of the pictures in detail and quickly determined the theme of the children's project. The history of Midland Station had obviously been the assignment. Grunting, he traced the crayon stroked images of his town's past, the third graders doing an excellent job of depicting the stages of economic development.

Midland Station, Texas began life as little more than a train depot for the Texas Pacific Railroad a score before the turn of the century. The sleepy, one-dirt-path town didn't remain a speck on the map for long, and quickly grew in prominence. Due in part to the growth of the stockyards in Fort Worth, Midland Station became a prosperous loading center for the local ranchers to transport cattle to the larger metropolitan areas to the east. As such, it grew in prominence and was soon designated the county seat.

Additionally, the village enjoyed the distinction of a geographical formation named the Spraberry Trend. Discovered a short 60 years later, it provided the catalyst for the city to expand exponentially, eventually attracting more than 100,000 inhabitants who called it home.

The Trend was named after one Mr. Abner Spraberry, a local rancher who happened to own the land where the oil was first discovered.

For the first 40 years after the detection of Texas Tea beneath the semi-arid grasslands, the Trend was thought to be the biggest petrochemical head-fake in history. At one point in time, the US Department of Energy descried the Spraberry Trend as the largest *unrecoverable* oil reserve in the world.

Wells by the thousands were sunk into the earth's crust, and practically all of them found oil. Time and time again, great celebrations were held and investor propaganda was generated en masse.

But inevitably, something unforeseen occurred - the wells would stop producing. Independent oil companies went bust by the score. Every few years, the cycle was repeated, typically reinitiated by some advancement in technology that promised access to the ocean of black gold sitting beneath the town. For decades, those expectations were never met.

Midland Station and her sister city, Odyssey, didn't boom, and they didn't wither. The endless cycles of drill-produce-bust kept enough money flowing through the local economies to provide for steady, but unspectacular growth. It wasn't until the late 1980s that a technique called "fracking" was used to access the oil below. Spraberry finally began to produce steady, profitable results. The Trend remains the third largest known reserve in North America.

Cameron looked at his watch and decided he'd spent enough time gazing at the museum of child art. He had a full schedule on his calendar today and needed to stick to his agenda.

Another few doors down, he found a neatly printed index card with bold black letters indicating that he had indeed arrived at Mrs. Evan's 4th grade classroom. Through the closed door, he could hear murmuring of distorted voices reciting multiplication tables.

Bracing the heavy box he carried against the frame while knocking twice, Cam reached for the door and entered the classroom. His presence immediately drew the attention of 31 pairs of young eyes. Mrs. Evans was also interested in the interruption, her annoyed look instantly replaced with a broad, welcoming smile. She rose from her desk and approached, offering her hand as a greeting.

"Good morning, Mr. Lewis. Welcome to our class."

Cameron placed the box by the door and accepted the teacher's handshake. "Good morning, Mrs. Evans. Thank you for inviting me."

Turning to face her students, the kindly looking teacher announced, "Children, we have a very special treat this morning. This gentleman is Mr. Cameron Lewis, the Chief Executive Officer and Chairman of Lewis Brothers Oil. He's taking a few minutes away from his extremely important job to stop by our school and talk with all of you about the history of Midland Station."

Over the years, Cameron had addressed numerous audiences. His oratory biography included hostile investors, angry customers, greedy Wall Street executives, and countless other speaking engagements. Despite all of that experience, he always found himself in pensive frame of mind during these monthly visits to the local elementary school.

The young minds seated before him were fully capable of asking any question, and often did so without regard or filter of social amenity, political respect, or fear of insult. More than once, a topic had been broached by one of these innocents that had caused him pause. It was common for pointed, difficult inquiries to be aired – queries that no adult within 50 miles would dare verbalize to Mr. Cameron Lewis.

Despite the world having gone to hell... regardless of the troubles that faced his company and the city... the most powerful man in the area still made the effort to engage these completely uninhibited minds. He considered the visits an educational opportunity for both him and the children.

Mrs. Evans wasn't a child and most definitely understood the rank of her visitor. Without hesitation, she rolled her desk chair to the center of the room, indicating Mr. Lewis should sit and relax.

"We've been studying our regional history, Mr. Lewis. We've spent the last few days focusing on the influence of oil and natural gas on our community. This morning, I lectured the children briefly on the role of your family and their part in enabling the growth of Midland Station."

My family, thought Cameron. *So glorified and endeared now - if people only knew the truth. Grandpa Lewis was a bully and a ruffian at best. My father was, to use a polite term, a scoundrel. No skirt was safe. Bet the history lesson didn't mention any of that.*

"Thank you, Mrs. Evans," began the local celebrity, the volume of his voice slightly elevated to compensate for the drone of the generator in the background. "My family, like so many here in Midland Station, labored tirelessly and believed in our town. My grandfather started as a wildcatter and worked on some of the earliest exploration activities in the area."

And so Cameron James Lewis began his well-rehearsed, carefully simplified presentation to the children. Despite the pictures of derricks, men in hardhats and supertankers hanging in the corporation's downtown lobby, Lewis Brothers Oil really wasn't an exploration company. In the terminology of the trade, LBO was a downstream player. After losing practically everything twice during the Trend's many cycles of boom and bust, Cameron's grandfather had prudently decided to wait until others had located and pumped the black gold out of the ground before getting involved. LBO would then step in and offer transport, testing, refinement, and delivery of the product. Exploration was simply too risky. While the rewards weren't as big as tapping into a gusher, there wasn't any financial downfall when the hole went dry. The company experienced steady growth every year and established itself as a major corporate citizen of Midland Station.

The 1980s was the decade for consolidation, and Cameron's father had navigated the minefield of acquiring smaller competitors with a deft and crafty hand. LBO doubled in size by utilizing leveraged buy-outs and other non-organic growth strategies.

The 1990s was all about technology. Cameron was just entering the business during those years, and as demanded by family tradition, he worked his way up from the bottom. His insight opened his father's eyes to the power of computer systems, automation, and the internet. Again, the company swelled the ranks of its employees, bank accounts, and prominence in the community.

By 2005, LBO was the single largest employer in Midland Station and an 800-pound gorilla roaming the town's political landscape. Anyone running for any office in Midland Station kept the company's best interest at heart. It was either that, or face an opponent who enjoyed the enormous financial backing of the firm in the next election.

In 2007, Cameron took over the helm after his father suffered a nearly fatal coronary episode. There was little doubt the heart attack was in no small part due to the boss's leggy, buxom personal assistant… Well that, accompanied by far too many steak and bourbon lunches, and the often-refilled humidor of illegal Cuban cigars residing on the man's desk wasn't a recipe for longevity.

The recession of 2008 hit the city of Midland Station hard - the Second Great Depression a few years later, a sledgehammer. The city's government wasn't overly efficient to begin with, a condition resulting from decades of suckling from the breast of the local oil economy. When the real estate bubble popped, the local government found itself with a rapidly eroding tax base, huge amounts of debt, and high unemployment.

LBO, with Cameron at the wheel, did what corporations always do – it took steps to survive. The company had no choice but to supplement a serious decline in city services. Private security became necessary to protect the firm's many facilities spread throughout town, the result of the shrinking police force. Before the collapse, LBO had been forced to invest in commercial fire protection, security, and even medical facilities for its employees.

Of course, Mr. Lewis didn't present detailed, factual history to the children. He kept things simple and upbeat – a thespian-grade delivery designed to put a positive face on both LBO and the future of Midland Station.

Finishing the canned portion of his talk, Cameron cleared his throat and asked, "Does anyone have any questions?"

The first hand shot up, belonging to an eager looking, curly headed girl in the front row. After acknowledging her with a nod, the tiny voice inquired, "Why didn't the army come to help us? My mom said the soldiers went to other places."

"Our army wasn't big enough to go into every city. While Midland Station has a lot of people living here, we're not nearly as big as Dallas or Houston, so they sent their soldiers to help those places."

Another question from the first row, "We will ever have Cartoon Network on television again?"

Cameron had to smile at that one; he missed the Cowboy football games himself. "I think we will one of these days, but it won't be soon."

A tussled looking boy in the back row, "I heard my mom and dad talking. And, well, my dad's worried that you... that you have too much power in Midland Station. He said it reminded him of the company towns in... ummm... West Virginia. He kept talking about coal miners and stuff. He said you were a dictator."

"Billy!" interrupted Mrs. Evans, "That's not polite. Apologize to Mr. Lewis this very moment, young man."

Cameron waved off Mrs. Evans, a curt gesture and a smile signaling the schoolmarm that he wasn't insulted at all. *Well*, thought Cameron, *there it is. The primary reason I'm here. The undercurrent has been rumored for weeks. Now little kids are saying it aloud.*

"Your father has every reason to be concerned, Billy. I'm sure it looks like my company is trying to control everything in our town. I want all of you and your parents to know - tell them I said this in your class today - I don't want to run a town. I want to run an oil company. When things get back to normal, I'll be the happiest person in Midland Station."

Spinning in the chair, Cameron stood and moved to the box he'd carried in. Moving the heavy container to Mrs. Evan's desk, he opened the top and then looked over the curious students. "I've brought everyone a little surprise today. It's a gift for you and all of your families."

Reaching inside, Cameron pulled out a bright blue can of SPAM and held it up. Surprised smiles flashed across the classroom, every single child brightening. A couple of the children clapped their hands with excitement, while the sounds of others sharply inhaling filled the room. Even Mrs. Evans was aflutter, unable to prevent herself from peaking over the edge of the box, obviously trying to ascertain if there might be enough for her to take one home. There was.

As Cameron passed out the prized, scant cans of meat, a sense of melancholy began to overshadow the joy of giving. *A year ago, these kids wouldn't have even known what a can of SPAM was. Now, they practically fight over junk food*, he thought.

Strolling to the waiting car, Cameron couldn't help but reflect on how he, his company, and the sleepy settlement of Midland Station had deteriorated to the point where children reacted to an offer of canned meat like he was passing out bags of gourmet chocolate truffles.

As he ambled to the idling SUV, he was joined by the two security men, the bodyguards abandoning their positions at the school's entrance.

"Everything okay, sir?" asked Lou.

"Yeah… It's just as I suspected – the natives are getting restless."

Lou misread the comment. Wrinkling his brow, the muscular man responded, "I think it's a good idea if you keep Barry and me with you from now on, sir."

Dismissing his employee's concern, Cameron said, "Oh, it wasn't that, Lou. None of the little kids threatened to kick my ass or anything. It was one of the questions they asked that concerns me. I was compared unfavorably to a dictator."

Grunting, Lou relaxed, happy his boss hadn't been in immediate danger.

"Still, sir. I would feel better if you allowed at least one of us to remain…"

Cameron stopped walking, the reaction interrupting his man. "Lou, I know you only mean the best, but I can't stroll into an elementary school surrounded by armed security. Those kids going home and telling their parents about that would only make the situation worse."

A curt nod was Lou's only response. He knew better than to debate with Mr. Lewis.

The trio entered the SUV and were soon leaving the school's sparsely populated parking lot. As the driver rounded the building, Cameron spied a line of school busses waiting for the children to board. *At least we've got gasoline and diesel,* he thought. *Too bad you can't eat it.*

As the SUV sped through the mostly abandoned streets of

Midland Station, Cam's thoughts centered on food. The population of Midland and Odyssey combined was well over 100,000 before the downfall. When the electricity had first cut out, no one had really been overly concerned. Summer thunderstorms and the occasional grid failure had caused similar outages before. The terrorist attacks, radical steps by the federal and state governments, and the riots erupting along the eastern seaboard were all thousands of miles away, and while concerning, didn't impact daily life in the region.

Two days after the power failure, the mood was almost festive. Neighbors were feverishly barbecuing the assorted thawed meats from their freezers and loosely organizing block parties to share the over-abundance of prepared food. After five days without lights and air conditioning, serious concern began to set in, and folks started hording what little was available. When word began to spread that the electric company's Houston headquarters had burned due to an out-of-control fire in the city, general panic erupted.

The city's police force had already been decimated by staff reductions, and the fire department hadn't fared much better. After seven days of indiscriminate civil unrest, the entire city government collapsed. Some police officers died bravely in the line of duty, while others melted into the general population. Lawmen had families – and those loved ones had to eat, too.

The news that Austin was in worse shape than Houston and Dallas didn't help. When word spread that the governor and most of the state's elected officials had been killed in the violence, full-scale looting broke out in Midland Station. But it wasn't until the mayor was bludgeoned to death while sneaking out of town with his family, that a complete vacuum of leadership destroyed what little order remained. Lewis Brothers Oil mobilized its employees and security teams to protect its assets.

Cameron's view out of the SUV's backseat bore witness to the violence that ravaged his hometown. Entire blocks of commercial buildings had burned to the foundation, most as a result of arson. The president of LBO remembered those times as if they were yesterday - the panicked managers, the employees showing up at the well-guarded entrance to his home begging for help, the general daily chaos.

Eventually, the civil rage burned itself out. Those with pent up frustrations either starved, died, or quit due to exhaustion. Each night, fewer fires burned on the horizon, the echoes of gunshots and screaming victims eventually becoming the exception and not the rule. Cameron remembered thinking the worst was behind them.

He began mobilizing LBO's resources, organizing his people, and making plans to salvage what was left. That's when the ugly, inhumane beast of starvation reared its monstrous head.

As he and his security team navigated toward the company's downtown offices, they passed one of the mass grave sites. The once well-manicured, uniformly level lawn of the neighborhood park was now deformed by a raised mound of earth nine feet wide and two city blocks long. Grass and other ground cover had healed the scar somewhat, but it was dreadfully clear to everyone that the location was the final resting place of hundreds of their neighbors and family members. People were dying in such numbers there simply wasn't any other way to dispose of the bodies.

The death toll mounted in the hospitals and nursing homes. Gallant, dedicated caregivers tried desperately to save as many as possible, but the combination of overwhelming casualties from the violence, a shortage of medicines, and the lack of food deliveries resulted in the disintegration of the healthcare system. Nurses and doctors struggled to reach their hospitals because the roads were thick with rioters, fires, and vandalism. Those that did manage to report faced untenable numbers of wounded, feeble, and dying. Soon the generators ran out of fuel, the cafeterias served their last morsels, and pharmacy shelves were barren. The only thing that wasn't in short supply was bodies.

The next wave of casualties consumed the nation's elderly. Many couldn't fill critical prescriptions and few had more than a couple of days' worth of food. Family members helped the lucky ones, but their children and grandchildren soon suffered from bare pantries as well.

If hunger were a monster, disease was the titan of death. Within 90 days, the combination of unburied bodies, malnutrition, raw sewage, untreated water, mountains of garbage, and a lack of medical care resulted in a horrendous toll. Every germ and virus began to thrive in the petri dish that was Midland Station. Within 120 days, the city of 100,000 became a semi-ghost town of less than 20,000 stick thin, wandering zombies who mostly roamed aimlessly about, randomly looking for something... anything to eat.

Food, thought Cameron as they approached the sequestered downtown region and LBO's headquarters. *It always will be about food.*

"Are you okay, sir?" The concern in Lou's voice indicating he had detected his boss' mood.

"I was just thinking about Isaac Newton, Lou. He was a smarter man than most give him credit for."

"I know who Newton was, sir, but I don't follow."

"Newton's third law, *Actioni contrariam semper et æqualem esse reactionem* - To every action there is always an equal and opposite reaction. I think that law was in full effect for Midland Station. We sit on one the world's largest oceans of oil, yet our town is in a fruitless sea of isolation. Oil is our action; lack of agriculture is the opposite reaction."

Cameron glanced at Lou, the expression on the muscular man's face indicating he couldn't connect the dots. Smiling, the executive added, "We're oil rich and food poor. We're paying for the abundance of one necessity with the shortage of another."

Lou paused for a moment and then surprised his boss. "I'm sure there are places that have food and would trade it for gasoline. We need to barter more."

"Lou! Very good. That's exactly what we're trying to do. The problem is finding enough food."

The only thing going Midland Station's way was the refinery. *Refinery is actually too strong a word,* thought Cameron. *It's more like a large-scale test lab that can refine oil in small amounts.*

Gasoline had disappeared in 10 days. The hospitals, running purely on generators, had consumed most of the town's diesel supply in about the same period. One of Cameron's first actions had been to secure and then restart the lab's refining process.

Originally built to provide a service for LBO's customers, the lab could grade, classify, and certify small samples of oil and natural gas produced by the local wells. A mini-refinery, compared to the commercial facilities scattered along the gulf coast, at full capacity the lab could refine 150 barrels per day. This was a miniscule amount compared to the 50,000-100,000 barrels per day common in Texas and Louisiana, but those facilities required extreme amounts of electricity to produce product. Cameron could run his lab off portable generators.

LBO's engineers had worked round the clock to double that output. The effort resulting is a surplus of gasoline and diesel fuel. *But you can't eat MOGAS*, thought Cameron.

The founding fathers of Midland Station probably didn't realize they were establishing a town right in the middle of a climate zone that enabled very little food production. While cattle ranching was a vast industry, the modern day business of livestock depended on dietary supplements and food sources beyond what grew naturally on the land. Transportation was a necessity as well. Without fertilizer, pesticides, diesel, and grain shipments, agricultural production within reach of the city all but ceased. Lack of electrical power for irrigation sounded the final death knoll.

Some local farmers and ranchers ventured into town, offering to barter food for fuel and other available resources, but the supply didn't nearly satisfy the demand. The 20,000 surviving residents required a minimum of 60,000 pounds of food per day. Before the collapse, the average American consumed 5.5 pounds per day, but that was a time of luxury and waste. Twenty tons of food per day, seven days a week, 365 days a year was a monumental problem for the community.

After the worst of the rioting and outbreaks of disease, a vacuum of leadership drew down the resources of the entire community. Some neighborhoods banded together, armed men patrolling the streets to thwart looters and cagey strangers. Other small organizations, such as churches, synagogues and the VFW tried to fill the void, but the scale of the problem was beyond their reach.

Lewis Brothers Oil was a natural candidate to fill the void. The huge corporation had a command and control infrastructure in place, with Cameron at the top. LBO employees fared better than other citizens; LBO's facilities were well protected during the riots and had survived relatively unscathed. To a desperate, downtrodden population, the company became their only hope.

Cameron didn't want to run the local government. He had no wish to manage the entire town. But that's what happened in Midland Station. LBO organized food availability, generators for electrical power, medical care, and logistics for the community. The company's earthmoving equipment dug the mass graves while LBO managers rallied the neighborhood to bury the dead in order to halt the further spread of disease. LBO generators powered the pumps that refilled the water towers so residents could drink and bathe.

After the complete deterioration of the American economy, Midland Station gradually evolved into exactly what the young boy at the school had called it - a company town. Like the small settlements in the West Virginia coal belt, every resident worked, ate, drank, and motored at the pleasure of the company. People shopped at the company store, were treated by company doctors, and used currency that was printed on company machines.

At first, the citizens embraced the effort. Anything was better than what the community had just endured, and the spirit of cooperation was high. However, that all changed when things didn't improve.

The grind of the daily routine deteriorated the community's spirit. There was no belief in a more promising future. Hope gradually evaporated, replaced with frustration and apathy.

The inevitable abuses of power only served to exacerbate the situation. It was difficult enough for elected officials to remain within the guidelines of civil service. Those holding authority in Midland Station now were LBO managers who didn't have to defeat an opponent in the next election. The police, actually private LBO security personnel, no longer worried about watchdog groups or internal affairs investigators reporting directly to the mayor. The checks and balances in place prior to the economic collapse no longer existed, and the morale of the populace suffered for it.

Justice was harsh and often metered by company men, not elected professionals schooled in the ways and means of the law. Key LBO employees lived better lives, ate better food, and received better work assignments than their non-company neighbors.

Cameron James Lewis knew and understood all of this. It was

why he had begun the public relations campaigns like this morning's visit to the school. In his mind, there wasn't any other solution. He and his staff had debated, analyzed and proposed numerous different cures, but all led to even more horrendous and complicated situations – at least in Cameron's mind.

One recent suggestion included holding elections to install a new city government. That idea, floated during a management meeting, engendered a withering outburst from Cameron. "I'll be damned if I'm going to forfeit company assets to some dipshit new mayor. Let's say we did have elections and some clown won. What's he going to do? Where's he going to get food? A city government would seize everything my family has worked almost 100 years to build. LBO is the only thing that's working and keeping the community alive. There is no way to predict what would happen if someone outside the company seized control."

The SUV pulled into the headquarters' underground garage where Mr. Lewis' assistant waited with a tablet computer and forced smile.

"What's up, Linda?" Cameron stated more than asked.

"Your first appointment of the afternoon is waiting for you, Mr. Lewis. He's early."

Rubbing his chin, Cameron studied his secretary's expression. "Is everything okay? I mean... I'm wondering why you decided to wait down here and not at your office."

Shifting her weight from one foot to the other while staring at her shoes, the woman responded, "That man makes me uncomfortable, Mr. Lewis. I'm not sure why, but the way he looks at everyone makes me shiver."

Nodding with a knowing air, Cameron motioned for Brenda to walk with him. "I understand. He is a bit of a character and operates at the lower levels of society."

The executive and his entourage rode the elevator to the top floor of the 14-story building. With his security detail in front, Cameron entered his private office to find a guest surveying his environment through the suite's floor to ceiling windows.

"Good day, Mr. Lewis."

Cameron ignored the greeting, hanging his jacket on a hook behind the door and then moving immediately for his desk. "I'm not happy with our arrangement, sir. You've been late on the last two deliveries. Yesterday's was considerably short on product."

"And I accepted less payment for the product. We had equipment difficulties," he answered. "It happens."

"When we entered into our contract, you promised to deliver 10,000 pounds of food per week in exchange for gasoline, generators, liquor – and of course the continued care of the patient. So far, you've missed that mark half the time. I'm feeling the need to cancel our contract and secure another supplier."

"Mr. Lewis, we'll catch up. We've found a new source that should provide a significant amount of goods."

"Where you get the food isn't my concern, sir. I've got 20,000 hungry people, and they're getting restless. I need you to hold up your end of the agreement."

West Texas
January 17, 2016

Theodore Bonaparte Belou rubbed the five days of gristly, salt and pepper beard darkening his chin. Unlike so many men of the times, Mr. Belou's facial growth had nothing to do with lack of access to shaving accessories, his appearance and habits relatively unchanged since well before the collapse. *Why waste the edge of a perfectly good razor more often than need be*, had been his motto for years.

The elder man's eyes scanned row after row of discarded machinery, rusting metal and broken components randomly deposited across his 20-acre patch of West Texas paradise. He was searching out his son, waiting to see if a critical part could be salvaged from the yard. Another truck had broken down, the loss disrupting their business enterprise and drawing the ire of Mr. Cameron Lewis.

The product of a Louisiana Cajun father and a Nationalist French mother, Mr. Belou had located to this very swath of arid sand 46 years ago. Chasing fortune and sick of the damp Louisiana swamps, the latest oil boom in central Texas had lured the young man away from his boyhood home.

Rig-boss, after foreman, after field manager had turned him away. There were droves of men seeking jobs, and most had experience in the oil field. A discouraged Teddy had been just about ready to return home when one sympathetic supervisor had pointed to a rusting heap of drill pipe and busted valves scattered nearby. "Haul those off for me, boy, and I'll pay ya fifty dollars cash."

"Where would I haul them, sir?"

Pulling a pencil from above his ear, the man tore a corner from his brown lunch bag and began sketching a map. "This here land is leased by our company for storage. Dump that junk along there. No one ever goes out that way, so put it anywhere."

And he did.

The $50 paid for a bag of food and a full tank of gas in his beat-up old Chevy pickup. It also inspired an idea. The next few days, Teddy visited rig after rig, offering to haul off scrap, trash, and junk. He had been stunned at how quickly clientele had been established. Sleeping in his truck and occasionally showering at the truck stop, Teddy survived. The roll of money stashed inside his glove box grew larger by the day.

A few weeks later, he pulled into his original customer's location, the Edwards #14 rig. Shocked at finding the worksite all but abandoned, Teddy made for the small mobile home that served as the rig's office. After knocking on the door, he was greeted by the agitated foreman. "We're shutting down, Teddy. The money ran dry just like the well. The investors have pulled out. Anything that's left after midnight tonight, you can haul off."

"What about the land where I've dumped the scrap?" Teddy asked.

"That lease was paid in full for 99 years, Teddy. If you're camping out there, no one should bother you for a long, long time."

The next morning, Teddy's truck was seen pulling a relatively nice house trailer toward the junkyard. He took full possession of his new home that afternoon, discarding the few reminders of Edwards #14.

Over the years, Teddy became known as T-Bone. He wasn't sure how he earned that title. It might have been because of his given name. Perhaps it was due to his claim to fame – his personal, entrepreneurial effort - running what many of the locals referred to as a boneyard. Regardless, Mr. Belou embraced the handle – it sounded more like a proper Texas name, and he liked fitting in and staying under the radar.

T-Bone quickly diversified his stream of income, adding spare parts sales to his junk hauling enterprise. The improved business model ensured that T-Bone made money regardless of the direction the iron moved. Within a year, he hired another oilfield drifter to help. At 18 months, he expanded his small business again, broadening his "commercial fleet" by acquiring a second truck with more towing capacity.

Movement in the distance interrupted T-Bone's reminiscing about the good old days and snapped his attention to the present. His oldest son was sauntering back toward the house empty-handed, the firstborn's disappointed shuffle a redundant indicator that their truck was going to remain out of service until a suitable widget could be salvaged.

As he watched the now middle-aged man return, T-Bone couldn't help but notice how much Lyndon reminded him of his mother.

Three years after his first haul, T-Bone had decided to venture home for the Christmas holiday. Swelling with pride at his success and sporting a truck that was only two years old, T-Bone had made the drive to rural Cajun country brimming with gifts, new clothes, and the confidence of a "home-town boy done good."

At first, his family's reception had been icy, indicative of skepticism born of poverty-induced disappointment, some uncles even openly condescending to him. "Ain't no way an uneducated boy like you has got spending money in his pockets. You been out robbin' banks, son?" Another had voiced his disdain with "Nobody here got no use for a show off, Teddy."

Angry, frustrated and ready to bail, T-Bone had toughed it out. Vowing to head back to Texas first thing after the presents were opened, the young man had withdrawn, opting for the solace of isolation over the festivities of the family reunion. He had no way of knowing that his life would change forever on that Christmas morning.

Eva's father was an uncle's old army buddy who was passing

through. Sitting on the porch swing, T-Bone would never forget watching the off-green Ford LTD with its clanking muffler pull into their lane. When the rattletrap old junker finally smoked to a stop, the image of the leggy beauty that climbed out of the backseat would be imprinted in his mind forever.

The young girl's family led a simple, pastoral life, surviving mostly off the land with a little help from the county when times were really bad. Her dream of escaping to the far away Lone Star state was an idealistic concept Eva had nurtured since she was a youngster. A mystical place where jobs were available for the asking fueled bedtime stories about a land of milk and honey, intriguing the little girl who sometimes fell asleep with a rumbling tummy. While the security of a constant food supply would have been romantic notion enough for Eva, her suitor's genuine infatuation sealed the deal.

T-Bone would have considered kidnapping the girl if her desire to escape a mundane, and sometimes precarious, existence hadn't been compelling enough. He was relieved to find the new love of his life eager to make her own move. On New Year's Day, Eva secretly left a note for her parents and slipped out the back door to T-Bone's idling getaway-truck. As soon as the Texas state line was in their review mirror, the two tied the knot in front of a Justice of the Peace in Beaumont. The newlyweds honeymooned in a swank Houston hotel, Eva fascinated by what T-Bone called "room service." What began as a young man's fancy quickly grew into a deep love and affection on both sides.

Lyndon had been born nine months later.

"Dad, that tie-rod isn't going to fit. I guess we're down to a single truck until we can find a 2004 Ford V8 lying around somewhere." T-Bone shook his head, "Tell the boys to keep a look out for another vehicle to *salvage*. Given how strong *business* has been of late, we need something a little bigger anyway."

Lyndon grinned at his father's phrasing, knowing all too well that "salvage" meant steal or loot. He wasn't embarrassed or surprised – the Belou clan had crossed the ethical line to do what it took to get by, even if it meant bending a law or two to put food on the table.

Sauntering up to the porch, Lyndon eyed his father with a certain amount of pride. The man had worked his way out of the hopeless cycle of poverty that had plagued their family for generations. Despite having to fight for every inch of ground, Teddy Belou had never been bitter, never given any indication of quitting - even when he was unjustly sentenced to two years in prison. *That actually motivated him*, thought Lyndon. *That's when he started living as if it was every man for himself.*

The story had been told a hundred times. T-Bone being asked to remove equipment that seemed in better condition than most of his loads...the Sheriff pulling into the bone yard a week later...T-Bone being handcuffed and hauled off to jail.

As it turned out, the oil company had asked T-Bone to haul off that nice looking machinery because they were desperate for money and reported it stolen in order to collect the insurance. Both T-Bone and the rig's manager claimed they were innocent. In the end, the district attorney convinced the jury that both men had conspired in the scandal and both were sentenced to two years at Huntsville.

Lyndon had been nine years old when the police had taken away his father. He already had three younger brothers, and his mother struggled desperately to make ends meet.

T-Bone returned from Huntsville a changed man. Aggression replaced a laid back, mellow demeanor; a drive to dominate superseded his sense of fairness. Before his internment, T-Bone believed the best business arrangements were those that benefited both parties. Afterwards, he wasn't satisfied unless he screwed the other guy. The business suffered, but he didn't seem to care. The only people who weren't targets of T-Bone's new assertiveness were his wife and children. *To hell with everyone else.*

T-Bone scowled at his first-born and scratched his stubble. "We've got to acquire something bigger, Lyndon. Our customer is demanding more and more merchandise, and we both know what will happen if we can't deliver. This bullshit of a pickup load here and there isn't going to cut it. We need a truck of some sort – something big and heavy that will haul a lot of weight."

Lyndon tilted his head, his face brightening after a moment of thought. "I think I know exactly where to find just the truck, dad."

Alpha, Texas
January 17, 2016

Diana shifted her weight, the motion eliciting a loud squeak from the folding metal chair. She was thankful no one could hear the seat's outburst, a fringe benefit of the musicians playing nearby. *A brass band*, she thought, *who would have thought we'd ever have the time or a cause for a band*?

She exchanged glances with Nick, who made brief eye contact and winked before turning his attention back to the musicians. A reasonable rendition of John Philip Sousa's *The Thunderer* rolled across the lawn to the delight of the gathered citizens of Alpha, the throng of election-eve voters practically filling the city park.

While Nick tapped his toe to the march, Diana's attention wandered through the crowd. She was reminded of old black and white photographs depicting elections from long ago. While she couldn't remember any details of the time or place, the grainy pictures reflected a carnival-like atmosphere – a gala event. Alpha, Texas was experiencing its own version of those times – practically the whole community was on or near Main Street - reclining on blankets or lawn chairs and otherwise perching wherever else they could improvise a seat along the strip. There were even three sets of legs swinging happily beneath a low branch belonging to one of the park's large elms.

Food vendors, balloons, and even a man offering pony rides for the children bordered the throng. It was almost as if everyone was looking for an excuse to get together and have a celebration. *Now where on earth did someone find helium to inflate balloons?* The deacon wondered.

The band finished its patriotic refrain, and immediately the master of ceremonies strode to the podium, glancing at his notes in preparation of introducing the next candidate after the applause died down. Leaning toward Nick's ear, Diana whispered, "This reminds me of the old West and how elections were a big party back then."

Nick smiled and nodded, whispering back, "You're right. Hey, but didn't they do the same thing for hangings?"

Diana rolled her eyes and then returned her attention to the platform.

"Citizens of Alpha, Texas, before I introduce the last candidate of the evening, I feel obliged to say a few words. There isn't a resident of our town who doesn't owe this woman a deep debt of gratitude. Were it not for her, every single one of us might be living under the tyrannical rule of outlaws and criminals. Were it not for her, many of us would have perished from lack of food or water. Regardless of the outcome of this monumental election, I believe I speak for everyone present as I express my sincere gratitude to Deacon Diana Brown!"

Thunderous applause and shouted encouragement erupted from the park as every citizen stood and clapped, whistled, and nodded toward the stage. Diana flushed immediately, her cheeks turning an even darker shade of crimson as she sensed Nick standing and clapping beside her. The outburst was so unexpected, Diana could only smile, nod, and mouth the words "Thank you," as she surveyed the supportive faces of her friends and neighbors.

After what seemed an embarrassingly long time, the speaker continued. "As all of you know, Diana has sacrificed so very much for our town. She has shouldered every burden, made the difficult decisions, and demonstrated sage leadership during these troubling times. She organized our people when disaster left nothing but a stunned, directionless humanity. She united us when our freedom was threatened. Her courage enabled Christians to fight, and her wisdom brought combatants to Christ. I speak purely from the deepest core of my heart when I say, 'Thank you, Miss Brown. Thank you for all you've done.'"

Again, the crowd rose to its feet, shouts of encouragement piercing the din of clapping hands. The man at the podium waited a short period and then quieted the crowd by raising both hands. As the applause began to settle, Nick bent down and whispered, "So much for getting to see a lynching tonight."

"Without further ado... ladies and gentlemen... may I present the candidate for mayor, Deacon... Diana... Brown!"

Taking short steps on somewhat wobbly legs, Diana managed to stroll across the stage without stumbling. She was somewhat relieved when she reached the lectern, the wooden stand representing a protective shield from the raw emotion emanating from the crowd.

Nodding, smiling, and unfolding her prepared remarks, the reserved speaker kept repeating, "Thank you, thank you so much, thank you," as the ovation continued.

"Citizens of Alpha," she began. "I have a few, very simple goals should you see fit to elect me as the next mayor of our wonderful town. First and foremost, I want to establish security. History has taught us that without rule of law, nothing will get accomplished and recovery will be stunted. Storekeepers won't trade if they're being robbed. Farmers won't plant if the harvest is looted. We have only to look back at our own history of a few months ago to know that fear grinds civilization to a halt. As a society, we cannot better ourselves if we are threatened every single day of our lives."

Pausing briefly, she waited until the sounds of agreement and support died down before continuing.

"My second priority is to configure our government in a way that enables every citizen of Alpha to become self-sufficient. I will establish adult education that addresses the critical ability to produce food. It is beyond the reach of our government to feed the people. My philosophy will be to train fishermen, not deliver fish."

Again, the crowd signaled its approval with nodding heads and clapping hands.

"Finally, I want to proclaim our future government's position regarding assistance. We, as a community, will be measured by how we treat the most desperate of our citizens. We, as a *society*, will be morally graded on the quality of life of the least fortunate of our people, not the most affluent. A focus of my governance will be to enable our churches, private organizations, and charitable individuals to be the first responders for the desperate and downtrodden. I'll allow no citizen of Alpha to starve. I'll not deny basic necessities to any law-abiding individual, but I will only deliver those resources as a last resort. My intent is to set our fledgling democracy on a path that enables self-reliance, not dependence or entitlement."

Diana chanced a quick glance at Nick while waiting for the crowd to settle, her friend flashing a quick thumbs-up signal for support.

"As you all know, there is a practically endless list of projects, tasks, and priorities for our community. Some of these worthy endeavors can only be accomplished with the backing and management of government. Reopening the schools is one such example, the repair and availability of a fire department is another. These civic uses of our limited resources will benefit all of us, and that's what I want to achieve. If we all pull together, my office will be able to focus on organizing and prioritizing improvements that will ensure all of our lives continue to improve!"

The noise from the crowd grew, Diana stepping back and waving her appreciation. On her way back to Nick's side, she tried to make eye contact with as many folks as possible all the while again repeating "Thank you," to the supportive throng.

The presentation part of the agenda complete, Nick and Diana made their way from the stage and began mingling with friends and neighbors. They sampled food, shook hands with dozens of people, and generally enjoyed the spirit flowing through the crowd.

Kevin approached his dad, the surrounding excitement contagious. "Dad, I have never seen anything like this. The enthusiasm here is electric. Everyone seems to approve of what Diana has already done for the community. So why did Diana speak to the crowd like that? She seems to have this election in the bag. I mean, I didn't think anyone else was even running for the mayor spot anyway."

"She doesn't want it to appear like she's taking it for granted. And she doesn't just want to run on her history, she wants to unveil her vision for the future."

"So she can lose?"

"No, I don't think so. She's running unopposed. I guess someone could write in another person's name, but that's unlikely."

Kevin was puzzled by his father's answer, but decided not to pursue it further. Nick looked down at his son's confused expression and said, "Don't worry about it, buddy. I've been studying elections since I was your age, and I never have figured it all out. Politics is a really weird business. You and I will stick to honor, integrity, and living a simple, happy life. We can leave all the complex stuff to other people."

Brightening, Kevin asked, "That sounds like a plan, Dad. Hey, how about we work in some trigger time once I'm healed?"

Nick tousled his son's hair, "*That's* my boy."

A line of people snaked down the courthouse steps, the generally upbeat crowd utilizing the time to gossip, solicit for favorite candidates, and exchange a few words with neighbors. The ballots were much less complicated than those of recent years, consisting of a single sheet of paper copied on one of the machines in the former clerk's office.

Someone had taken a series of shoeboxes and cut slits in the top. Each voter was issued a pencil, had his or her name checked from a list, and then was escorted to the "booth," which was essentially sheets of dark blue plastic hanging from the ceiling to provide privacy. Once the voter's selections were made, the secret ballot was folded, deposited into one of the boxes, and the voter's hand was stamped.

The election process didn't have anything to do with the queue inching along. That minor inconvenience was prompted by the friendly banter and casual conversation taking place at the registration tables. Clearly, this election was the social event of the season in Alpha, fostering a sense of community that had not been on the agenda in years. It seemed every voter knew every election worker and wanted to catch up on the latest about kids, family, and local news. And for the few new settlers in the village, there might as well have been a welcome wagon pulled in front of the courthouse. The scene looked more like a block party than a polling station.

The rules had stated that anyone in line by 12 noon could vote. Nick looked at his watch and realized it was quickly approaching that time. He motioned for one of his security helpers to follow and then assigned the man to close the end of the line.

"What should I do if any stragglers show up?"

After thinking about it for a bit, Nick answered. "Look at your watch, smile, and say, 'I think my watch is fast. Go ahead and get in line.'"

"So there really is no deadline?"

"Nope. I don't want a single person to miss a chance to vote. It's the way we do things. I'll stop back by around 1:00 and see if folks are still drifting in."

"Bring me back a jar of water on your way, if you think of it. It's starting to warm up."

Terri fumbled with the lace of Bishop's boot and lost her balance. Bishop's right hand shot out and grabbed her shirt, gently tugging until she had steadied herself.

"Aren't we just the pair," she giggled, returning to her task. "Between my baby-tummy and your bum side, we could be the stars of a situational comedy. Better alert Hollywood."

Bishop smiled, "We are pitiful. Thank goodness you're not really, *really* pregnant yet, or we would really be in trouble."

The boot tied and Bishop's pullover shirt adjusted, the couple left the hospital room and ventured outside. It was Bishop's fourth day of walking, the confines of his floor and then the complete hospital building having already been explored on previous tours.

"Where to?" Terri inquired, hoping to see something different today.

"Let's head for the parade ground over by our old quarters. That's a nice grassy area."

"That's a great idea. I like the softer ground – it's easier on my back."

As the couple meandered along, Bishop looked down at his bride and commented, "Terri, I woke up married to a different woman. I want you to know I love this new gal just as much as the old one."

Frowning, Terri asked, "What do you mean by a different woman? Let me get my rifle before you answer that, mister."

"Seriously, you've changed. Before I was shot, you could care less about politics, leadership, and government. Now, that's all you want to talk about. I can't remember your even being interested in the evening news before. Now all our conversations inevitably take a political turn."

To emphasize his point, Bishop pointed to the book Terri carried in her hand. "'The Rise and Fall of Modern Empires.' Really? That's some heavy stuff."

Waving him off, she dismissed his observation, "Oh, the Colonel brought that over for me. He and I talked a few times while you were off in la-la-land. He's quite the fascinating man."

Bishop stopped mid-stride, facing her with a smirk. "Now I know I'm in trouble. You've been talking politics with the Colonel?"

Terri laughed, tugging his arm to continue their stroll. "You know I'm doing this just to understand, don't you? I need to make sense of why Wayne and Senator Moreland acted the way they did. I need to have an understanding of what prompted all that happened."

Bishop's voice was serious when he responded. "The man who kidnapped you did what he did out of a lust for power. I don't think it's any more complex than that."

"But what motivates that thinking, and how do we avoid it? How do we keep from repeating the same mistakes again and again?"

Bishop made a pistol out of his good hand and fired a pretend round in the air. "Revolution is the only cure I know of."

"Revolution isn't a cure; it's a reset," Terri retorted. "If you follow the Colonel's logic, revolution only makes the societal pie a bit smaller, and thus the hunger for power is downsized to match the size of the pie."

Half playing, half-serious, Bishop snorted, "Still – the job gets done."

"And a lot of people die. And a lot of destruction takes place."

"I'm not a radical, Terri. You know that. Even when things were at their worse, you didn't see me spouting off about armed revolt. Still, my experience has been that once men taste that ultimate power, you'll not stop them, short of forcefully taking it away."

The couple continued walking, Terri musing over Bishop's point of view. Finally, she offered, "The Colonel believes you can only control the problem by limiting the size of any single man's influence. He said that's why state's rights were such an important part of the founding father's thinking.

Bishop paused, his gaze intense. "Well, I'm certainly not as educated as the Colonel. I don't have the benefit of formal teachings or scholarly influences, but I can tell you one thing that is fact. Power... corruptive power... requires an enemy. For it to feed freely and proliferate unchecked, there must be some overt threat. Power bathes gloriously in the limelight of fear."

"Why? Because the fear distracts the people – diverts their attention from the power snatchers?"

"No. Because people do crazy, stupid shit when they're scared or threatened. They give over control of themselves to some politician or king in order to win or survive."

"So how do you stop what the Colonel calls 'the beast?'"

"You can't stop it, you can only control it... minimize it."

"Okay, then how do you *control* the beast?"

"Control fear, and you limit the power others have over you."

Alpha, Texas
January 18, 2016

Piles of paper ballots covered the large folding tables scattered throughout the main courtroom. Volunteers hustled here and there, some with clipboards, others carrying laptop computers glowing with spreadsheet software on their displays.

Originally, the jury box had been reserved for the candidates, the elevated seating chosen for its superior vantage to observe and validate the counting process. Diana had been insistent that anyone running for office be present to witness the ballot count. She didn't want any notion of cheating or favoritism – any conspiracy undermining the effort to organize Alpha's first post-collapse election. Yet, as the count progressed, the comfortable jury seating remained mostly unoccupied. The polished oak rails bordering the 13 leather chairs were apparently too restrictive for the restless legs of anxious citizens who had thrown their hats into the ring.

Diana, despite running unopposed, hustled around in a whirlwind of nervous activity. While the voting had proceeded without issue, coordinating the final tally of over 2,000 paper ballots was a significant undertaking. By mid-evening, every available flat surface was littered with coffee cups, computer cords, dull pencils, and tally sheets.

The voters of Alpha had been invited to witness the proceedings as well. Every row of benches in the cavernous room filled to capacity, and most of the walls were lined with a standing room only crowd. A polite, but constant murmur arose from the onlookers, a nervous bout of laughter punctuating the air every now and then.

It was 8:37 p.m. when the final spreadsheet was printed out. Five minutes later, Diana set down her marker and picked up a stack of poster-sized cardboard signs, neat rows and columns of names and numbers handwritten on their surface.

Without making eye contact with anyone, the deacon marched down the center aisle of the courtroom, closely followed by Nick, who held a large roll of duct tape in his hand. The throng of gathered citizens made an opening for Diana to pass, eager eyes trying to steal a peek at the results tucked under her arm.

The main lobby of the courthouse was also full of people milling about, in anxious anticipation of the election results.

Nick's height came in handy, his arms stretching high to adhere the poster where the crowd could read the results. As the gathering converged to get a closer look at the tally, the former Green Beret had no problem clearing the way for Diana so she could continue mounting her other signs.

When they hung the second poster, Diana leaned in close to Nick and whispered, "I hope we don't have any sore losers. It would be a shame for this election to cause a divide and set this recovery back."

"I think you're worried about nothing. Most of the folks who ran for office did so with hesitation. I mean, who has the time to grow food, take care of a family, and help run the town? I would bet most of them will be relieved not to have to worry about it."

Pete's Place was the hub of activity for Alpha's smaller neighbor to the east. The election in Meraton had been a far simpler affair, given there were only a few hundred residents in the entire town. A mere three unopposed candidates were on the ballot, two for the council and one for the mayor, Pete.

No one even bothered to post the predetermined results.

Still, a spirit of community and participation filled the air, some of the joy directly attributed to the free moonshine being distributed from the bar – after the polls had closed, of course.

Pete was in a fine mood despite having endured three days of relentless teasing. After being begged by just about everyone in town to put his name on the ballot, the bartender had been on the receiving end of constant, good-natured ribbing.

The restricted scale and obvious outcome didn't diminish the importance of the event. There wasn't a single person in Meraton who didn't appreciate Pete's initiative to hold an election. The fact that he didn't consider his post a foregone conclusion wasn't lost on the fledgling community.

Always the conscientious civil servant, Pete started making coffee when celebratory pistol shots rang out, the post-election revelers on Main Street firing into the air. The mayor-elect shook his head as he closed the tap, commenting to a nearby patron that wasting ammo in this day and age simply wasn't proper civic policy.

Unlike Meraton, Alpha's celebration of democracy was far more formalized and much quieter. Winners and losers alike were greeted and congratulated by the crowd that swelled in the street outside of the courthouse. Promises of "I'll do my best," and "I will need your support," filled the air.

Diana made the obligatory rounds, shaking hands, exchanging

hugs, and kissing cheeks. Like Meraton, not a single soul missed the point that she had organized and been the driving force behind the resurrection of the election process.

The simple act of casting a vote... of having a choice... of participating in the future was an uplifting experience by all involved. As Diana worked the crowd, she noticed folks' chins were raised, eyes were brighter, and smiles flashed just a little bit wider.

After finishing the tour, the deacon turned to Nick and Kevin. "I'm done. I'm tired to the bone and just want to sleep for a week. Will you escort me back to my castle, kind sirs?"

Nick bowed at the waist, "Yes, my liege."

Swatting his shoulder, Diana protested, "Now stop that!"

Kevin, joining the joke, bowed as well. "Your wish is my command, Your Majesty."

"I'm going to order both of you thrown in the dungeon if you don't knock it off. Of course, I'd have to build one first," she snickered.

Grinning widely, Nick swept his arm in front of the town's mayor-elect. "As you wish, my lady."

Chapter 4

Beltran Ranch, West Texas
January 22, 2016

The plank-board fence surrounding the corral was serving double duty this evening. In addition to its obvious function of livestock control, it was also supporting one Mr. Carlos Beltran. One of the elder rancher's dusty, worn boots rested on the lowest cross member while his arm sought comfort in its familiar and time-worn position, draped casually along the top rail.

The rancher's gaze was focused on nothing special, his eyes fixed on a point in space somewhere between the black foothills of the Glass Mountains to the west and the sun that was about to drop behind them. The dirty, weather-faded Stetson protecting his head rested in a way that announced it wasn't a decoration. The rings of sweat salt, frayed edges, and tired looking brim declared it was an essential piece of equipment, as important as a rope or gloves.

Mr. Beltran stood motionless, an island of stoic calm surrounded by a riot of swirling flesh, baying animals, and shouting men. The corral was filling rapidly with longhorn cattle, hundreds of the huge beasts being funneled into the fence's confines by harassing cowboys and their nimble footed steeds.

As the last of the herd was driven in, a single horseman galloped toward the ranch's owner. The rider pulled up short, dismounted gracefully, and approached his boss. A few steps away, the large-framed, wiry cowboy moved his hat to his midsection as a sign of respect. "Count's all done, Mr. Beltran. We're nine head short."

Carlos didn't immediately acknowledge the report, his gaze drawn to the ocean of bovine flesh circling in the corral. "They're thin, Mack. Awful thin. Before long we won't have anything but bones, hide, and hooves."

"Yes, suh. They're moving slow too, Mr. Beltran - there's no fight in 'em."

The older man regarded his spread, head moving slowly from right to left as if he were taking it all in for the first time. In reality, he was thinking about his ancestors and the tribulations that always managed to plague this land. It seemed that every generation of his family faced a test, some challenge delivered by man or nature, sometimes both. Now his ranch was facing yet another trial for survival.

A Beltran had ramrodded this 180,000-acre outfit since before the American Revolution. Originally migrating north from Mexico, no one in the family knew for sure why they had relocated. While some ventured it was the lure of unclaimed range, others believed it was to escape oppression at home. A few inside jokes speculated that criminal escapades had resulted in a hasty trip northward. The true reason was long lost in the memories of seven generations that had lived and died on the property - the truth buried in the family graveyard that resided just over half a mile from where Carlos stood. It didn't matter. The clan was here... and here to stay.

Whatever had driven his forefathers to settle in West Texas must have been an extreme motivator. The arid, high desert range was a harsh, unforgiving land. Even the southern Comanche Nation that dominated central Texas at the time didn't settle the area. While Carlos' grandfather had shared riveting, fireside tales of painted warriors and desperate gun battles, in truth the larger Indian settlements were miles to the north where the terrain was far more hospitable. Still, there was no doubt about the occasional raiding party trying to push the settlers out, sometimes coming frightfully close to succeeding.

Water was scarce here, and the sandy soil supported little vegetation. The summers were blistering hot, and the winters bone numbing cold. Perhaps the reason why the land had been unclaimed had something to do with its being practically worthless. On days like today, Carlos wondered if it were cursed.

"Mr. Beltran, do you want me to fetch the doc?"

Carlos knew the foreman meant the ranch's resident veterinarian. The animal doctor had lived in one of the spread's secondary haciendas for over 30 years, a necessary investment for an outfit the size of the Beltran operation.

"Naw, Mack. I don't think that's necessary. Any fool can see they're just not getting enough to eat. I don't think the doc has any grain stashed away. Besides, isn't Jobo's wife in labor?"

"Yes, suh, she was last I heard. I hope this one is easier than the last."

Relieved at the change of subject, the old man smiled. "What's this... his fifth?"

The foreman shook his head with a sly grin. "You would've thought Jobo and the missus would have figured out what was causing that by now. I just hope this little one pops out all proper like. Jobo wasn't worth a shit for a week after that last birth went haywire."

The old rancher nodded, recalling the bottle of his best whisky Doc had consumed after having performed an emergency C-section on a human female. Mr. Beltran smiled, remembering the man's shaking hands and shortness of breath after the procedure. While it was all part of life on a remote ranch, a fifth of strong medicine had been required to settle the reluctant physician that day. He might be a vet, but over the years, he'd been forced to work on his share of two-legged animals as well.

"Mack, there's no choice but to cull this herd. Without outside grain deliveries, our land just won't support this number of head. What I'm worried about is losing all of them before spring. They're weak now, and one strong virus could spread like wildfire, maybe kill every last animal."

Mack nodded his understanding, but offered no comment. His confidence in the boss was supreme, especially when it came to livestock. No one in West Texas knew more about cattle. It was common wisdom that a wise man neither ignored, nor argued with Mr. Carlos Beltran when it came to beef on the hoof.

"Did you find the nine missing carcasses?"

"No, suh. We only found one, and the turkey vultures are now fatter than our steers."

The foreman's response drew a sharp look from the boss. "Only one?"

"Yes, suh. I can't claim we searched every last square foot on the north range, but I don't think we missed any dead animals. The vultures circling overhead make them easy to find. For sure we didn't overlook eight live ones."

The old cattleman's spine stiffened at the statement. For the first time in the conversation, Mack felt the withering, direct focus of Mr. Beltran's gaze. "Any sign of the rustlers?"

"Yes, suh. Two of the boys surprised them, but the poachers made off before our men laid eyes on them. It has to be the same crew that hit us last week. They're using trucks and know what they're doing. They also used explosives to drop the south wall of the Rio canyon. We were almost underneath the demolition. I had one man hurt, but not bad."

"They took six animals last week, eight more now. That's not just some wandering desperados. It would take 100 people to eat that much beef, even the skin and bone kind like these."

"Do you want me to assign some men to watch the herd when we drive them back to the range?"

The question was a valid one. Someone was stealing Beltran property, and a lot of it. Normally such an act would be akin to declaring war and result in armed cowboys searching for the culprits. Law enforcement was thin in this part of the country, and most of the large ranches depended on their own men for protection. When the rare trouble did arise in West Texas, the sheriff was summoned - but no one counted on a deputy arriving quickly.

Not long ago, even a hint of rustling would have been cause to hunt down the perpetrators. Now that the world had gone to hell, Carlos hesitated.

"Mack, in a way those poachers are doing us a favor. We can't eat all the beef ourselves."

The ranch hand nodded. "Still don't sit right with me, Mr. Beltran. If this pace keeps up, we won't have to worry about culling the herd; there won't be anything left."

The older man looked at the disappearing sun and motioned for his employee to follow. "Walk back to the big house with me, Mack. I want you to show me on the map exactly where you found the dead animal and what ground you covered."

The two men made their way through the core of the Beltran Ranch, ambling past an assortment of outbuildings, homes, sheds, and other small structures. Over 60 people lived on the property, their residences scattered around the original homestead. Manufactured homes, house trailers, stick-built bungalows, and adobe bunkhouses provided shelter for the workforce. More than a dozen barns, workshops, stables, and offices rounded out what was essentially a small, privately owned village.

Many of the residents had been born on the property, some being third generation employees of the Beltran family. Like any small community, people married, reared children, and formed a close-knit society. Any man was welcome to leave the employment of Mr. Beltran, but few did. There was one exception – those serving in the armed forces of the United States. Almost every able-bodied male and most of the females served. It was a proud tradition, as well as a chance to grasp a different view of the world.

The pair continued their progress through the central lane until they approached the big house. While Mr. Beltran and his family maintained private quarters inside the structure, the building served an additional purpose. The ranch's main offices for accounting, sales, procurement, and family services were all located within. Buyers from the Fort Worth stockyards would conduct their business there as well. Millions of dollars of fuel, food, equipment, and machinery were purchased within its walls. Merchants and breeders alike sampled the West Texas hospitality extended amid her upscale, eclectic farmhouse setting.

Kicking the dust from their work boots, Mr. Beltran and Mack entered the premises via the main entrance in front. Only the ranch's owner and his immediate family used the private side door. A reception area welcomed the two men, adorned with the same phone system, guest chairs, and office equipment that would greet visitors to almost any corporation in the world.

The pair headed immediately for a conference room just a few doors down. The hallway was lined with portraits of the ranch's previous masters. The early generations of Beltran men were depicted on oil painted canvasses, while their descendants posed for photographs. Mack pushed open the double doors that led to what everyone called "the boardroom," a chamber dominated by a large table of polished red maple, surrounded by high back leather chairs. A speakerphone, video projector, and crystal serving set resided on the glossy surface.

All four walls resonated with purpose - to educate the visitor of the scope, heritage, and mission of the Beltran Ranch. One wall was virtually eclipsed by an oversized, comprehensive map of the property. The opposite side of the room was filled with a pictorial history of the ranch, including antique tintypes and cabinet card photos, as well as faded black and whites from the mid-20th century, and a few larger, more recent pictures that captured the past in full color. Another surface was covered in military memorabilia belonging to those who served both the United States and the Confederacy.

While Mr. Beltran poured himself a glass of tea, Mack couldn't refuse himself a curious glance at his own image on the wall of honor. It wasn't much - a poor snapshot taken years ago - his graduation from Army Ranger School at Fort Benning. He could still remember every vivid detail of that day so long ago. He had been so proud and yet so tired. The two deployments to Iraq that followed had dulled his ego, but not his weariness.

His grainy portrait hung directly below another that he had studied several times. A young Corporal Carlos Beltran stood shirtless with flak jacket and M16 rifle, the vegetation of a remote Vietnamese jungle providing the backdrop.

"It was 103 that day," the boss' voice sounded over his shoulder. "I think the humidity was over 90%. You couldn't tie your bootlaces without busting a sweat. That picture was taken about a month before we lost Jonesy."

"That war sucked," was Mack's only comment.

"They all suck! And I was so full of bullshit pride and worthless patriotism, going to defend the honor of the United States of America." Mr. Beltran paused, the memories flooding his mind. "You know as well as I do, all that BS means nothing. It wasn't long before all I cared about was the men serving next to me. It wasn't flag, or God, or country. It was the 18-year-old kid trekking through the rainforest with me. The grunt eating dirt and drinking in lungs full of cordite smoke. He's what mattered... and nothing else."

Mack turned and faced his mentor, nodding. "Yes, suh, I do understand."

"It's just like the ranch," the boss continued. "All that matters is the people here. If we don't take care of each other, no one will. Nobody will give a shit. There won't be any rescue or miracle;

we're responsible for our own survival."

Mack nodded his agreement and watched as Mr. Beltran turned and stared back at the big map. The foreman wasted no time and moved to point at a spot on the northeast boundary of the property. "Here," he announced. "We found the herd grazing in this region. The one carcass was in the same general area."

The old rancher rubbed his chin, studying the depicted area. Mack moved out of the way, as Mr. Beltran raised his arm. There's only one way in and out of that section. I think we've solved our mystery. Someone from Fort Stockdale is using my herd for a grocery store."

Mack followed Mr. Beltran's finger and raised his eyebrows. "That would make sense, suh. We've not heard much from up that way for months. Anyone left in the town has to be getting desperate. What do you want to do?"

Carlos turned away from the drawing and stared at the wall of honor. The fact that many of the displays represented accolades awarded posthumously didn't escape his attention. He turned back to Mack and announced, "We don't want to start a war. I've got a bad feeling about this, and until we're for sure, I want to tread carefully. Besides, feeding our animals is a higher priority right now. Without some feed, we can hunt down rustlers all we want, and it won't do a bit of good."

Mack only nodded, waiting for the boss' orders. He didn't have to wait long.

"Mack, I want you to assign two men to follow the herd. They are to observe and scout only. They are not to engage, and I want you to make that absolutely clear. I'm going to take a couple of the boys and head to Meraton in the next few days. Maybe that bartender everyone keeps talking about has heard of some grain or other food source. You're in charge while I'm gone."

Mack didn't like the idea. In a tone tempered by respect, he objected, "Suh, I would prefer if you let me or one of the other men go into that town. That's a dangerous place, and a successful man such as yourself might be a target. It hasn't been that long since we lost a man there to bank robbers. There have been shootouts, dopers, and all kinds of riff-raff roaming around that place."

Mr. Beltran nodded, secretly warmed at his employee's desire to protect him.

"I'll take a couple of the boys with me, Mack. Get Slim and Butter – they'll keep me out of trouble."

"Yes, suh."

Fort Bliss, Texas
January 23, 2016

The third week of the Moreland presidency brought about more changes for both Bishop and West Texas. The elimination of the last artificial object from Bishop's body was one such monumental event. The couple celebrated the absence of the restraint pinning his left arm against his chest by slow dancing around the room while his wife hummed a waltz. Bishop's rehabilitation had progressed well, helped in no small part by his and Terri's long afternoon strolls around the base. The only remaining visible sign of his injury was in his hesitation to use his left side. The doctors and physical therapist had promised that condition would improve over time.

During this period, the couple enjoyed more one-on-one time than ever before, meandering hand-in-hand and chatting about whatever came to mind. Bishop's first conversational priorities had been his wife's mental well-being. He had quizzed her repeatedly about the ordeal she had endured, always listening with great intensity. Once he had assured himself that Terri wasn't badly scarred, the next consuming topic of discussion had been the baby's condition. The base hospital had performed an ultrasound on the fetus, resulting in a good report. The electric shock of the Taser hadn't impacted the unborn child in any measurable way. While the doctors couldn't guarantee the prognosis, their comforting words eliminated some of the couple's concerns, but not all. Like all expectant parents, they wouldn't be for sure about the condition of their firstborn until the baby made an up close and personal appearance.

Terri didn't tell Bishop everything about her experience as a hostage, at least not at first. She knew her husband well. While Bishop's protective nature often made her feel secure, his physical condition warranted a gradual exposure of some details. Her communication was throttled by visions of the thin stitches next to her man's heart, those scrawny pieces of life-saving thread always at the forefront of her mind. Her measured disclosure of the facts wasn't all for Bishop's sake, however. While the visible signs of her beating were long gone by the time he regained a lucid state, Terri's psychological bruises remained. When she finally revealed the full story, her mate remained silent, eyes focused on an empty point in space. Terri knew the lack of external reaction was a façade, cold waves of fury resonating from her husband and chilling the air.

Eventually Bishop exhaled, lowered his head, and spoke. "Terri, I'm sorry I wasn't there for you. I would give anything to change what happened."

"It's okay, Bishop. I'm fine now. There wasn't anything you could have done. A lot of people are suffering through worse - every single day."

"I guess I should focus on the fact that we made it – that we're still together."

Terri nuzzled her head into the crook of Bishop's neck and sighed. "That's how I'm coping with it all. That's really the important thing to me. I want to be with you forever."

The next day dawned with the doctors telling Bishop it was time for him to leave the hospital. The surprise news left the pair with a difficult decision about where to go. Bishop was uncomfortable heading back to the ranch one handed, and Terri wasn't quite ready to return to Meraton. They finally decided on a short vacation to Alpha, hoping Nick and Diana wouldn't mind two recuperating guests.

During the dismissal process, one of the staffers relayed the message that the base commander would like a word with Bishop before he was transported off base. The request wasn't unexpected.

The couple entered General Westfield's reception area a short time later. They found the same protective major, busily administrating the commander's affairs. Unlike previous visits, the officer didn't project any attitude toward Bishop, promptly escorting the two into the main office without incident.

"Our paths cross again, Bishop," began the general officer while extending his hand. Nodding at Terri with a smile, he added, "Ma'am."

"Good morning, sir. I was told you wished to have a word?"

With a hesitant glance at Terri, the general opened his desk drawer and produced a small brown paper bag. "I've got something of yours here, Bishop. I've been keeping it for you."

Bishop peeked inside the bag, locating his knife and scabbard. The act of kindness made him smile. "Thank you, sir. I have a long history with this steel."

"I know, Bishop. The Colonel has entertained me with stories about some of his prior work. Your name drifted into a few of the tall tales."

Terri was curious, "How's the recovery going, General?"

Westfield's response surprised the couple. The normally stoic officer grimaced and responded, "Not well. While there isn't any threat of additional infighting, the operation to focus all available resources on the Mississippi delta isn't progressing as planned. A few of the cities along the Eastern Seaboard erupted in violence as the military pulled out. What little of those communities that are left aren't happy with the feds focusing the vast majority of their resources elsewhere."

Bishop could understand the unrest. According to the last information provided by the Colonel, the military was barely keeping order in some of the huge population centers. Pulling those troops out in order to jump-start the nation wouldn't be a popular decision. Still, the heartland was the only place that had all of the necessary resources of nuclear power, transportation, agriculture, and fossil fuel refining. From Bishop's limited perspective, the plan was a good one. Get the center of the country functional again, and use that as a base to spread the recovery east and west.

The general continued, "What is truly disturbing is the level of causalities being reported. Starvation, disease, and civil unrest have taken their toll. Some estimates claim we've lost over 40% of the population."

Terri inhaled sharply, covering her mouth at the shocking figure. "That's over 140 million people, General. That's unbelievable."

"It's just an estimate, but believable. There's simply not enough food. The northern states have experienced a hard winter so far, millions of people trying to survive without heat or fresh water. The president is trying to get a crop in the ground this spring, but we won't realize the benefit of that until harvest time. I fear that number of casualties could grow considerably by then."

Suddenly Bishop felt his problems were insignificant compared to so many. The general wasn't done. "I know we are burying over a 1,000 bodies a week out in the desert ourselves. El Paso won't exist in another 12 months. Things are worse across the border, I hear."

Terri was still trying to comprehend it all. "General, surely there are other sources of food. What about fishing or the millions of head of livestock?"

"There's precious little fuel being refined. So far, a single nuclear power plant has been restarted, and it's only generating at 30% capacity. Without fuel, the fishermen can't work. And even if they could, there's no way to transport the product to the cities. I'm going to begin rationing here at the base today. We're running short of fuel, food... hell... just about everything. My battalions in Phoenix and Denver are barely receiving enough resupply to feed themselves, let alone the few million people left in those towns. According to my commander in Arizona, the nightly funeral pyres can be seen from 10 miles away. I'm bringing them home next week before there isn't enough fuel for them to return."

Bishop didn't know what to say, looking down in silence. After a brief pause, the general continued. "Bishop, I'm sorry, but I can't fly you out of here. Surface transport via a couple of HUMVEEs is the best I can do right now."

"Thank you, sir. That is most kind. A ride to Alpha would be appreciated."

The base commander rose from his chair, a clear signal that the meeting was concluded. After shaking hands, Terri asked one more question, "General, what will you do when the food runs out here at the base?"

"That's a very good question, young lady. I wish I had an answer to that."

Alpha, Texas
January 23, 2016

The migration to Alpha was in full swing when Bishop and Terri arrived via HUMVEEs. The two coyote brown military transports caused quite a stir among the people waiting to enter town. After a few moments, the men staffing the northern entrance to Alpha waved the Army drivers past. As they entered town, the couple was shocked at the changes since their last visit to Alpha only a short time ago.

There were a few cars on the streets, most trying to navigate the blinking traffic lights and rusting relics that still littered the pavement. Storekeepers were sweeping piles of glass and other debris from the sidewalks while other men covered broken windows with sheets of plywood. Squeals of delight drifted from a nearby park as youngsters commanded the monkey bars and jungle gym under the watchful eye of their mothers.

"We leave town for a few days, and Nick messes things up," Bishop commented.

Terri grunted, unable to tear her eyes from the miracle that was Alpha. "Are you sure these soldiers didn't take a wrong turn? What happened to our favorite ghost town?"

Even the military drivers were impressed with the scene unfolding before them, one man asking his sergeant if they could stay in town overnight and see the sights. Eventually, Bishop and Terri were dropped off at the courthouse where they found Alpha's "First Couple." Bishop was being carried to a waiting medevac helicopter the last time Nick had seen him. The big man was so happy to see his friend alive, Nick's eyes watered up, and he turned away. Bishop was polite and didn't comment, his throat being a little tight as well. Anyone who had been watching the two would have been touched by the brief, but telling hug the two men shared, each slapping the other on the back to signal its end.

"I was going to ask if you would mind hosting a couple of tourists," stated Terri, taking in the flurry of activity, "but it looks like there might not be any rooms at the inn."

Diana smiled and hugged Terri. "Of course you two can stay here anytime you wish. We've got plenty of space."

Almost an hour passed as the two couples caught up on the events of the last few weeks. Nick assured Bishop the wounded man's truck and weapon were safe and well cared for.

"My dad always made me fill it up when I borrowed his pickup," teased Bishop. "I assume you have topped off the tank?"

Nick and Diana were still using the church as their quarters, and it was decided Bishop and Terri would join them there during their stay. Most of the congregation had moved back into their own neighborhoods after the siege had been broken, and the religious compound seemed almost deserted and tranquil in comparison to the couple's previous experience there. Diana remarked that the sanctuary had reclaimed its peaceful persona and now was most often visited by new arrivals to the community as a site for quiet reflection in a world askew. Additionally, the mayor shared her plan to repurpose a few of the Sunday School rooms for her self-reliance skills training.

"Well, we want to help out with the reconstruction," Terri declared. "We will pull our weight and help with the workload."

Bishop nodded at his restricted left arm, adding, "If there's anything a handicapped guy can do, I'm willing to try."

Nick grunted, "Oh, come on now, Bishop. That little old injury to your ear isn't all that bad. Besides, you have another perfectly good ear anyway. And you know, most folks your age expect to lose hearing as they get a few years on them. Don't worry, my friend. We can still find some way you can help out around here." A smirk flashed briefly on his face before the former operator's serious expression returned, and he continued. "Wait! I got it! You can help with the quilting bee at the library. No one really talks there anyway, so your missing ear won't be an issue there. How are your sewing skills?"

Bishop smirked and cupped his ear. "Could you repeat that, sonny? I couldn't be sure, but it sounded almost like you said you were denying me access to those close-in parking spots?"

Bishop, tired from the journey, headed off with Nick to find, "any comfortable horizontal surface." Terri felt a strong urge to be out and about, a victim of hospital-induced cabin fever. She decided to get a feel for Alpha's new popularity, keenly interested in how the town was handling the boom. The greeting she and Bishop had received as they entered the community sparked her interest in discovering how Diana had organized the processing of new arrivals.

"It's a work in progress," commented Diana. "We interview each new settler about what they did before the collapse. We document what type of skills and education each person has. Then we match folks with housing, municipal projects and self-reliance training. We are still refining how this procedure works."

"What kind of improvements are you working on?"

"I don't really know all of them. After our electric grid came back up, we were flooded with people approaching us with new ideas for our reconstruction and reorganization. One group is working on cleaning out two of the school buildings so we can start classes again. Another family solicited help converting their taxidermy business into a butcher shop. And believe me when I tell you that we need a butcher *yesterday*. Plus, we have teams taking inventory of abandoned buildings while other crews are listing the contents that haven't been looted. This flurry of activity makes it difficult to keep track of what everyone is doing so that we can effectively match people to jobs."

"How are you feeding everyone?"

"Pete is sending vendors our way. When merchants don't sell all of their goods in Meraton's market, he suggests they drive up here and trade with us. So far, the church has been buying all the food we can get from those suppliers in addition to two of the local ranchers who are providing beef and chicken. We've planted over a dozen gardens, but it will be a while before they produce. Hunters have been bringing back the occasional deer, and we have two teams who have been foraging the local forests for anything palatable."

Terri thought about the organization for a while as the two women strolled up and down Main Street, waving to friends and noting the progress.

Terri said, "Diana, I want Bishop and me to pull our own weight. He's limited in what he can do, but maybe we can help you keep track of some of the initiatives you are organizing."

"Sounds good to me. I find myself completely overwhelmed by

the workload. I'll take any help I can get."

"I want to get going first thing in the morning. Where do you suggest I start?"

After pondering Terri's question for a moment, Diana pointed toward the courthouse lawn. "Meet me up here in the morning, and you can work with one of the welcoming teams. That's really our most important job right now. Maybe you can figure out a way to streamline the whole mess."

After a quick breakfast, Terri rushed off to the courthouse and found Diana already hard at work.

"I'm working on my first new city ordinance, and it is one complex issue." Dianna announced. "I want very few laws for the citizens of Alpha, but I think all our folks have to participate in food production. While we all know that starvation is simply unacceptable, even the potential of a food shortage could destroy everything we're trying to build."

Terri agreed, "Hunger can be a negative influence on law and order, too. Desperate people do desperate things to avoid starving. But how are you going to legislate how food is produced?"

"We're not. We have to leave it up to the individual to determine if they want to hunt, gather, or grow – perhaps some combination of the three. What is absolutely critical is that everyone produces enough at a minimum to feed themselves and their family."

Terri's finger found her chin, her mind clearly processing information along her mental neuro-highway. "I think the biggest issue is going to be a lack of knowledge. Take me, for example. I was a city girl. I'd be unable to do any of those things to produce food for myself."

Diana replied, "In fact, the first formally sponsored training organized is going to address this topic. We're going to establish 'continuing education classes' on how to garden, hunt, or identify edible foodstuffs."

Terri grinned, "Bishop needs to attend the gardening class. His little patch back at the ranch was faring poorly when we left."

"I've been surprised at how many green thumbs we've got around here. Some residents have already planted oversized gardens that will eventually produce more than required by their families. They saw the need early. On the other hand, we've got a few people who are not naturally inclined to produce calories by any method. They represent a challenge to contribute to the anti-hunger initiative."

"Alpha should follow Meraton's model. For those who don't want to hunt or grow, gathering and bartering can be the answer. We can organize family trips to the valleys and gather food there. Bishop and I took a little hiking vacation up into the mountains a while back. It was like one of those old television commercials were they talk about harvesting nature's bounty. I bet there are some citizens who can act as tour guides and nature experts. If they can show people which nuts, berries, nettles, and greens are okay to eat, I bet your citizens would line up to attend a class like that. You might even be able to find someone who has knowledge of using herbs to promote health and wellbeing."

Diana nodded, "Yes, you are right. The classes need to address the need of our residents to promote attendance. But what do we hope the classes will accomplish? I initially thought we need to set food production quotas based on the number of family members, but that wouldn't work. Big framed men eat more than thinner individuals. Older people don't require the calories that growing teenagers consume, and our elderly are never going to be able to cultivate crops and hunt like our younger population groups. I've decided the best method of enforcement would be a results orientated measurement with occasional consultation. The rule would be simple: If you approach the council with a need for food, you better have a good excuse for drawing from the community chest and putting everyone else at risk."

Terri laughed at her friend's phrasing. "Garden plots will be the norm. Seeds should be readily available to everyone. Folks will need fertilizer as well."

Diana laughed, "You should attend our council meetings. Fertilizer isn't in short supply there."

Laughter broke the tension caused by the serious nature of the conversation, and the new mayor became serious again.

"Insecticides are going to be a problem. We'll have to try to keep the pests under control by using natural substances. One of our best growers said there are some plants that are known to deter hungry insects and damaging diseases. I want practically every occupied home in Alpha to have a plot of veggies growing on the premises. With our hot climate, we should be able to support a year-round growing season."

Terri was thinking ahead. "You can organize contests and have competitions for the best produce. They can be like the pre-collapse 4-H fairs. I remember going to those as a kid; whole towns would gather to show off the juiciest tomatoes or prize winning green beans. People even exchanged recipes, canning tips and shared growing and cooking tips."

Diana continued, "Domestic animals are also going to play a role. Goats, pigs, chickens, rabbits, and even a few dairy cows would contribute a bunch. I'm going to use some city funds and buy some goats at the Meraton market soon – I want it to be a common sight to see them grazing in city parks. Besides, their appetites can keep the grass down. We don't have the gasoline to power lawn mowers. Producing eggs, milk and meat... it can all work."

"I want to contribute too, Diana. Tell me what I can do to help."

After Diana gave her a quick briefing on all of the activities, Terri volunteered to help the welcoming committee.

The guys had taken off early this morning, Nick wanting to give Bishop a tour of his security arrangements. Diana pointed Terri in the right direction and then rushed off to attend a meeting on healthcare.

Terri was assigned to a table that had been set up on the courthouse lawn, a large sign declaring her area as "Station #4." As travelers arrived on the outskirts of town, they were directed to the courthouse after a brief screening to keep troublemakers and random rogue elements out of Alpha.

Once the refugees made their way to the courthouse, they answered a single page questionnaire. Based on their responses, the newcomers were then directed to a station where detailed acclimation could begin.

Terri was informed that Station #4 handled families with minor children, her on-the-job training being provided by the three kindly ladies who served as Terri's co-workers. She was also warned to expect the worst. As one soft-spoken volunteer put it, "Most of these folks have traveled a rough road after living on the edge the last six months. Be prepared to have your heart broken."

It wasn't long before Station #4 received its first customers. Terri noticed a family approaching across the shady lawn, the middle-aged man and woman apprehensive, and the children sluggish and shy. As they ventured closer, details of their individual condition shocked Terri to the point where her stomach began to churn.

The parents were dressed in rags. Previously a respectable outfit of blue jeans and polo shirt, the father's combo was now threadbare and tattered, the cloth so filthy it was difficult to identify the fabric. The mother's clothing was only a slight improvement, her tennis shorts and short sleeve blouse in complete disrepair. Stringy, filthy hair accented the sunken, hollow looking expression on the adults' faces. The stench of body odor was strong even in the outdoor environment.

Terri would guess the three girls ranged in age from four to eight years old. Their condition and demeanor caused Terri's eyes to water from emotion. Skinny, stick-like legs extended from under the soiled skirts. The children's clothing had seen far better days as well, but was at least recognizable. It was the girls' expressions hiding under layers of grime and filth that evoked such deep feelings inside of Terri. Most of all, it was their eyes that disturbed her; they were dead.

Of all the suffering children she and Bishop had encountered on their trip from Houston, nothing could have prepared Terri for the lifeless appearance of the children standing in front of Station #4. Despite working with her share of unwashed, hungry kids, she was horrified. She had interacted with young ones who were in danger, or sick, or without parents - none of those comparing to the state of these girls. It was as if they had withdrawn to the inner reaches of their minds and died, leaving their bodies to walk around like mindless, numb robots.

"Terri," whispered one of her co-workers, "you're staring."

Shaking herself out of the trance, Terri nodded. "Sorry."

“Welcome to Alpha, Texas… Mr. and Mrs. Hendricks. Please take a seat. I assume you’ve been offered food and water?”

The man hesitated before answering. “Yes, yes we have, and thank you.”

“Where are you originally from?”

Mr. Hendricks seemed to have trouble remembering, finally answering “Houston” after a long pause. The response focused Terri’s attention even more. These people might have been her neighbors less than a year ago.

Mr. Hendricks managed to expand on his history. “We… we were driving to my parent’s home in El Paso and couldn’t find gasoline anywhere. We stopped at every station for 50 miles, but no luck. We finally checked into a hotel. I don’t remember which one anymore. We ran out of gas the next day. Then some men came along in a truck and robbed us of everything we had. We wandered for two days and finally ended up at Fort Stockdale. We’ve been living at the labor camp ever since.”

“Labor camp?” asked Terri.

“That’s what everyone calls it,” interjected Mrs. Hendricks. “I think it was more of a concentration camp to be truthful.”

Each of the women working Station #4 was taking notes while trying to keep the visitors at ease. As the Hendricks’ family story unfolded, Terri found it almost impossible to write anything, so troubling was the experience of the people sitting in front of her.

At first, the people of Fort Stockdale had been helpful, kind, and welcoming. Much like current day Alpha, more and more stranded travelers wandered into the small town every day. When the delivery trucks stopped arriving, the locals began to worry. When the power wasn’t restored after two weeks, some of the natives became restless. When the grocery store was completely barren, things got ugly.

It was the county’s district attorney who took control. An educated, commanding woman, the DA had stormed into town with a handful of deputies, three cases of food, and a signed court order giving her control via declared martial law.

The town’s single hotel was requisitioned to be used for official business. Tents were collected from local citizens and pitched by a creek that ran along the edge of town. All non-citizens were ordered to take up residence in the tent city. Its occupants dubbed it "Shantytown."

At first, the water level in the nearby stream provided for the transplants. As the hot summer wore on without rain, the creek dried up. The men living in the tent city took to foraging for food and water – anything they could find. This activity was quickly stopped by the local law enforcement officers, a few of the stranded travelers being shot while arguing their cases.

The DA's promise to provide rations for Shantytown was never fully implemented. Despite every able- bodied adult being put to work plowing fields, chopping wood, and harvesting crops, it seemed like there was barely enough food and water delivered to the tent city for the residents to survive.

Terri noticed one of the girls scratching the back of her hand and realized the child was injured. "What's wrong with your hand, sweeties?" she gently asked.

The kindergartener, upon realizing someone was addressing her directly, immediately ducked and hid behind her mother.

"I'm sorry, ma'am. She's not been very social since she was stamped."

Terri tilted her head, "Stamped?"

The father interrupted, showing some emotion for the first time. "Branded is more like it. They branded my daughter for stealing food the children found. Those… those self-righteous animals."

The girl's mother pulled the young child around to face Station #4, softly brushing her tangled hair. "Show these ladies your hand, Carla."

With great hesitation, the girl complied, extending her right arm for the women and causing Terri to inhale sharply. There on the back of the dirty, tiny little hand was a deep scar in the outline of a "T." The sight reminded Terri of pictures she had seen of ranch brands freshly burned into calves.

"She and two other youngsters found a box of apples that had fallen off a truck. They brought the container back to Shantytown and shared the food. When one of the enforcers found the box and began asking questions, the children were accused of being thieves and stamped for punishment."

Terri's outrage caused her to respond a little too sharply. "Who did this? Who ordered the branding of a child?" she demanded.

The mother and father both responded at the same time. "The DA did, of course." Mr. Hendricks continued, "She runs the town and meters justice. If an adult is caught stealing, they are banished to the desert. First offender minors are branded, but if a child is caught a second time, the whole family is banished from the city."

Terri had to stand and walk away, her fury overwhelming the need to stay and help process the Hendricks family. As she blindly turned the corner, she ran headlong into Bishop, Nick, and Diana.

"Hey there, darling," Bishop began, "How's it go...." The expression on his wife's face instantly telling him something was wrong.

"Bishop," started Terri, her finger pointing at his chest, "I want you to go get our rifles right now. We are going to go kick some ass."

"Whoa there, young lady. Slow down. What's wrong?"

"Bishop, there's some asshole who is branding children and starving adults. She's running some little town not far from here, and it has to be stopped – right now."

Placing his hand on Terri's shoulder, Bishop tried to steady his wife. "Terri, please calm down. What the devil are you talking about?"

Terri began sobbing and buried her head in Bishop's shoulder. Diana sighed and attempted to explain. "I think your wife has just encountered some new arrivals from Fort Stockdale. From what we have heard, the woman running the show up there apparently uses some unjustifiably harsh discipline. We started hearing similar stories a few days ago."

Nick looked puzzled. "She's branding people? Like using a hot iron to burn a ranch's mark on cattle?"

Diana nodded, "Yes, from what we've heard, they use it to identify and deter criminals."

Terri managed to gather herself and pulled away from Bishop's shoulder. "Go around the corner and talk to that family sitting over there. Those Fort Stockdale animals branded a five-year-old girl whose only crime was finding a box of apples. She sure as shit doesn't look like any criminal to me."

Diana soothed Terri's shoulder. "I know you're upset, Terri. I was too when I started hearing what was going on up there. We've had quite a few people show up from that hellhole this week."

Again, Terri looked at Bishop with hatred burning in her eyes. "Come on, Bishop, I want to go and set those people free. I want to go right now."

Bishop pointed to his arm and sighed. "Terri, I saw some pretty ugly stuff when we went to Fort Stockdale to turn on the electricity. I know how difficult it is to handle things like that. But I'm not ready or able to fight anyone. I can't even put on my own pants right now."

It took Terri a few moments to digest Bishop's words, but eventually his meaning registered with the irate woman. She nodded, sighed, and rubbed her eyes. "I'm sorry, everyone. The story I just heard from those people reminded me of being a hostage. It hit a little close to home. Besides, I guess being a hormonal pregnant mess is causing me to get a little more emotional than usual where children are concerned."

Bishop looked at his wife, "You okay, babe?"

Nodding, Terri sniffled and then replied, "Yeah. I'm good."

The foursome proceeded back toward the newcomer processing area just as the Hendricks family was finishing up. Diana approached Alpha's newest residents with her hand extended and introduced herself as the city's mayor.

"Miss Brown," stated one of the workers at Station #4, "Mrs. Hendricks is a registered nurse."

"Outstanding," Diana declared with a smile. "I'm sure these ladies told you we're trying to improve our medical capabilities. I just returned from a meeting on that very subject. Your experience will be welcome here."

A golf cart pulled up, the volunteer driver approaching the station. One of the workers handed him a slip of paper containing an address. "1201 South Oak Street," he repeated. "I used to live on South Oak years ago. It's a fine neighborhood." With that endorsement still hanging in the air, the family was shown to the waiting cart and escorted to their new home.

Diana watched as the newcomers sped off in the electric transport. After a bit she turned to her friends and declared, "There will be a 'Welcome to Alpha' box at their new home. It will have a few basic commodities like toothpaste, soap, and a few cans of food. There are instructions on where they can go to find clothing and other supplies. We'll give them a few days to get used to things and then try to integrate them into the work force. It's the best we can do right now."

"Those people looked pretty shell shocked to me," Bishop said. "How long is it taking the average refugee to become productive?"

Deacon Brown sighed, "That's part of the problem. Most of these people are barely walking, and many of them have severe health issues beyond malnutrition. We have to feed and care for them, and it's becoming a drain."

Bishop understood. "You can't turn them away. We'll just have to figure out how to make it through somehow."

Fort Stockdale
January 24, 2016

District Attorney Patricia Gibson looked at the dusty diploma hanging across from her desk. The document had once generated extreme pride for the small town girl, a significant achievement surpassed only by her election as the county's top legal authority just over a year ago. The sheepskin proclaimed her award of a Juris Doctorate from the University of Texas School of Law. Not an insignificant honor for the first member of the Gibson family ever to attend an institution of learning beyond Central High School.

Hardly a morning went by that Pat didn't think to take the damned thing down. It was a reminder of a better time and a full life –

thoughts that now could anger her to the point of making bad decisions. *Lord knows there have been enough bad decisions already*, she thought. Glancing one last time at the "To Do" list penciled in the open calendar on her desk, she stood and brushed a few breakfast crumbs from her blouse. It was time to get to work – the men would be waiting on her.

DA Gibson squared her shoulders and stepped outside. The sun was already a quarter high in the eastern sky, and the sudden brightness cause her to flinch, raising a hand to shield her eyes from the glare. She was greeted with a chorus of "Good morning, ma'am," from the gathered onlookers.

Glancing around until her eyes acclimated to the brightness, Miss Gibson inventoried the men who stood in a semi-circle around the side entrance to the Pecos County courthouse. She knew all of the six onlookers well. Four of them were what the citizens now called enforcers, ex-lawmen who didn't bother with a uniform anymore. Long guns and badges were the only remaining hint of their pre-collapse responsibilities.

The fifth man was the town's resident electrician who was standing next to the warden, the person responsible for the refugee camp.

"What's on the agenda this morning, gentlemen?"

The electrician stepped forward and spoke first. "Ma'am, I'm on my way over to the Jones place again. We're going to take another shot at making that water well work. I've got the battery-wagon all charged up."

Pat thought about the man's statement for a moment before replying. "Are you sure we've corrected yesterday's problem?"

"Yes, ma'am. One of the batteries shorted out. I had to requisition another from the storehouse."

"Another one? Isn't that three already this week?"

The man avoided Pat's gaze, choosing instead to look down at his dusty boots and mutter, "Yes, ma'am."

Buying time to think, Miss Gibson glanced at the nearby horse-drawn wagon. Stepping over to the contraption, she studied the contents of its bed. Rows of automobile batteries rested on the wooden floorboard, each connected in a series with heavy cables that in a former life had been jumper cables. At the rear was another larger, green metal box that the engineer called an "inverter," a device used to convert the electricity generated by the batteries into more usable current.

Turning back to the nervous electrician, she asked, "How many batteries are left in the warehouse?"

"I'm not exactly sure, Miss Gibson. I would estimate there are about 20 left."

Pat wasn't happy with that answer. "You would *estimate?* You can't *count* to 20? I want to see those inventory sheets on my desk first thing in the morning. Every single battery had better be accounted for, or we will be hunting for a new electrician. Do I make myself clear?"

"Ye... Ye... Yes ma'am," stuttered the linesman.

DA Gibson stepped closer and pointed with her finger. "If I find that you've been trading our precious batteries for something like whiskey, you'll have more to worry about than finding another line of employment."

Pat's threat caused the enforcers to chuckle, but they all knew it wasn't a laughing matter. Shortly after the collapse, the DA had organized a seizure of every unused automobile battery in town. The move had saved hundreds of lives.

Unlike many small towns, Fort Stockdale's water wasn't supplied by a single well. The berg's location on the high desert plains had forced the city's planners to drill several smaller wells into the pockets of life-giving liquid trapped in the limestone below. When it became clear that the electrical service wasn't going to return quickly, DA Gibson had organized a mobile power plant that traveled around the town and pumped water into the above ground storage tanks.

At first, a pickup truck had been used to haul the life-sustaining cargo. Gasoline generators charged the battery banks overnight, and then the truck drove from well to well, hooking up the power and pumping the neighborhood's tank full. When the gasoline began to run out, horses were substituted. Eventually, wood gas had to be used to run the generators.

Despite being a town of over 8,000 people, the number of car batteries scavenged had been remarkably slim. Most of the automotive parts stores in town carried a minimal number of replacements. Even the big box store chains with extensive auto repair facilities produced fewer than expected quantities. Still, the system worked, and the people had water – for the most part.

The population didn't remain at 8,000 for long.

Food had been a completely different challenge. Little local produce was cultivated in the surrounding countryside, and the local cattle population was quickly depleted.

DA Gibson had instituted rationing, seized private property, and taken control of a local government that had completely disintegrated in a matter of weeks. It was the most difficult moral dilemma she had ever faced. Not only was the workload extreme, the ethics of the entire process went against her grain. She had become a lawyer to protect people's freedoms, not take them away. She had worked two jobs, studied all night, and avoided interpersonal entanglements in her resolve to protect the American way of life. To find herself in a situation where so many lives depended on her violating those rights was demoralizing at best.

But there hadn't been any choice.

It seemed like every single day had required life and death decisions. Who received medical care, and who suffered with pain? Who received food and who went hungry? What should be done with a man caught stealing food? What should be done with a woman accused of killing her neighbor?

The town's mayor had been killed in the first wave of violence that swept the small town. Desperate, starving citizens without water demanded the city do something – anything. The protest had turned violent, first with rocks, then bottles, and eventually gunshots. The elected official had died in Pat's arms.

Something came over her that fateful afternoon. The ring of deputy sheriffs and city police officers was being pushed back, law enforcement's struggle failing to keep the swelling throng of angry residents away from the courthouse. DA Gibson remembered the fear she felt from the mob. She watched a police officer fall, not 20 feet away, and then stared in horror as the man's body was literally torn apart – such was the ferocity of the horde.

In less than 15 minutes, the Chief of Police turned to DA Gibson and screamed, "What do you want us to do? We can't hold out much longer."

"Why are you asking me?" she had shouted over the clamor of the crowd's howling fury.

"Because everyone else in the chain of command is dead."

Terrified - positive she was going to die horribly at the hands of the very people who had voted her into office, those fateful words had rolled out of her throat. "Fire into the crowd, Chief. Disburse those people by any means necessary."

The blood spilled that afternoon had stained the streets of the courthouse square for weeks before enough rain fell from the arid Texas sky to wash it away. When the light was just right, DA Gibson thought she could still detect dark areas on the pavement, remnants of the desperate ones who fell that day. She prayed that time would fade the visions of carnage from her memory.

Since that event, DA Gibson had ruled Fort Stockdale with an iron fist. She considered her soul already lost and went about running the town's business without emotion or compassion, every decision based on the cold, hard logic of what would keep the most citizens alive for another day.

Suicide was always on her mind.

Meraton, Texas
January 24, 2016

Pete's Place was doing a brisk early evening business. The warmer-than-normal West Texas day had brought the crowd hustling in for a cold one as soon as the market had closed. *Cold one*, thought Pete. *I didn't think I'd ever serve another frosty beverage again. Thank heavens for electricity!*

The bar's patrons filled every stool and table, the smell of cigar smoke, leather, and gun oil permeating the small establishment. The early hour prompted most patrons to be on their best behavior, the din of conversation, laughter, and good times reverberating throughout.

Pete was busy behind the bar, fulfilling the traditional role that included being a good listener, janitorial service, and server, ensuring glasses stayed full. With one towel over his shoulder, and another in his hand making small circles on the bar, he didn't notice the new arrivals at first. It wasn't until a hush fell over the place that he looked up to see three strangers entering his establishment.

The first gentleman to breech the threshold was a tall man. Pete guessed the stranger topped 6'4" and was well over 200 pounds. A dark Stetson angled slightly down in the front shadowed the man's face, but nothing could hide the muscular chest that bulged underneath the fellow's plaid shirt.

Behind the first, entered a second gentleman. This guy was older, not as tall, but still a formidable looking character. Tuffs of gray hair showed beneath the worn brim of his headgear, a rock-like jaw projecting determination and authority. *He's the boss*, thought Pete. *I can see it in his eyes.*

The trio of strangers was rounded out by a thin, wiry looking cowhand. Not overly large or heavy, Pete's instincts bristled when he looked into the man's icy, dark-green eyes. *Here's the dangerous one*, the bartender judged, *this man's not afraid of anything because he's seen it all before – and he won.*

Pete slid half a step down the bar, positioning himself within easy reach of the sawed-off shotgun residing there. He was just about to reach for the weapon when one of the customers called out. "Mr. Beltran! Welcome sir! I've not seen you in Meraton for a long time."

The older man in the middle removed his hat and smiled at the greeter. "Hello, CJ. It has been a while at that."

Following their boss' gesture, the two cowpokes removed their hats, and the general atmosphere relaxed. Several people moved to greet the famous local rancher, Pete counting no less than four of the ladies kissing his cheek.

The big, burly cowboy stayed close to his boss, never more than an arm's length way. The thin man headed directly for the bar. Pete asked the age-old question, "What will ya have?"

He received the age-old response, "What do you have?"

"We've got locally brewed beer. It's not bad. I've got bathtub gin and moonshine whisky. There's still a pot of coffee that's drinkable, and I could even come up with some cold water if you're the designated driver. What'll it be?"

"Beer for all of us, please."

While Pete filled three mugs, he studied the stranger. The man's intense gaze panned the room, scrutinizing the crowd as his boss moved and greeted almost everyone there. It was clear to the ex-Philly cop, now turned barkeep, that his latest customer was a professional. The man's eyes constantly probed low, always looking at hands and waistlines, never at faces. Faces couldn't hurt his boss – hands could fire weapons.

Pete slid three mugs full of cold, brownish liquid across the bar, each container boasting a slight overflow of crème-colored head. "Where'd you get your training?" he casually asked.

An odd expression crossed the ranch hand's face. Pete could see the displeasure in the man, a look of annoyance that anyone had noticed his presence. *Another sign of a pro*, thought Pete.

"I'm not sure what you mean, sir."

Pete snorted and then flashed a friendly smile. "Don't worry, son. I was a cop before I started filling mugs. I can spot someone with training a mile away. I won't tell anyone; your secret is safe with me."

Flashing an understanding smile, the cowboy peered down at his beer. "I was recruited out of the Army by the State Department. I worked in the asset protection service before I decided to come back to the ranch. I missed the work, and Mr. Beltran was kind enough to take me back in."

"Well, welcome to Pete's Place. It's rare we have any trouble here, so sit back and relax. Enjoy your beer."

With a twinkle in his eye, the cowboy motioned to the bar with his head. "Speaking of trouble, what's that you got behind the counter there? A 12-gauge? Shortened barrel? Pump? At least that's what I would guess you thought about reaching for when we first came through the door."

It was Pete's turn to be surprised. "Now how did you know I had a shotgun back…."

About then, Mr. Beltran and the big cowboy returned to the bar, each accepting a mug from their friend. Mr. Beltran took a long sip, smacked his lips, and announced, "Not bad, not bad at all." The elder rancher then extended his hand to Pete and volunteered, "Carlos Beltran. You must be Pete."

Grasping the offered hand, Pete nodded. "Yes, sir. That would be me. Welcome to Pete's Place."

Mr. Beltran nodded to the large man on his right, "This is Butter," and then to the slighter man on his left, "and this is Slim."

"Butter?"

The big fella shyly looked to the floor and muttered, "I can't help it – I know it isn't as healthy as green, leafy vegetables, but I just like butter. Is that such a bad thing?"

Slim grunted, "Don't let him fool you. He eats butter on *everything*. He eats butter on pizza. Even with his questionable eating habits, he was also an undefeated state champion wrestler who was a shoe-in for the Olympic Team before everything went to hell. Probably would have gotten his ass whooped by some smelly Russian dude, though."

Butter straightened at the jab, an argument forming in his throat. The retort never made it out though, Mr. Beltran placing his hand on the big cowboy's forearm, ending the debate.

After everyone had shaken hands, Pete moved on to serve other customers, his social instincts deciding the three newcomers wanted privacy in addition to quenching their thirst.

Less than an hour later, the lights blinked once and then dimmed. The event caused several customers to sigh, a few taking in the electrical pulses before lamenting, "It's that late, already?"

Pete pulled a box of candles from the bar and began passing them out. "Time for 'ambient lighting,' folks. The beer will stay cold even after the electricity goes out."

Despite the quick dispersion of candles, the windmill's lack of power generation was an unofficial notification that it was time for many of the folks to head home. Some had long commutes, while others had chores best accomplished before the day became too warm, and thus needed to retire early. It was a symptom of country life.

After a hearty round of "Good nights," and "Be careful," Pete moved around rapidly, picking up glasses and wiping down tables. The three visitors from the ranch remained, talking quietly among themselves at the end of the bar.

When Pete returned to see if any of their glasses needed refilling, all of the men politely declined more beer. Mr. Beltran had something else on his mind, however. "Pete, when you have a minute, I'd like a word."

Placing both hands wide on the bar, Pete smiled and replied, "Sure, Mr. Beltran. What can I do for you?"

"Pete, the reason why we've come into town is that I've got a problem out at the ranch. I was hoping you might have some idea of a solution."

The bartender's face became serious. "Mr. Beltran, whenever this town has needed help, you've been more than generous. Every single person in Meraton is in your debt. If there's anything I, or anyone else can do, we'll be glad to return the goodwill."

Carlos waved off Pete's words. "Oh, now. We've not done anything one neighbor wouldn't do for another. That's the only way folks get by in this land, helping each other out."

The old rancher sipped his beer and then looked Pete straight in the eye. "My cattle are starving. We're going to lose the whole herd if we don't find a way to feed them before the spring rains come. I've got to find another source of feed, and several tons of it."

Pete shook his head, "Sorry to hear that. Most of the other ranchers around have been bringing butchered beef in to the marketplace on a weekly basis. I've heard more than one say they're reducing the number of animals in their herd. I'm assuming the numbers you're talking about are far beyond anyone else's problem."

"We've got 15,000 head total. Our land, even after the rain

greens everything up, will only support about 8,000 without an outside source of food. I need about 30 tons of corn or hay, and I need it pretty quickly."

"Mr. Beltran, it's late now, so why don't you and your men get rooms down at The Manor? In the morning, you and I will tour the market and see if anyone has any ideas. We'll also radio Alpha at first light and let them know what's going on. You've got a lot of friends there as well. I hope someone has a solution that will work for you, sir."

The old rancher looked away, an unusual expression crossing his weathered face. Pete couldn't read it. "Is there something wrong, Mr. Beltran?"

"No, no sir. It's just I'm not used to asking for anyone's help. It's an uncomfortable feeling."

Pete dismissed his customer's concerns. "Trust me, sir. The people of Meraton and Alpha would welcome the opportunity to help you and the ranch. You've always been there for us. Like you said, it's the neighborly thing to do."

Chapter 5

Meraton, Texas
January 25, 2016

Pete rose early, quickly running through the tasks to prepare his business for another day's trade. He had tossed and turned most of the night, desperately trying to think of a way to help Carlos Beltran. He just couldn't think of a workable idea.

Leaving the bar and moving along Main to The Manor, he wasn't surprised to see Betty's three guests already awake and lounging on the front steps of the hotel. "Good morning."

The greeting was answered by all of the men, and then Mr. Beltran expanded. "We've had good coffee, good eggs, and good conversation with the proprietor of this fine establishment already this morning. A fine start to the day."

Betty appeared behind the men, her hand grasping a pot of coffee. "Anyone need a refill? Oh, good morning, Pete. Need a cup of coffee?"

Pete declined the offer, reassuring Betty that he'd take a rain check. Saying her goodbyes to the guests, The Manor's manager hurried back inside.

"What time does the market open, Pete?"

"It's typically in full swing by nine. I thought we'd send a message to Alpha first. After that, we can talk to the folks while they're setting up."

"Sounds like a plan."

The four men strolled a few blocks down Main and then crossed the road at Cherry Street. Meraton's sole HAM radio operator resided at the end of Cherry and was normally an early riser.

All four remained silent during the trip, each man keeping his early morning thoughts to himself. A few blocks later Pete paused and pointed to a single-story brick, ranch style home, the property's only noticeable feature being a 50-foot tower topped by an unusually shaped antenna.

Dennis Levine answered the knock on his door with a sleep-filled, gravelly voice that somehow managed to relay curiosity and annoyance in the same tone. "Pete? Is something wrong?"

"Good morning, Dennis. I have Mr. Beltran and two of his men with me. We have a message we need to get off to Alpha. Is your equipment running this morning?"

The front door opened a few inches and then all the way. "No, I've not turned it on yet. It'll take a few minutes to warm up. Come on in."

The four visitors entered a modest living room, Mr. Levine already sitting at what had once been a dining room table, but now more closely resembled a radio station's control room. Numerous black boxes, rows of switches and dials, and a maze of wiring filled the space.

A sleepy sounding voice called out from the back of the house, "Dennis? Is everything okay?"

Cupping his hand beside his mouth, the radio operator answered, "Everything's fine, Marie. It's Pete and some friends needing to send a message. Go back to sleep."

Dennis began flipping switches and turning dials. Taking a pad and pen, his eyes surveyed Pete's face for instructions. "What's the message?"

"The dispatch is for Diana and Nick. Tell them Mr. Beltran is in Meraton and has a serious problem. He's losing cattle and needs several tons of feed. Ask them if they have any ideas on where we can find a source to keep his livestock from starving."

Pete looked up at Carlos, "That sound about right?"

"Yes, that pretty much covers it. Please add that I appreciate everyone's time."

"I'll send it first thing after the radio's tubes warm up," promised Mr. Levine.

The conversation was interrupted by a rustling sound from the back of the house. Everyone but Slim ignored the disturbance, all of them assuming Mrs. Levine had decided to stay awake. Mr. Beltran was just reaching to shake Mr. Levine's hand when Slim yelled out, "GUN!"

Pete half turned in time to see a rifle barrel rounding a corner before the room erupted in movement. Slim produced a Glock pistol from his beltline, the handgun raised and aimed in a blur of motion.

Butter moved to shield his boss, the effort causing him to step through a cluster of wires feeding the tabletop menagerie of electronics. The big fellow's foot hooked in a power cord, pulling the attached black box onto the floor.

Mr. Levine ducked under the table, his mind finally settling on the thought that someone was going to shoot his wife. He managed a weak and pleading, "Wait!"

"Come on out, now," Slim's voice stated with authority. "Move real slow, and no one will get hurt."

A head showed around the corner. A patch of rustled gray hair appeared, soon joined by a pair of bushy eyebrows peeking for only a moment before ducking back behind the wall. "Dennis," a distant, nervous voice sounded, "you okay? What's going on over here?"

It took a moment for the terrified homeowner to respond. "Dean? Dean is that you? What in God's name are you doing?"

"I saw all these strangers walking up to your house, Dennis. I thought you were being robbed."

Mr. Levine held up a shaking hand, his eyes wide with fear. Looking at Slim, he managed, "That's my neighbor. He's a little nosy, but you don't need to shoot him for it. Please don't kill him, mister. Except for grilling Texas' worst barbecue, he's not *really* such a bad guy."

Pete knew the man as well. "Dean, it's me, Pete. Put that damned gun down before these men scatter your insides all over Marie's carpet. Nobody is being robbed."

The town's mayor walked toward the corner, shaking his head in frustration. Slim watched as Pete's hand reached out and snatched the barrel of a weapon. He soon returned with an embarrassed, older man wearing a nightshirt, shorts and bright pink slippers. Pete couldn't resist. Pointing down at the intruder's feet he remarked, "Love the shoes, Dean. You wear those every day or did you save them especially for the apocalypse?"

Dean glanced down and then flushed red. "I guess I put on the wife's shoes. We had the curtains drawn, and it was dark in the bedroom."

Pete handed the man his rifle back, his tone stern. "You'd better get back home, Dean. Your better half might come looking for you and someone might get hurt - probably you for sneaking out in her pink bunny slippers."

Turning back to Dennis, Pete questioned, "Are you okay?"

The man answered with a nod and then began to immediately reassemble his equipment. Mr. Levine's face expressed concern over the box that had landed on the floor, cradling the hardware like a mother would comfort a child with a skinned knee.

"Is your equipment okay, sir?" asked an embarrassed Butter.

"I... I... don't know yet. I think so."

Pete stepped over, placing a comforting hand on the radio operator's shoulder.

"Do you have the message straight?"

"Yes, yes, I sure do."

"Okay, Dennis. Sorry to have bothered you and sorry about the commotion. We'll be on our way."

Pete and his guests exited the radioman's home, making their way back toward Main Street and the preparations to open the market.

After a short period spent gathering his wits, Mr. Levine finally checked his frequencies and centered the microphone. "Alpha... Alpha... This is Meraton. Come in, please."

It was 20 seconds before the small speaker hissed static, "Dennis, is that you?"

"Yes, of course it's me. Who else would it be?"

"There must be sunspots or something this morning, Dennis. Your voice sounds odd, and I'm not catching every word."

"Never mind that, Phil. I have a very important message for Diana and Nick. Are you ready?"

"Please repeat that, Dennis. The message broke up. All I heard was 'Important,' and 'Diana and Nick.' What's going on?"

"Look, I've had a helluva morning already, my friend. I had armed men in my house. They're in Meraton. They almost shot my neighbor. They're from the Beltran ranch, and Mr. Beltran has a serious problem. He needs help. He needs food for his cattle, and a ton of it. Pete wanted to know if Nick or Diana had any ideas on how to help."

The Meraton broadcaster waited on his friend in Alpha to respond, but he never did. Mr. Levine hailed his counterpart again. "Alpha? Alpha? Are you there?"

No response.

Checking the lights on the various electrical components, Mr. Lavine noticed one critical lamp was no longer glowing with power. "Damn it! That's the piece that got knocked on the floor."

Forgetting all about the message, Dennis immediately moved to unplug the malfunctioning box and then headed to his garage with the hope of repair dominating his thoughts.

Phil looked at what he had written down, no longer craving coffee or more sleep. Anxiety caused his hand to shake the pencil as he mentally reviewed the unusual transmission. Something was really wrong in Meraton, and he needed to find Diana or Nick.

Thoughts of combing his hair, putting on socks, or brushing his teeth forgotten, Phil rushed from his home on South 4th and headed directly for the church six blocks away.

There were several residents already awake and milling about, a few of them greeting Phil as he rushed by. The radio operator ignored his neighbors; panic welling as he worried that his friend

Dennis was in serious trouble.

Pushing through the front doors of the church, Phil was relieved to find Diana and Nick talking just inside the lobby. "Nick! Diana! Meraton is under attack! I just received a transmission from Dennis, and now he's off the air."

"What? What do you mean by, 'They're under attack'?"

Holding out his paper, the anxious messenger showed Nick the words. "See? See here. Dennis' words were breaking up. I kept hearing pops that might have been gunshots, but look at what I did hear. 'Armed men in my house… Meraton… Help… Beltran ranch… Help… Ton… Men.'"

Diana asked, "Can you verify his message? Can't you get any more information?"

"He went off the air after this. He's neither broadcasting, nor receiving."

Nick looked at Diana, Alpha's Mayor responding immediately. "They came to our aid when things looked hopeless. Gather up as many men as you can. Use the emergency gasoline supply, and go help them, Nick."

The big man nodded, "On my way."

Reaching for the ever-present radio on his belt, Nick began transmitting instructions before he reached the door.

Nick looked out over the multitude of men gathering for the trip to Meraton, the football field at Alpha High School an ant mound of bustling activity. Men hurried here and there, taking instructions from their team leaders and making sure equipment was ready and stowed in the proper places. Motor noise, shouted orders, and banging equipment accented the visual image of what amounted to a small army preparing to move. Trucks and vehicles of every description delivered both men and materials while volunteers waved arms and shouted orders to control the flow of traffic.

The gathering of men and machines being assembled for the mission was impressive, especially given the size of the town. Deke had even offered up four of his men to help.

Nick looked up to see Terri approaching the field, a rifle slung over her shoulder, and a determined look on her face.

"And just what do you think you're doing, young lady?"

"I'm going to help. Bishop isn't well enough yet, but we intend to pull our weight – just like everyone else."

Nick smiled at her gumption, and then shook his head. "You don't have to do this. You and Bishop have done more than your share."

"Are you saying you don't need experienced fighters?"

Nick knew where the conversation was headed. On more than one occasion, Terri had proved herself the equal of most any man in a gunfight. He had witnessed her skillset personally.

"Terri, I can't in good conscience allow a pregnant woman to enter a battle. I don't care a rat's ass about honor, equality, or the fact that every female left in the country needs a pioneering spirit to survive. Intentionally putting you in harm's way goes against my grain."

Terri's expression softened, her friendship with Nick strong. "Are you going to scout the town first?"

"As a matter of fact I am."

"Let me go in first. I know the people there better than anyone on your team. I'll know if something is wrong. If there are lawbreakers around, their suspicions are less likely to be aroused by a pregnant girl."

Nick thought about the idea and had to admit she was right. Still, the mere chance that something could happen to her made his stomach churn.

Terri touched Nick's shoulder, interrupting his thoughts. With a serious tone, she reminded him, "Nick – the people in Meraton are my friends, too."

That was the clincher, the final argument he couldn't debate. Still, he had conditions. "Terri, so help me God... if there's even the slightest indication of trouble, I want you to find a safe corner and hide. Promise me you'll not do anything brash or foolhardy."

"Promise."

As an afterthought, Nick asked, "Where's Bishop? I assume he knows what you're planning?"

Terri waved him off, "Oh, I would have told him for sure, but Bishop left to check on the ranch first thing this morning. He won't be back until much later this afternoon."

Oh great, he thought. *I just told my best friend's wife she can tag along and gather Intel on criminals prior to a skirmish. That's just great.*

He shook off the concern over Terri and jumped back into organizing his men. Heeding Deke's advice, Nick had decided to arrive in Meraton with a show of overwhelming force. Normally, 10-20 men would be enough to handle practically any situation, but today almost 50 were going to make the trip. If Meraton and the Beltran ranch were calling for help, the situation must be extremely serious.

Nick paced over to one of his team leaders and said, "Good morning. Has everyone in your group been briefed on the plan?"

The man nodded nervously, "Yes, sir. Our job is to approach from the north."

Nick smiled to relax the man, and then lowered his voice to a whisper. "We don't know what we're walking into, but your guys are well trained, brave men. It could be just a few drunken nomads trying to shoot up the market. No one knows. We'll be okay, if we just stick together."

Two 18-wheel semi-trucks were requisitioned to provide transport for equipment. Six ATV units were wheeled onto one trailer, while packs, equipment, and supplies filled the second.

A school bus would provide the majority of the men a ride to the outskirts of the troubled town. A pickup full of shooters was designated to escort the convoy, with a string of 4-wheel drive pickups bringing up the rear. Nick sighed, thinking about the amount of fuel that was going to be consumed during the endeavor. Refined fossil fuel, gasoline and diesel, was going to be their choking point, and everyone knew it. He began to question the wisdom of today's investment, but then thought about all of his friends in Meraton. *If we ever called for help, I'd want them to respond like this*, he decided.

An hour later, the convoy rolled out of town, a parade unlike anything the citizens of Alpha had witnessed in a very long time. Diana and Kevin stood, watching the procession, waving at the vehicles as they passed.

"Should I have delivered a rah-rah, go get 'm speech?" asked Diana, trying to lighten the mood.

Kevin didn't respond, silently cursing the wound that prohibited him from being at this father's side.

Bishop turned off the truck, his routine of covering his tracks and disconnecting the booby traps complete. The morning sun glinted off the camper's shell as he walked toward what had been their home for several months. Everything looked undisturbed.

His first thought was of the Bat Cave, really a rock room that he had modified with a heavy steel door and locks. His weapons, the bank robber's gold, and all of his other equipment was untouched.

Next, he checked the camper, and while dusty, it too had not received any visitors since he and Terri left in a rush. He gathered up the small amount of food that could possibly spoil in the next few weeks, and set it aside.

The hot tub was full to the brim thanks to the constant trickle of water dripping from the rock shelf above. He gingerly bent down, scooped a handful of clear, cool, spring water, and drank his fill. They had celebrated Christmas here just a few weeks ago, the memory of Terri's childlike excitement bringing a smile to his face.

The garden was the only casualty. His meager plantings hadn't survived the absence of irrigation. If the number of tracks were any indication, the local rabbit population had been busy with a harvest of their own. *At least all that work hadn't been a total waste of time*, he thought. *The jacks probably managed a few nibbles before the sprouts completely shriveled away.*

By the time he loaded the truck with ammo, some gun cleaning supplies, and spare clothing for himself and Terri, Bishop was exhausted. His throbbing shoulder and left side warned him that he was overdoing it.

Assessing the strength of the sun and the heat, he decided a nap was in order, despite the early hour. The Bat Cave would be cool and shady. There was a cot in there that was far from a torture device, so he locked the truck's bed and made for one of his favorite resting spots.

Bishop entered the refreshing stone chamber and closed the door behind him. Unfolding the old makeshift bed, he fashioned a pillow out of one of his packs and gently lowered his aching frame onto the sagging, olive green canvas.

Ten minutes later, a gentle rasp of snoring added its voice to the desert's morning choir.

Two miles outside of Meraton, Nick motioned for the driver to pull over. The team leaders dismounted and met Nick along the side of the road where he repeated the plan to ensure everyone understood.

"This is very simple folks. Team 1 is going to head off across the desert in their four-wheel drive trucks. They'll dismount and approach Meraton on foot from the north. Team 2 is going to wait right here until Team 1 is in position. Everyone clear on that?"

Nick surveyed the circle of attentive, nervous faces but didn't see any problem. He continued, "I'm going to give Terri a ride into town and drop her off. She is going to try to get us some intelligence on what's going on. She'll have a radio, and we can all hope to have a better picture of the threat before we move in. Is everyone clear on that?"

Again, the circle of men nodded their understanding.

"Let's do it!"

Nick watched as men hustled off, some nervous, some showing outward fear, and others calm, cool and collected. *Just like any other group of soldiers I've led*, thought Nick. *They'll all do fine.*

A few minutes later Nick pulled into a vacant lot on the edge of Meraton. In the distance, he and Terri could see activity on Main Street, but couldn't make out many details.

"It looks like the market is opening like usual," observed Terri.

"Hard to tell from here. I don't want to get any closer in case someone gets curious. You good?"

Smiling, Terri patted her pistol and then pointed at the small radio beside her in the seat. "I'm good." She picked up a baseball hat and proceeded to tuck her hair under the hat. A pair of sunglasses rounded out the disguise. "There's not that many pregnant ladies walking around," she noted, "but this little get-up might keep a few folks from recognizing me."

She reached for the door as Nick said, "Good luck. I'll be standing by."

Terri approached the edge of the market, trying to measure her stride and appear casual. The tables, booths, and vendor display areas were bustling with activity as the shopkeepers went about setting out their wares. Her first observation was everything looked normal.

Meandering toward The Manor, Terri noted three strangers talking with Pete and Betty on the sidewalk. Something wasn't quite right. Pete's body language was stiff, and Betty seemed nervous. Switching her focus to the men she didn't recognize, she immediately noticed one of them carried a pistol, the holstered weapon peeking out as the fellow raised his arm to point.

Almost everyone in Meraton was armed, by either shouldering a rifle or carrying a sidearm on a belt, so that observation wasn't especially concerning. What she saw next made her heart race.

Two men approached the strangers, casually walking along and apparently doing a little window-shopping. Both of the gentlemen wore revolvers on their belts. When they approached the group surrounding Pete, one of the strangers moved to intercept the shoppers, his hand moving closer to the weapon at his waist. The large stranger also stepped in the same direction. *They're bodyguards*; Terri sensed immediately, *they're protecting the older man. He's in charge.*

The two shoppers evidently felt the intimidation and changed their direction to keep their distance.

Terri continued through the market, slowly sauntering by several tables while pretending to shop. Other than the three men talking with Pete and Betty, she couldn't see anything out of the ordinary. Cutting down a side street, she found a quiet spot and pulled the radio from under her maternity blouse.

"Nick, are you there?"

"I'm here, Terri. What's going on?"

"There's definitely something weird here. I see three hard-core strangers on Main Street, and everyone is nervous around them. It reminds me of when the bank robbers were in town. People avoided them or looked away. Other than that, everything looks completely normal."

"Our teams are still about three minutes from moving in. Is it safe for you to keep scouting?"

"Yes, no one has even noticed me. The market is alive with activity right now, so I can easily sneak around a bit more. If I see anything else, I'll let you know."

Terri slowly made her way down Main, her eyes always watching the group surrounding Pete and Betty. Pete's body language clearly showed he was nervous around the men, his motions animated - just a little more rapid than normal. She scanned the rooftops, checked the side streets, and even managed a peek inside The Manor's gardens. Everything seemed as it should except for the three men with Pete and Betty.

As Terri approached, two children ran past laughing. The little one's mother was close behind, trying to catch up with the excited youth. The encounter changed Terri's perspective as she looked around the market. *There are women and children all over the place*, she thought. *If somebody starts shooting, people are going to get hurt. A lot of people are going to get hurt.*

"Nick, I can't find anything out of the ordinary except for those three guys. I've looked high and low. I'm not sure this is such a good idea."

"Suggestions?" squawked the radio's small speaker.

"The market looks like any other day, Nick. Maybe I'm missing something. Why don't you come in? Maybe bring another man with you and see for yourself?"

"Okay, on our way."

Five minutes later Nick and one of his men arrived, making eye contact with Terri across the street. The trio met up in front of a booth selling used clothing, and Terri pretended to browse while Nick's eyes scanned the street.

"Wow," the big man commented, "two of those guys standing beside Pete are some serious protection. But you're right; I don't see anything else wrong."

"Do you think they're holding Pete and Betty hostage or something?"

"Hard to tell, but given the message we received and how things look, I'd say that's a possibility."

Terri folded a shirt and placed it back on the table, smiling at the vendor. She and Nick turned away, and pretended to head to the next stall.

"I can get near to them. I don't think they'll pay much attention to a woman, especially a pregnant one."

"You saying you want to try and take them down quietly? I don't know about that, Terri. That's always difficult to do. Well trained teams of professionals struggle with that sort of operation."

"If I can get behind them, and you approach from the front, we can find out what's going on real quick. I think it beats flooding the town with 50 guys brandishing weapons."

Nick thought about her suggestion and had to agree. It just didn't seem like anything was seriously wrong in Meraton, and there were numbers of innocents roaming the streets.

"Okay, I'll follow your lead. Be careful."

Terri split off from Nick and his man, slowly making her way along the avenue. Browsing goods, asking a quick question of a vendor, she tried to act like the typical marketplace customer. Her pulse quickened as she approached what Bishop would surely call the "objective," her mind questioning the wisdom of the entire affair more than once.

Slim didn't care about the conversation taking place between the bartender, Mr. Beltran, and the hotel manager. The three of them had been comparing the differences and similarities of their respective business models for 15 minutes, and he had lost interest long ago.

His job was to protect Mr. Beltran and the boss' insistence on standing out in the open with so many armed people walking around was grating on his nerves. Still, the people on the street seemed peaceful enough, most of them uninterested in Mr. Beltran or the ongoing debate.

Butter didn't seem to mind, the big guy's attention occasionally drifting off, focusing on a passerby or some other activity in the market. *But that's just Butter*, he thought. *If there's trouble, I know he's got my back, but he won't be the first one to see it coming. That's my job.*

Movement caught Slim's eye, and he glanced up to see a woman walking down the street in his direction. Tensing for just a moment, he relaxed as he noticed her hands were empty, and she was with child. He normally would have moved to block such a close passage to his boss, but decided to give the lady a break and let her continue down the sidewalk – his western sense of honor giving special consideration for a woman in her condition.

He immediately dismissed the pregnant lady when he saw a very large, physically fit gentleman crossing the street on a vector that would bring him close to Mr. Beltran. Butter saw it too and moved to intercept. Slim's heart jumped just a little when a third man appeared around the corner, his purposeful stride heading right at the boss.

Butter blocked the big guy's path four steps away from Mr. Beltran, the tall cowboy meeting the newcomer eye to eye. "Good morning, sir," Butter managed to say while holding up his hand in a semi-friendly gesture. Nick smiled, and then both of his hands shot out and grabbed Butter's wrist.

Several things happened at once. Butter's wrestling instincts and raw physical strength surprised Nick. Rather than the man going immediately down, Butter twisted perfectly and moved his free arm to block Nick's hold. The ex-operator countered by throwing his leg behind his opponents, and both men collapsed in a heap - right in the middle of the street.

Slim, having confidence in Butter's ability to disable his foe, drew his weapon, and shoved it in the face of the third member of Nick's team.

For a few moments, everyone's attention seemed to be drawn to the wrestling match. Nick decided grappling with the big, amazingly strong cowboy wasn't such a good idea and began to strike. Butter, shocked at how skilled his opponent seemed to be, arrived at the same strategy. Fists, elbows, and palms flew through the air as the whirling ball of tangled combatants rolled across the pavement. Thuds and grunts sounded as blows landed and counter strikes were thrown.

It was the sound of Mr. Beltran's voice splitting the air that stopped the contest. "Butter! Stop!"

Everyone turned to see Terri standing with her pistol pointed behind Mr. Beltran's ear, the old rancher's hands in the air. She nodded toward Slim. "Put that weapon down, or I'll shoot this man."

Slim's eyes darted between Terri and the man he had covered, all the while thinking, *Fuck! The damned pregnant woman…I can't believe I fell for that one!*

Pete's voice interrupted the standoff. "Terri? What the hell are you doing, Terri? Put that gun down right now. That's Mr. Carlos Beltran you're poking with that piece."

Terri threw a glance at Betty, her friend smiling and nodding. "It's okay, Terri. Everything's fine."

Terri looked from face to face, obviously confused. “Pete, are you sure? We received a message over the HAM radio. We thought Meraton was under attack.”

“What are you talking about? We sent a message saying Mr. Beltran had a problem, but no one’s under attack. Please put the gun away.”

Slowly, Terri lowered her weapon, and everyone exhaled. Slim did the same with his iron, his eyes still focused on the pistol that had been touching his boss’ head. Nick disengaged from Butter, the two men wearily eyeing each other while straightening their clothing and brushing off road dust.

Mr. Beltran slowly turned to face Terri, reaching to tip his hat. “Carlos Beltran, ma’am. Nice to meet you… I think.”

Everyone laughed, and then Terri tucked her pistol away, an embarrassed look on her face.

Not knowing what else to do, Terri gave Nick a helpless look and noticed he was bleeding from the nose and a sporting a cut on his cheek. Moving to check on her friend, she said, “Nick, you’re hurt. Let me take a look.”

“I’m okay,” grunted the big man while throwing a glance at Butter. “I had it under control.”

“Bullshit,” responded the ranch hand, spitting a mouth full of blood onto Main Street. “But I’ve got to admit – you’re as strong as an ox. Where’d you learn to wrestle like that?”

Nick shook his head while wiping his nose-blood on his sleeve. “I was getting ready to ask you the same, exact question. Lawd have mercy; you’re a handful.”

Within a few minutes, hands were being shaken and apologies exchanged. The miscommunication was cleared up as everyone regretted the entire affair.

“Might as well salvage what we can out of this,” Nick observed. “I’m going to radio my men and tell them everything’s okay. Hell, we can even let them shop at the market for an hour or so before we head back to Alpha.”

Chapter 6

Alpha, Texas
January 25, 2016

The truck's original purpose had been to haul gravel and other miscellaneous fill for the Texas Department of Transportation, or TEX-DOT. The dual-axle, diesel powered behemoth was capable of carrying almost 40,000 pounds of payload inside its 15-foot long steel bed and had served the local highway maintenance crew well for over 200,000 miles.

To the men operating the checkpoint, the image of a large truck approaching wasn't anything new. Over the past few weeks, every conceivable type of transport had passed by their location. The virtual parade of newcomers arrived via long-haul semis, horse-drawn wagons, bicycles and every type of vehicle imaginable.

Just a few days ago, two men leading a pair of fully loaded Army mules plodded right up to the checkpoint. The beasts were burdened with a mismatch of boxes, suitcases, tarps, and bags, all of the cargo crisscrossed with scraps of rope and baling twine. There was even a metal drinking cup hanging from one animal, each footfall generating a musical pinging sound that somehow added to its character. Someone had facetiously inquired if the two travelers had been prospecting, but the joke had fallen flat.

Even when the approaching truck cleared the heat mirages distorting the atmosphere, it still wasn't worthy of note or concern. Nick had set up the checkpoint to help the flow of refugees, not as a roadblock. Two pickup trucks sat parked at careful angles, their spacing requiring a motor vehicle to slow and steer around them, but anyone could pass through. While armed, the volunteers who worked the checkpoints were more akin to greeters than sentries.

"He better slow down," observed one of the volunteers as he stepped out of the shade to welcome whoever was driving the big truck.

"Are those people riding in the bed?" asked his partner.

The response was a bit slow in coming because both men realized something just wasn't right. The drone of the approaching diesel engine was increasing, and odd shapes resembling human heads appeared over the front edge of the bed. Twinkling flashes soon followed.

“Get down!”

The warning came as several bullets slammed into the ground near the two watchmen. Diving for cover while trying to ready their weapons, both men stared in horror as the massive, accelerating truck slammed into the first and then the second pickup. The checkpoint's vehicles were no match for the kinetic energy imparted by an 18,000-pound steel ram traveling at close to 60 mph. Both the new Ford 150 and the classic 1954 Chevy pickup were flung aside like Matchbox toys, the more recent model rolling over twice before coming to a stop in the desert sand.

One of the volunteers was pinned beneath his own vehicle, his scream drowned out by the deafening protest of crushed metal, racing engine, and discharging rifles. The surviving man stood for better vantage and reached for the 2-way radio on his belt.

“Alpha! Alpha! We have a dump truck full of several men heading for the center of town and shooting multiple weapons. J.J.'s hurt! I need medical help.”

Diana was in the church office, discussing work assignments with a group of volunteers. When distant popping noises reached her ears, the deacon stopped talking and raised her head for a brief moment but wasn't concerned – with the amount of hunting and the slaughter of cattle in town, gunfire didn't necessarily mean trouble. The panicked radio call quickly changed her demeanor.

Racing for the front of the building, she paused to gather up her own rifle and a small bag. There was already a full magazine in the AR15 and several more ready in the satchel. Hesitating for the first few steps while draping the strap over her shoulder, the town's mayor was running at full speed in seconds.

As Diana bounded down the church's front steps, she spied two men climbing into a waiting golf cart, gun barrels pointing into the air. Yelling for them to hold up, Diana jumped onto the back bumper and signaled the driver to floor it.

Additional gunshots rang out in the distance. Their echo, combined with a woman's scream and the muffled roar of a big diesel engine, told the driver which general direction to steer. The small, almost silent cart raced for the center of town, the bedlam of conflict seemingly emanating from the courthouse.

Along the way, Diana noticed several men and a few women heading in the same general direction – all of them with determined expressions accompanied by loaded guns. The town's recollection of being overrun by ruthless, escaped convicts was still at the forefront of everyone's mind.

Before the electric cart could travel the 12 blocks to the courthouse, the echoes of disturbance seemed to fade away. For a moment, Diana held out hope that it was all some sort of misunderstanding. As they approached Main Street, those thoughts were quickly dashed.

Men, women, and children scurried from porch to pedestal, seeking shelter from the angry reverberation of the oversized vehicle and the impending rain of bullets pelleting the buildings adjacent to the courthouse. As the city's center came into view, Diana determined that a colossal dump truck had crashed through a hedgerow, two parking meters, and a trash can, finally rolling over a landscape island of crepe myrtles in front of the building's main entrance.

Pointing to an alleyway, Diana instructed the driver to stash the cart. All three responders climbed out and carefully began making their way closer to the disturbance. Using any available cover, the trio dodged from parked car to fire hydrant to building doorway as they sought a reasonable vantage point. They were soon joined by a fourth man who approached them hastily, motioning for Diana to stay put.

Between gulps of breath, the man reported that the dump truck had deposited at least a dozen armed men into the courthouse. The witness went on to say that he hadn't seen anyone leave the building since the invasion.

Before the panting man could continue, movement across the street drew Diana's attention. Behind the bumper of a nearby car, Bishop adjusted his position to get a better vantage through his riflescope.

"I thought you were at the ranch," she yelled.

"I just got back," Bishop replied. "Don't you guys ever have a quiet day around here?"

Ignoring the sarcasm, Diana glanced at the rest of her party and issued instructions to them. "These guys seem to have concentrated all their energies on the courthouse. Let's coordinate our efforts and surround the building to force their hand. Radio me if you see any movement. Engage the potential witnesses to find out how many of our folks were inside when these intruders overran the building."

Without waiting for any acknowledgement, Diana ducked low and dashed across the street to join Bishop.

"What is going on?" Bishop queried, not having any awareness of the event prior to the last five minutes.

"I'm not certain, but from what I can piece together, that truck busted through the checkpoint and made a beeline for the courthouse. You can see as well as I can it didn't show any respect for our parking laws. A witness just informed me that close to a dozen armed guys jumped out and ran into the courthouse. That's all I know."

"Why? What are they after? Any clues?"

"No idea, Bishop. I have a funny feeling we'll find out soon enough. I'll also predict we won't like the answer to that question."

A funny look crossed Bishop's face, and then he turned and locked his gaze at Diana. The mayor almost recoiled from his *stare. This man doesn't resemble my friend, she thought. It's his eyes. Dark, predator-like eyes without soul or fear.*

"Is Terri in the courthouse?" came the icy question.

Diana understood at once. "No… no… she went to Meraton with Nick and the men." He relaxed instantly. She started to update him on the rescue of the neighboring town when movement drew the pair's attention.

A man suddenly appeared on the courthouse steps holding a

large frame revolver and tugging one of the town's volunteers by the hair. The stranger forced his hostage a few steps outside and then yelled, "Who is in charge here?"

Glancing at Bishop, Diana shrugged her shoulders and started to rise, but Bishop's hand pressed down on her shoulder. "I'm not so sure that's a good idea."

The kidnapper was clearly impatient, quickly adding, "Come on out, now. I know it's a woman running this show. Come on out, or I'll kill a few of my guests to show you we are serious."

"I'll go with you," Bishop said and stood up.

The two citizens of Alpha paced slowly down the street, Bishop being extra careful to keep his rifle pointed down, an indirect threat.

"That's close enough," sounded when the pair was within easy range of conversation. "I'll make this plain as day," the man began. "I've got 15 men with me, and we need food, guns, ammo, or anything else of value you've got laying around. Fill up that truck, and we'll be on our way. Fuck around, and people will die."

Diana didn't hesitate, "There's not enough food or fuel in all of Alpha to fill your truck. We're on the edge of starvation ourselves."

"Bullshit! I've had two of my cousins scouting this town for days, lady. We know y'all are eating like kings around here. Fill up the fucking truck, or I'll start littering this pretty front lawn with the bodies of your friends and neighbors."

"Let the people inside go, and I'll take their place," Diana offered.

A sneering laugh was the response. "Lady, I may not be wearing my Sunday best, but don't underestimate my intellect. Stop trying to buy time, and start filling that truck. We know you've got beef, flour, bags of rice, and pine nuts. My men saw them. Guns and ammunition work, too. Anything else, you need to clear it through me."

The man started walking backward toward the courthouse's double door entrance, dragging his panic-stricken, sobbing captive with him. After a few steps, he paused and made deliberate eye contact with Bishop. "I know what you're thinking, Bubba. I know you're some badass swinging dick around here. I've got one word for you – *'Don't.'* Don't try any heroic shit, or people will die. This ain't our first rodeo… we lost all reservation over killing months ago."

A few moments later, the man disappeared inside the limestone building.

Bishop pulled Diana out of the direct view of the courthouse, moving around the corner of a nearby building. Addressing the clearly frustrated woman, he shook his head and said, "I don't think he voted for you," and then added, "This isn't good. Not good at all."

Diana nodded, "No kidding. Any ideas? My week-long, on-the-job, volunteer mayor training didn't exactly prepare me for negotiation and rescue," contempt dripping from her words.

Bishop didn't look at her, instead maintaining his gaze fixed toward the street. "They couldn't have picked a better place to hole up. That structure was built as a fallout shelter back during the Cold War. The walls are thick, the windows small, and there's clear ground all around the place. If they position their men well, we can't even get close to the courthouse without their seeing us coming."

Diana paced around for a bit before responding, "It sounds like I'd better give orders to start gathering food."

"Yes, I think that's the safe thing to do. I can talk to Deke. Those contractors are the best-trained people around. Maybe one of them will have an idea."

Bishop started to turn, but Diana clutched his shoulder. "If we give those thieves that much food, there won't be enough left for the town. Even if we clear out our reserve, I don't know if we can fill that truck."

"I know," Bishop replied. "Buy me some time. Play along as if we're giving in. I think we need to get some professional advice here."

Diana set off, issuing instructions and consoling family members of the people being held hostage. Much of the food available wasn't easily transferred from its storage location to the courthouse. There were four sides of beef at the taxidermy-turned-butcher, several bags of harvested wild greens and some boxes of canned goods being prepared for distribution. One by one, volunteers began carrying loads of foodstuffs, and at Diana's request, left them lying on the ground in close proximity to the truck.

Bishop made for the hotel where the Darkwater contractors were staying. As he zipped up in a borrowed golf cart, he found most of the operators standing outside, curious at what all of the commotion was about.

Bishop quickly explained the situation.

Deke whistled, "This really *is* the wild, wild West."

"No shit," Bishop added, "Any brilliant ideas?"

Deke shook his head, "Hostage rescue is a tricky business, slick. Takes special training and equipment. I know a little bit about the methods, but for sure, we don't have the equipment. Snake cameras, radios, or cell phones for the negotiator to talk to the crazies - we don't have any of that stuff."

The group continued to float a few ideas, but Bishop didn't hear anything that had a good chance of working without getting a lot of innocents killed. He thanked the contractors and made for the cart when Deke offered, "We've got thermal imagers. They won't show much through the limestone walls of that building, but they can see heat through glass most of the time. I don't know if that's any help."

Bishop scratched his chin, an idea starting to formulate. "Thanks. I'll keep that in mind."

Bishop located Diana two blocks down from the courthouse, the mayor directing several workers while trying to maintain control of the situation.

"Give me good news," she said.

"I can't just yet, but I've got an idea. I need some time."

"Gathering up that much food is going to take a while. I've got a couple of the men looking for older guns no one uses anymore."

Bishop noticed the sides of beef that were being stacked nearby. Each slab of meat was wrapped in thick cheesecloth. Looking back at Diana, he said, "Don't load those until I get back.

Ignoring Diana's questioning look, Bishop hustled off in the golf cart, heading back for the church. He had spied a pair of old stereo speakers in the maintenance shed and made a beeline directly for them. A small amount of work with a screwdriver resulted in successful retrieval of the speaker's magnet.

The next leg of Bishop's scavenger hunt involved his load gear. Bishop carried a flashlight designed with interchangeable settings, one of which was infrared. All the time cursing having only one useful arm, he retrieved some para-cord, and with great effort securely attached the magnet to the body of the flashlight. He replaced the batteries with fresh, recharged units and then tested his device on the metal porch railing.

The next stop was the church infirmary. During his visit to have his wound cleaned, Bishop had noticed a box of chemical heating pads sitting in the corner. Normally used for sore backs or aching muscles, the devices contained small bags of iron powder that when squeezed, combined with carbon and water, producing heat for several hours. He gathered up the box and headed back toward the courthouse.

Bishop recruited a passerby to help him carry the box to Diana. The deacon peered inside and flashed Bishop a puzzled look. "Are you worried the beef has a slipped disc?"

Bishop grinned, and replied, "No, but I do believe those heating pads will show up on a thermal weapon's site. They should shine like beacons in the night."

"I used thermal guidance systems in the Navy," she replied, "I didn't know we had anything like that in Alpha."

"The Darkwater guys have them. I also want to hedge our bet,"

Bishop said, holding out the flashlight. "This torch shines an infrared strobe. We need to stick its magnet on the truck some place where it won't be noticed. The beam should be pointed skyward."

Deacon Brown looked Bishop in the eye and nodded. "I see what your plan is. You intend to let them out of town with the food and then hunt them down after we have all of our people back. Very good."

Bishop looked down, disappointment crossing his face. "I just hope Nick and Terri are back soon. I can't help you chase these assholes down, but at least we should be able to find them. Maybe the Darkwater guys will help with the dirty work."

Diana put her hand on Bishop's good shoulder and reassured her friend. "You've given us a chance, Bishop. Not only will we need this food back, but we can't have rogue hostage takers roaming the streets."

Deacon Brown maintained eye contact with Bishop until he acknowledged her words with a nod. She then immediately turned to her workforce and began issuing instructions regarding the heating pads. A few minutes later, all of the chemical devices were hidden inside bags of food, closely intertwined with the cheesecloth wrappings, where their presence was inconspicuous.

Movement from the front of the courthouse drew everyone's attention as the same man appeared, this time with a different female hostage as a shield. "Listen up! I've been watching you gather the loot, now it's time to start loading the truck. We've no doubt worn out our welcome by now."

Diana stepped forward and announced, "I'm not putting one calorie on that truck until we talk about how the exchange is going to go down. I want my people back."

"First, you're going to assign a couple of strapping, young men to pack those sides of beef for us. After that, I'm going to send one hostage out of the building at a time. Each one is going to load his or her share of that food onto our truck. As the loading is completed, I will give permission for that person to return to you. We are going to keep two hostages with us. That way, you won't get a wild hair up your ass and try to ambush us on the way out of town. I'll drop off the last of my charge five miles outside of the city limits. You can pick them up at your leisure."

Diana thought about the terms for a moment before responding. "Agreed. Let's get this over with."

Realizing the obvious choices for loading the dump truck, Bishop quickly hustled one of the bulked men out of sight. He explained to the fellow where and how he wanted the flashlight mounted. Bishop turned on the device, setting it to strobe an infrared beam. He handed it over, wishing the deliveryman the best of luck.

The man carrying Bishop's flashlight made sure he was one of the crew that hopped up into the bed of the truck. As the second side of beef was hefted up, he and another man dragged the heavy load toward the front near the cab. Bishop was watching closely as the two men played it perfectly. The beef seemed to slip from one guy's hand and land on his partner's leg. Shouting out, the injured fellow reached for the edge of the dump-bed and stuck the flashlight between the cab and the front of the steel box. He even managed to stick it pointing perfectly skyward. Mission accomplished!

The rest of the hostage exchange went smoothly, but Bishop didn't hang around to witness the proceedings. Speeding off again in the cart, he traveled the side streets of Alpha until he found the address of one Mr. Hugh Mills.

In performing her municipal duties, Terri interviewed quite an interesting assortment of folks, in the hope of assimilating refugees and residents alike into the public works program. One of the most interesting of Alpha's citizens, Mr. Mills was quite the charmer, in his late 50s, and a widower. He explained to Terri that back in his old Air Force days, he used to fly C-130s all over NATO.

"I hope that husband of yours knows what a lucky guy he is to be hitched to a stunner like you, Ms. Terri," the old gentleman had told her. "I sure do miss my Janet," he continued. "You know you just assume that the ones you love will always be here." Recently retired, he had flown a few small commercial stints, avoiding full-time employment so that he and his soul mate could cruise or jet away to exotic locales. But that changed when Janet was killed by a drunk driver. Bishop found the man working in his garden and introduced himself.

Bishop announced himself as "Mr. Terri" and explained his strategy to the pilot, relieved when the man's eyes brightened. "Bishop, I'd be glad to pay back the people of Alpha for all they've done for me. Besides, I could use a little adventure. I should probably tell you though, I have not flown at all since my wife's death last year. My heart just wasn't in it. But without any other traffic around, I should be able to get my bearings pretty quickly. The other issue is that I don't know what condition my plane is in. I figured it was pointless to walk out to the airport since I didn't have enough gasoline to get her in the air anyway."

Bishop invited Mr. Mills to take a ride with him out to the hangar, and his new acquaintance happily agreed to go. The two men hopped into a golf cart and proceeded to the north side of Alpha.

Arriving at the airport reminded Bishop of the gunfight that had occurred on the premises just a few, short months ago. Alpha had been ruled by thugs at the time and he had invaded their turf to scavenge medical equipment to save his old boss. It had been a desperate fight while one of his party had found and readied a plane.

Steering onto the main tarmac, Bishop noted his getaway dune buggy remained right where he'd left it. The engine had suffered too much bullet damage and sputtered to a violent end. Bishop hurried by the converted HUMMER, swiping the dust from the hand-painted logo on the hood as he passed. Ignoring the broken glass and rusting bullet holes, he whispered, "You deserved better," under his breath.

The remainder of the airport looked untouched. Hugh wasted no time hopping out of the cart and hustling into the massive storage shed where several aircraft were accommodated.

Before Bishop could follow him, Mr. Mills exited the facility, shaking his head. "It's here and appears undisturbed. All that we need is some gasoline."

"I can handle that," Bishop boasted. "I've got connections with the city council."

The two men sped back to Alpha where Bishop exchanged the

golf cart for his pickup truck. His first stop was to find Diana.

"You want to requisition gasoline for what?" Diana asked.

"I want to get one of the airplanes functional and use it to find the devices we hid on that truck. I think we can find our crooks a lot faster from the air."

"At night?"

"Yup. The contractors have infrared for heat detection, and I have night vision. The welcoming committee had a pilot listed – that's Mr. Mills standing over there. In the long run I think we'll use less fuel tracking the extortionists from the air than searching the entire desert in trucks."

"Okay, Bishop. I sure hope this works. I'll send men to the church and have them take the spare cans from the maintenance shed. We'll bring them to the airport."

Bishop spread his hands, "I would put the odds at 50/50 that we'll find the thieves. But something you said the other day made me think that having a functional airplane or two wouldn't be a bad idea anyway."

"Something *I* said?"

"When you compared our little shindig here to Alaska, it made me think. They use small aircraft a lot there because of the terrain's inaccessibility and the often-impassable roads. If we develop airborne capabilities, it could solve all kinds of issues. Medical emergencies, resupply, and security – the possibilities are practically endless."

Diana pondered Bishop's idea and nodded. "I see what you mean. I bet Nick will love it. Okay, Bishop, you'd better get going. Good luck."

Bishop's next stop was the hotel where the contractors were housed. Deke gathered his gear, throwing his rifle, pack and other equipment in the bed of Bishop's truck.

A short time later, Bishop and Deke stood, watching Mr. Mills while he made ready in the cockpit. Smiling, the pilot nodded at Bishop and yelled, "Everything appears to be in good shape. If you can give me a jump, I think she'll start right up."

The engine sputtered and paused for a few rotations and then roared to life. Hugh studied the gauges and controls for a bit before giving his spectators the thumbs-up sign through the window. Bishop yelled over the engine noise, "Deke, let's roll."

The sun was just dropping behind the Davis Mountains to the west as Bishop and Deke squeezed in the tiny cockpit. Bishop spread a small map across his lap and pointed out his flight plan for the two men. "The way I figure it, that truck can only travel at 50 mph or so. They have a 45-minute head start, so that means they have to be within 50 miles of Alpha by the time we get airborne. We know they headed north out of town, so our search area can't be that big."

"I'm assuming you don't want them to know we're flying around?"

"That's right. As far as we know, no one has tried anything like this. Deke's got a thermal monocle, and I have a light amplifying device. We have no idea of their effective range, but it's probably 5,000 feet or less."

Hugh thought for a bit and then smiled at his passengers. "My instructor flew scout plans very similar to this one in Vietnam. He taught me a technique for fun, and I never thought I would use it. But I think it is a strategy that could apply here. Basically, I'm going to climb to 6,000 feet above the ground and then coast down to 3,000. We won't make any engine noise that can be heard on the ground that way."

Deke's eyes widened at the pilot's statement, the contractor muttering, "Coast?"

Mr. Mills chuckled and responded with a simple, "Trust me."
"That's what they all say."

Hugh rolled the airplane across the tarmac and positioned the small craft directly in the center of the runway. The wind was dead calm, so the direction for takeoff wasn't an issue. "Here we go," the pilot announced as he increased the throttle. In a matter of moments, the three were looking back at the hangar from a lofty elevation.

The air was smooth, and the plane appeared to be running well as they gained altitude toward the east. While Hugh worked the controls and monitored the GPS, Bishop and Deke turned on their spotting devices and began adjusting focus while trying to acclimate to the height. In the fading light, each man picked an identifiable object on the ground and then compared the appearance while viewing through the respective scopes.

"It's a little hard to get accustomed to everything being so small," announced Deke. "But I think my thermal is working pretty well."

"Same here," responded Bishop. "I've got a 3-x zoom on the PVS-14, so that's helping a little."

After climbing to 6,000 feet, Mr. Mills announced, "Okay, fellas – I'm going to drop the power and glide for a while. You guys search, and I'll watch the instruments so we don't hit the ground."

"Sounds like a plan," Bishop commented from the back seat.

"I like the part about you watching the altimeter," added a nervous Deke.

Nick, Terri and the posse arrived back in Alpha just as the searchers had achieved flight. Nick's frustration at the wasted time, effort, and gasoline was quickly forgotten as Diana briefed everyone on the events of the afternoon.

Terri and Nick stood listening in silence until Diana recounted Bishop's effort to conceal homing signals in the truck. "He did what?" was Terri's initial reaction.

Diana ignored the question and continued, her friends interrupting again when she relayed the ongoing airborne search plot. "He went where?" Terri asked, not really expecting an answer.

Nick didn't give Diana time to respond, "Wow, we leave town for a couple of hours and everything goes to hell in a hand-basket. Got to hand it to Bishop, if that scheme works, we might be able to eat for a few more months. That was pretty quick thinking."

"You better tell the posse not to get comfortable. If Bishop and Deke locate the crooks' stash, we will need to mobilize quickly."

The plane was on its third glide across the field of study when Deke's excited voice sounded out, "Got 'em."

Bishop quickly switched sides and brought the scope up to his eye. The green and white landscape below was harshly interrupted by a flashing bright beam reaching for the sky. It only took a few moments to center on the source.

Looking like a child's toy, Bishop could clearly make out the shape on the getaway truck as it bounced along. The strobe of the flashlight made the vehicle stand out like a hotel sign on the Las Vegas Strip, its beam illuminating a bright lime-green against the stark black background of the surrounding desert. It was impossible to judge what speed the driver was maintaining, but it didn't look as if they were in any hurry.

The truck was bouncing along what appeared to be a farm lane. Bishop checked the plane's GPS and then used a red light to verify the location against his map. He confirmed there wasn't any public road close to the route being traveled by the target below.

"How are we doing on fuel?" Bishop asked Mr. Mills.

"We can stay up for another two hours or so, maybe a bit more."

"Let's give them plenty of room just in case somebody down there has good ears."

Deke and Bishop exchanged devices, each curious what the other man was seeing. The truck below looked like a hefty, multi-colored blob with a disco light when viewed through the thermal scope. Not only could Bishop see the engine's bright red glow, the individual riders in the back were clearly discernible as they bumped along the rough terrain. The chemical heating pads showed an intense color of pink, obviously much warmer than the surrounding human bodies.

"If we had an armed predator drone on-call, I could save everyone a lot of time and trouble," offered Deke.

Bishop and Hugh grunted. "Probably not a good idea if you want any of the food back though," Deke added.

As Bishop reached to hand Deke his scope back, he noticed some familiar equipment mounted on the console. "Hugh, does the radio work?"

"Should," replied the pilot, reaching for the knob. The three men watched as the digital dial glowed to life. "It seems to work, but there's nobody to talk to."

Bishop dug around in his vest, his one good arm making the effort frustrating. He eventually located a piece of paper with several numbers written on it. Passing it forward to the pilot, he asked, "Will that radio broadcast on any of these frequencies?"

Hugh reached up and turned on a red light, the color necessary to avoid losing his night vision. Scanning the list, he eventually responded. "Sure, one of these is an aircraft emergency channel. Who are we going to call?"

"The HAM radio operator in Alpha. He can update Diana on our status so she can start planning where to send the cavalry."

Hugh turned the dial until the large red numerals indicated the correct frequency. As he lifted the microphone, Bishop said, "Hold that for a minute – I've got another idea. They're heading east, northeast. Let's fly ahead of them on the same course and see if we can figure out where they're going. That would be more important to Alpha than where they are right now."

Deke agreed, "If they've got some sort of camp or base, it would also be good to scout another route in. They're probably watching their backs."

Mr. Mills adjusted the controls, and the small plane gently dipped one wing and banked toward the east. Forty minutes later, Deke detected several glowing globs of heat through his device and pointed out the location to Bishop.

"I can't make out much detail at this height," he reported. "Any chance we can glide in a little closer?"

"I can take you right over the top of them if you want. I don't want to get too low though. There might be power lines or something else sticking up that would ruin our day."

Hugh banked the craft again, pulling a large, slow circle over the open desert and building altitude. A few minutes later, he shut off the engine completely, the act causing Deke's head to pivot sharply.

"What are you doing?" the contractor protested.

"It's okay, Deke. We just became a glider. It's cool."

Bishop had to admit he liked the reassuring vibration of the plane's engine a lot better than the sound of the air rushing past at over 100 mph. Mr. Mills seemed confident and calm, so he decided to focus on the scouting and not the ground.

"Their camp should be coming up on the starboard side here shortly. We're going to be low, so you should be able to get a good look."

Sure enough, Bishop and Deke spotted what appeared to be a cluster of machinery and piles of metal randomly stacked around a central group of house trailers, campers, and a single ranch-style home. Deke detected at least 19 heat signatures of people within the compound.

Bishop's view provided a little more context. "It's a junkyard. Alpha was robbed by a bunch of scrap dealers? That doesn't make any sense."

"Scrap dealers need food, too," responded Deke.

"I don't think so. Counting the people on the truck, their little gathering down there has 30 people, tops. Why demand so much food? That number of people couldn't eat that much food in three months. Why take the risk of stealing more than you need?"

"Maybe that's not where the dump truck is headed," offered Hugh.

Bishop said, "You might be right, but there's nothing out here for miles. Let's go back and follow them in to make sure."

Forty-five minutes later, it was obvious the stolen food was indeed heading directly for the boneyard.

Bishop rubbed his chin, "Let's head back. We can radio the others on the way, and they can rally the posse."

Looking at his charts, Hugh commented, "It will take us 90 minutes to get back as the crow flies."

A scowl crossed Deke's face, "Ninety minutes by air? That means it will take a team from Alpha at least four hours to get here. That food could be long gone in four hours. We need to keep eyes on that cargo. Can we radio and stay up here?"

The pilot shook his head, "No, no way. I have 120 minutes of fuel left with a 10% reserve. We can stay up here maybe another 35 before heading back, and that's pressing it."

Deke's face brightened. "Can you land?"

Before Hugh could answer, Bishop interrupted. "What are you thinking, Deke?"

"If we can land a few miles away, I could run to their location and keep an eye on things until the cavalry arrives. That eliminates any chance of our food making another get away."

"And what are you going to do if they try and move the food?"

"I'll disable the truck and let them chase me around the desert for a while - if they want. Don't worry about me, Bishop. I've been chased before. I know how to discourage pursuit."

Bishop's mind went back to the time where he had fought Deke and his team in the desert. The episode sent a cold shiver down his spine. *I wouldn't want to be in the junk business if it comes to a fight down there*, he thought.

"So, Hugh, can you land?"

While Bishop and Deke had been discussing the issue, Hugh had been studying his ever-present chart. "The closest I can get you is I-10. The junkyard is 3.1 nautical miles south of the interstate. Is that too far?"

"No problem," stated Deke.

While Hugh angled the plane toward its new destination, Bishop and Deke scoured maps, radio frequencies, and signals. An alternative hook-up point was established.

"I'm going to do one fly-over the road to make sure there aren't any cars in the way. Can you guys use those fancy doodads of yours to make sure we're not going to run into anything?"

A few minutes later, Hugh touched the small plane down on the eastbound lane of an abandoned I-10. Deke hopped out of the plane, and Bishop extended his good hand. As the two men shook, Bishop confessed, "I wish I could go with you, dude. I'm barely hanging in as it is."

Deke nodded, replying, "You took one hell of a hit, brother. Even if you were only 50%, I'd welcome you on my team." And then Deke was gone, trotting off into the night.

Bishop climbed back in the plane, nodding to Hugh. "Can you find your way home okay? I'm going to take a nap."

Nick took the paper from Phil's hand, the HAM operator excited over the message. "You're sure of these coordinates?" The question carrying more negative tone than Nick had intended.

"Yes," Phil snapped, "I'm 100% for sure. The pilot's transmission was crystal clear. That whole Meraton wild goose chase wasn't my fault, man."

Waving off the man's concerns, Nick apologized. "I'm sorry, Phil. With resources limited the way they are, that kind of miscommunication was bound to happen. I know you're doing your best."

"It's not easy being the telephone operator and emergency dispatcher for the whole territory, you know," Phil grumbled as he shuffled back home.

Turning to Diana and Terri, Nick studied the message again before calmly stating, "Here we go again."

Terri was worried about Bishop. "Did the transmission mention anything about how he's doing? He should be in bed resting, not flying all over the desert chasing blackmailers."

"No, Terri, but I'm sure he's fine. The guys will be back at the airport in an hour. We need to gather up the men and meet them there. They're requesting we shine some headlights on the runway to help them in."

One hour later, Nick and four truckloads of his best men were parked along the runway at Alpha's regional airport. Each vehicle was strategically parked to illuminate the landing strip for the incoming flight. Hugh brought the plane in perfectly, the single engine craft coasting to a stop outside the main hangar. Terri was there waiting for her husband.

"Oh my gosh, Bishop. I can't believe you went after those criminals in your condition. Are you okay?"

"Yes, I'm fine hun. Tired, but fine."

"Remind me again now. Which arm hurts, Bishop?"

Not really understanding his wife's question, Bishop pointed to his left arm.

"Good," stated Terri before punching his right shoulder. "Don't ever pull a stunt like that again while you're still sick. Now, come on. I'm putting you to bed, and I'm going to hire Kevin to babysit your wayward ass - to make sure you don't try and sneak out again and go play with your friends." With that, Terri pivoted and strode with purpose back toward their waiting truck.

Bishop shook his head, and then made to follow his wife. While hustling to catch up, he couldn't control himself and asked, "Are you going to tuck me in and help me get to sleep? You know - the good way to make me sleepy?"

Terri turned her head and responded over her shoulder without breaking stride. "Tell me again. Which arm hurts, Bishop?"

"They both do now."

Deke decided to jog the three miles to the boneyard, taking an easy pace across the flat terrain. As his GPS indicated he was close to the target, he slowed and proceeded with more caution. The piles of scrap metal, discarded machinery, and random junk actually made his approach relatively easy. It appeared as though whoever had unloaded the scrap had taken the easy way out and avoided the few natural undulations that rippled the landscape.

Another factor that assisted him greatly was the aerial reconnaissance. Having a solid mental picture of the layout of the place allowed him to expedite his penetration without sacrificing safety. He also had a clear mental map of his regress, should a retreat become necessary.

A hefty, haphazard pile of what appeared to be discarded drainage pipe provided the perfect cover. The twenty-foot long sections were easily wide enough for a man to crawl through. Using his infrared flashlight and the FLIR scope, Deke checked to make sure he wouldn't be disturbing any of the local wildlife before he entered, the thought of encountering a rattlesnake in such a restricted area unsettling.

His pipe-hide was less than 100 feet from the dump truck that was parked in the middle of the main cluster of homes. There were few lights inside any of the residences, and it appeared as though everyone had turned in, given the late hour.

Deke double-checked his compass and watch. It was questionable whether the sun would be rising before the men from Alpha would arrive. The last thing he wanted was to be trapped inside the tube, his position fully illuminated by the light of a new day. His compass indicated he was facing almost due south, so he would be neither exposed, nor blinded at sunrise. Still, he decided if the boys from Alpha didn't show up 30 minutes before dawn, he'd back out of the pipe and seek a better position.

An hour later, flashing light in the distance drew Deke's attention. It quickly became obvious that another vehicle was approaching and didn't feel the need to be sneaky about it. Headlights illuminated the compound, the twin beams signaling the emergence of a large flatbed truck. The driver pulled in alongside the dump truck and honked his horn twice.

Three armed men jumped down from the bed and milled around the back of the truck until movement and light from the main house acknowledged their arrival.

"'Bout time you guys showed up," came a greeting from inside. "We gave up and went to bed."

"We're here now; let's get this done. I've got to get this load back to Midland Station before dawn, or my ass is in a sling."

"Hold yer horses. We'll get it moved over. Do you have the fuel?"

"Of course we've got the fuel. Ten drums of gasoline and five of diesel. Just like the agreement says."

Deke's heart raced as he watched a few sluggish men from the surrounding trailers join the crew. Rubbing the sleep from their eyes, yawning and complaining, the men began lifting full 50-gallon drums via a winch mounted at the back of the flatbed. Each barrel was rolled out of the way, the apparent storage place directly in front of Deke's position. As soon as the last of the fuel was unloaded, the workers began transferring Alpha's food from the dump truck to the level transport instead.

By the time the food was being unloaded, a few women were awake, yawning, and chatting with one another. Two toddler-sized children left their mothers' sides and wandered closer to see what their fathers were doing - one child receiving a harsh warning to stay back and out of the way.

Disgusted and cursing under his breath, there was absolutely nothing Deke could do. The angle to shoot and disable the flatbed was blocked by hundreds of gallons of gasoline. He could back down the pipe and move for a clear shot, but with the flatbed's headlights pointing almost directly at him, his movement would be noticed immediately. He might disable the truck, but the villains would shoot him down in the process.

The combination of the women, children, and drums of MOGAS completely ruined Deke's plan. Sighing, he watched helplessly as Alpha's critical load of food drove off, Deke watching as the truck's taillights became two small red specks in the distance.

The residents of the boneyard opted for more sleep, the area becoming quiet again in a few minutes. Deke slowly backed out of the pipe and trotted off toward the highest ground between the junkyard and I-10. A small rise several hundred meters to the north would allow him to observe the compound and wait on the men from Alpha. He dreaded delivering the bad news.

Nick was of a foul temper when the Alpha convoy finally arrived. It had taken far too long for everyone to assemble, and then one of the trucks suffered engine problems. By the time he and his troop had hooked up with Deke, the sun was well into the morning sky.

After receiving Deke's report, the ex-Special Forces operator was obviously angry. "Fuck it!" he yelled, "Everybody on a skirmish line. Deke, you take your people in first. I'm tired of pussyfooting around with this bullshit. I want to talk to those people down there and find out where our food went."

Nodding, Deke gathered his men and proceeded down the rise toward the boneyard without comment.

The Darkwater team moved with impressive speed and grace, rolling across the desert like a well-coordinated machine. Each man knew his position, movement, and sequence as the four-member advance team ate up ground without excessive exposure. "Damn, those dudes are like ghosts floating across the sand," commented one man standing near Nick.

"That's how it's *supposed* to be done," was the big man's reply.

T-Bone had finally gotten some rest, his nerves settled for at least a few more days. Stepping stiffly toward the kitchen, he stumbled over one of the dogs curled up in its favorite spot, which always seemed to be directly in his path.

"Damn it, Zeus. Damn it all to hell."

The large animal raised it head, casting a sad look towards its master.

"Shit. I forgot to let you two out last night. What good are junkyard dogs that like to sleep in the house all the time?"

Forgetting about his coffee water, T-Bone made for the front door, shooing the animals outside. "Go on now Zeus. Get outside Hercules. Time for you to go to work and earn your keep."

Pausing for a moment to watch the pair of huge beasts trot into the yard, T-Bone shut the door, his attention returning to the stove and heating water for that first cup of coffee.

Deke actually heard the footsteps of the mass of flesh before hearing the growl. *I'm in a junkyard*, he thought. *Of course, they would have junkyard dogs.*

In a motion as fluid as an old west gunslinger, Deke reached to the small of his back and drew his Taser, just as the 150 pounds of muscle and fur rounded the corner and bared its teeth. Without hesitation, Deke fired the weapon. The two-pronged steel fork hit the watchdog square in the breast, the sharp metal points easily penetrating the animal's fur and skin. Two seconds later, the beast was lying on its side, tremors of shock still pulsing through its unresponsive body.

Deke bent beside the helpless animal and raised his knife, but then reconsidered. Sheathing the blade, he produced a roll of duct tape from a pouch and in less than thirty seconds had secured the animal's muzzle and legs.

Just as Deke started to rise, a low growl signaled the animal at his feet hadn't been alone. Reaching again for his knife, the operator braced for the animal's charge, but a second Taser dropped the dog instantly. Smiling, one of Deke's men stepped from behind an old, rusting derrick and nodded toward his boss. Deke tossed the man the roll of tape.

The main cluster of homes was secured within five minutes of Nick's arrival with the main force. One by one, Nick and a team of men would enter the trailer or camper, appearing a few moments later with wide-eyed, terrified residents clad in their nighttime attire. The roused citizens of the boneyard were herded into the center of the compound. Rifles and harsh grumbles forced the shaken people onto their knees with hands behind their heads. Mothers with small children were all placed inside of a single trailer and warned to keep the little ones quiet.

T-Bone was pulling on his boots when Lyndon's voice rang out. Like any parent, he detected something was wrong in his son's voice. "Dad, you better come out here."

Mumbling, "What the hell," the junkyard owner mentally prepared himself that the fuel was leaking or someone in the compound was sick. T-Bone pushed open the front door and immediately ran into Nick's rifle, the flash suppressor touching the bridge of his nose.

Before T-Bone could react, Nick grabbed the old man's shirt with one hand and yanked forward and down with significant force. T-Bone was on his knees instantly.

"You're damned lucky I don't just shoot your ass right now. You hurt one of my people, robbed us of all our food, and tore the hell out of two perfectly good pickup trucks. We've wasted a ton of gasoline hunting down your worthless carcass, and I'm short one night's sleep."

T-Bone looked up into Nick's angry face and said, "I wouldn't blame you if you did, mister."

"First of all, I want to know where our food went."

"Midland Station."

Nick growled, "I know that much. Where and who in Midland Station?"

"The guy that runs the whole town. Mr. Cameron Lewis is my buyer."

Nick motioned toward the drums of fuel. "Where does he get that much fuel? Is there a big storage facility there?"

"No, sir. They make the fuel there. There's a small refinery running 24-7. They use it to keep the generators running and trade fuel for food."

Nick turned away, clearly frustrated with the entire affair. As he glanced at the barrels of fuel stacked around the compound, another question popped into his mind. "Why? Why do you steal? Why didn't you bring some of this fuel into Alpha and offer to trade? Clearly, you can't use it all."

"We do trade with some folks, mister. But I couldn't take the chance with your town. Mr. Lewis put me on a deadline – if I didn't deliver enough groceries, he would take my wife off her dialysis machine. She would die. That's why we broke into your town. That's why I couldn't take the chance."

Nick tilted his head, trying to digest the answer he'd just been given. "So you're telling me this man in Midland Station has your sick wife hostage?"

"No, sir. He would let me take her anytime I want. He has the only functioning dialysis machine I know of. He keeps her on the machine as part of my payment."

"What type of man holds a woman's medical care over her husband's head?"

"Mr. Lewis runs Midland Station with an iron fist, just like he ran Lewis Brothers Oil. He was a ruthless businessman then and twice as hard to deal with now. Really, I don't blame him after what those people have been through. Half the town is burned down or the site of a mass grave. There are 20,000 people and not nearly enough food. There's rumor of revolt floating around the streets."

Nick considered the information, using the time to figure out what to do next. He finally decided to ask his prisoner the very question that dominated his thoughts. "And what should I do with you?"

The old man on his knees didn't respond. Part of Nick wanted the criminal to beg for his life, to grovel for mercy. The man was a thief. On the other hand, Nick understood part of the motivation. *I'd do anything to save Kevin's life*, he thought. *I'd do far worse than anything this man has done to save Diana.*

Nick turned back and ordered, “Stand up.”

After waiting until his captive was on his feet, Nick’s voice became low and mean. “I’m going to let you and your people live today, old-timer. I’m going to show mercy just this once. In exchange for the food you took from Alpha, we’re going to show up here tomorrow and take most of this fuel. Even with that, you owe me. I’m going to come calling one day to collect that favor.”

“I’ll pay, mister. I’ll pay up.”

“Don’t even think about coming near Alpha or Meraton again. We know who and where you are. There will be no clemency for you, or these women and children, if I hear of even a hint of bullshit out of you. Do you understand that?”

“Yes, sir.”

Nick spun around to the gathered residents still on their knees, shouting, “Do all of you understand what I’ve said?” Staring until every single head nodded agreement, Nick sent runners to retrieve the trucks.

Chapter 7

Alpha, Texas
January 27, 2016

"This guy in Midland did what?" a sleepy Bishop asked.

"He's got this guy's wife on a kidney machine. He's forcing the dude to deliver food, and keeping her on the machine is part of the payment," responded Nick.

Bishop yawned, holding open the door to the kitchen for his friend. "That's cold, man. That's frosty cold."

"According to this T-Bone character, Midland's people are starving. The government completely broke down during the collapse, and a guy running some big oil company stepped in and took over. T-Bone described the new boss man as ruthless."

Bishop found one of the church ladies had already made a pot of coffee, the cheery volunteer bustling about the kitchen humming "How Great Thou Art." After an exchange of smiles and greetings, Bishop and Nick took their cups and sat at an empty table.

"I'm not surprised. A single employer or two dominate many small cities. They would have all of the infrastructure in place to step in and take over. As far as the ruthless part, that's no big shocker either. I worked for a company that wasn't afraid to bare its fangs now and then. An old manager of mine once told me that corporations were the most ferocious foe on the planet."

Nick nodded, lost in thought.

"I'll tell you one thing," Bishop continued. "This dude in Midland is going to be an issue. Whatever is going on in Fort Stockdale, at least they keep to themselves. This guy running the show in Midland is aggressive. If your new friend T-Bone can't deliver the goods, he'll find someone else that can. Maybe the next guy raids Meraton and doesn't take hostages. He just comes in and shoots everybody and then takes what he wants."

Nick rubbed his eyes and yawned, "I've got to hit the sack. I'm getting too old for these all-nighters. Hell, I'm getting too old for this shit in general. I'm retired, ya know."

"Watch that language in this building, old man," a voice sounded over Nick's shoulder. Both men looked up to see Deacon Brown strolling down the aisle of tables. "This is still the Lord's house."

Diana retrieved her own cup of java and joined the two men. "So now Alpha has lots of fuel and no food. I don't think that's a good barter."

"I wouldn't say we've got a lot of fuel, but it will help a little."

Bishop sipped at his cup, lost in thought. The sound of shuffling feet caused the three to look up and find a much tousled-looking Terri scuffling sleepily into the room. Raising one hand in a half-hearted greeting as she passed, her demeanor caused Nick to grunt. "She looks like I feel."

Diana shook her head, "I wouldn't want to be with child during these times. What were you thinking, Bishop?"

The jab caused Bishop to stiffen, his mouth opening to defend himself, but Diana's raised hand stopped the words from rolling off his tongue, "Now, now," the Deacon interjected, "remember what building you're in."

Everyone chuckled at the exchange. Terri, joining the group and holding a steaming cup, asked, "What's so funny?"

The friendly banter, mostly at Bishop's expense, continued for a few minutes while Nick wound down from his adventure, and everyone else prepared for the day. Nick had just announced he couldn't hold his eyes open any longer when Chancy, the town's electrical expert entered the room.

"Oh, there you are. I've been looking for you, Diana," the slight man announced.

"Get a cup and join us, Chancy," Diana invited.

"Oh, thank you, but there's not time for that. I wanted to let you know that I was talking with some of the newcomers this morning. I thought I recognized one of the women from my days at the power company. I was right. Anyway, she told me that two of the electrical crews were stranded in Fort Stockdale. She said there's even an engineer with them."

Diana rubbed her chin, “Really?”

Chancy nodded, continuing, “She also told me that they had two fully equipped line-trucks. You know, the ones with the man-lifts you see repairing overhead electrical cables.”

Bishop said, “I wondered what happened to all those guys. They must have been deployed in force when the grid started falling over. I just assumed most of them finally abandoned ship and headed home to protect their families.”

Diana looked up at Chancy and asked, “So what would these two crews be able to do for us, Chancy?”

“If they have engineers with them, they would know the entire system and the location of spare parts. The woman I talked with said those crews along with everyone else at Fort Stockdale who didn’t live in the town were housed in some sort of labor camps. Ya know, we could really use those guys. The first thunderstorm that hits Alpha may knock out our precious electricity, and without maintenance equipment, there’s no way we can fix it.”

“You all know how I feel about what’s going on in Fort Stockdale,” inserted Terri. “They brand little children and crucify people. You saw the bodies hanging on the crosses yourself, Bishop. I say we go kick their asses. Set those people free. I’ll go get my rifle and lead the attack.”

Nick shook his head, “Terri, while we all appreciate your passion and sense of right versus wrong, we can’t become the area’s police force. Even if we wanted to, we don’t have the manpower or the resources to start a crusade.”

Terri’s expression caused Bishop to stiffen; he’d seen that look in his wife’s eyes before. He was trying to figure out a way to warn Nick that he had just fallen into a tiger trap, but was too late.

“Nick,” she began with a soft tone, “didn’t I just hear someone say that Midland Station was going to be a problem for everyone in the region?”

“Well… yes, I was saying that… but…”

“And weren’t you one of the strongest supporters of helping the newcomers relocate to Alpha?”

Nick began to sense he was in trouble, "Yes, I think that's a good idea, but…."

"So let me ask you this," Terri interrupted with the sweetest voice she could muster. "Which requires *less resource* – letting places like Midland Station and Fort Stockdale starve and abuse people and then try and salvage what's left, or becoming proactive and addressing the problem at the source?"

While Nick tried to figure a way out, Diana chimed in. "It's a valid point. Word of what we've got going on here in Alpha and Meraton is spreading. Even if refugees from other towns don't come here, the people running those places might decide to try and take what we've built."

Bishop shook his head in disagreement. "Preventive strikes aren't always a good policy. Look at the mess we created in Iraq, all under the pretense of stopping an enemy that was *going* to be a problem – in the future."

Terri said, "We made a mistake in Iraq, no doubt about it. The justification was there; the execution sucked. We should have cut off the head of the snake, not tried to eat the serpent from the tail up. I don't want to see my husband and the other good men of Alpha mount an invasion of Fort Stockdale or anywhere else. I don't want to bury the casualties. What I do want is to surgically remove the problem, and let the people decide. If we take out the tyrants ruling those hellholes, I'm betting the good folks will rise. You saw that right here in Alpha, didn't you Diana?"

Terri's remarks caused everyone to pause, the concept making sense on so many levels.

Nick finally broke the silence. Taking Terri's hand warmly, he said, "You are one interesting bank teller, young lady. I'm going to think long and hard about what you just said… right after I get some sleep. Good night, everyone."

Diana hugged Nick, having one last suggestion before he retired. "Nick, if I invite Pete and Betty from Meraton, will you man the barbecue? I think we need to make some serious decisions and involve everyone."

Nick nodded, "If there's any steak left in town, I'd be happy to cook out. Give me four hours rest, and I'll be good as new."

A radio transmission resulted in Pete and Betty agreeing to make a road trip to Alpha that very afternoon, both of the Meraton residents eager to see some different scenery after months of being cooped up in the same town. The running joke for the rest of the day was how to roll out the red carpet for the visiting dignitaries when they arrived at the courthouse. It was, as far as anyone new, the first bi-city conference to be held since the shit had hit the fan.

Nick kept his promise and set about preparing to grill that evening. Before the meat hit the flame, he had stalked around in secret, a desperate attempt to keep the contents of an old family marinade from Bishop's prying eyes. Bishop was relentless, constantly dipping a finger in the liquid and guessing at the list of ingredients.

"Is that mustard? Do I taste mustard in there?"

Nick smirked but remained silent.

"Come on, Nick. It's not like this sauce is a national security matter or anything," Bishop prodded.

"Sorry, buddy. There are some things a man doesn't share with anyone - his woman, how he picks the Super Bowl winner, and the secrets of his barbecuing greatness."

Pete beamed when Nick added just a touch of his moonshine to the mixture. "That should help tenderize the steak even more."

"I wouldn't get that stuff too close to an open flame," warned Bishop.

The girls sat at a nearby picnic table watching the playful banter, their reaction to the men's behavior alternating between grunted laughter and the occasional eye roll. In reality, it was the perfect setting for a cookout. The mid-winter day was closing with a beautiful red sunset, the air temperature so perfect no one noticed its presence.

Terri was happy to see Bishop relax. Friends, a gorgeous day, and the smell of cooking steak were therapeutic for both of them, a welcome reminder that good things still existed in the world.

Before long, plates were being heaped with spoonfuls of potato salad, canned corn, and homemade flatbread. Nick declared the steaks 5-star restaurant worthy, ready for the distinguishing pallet of the esteemed gathering. After the first bites, Nick's sauce proved worthy of its higher-than-top-secret classification. No one issued any wisecracks when Terri reached over and helped Bishop cut his meat, his fumbling one-handed attempts resulting in a prime cut nearly falling into the grass.

As the group ate, the topic of the recovery naturally entered the conversation. Terri courted the group's opinions about what the priorities of the communities should be.

"Thinking long term is probably wise," began Bishop. "High level projects that benefit everyone over a time frame of years, not weeks."

Nick nodded until finishing his swallow. "Energy is job one. We have electricity, but gasoline, diesel, and other fuels are in short supply. We have to figure out a way to get fuel. Without that, there's no transportation, and we'll be limited in everything we do."

Terri produced a piece of paper and began jotting notes between bites of food. Diana sipped her tea and asked, "What about security? Right now, everyone is getting along pretty well, but it won't last. Besides, we've got people on patrol 24x7, and that eats up a lot of manpower."

Pete agreed. "I was a cop for years. We're going to have to train a police force of some kind. We will probably need judges, too. I don't want to re-create the legal system mess we had before, but people are people, and conflicts are bound to arise."

Bishop stared into the distance for a while before remarking, "I know where there are a lot of cops. I can't comment on their attitude, but there's a whole bunch of them about an hour's drive from here." Bishop went on to explain about the Wal-Mart Distribution Center he had come across while walking to Fort Bliss. "The parking lot was full of police cars from several different departments. They were pretty smart taking over that place when everything went to hell."

"Maybe we should go and invite them to join our ever more

prosperous community," suggested Terri. "Maybe they would welcome a chance to live normal lives again."

Bishop was skeptical. "That little diplomatic mission would require some planning. I got the distinct impression that those guys were operating under 'a shoot first, ask questions later,' principle. You might be right, but we would have to be cautious."

Betty added, "I've got a feeling that diplomacy is going to become an important skill in the near future." Everyone had to agree.

The conversation continued late into the night before a yawning Bishop excused himself. "My apologies for being such a lightweight, but these medications kick my butt. I'll see everyone in the morning. Nite."

Bishop's exit broke up the gathering, but not before Terri had compiled a very strong list of the group's priorities.

It took Alpha's sole living mechanic a full day to restore the squad car to running order. While the town's police department normally boasted nine functional law enforcement vehicles, most of them were beyond salvaging due to a variety of reasons associated with the collapse of society.

Four had been wrecked, their drivers obviously succumbing to the toxic gas while traveling at a high rate of speed. Many of Alpha's residents had fallen victim to similar circumstances as the town's streets were still littered with the crumpled remains of an assortment of cars and trucks.

Three were simply too gross for anyone to attempt repairs. Officers on duty had died in their cars and had remained inside, their decomposing flesh rotting for months in the torrid Texas sun. Maggots had discovered the decaying carcasses and done their work, the chemicals from their larva adding to the destruction of plastic and metal inside the vehicles.

The remaining two cruisers were newer models, equipped with fresher seals, bearings, and more modern engines. But restoring even these more desirable units posed additional issues. While Alpha was in complete anarchy, scavengers had taken to spiking fuel tanks in order to access the precious gasoline stored within. Anti-siphoning devices, time, and general laziness had promoted the destructive habit that left all otherwise undamaged transportation worthless. Despite their relatively low mileage, any machine that sits unused for a protracted period of time requires extensive efforts to restore.

Once the two patrol cars had been located, one was stripped for spare parts – critical organ donations for its sibling. Eventually the mechanic had pronounced the remaining cruiser "good as new."

Of all the priorities discussed the night of the barbecue, it had been decided that obtaining a police force should be tops on the list. The false alarm at Meraton and T-Bones' robbery all contributed to the decision. Nick felt like his security volunteers would have more time for training if they didn't have to police Alpha's streets alone.

Bishop and Nick were like two schoolboys, readying to give the car a test drive. Neither man had driven a high performance vehicle in ages, and the general lack of traffic anywhere added to their anticipated delight. Nick won the coin toss, awarded the first session behind the wheel while Bishop was relegated to the passenger seat, the promised consolation prize consisting of controlling the lights and siren.

Deacon Brown was the spoiler. "Before you two young men go out and get into trouble, I want you to keep in mind one very important fact. The gasoline you burn is a critical resource to everyone here. It is life and death to all of us. So I trust you'll each keep cool heads and not be wasteful."

Standing beside Diana with her arms crossed, Terri added her voice of reason. "Bishop, you're not even close to 100% yet. If you wrap that fancy car around a telephone pole, I'm not taking you back to Fort Bliss to be patched up again. I am pregnant, and that is not an excursion I intend to make after a sophomoric joy ride gone bad. You sir, are an expectant father, and I expect you will act like one."

Both men assured the girls that they would be calm and reasonable, that a test drive was critical before their journey. After all, they would not want to risk a mechanical breakdown in the desert.

Nick started the powerful machine and pulled out of the church lot like a little, old lady leaving Sunday morning services. The two girls stood and watched the car's progress, neither of them believing for one moment that the guys were going to take it easy.

"I'll bet you lunch they have that thing at top speed before they're out of the city limits," offered Terri.

"No bet," Diana responded with a grin. "I saw the look in Nick's eyes."

Terri grinned, nodding her agreement. "It's okay – they need to have a little fun. I don't know about you and Nick, but for Bishop and me, the overwhelming task of getting society back on track can be a real killjoy sometimes. In a way, it's kind of cute how they act like teenagers now and then."

The two women started to turn back toward the church compound when the report of squealing tires and a revving engine sounded in the distance.

Terri glanced at Diana and flatly stated, "Dang. I wish you had taken that bet."

Bishop couldn't help himself. Despite his bravado-based promise that he wouldn't react to Nick's driving, no matter what his friend did, he had to reach up and grab the "oh-shit handle" located over the passenger window and stabilize his body. He was thankful his right arm still functioned.

After leaving the church, Nick resisted temptation a full six blocks before issuing a warning to Bishop. "Hang on," he cautioned. Those two words served as the only advance notice for a change in venue. And before Bishop could even inhale, the big man had floored the accelerator. The police car was fast... very fast. The machine had managed 90 miles an hour within seconds. Nick then slammed on the brakes and negotiated a screeching turn that Bishop was sure lifted the car up onto two wheels.

In short order, they were out of Alpha and on open road, Nick's foot never losing contact with the gas pedal. "How fast so far?"

Bishop yelled over the racing engine and rushing wind.

"A mere 138 and climbing," was Nick's calm response.

Bishop whistled and then remembered the lights and siren. He flicked the switches and then sat back, a huge grin on his face.

Nick was smiling as well, glancing over at his partner in crime while yelling, "And this is how we roll!"

A few miles outside of town, Nick let off the gas and announced, "This bad boy made it to 146. Gotta love a well-tuned V8." Letting the car coast for a bit, Nick slammed on the brakes and cut the wheel sharply. The squad car turned and slid, eventually coming to a complete stop pointed back at Alpha and leaving two stripes of smoldering rubber in the road. "Your turn, partner."

Bishop and Nick exchanged places, and to the surprise of his friend, Bishop put the car in gear and slowly accelerated back toward Alpha. "My 95-year-old grandma drives faster than this to church on Sundays. Is something wrong with the car?" Nick asked.

"Not that I know of," replied Bishop. "I just want to get a feel for her. I'm not as much of a gearhead as some people I know."

Bishop stayed well below the speed limit until they rolled into the edge of town. Once back to civilization, the driver came to a complete stop at an intersection and glanced at Nick. "Rides nice," was his only comment.

Nick was just about to tease Bishop when the motorist revved the engine hard while still holding his foot on the brake. Huge clouds of black smoke rolled from the car's rear wheels, the smell of burning rubber filling the interior. Bishop wiggled the steering wheel just slightly; the movement causing the back end to sway like it was dancing. When the rear wheels drifted to the left, Bishop let off the brake and cut the steering hard, causing the car to literally leap into a right hand turn. The g-force slammed Nick against his seatbelt, the strain eliciting a grunt.

Blazing down the abandoned side street, Bishop maneuvered through a series of twisting turns and hard braking that strained every bolt and seam of the police car – and the passenger. After three minutes, Nick was sweating, breathing hard, and holding onto the safety handle with both hands. When Bishop finally stopped, Nick looked over with wide eyes and exclaimed, "That was fun! Let's do it again!"

Bishop grinned, ready to agree but then the gas needle caught his eye. Tapping the dash with his finger, Bishop sighed and said, "We better not. We're probably in enough trouble as it is."

"Damned women. Can't live with 'em, can't live without 'em."

Bishop nodded, "Especially the ones who carry a pistol and can shoot."

The two wannabe racecar drivers returned to find the girls standing on the front steps of the church, disapproving scowls on their faces. Diana's arms were crossed while Terri's hands resided on her hips.

"We're in the shit now, bro," observed Bishop.

"If you had just a little more frontal lobe development - at least I committed my sins out of earshot."

Bishop threw his friend a look of "Yeah, right," and then opened the car door.

"Hi, honey," Bishop cooed, attempting to make his voice as innocent as possible.

"What's up?" Nick asked Diana.

The two women looked at each other, and Terri rolled her eyes. Without further comment, the pair pivoted and strutted with purpose back inside the church. After a suitable period for cooling off, the two guilty men sucked it up and went looking for their mates.

"Does the church have a doghouse?" Bishop inquired.

"Not that I've noticed, but not to worry. There's plenty of empty housing around town."

"We could always go stay with the contractors over at the hotel.

At least the conversation would be interesting."

Eventually the duo found their significant others searching through boxes of clothing, the items collected from unoccupied homes and sorted by size for newcomers.

"We need to look professional," explained Terri.

"You don't want us look like just any old off-the-street politicians, do you?" added Diana.

Thirty minutes later, the four members of the Alpha Chamber of Commerce were on their way to visit the Warlords of Wal-Mart. Unlike the typical pre-collapse business meeting, all four of the visitors were heavily armed, Nick in full combat load – just in case.

The drive via unused, smooth Texas highway was much quicker than Bishop's previous trip on foot. He joked to Terri, "This cheapens the entire affair. You guys don't know how much you're missing by not suffering through the pedestrian route."

Terri replied, "Thirst, hunger, insects, and bullets all come to mind. I'll stick with the quickie tour, thank you very much."

The I-10 exit used to access the huge distribution center contained scattered remnants of abandoned cars and trucks. In the daylight, Bishop noted the roadway clutter didn't look nearly as ominous as it had when he came this way at night.

"I'm pretty sure these guys have the road booby-trapped, Nick. Proceed with caution."

"You had better get out and clear it for me," suggested Nick. "Just in case."

Bishop exited the back seat and began walking in front of the police cruiser. They hadn't rolled more than a few hundred feet when Bishop discovered the first tripwire. Tracing it back to the source, he found it connected to a roadside flare and easily disabled the device.

One additional early warning system was discovered before it was time to leave the interstate and proceed along the surface road to the warehouse.

Diana turned on the strobe lights when they were within observation distance of the giant building. "Just to make sure they think we're cops," she commented.

"Are you sure there wasn't a doughnut delivery truck available in Alpha?" Bishop asked. "We could have at least set a box of chocolate frosted on the hood as a sacrificial offering. I'm sure they would smell it from here."

Nick slowed the car as they approached a sign in the middle of the road. It read, "No food, no water, and no barter. Stay away or you will be shot without question."

While Nick paused to let everyone read the warning, Bishop tapped him on the shoulder and pointed to the side of the road. Two human skulls and a scattered assortment of other bleached skeletal remains littered the area. "They mean business," was his only comment.

The roofline of the complex was barely visible on the horizon. Nick judged its distance to be at least 1200 meters, the assessment eliciting a whistle. "If they have sharpshooters who can acquire a human target at 1200, they're damned good. That would take at least a .50 caliber weapon."

Bishop replied, "I remember seeing a SWAT van parked in the lot. It wouldn't surprise me if they had lots of long-range toys on hand."

The four agreed to continue, hoping that the police vehicle and flashing lights would grant them safe passage. At 600 meters, everyone began to relax.

"I'm telling ya," Bishop offered, "doughnuts would be like a passport to these guys. Are you sure you don't want to go back and fry some up?"

At 200 meters, they could see activity around the building. While it didn't look like anyone was rolling out the red carpet, no sniper bullets slammed into the car.

"How do you expect them to react when they realize we're not cops?" asked Diana.

"Depends. Does anyone here even smell like a glazed or sprinkled?" Bishop muttered. Terri leaned across the seat and whispered, "Which arm hurts, Bishop?"

"Hmmm ... I plead the fifth."

Terri hit his right shoulder anyway.

Nick grunted, "Hopefully some of the paranoia is gone by now. They aren't exactly on the scenic route, and other than Bishop's little raid, they probably haven't had visitors for months."

The facility was surrounded by a heavy gauge fence with the access blocked by a gate made of similar wire mesh. The access was closed and guarded by six eager-looking, young men covering the car with AR15 rifles.

Nick parked about 50 feet away and took the cruiser out of gear. Before Bishop could stop her, Terri opened the door and stepped out of the car. "I've got this," she announced.

Nick and Bishop reached for their door handles, but Diana stopped them. "You guys getting out in all that gear is going to freak their cookies. Stay put. They're not going to shoot Terri without any warning."

Nick rolled down the windows so they could at least listen.

Terri had ventured about ten steps toward the gate when one of the men yelled out, "Can't you read, lady? That sign back there was pretty clear. We don't welcome trespassers here."

"My name is Terri, and I have the mayor of Alpha, Texas with me. We've come to make you gentlemen an offer... an offer you might want to seriously consider."

The men at the gate didn't seem impressed. "What could you possibly offer us?"

"A job... employment... a home... schools for your children. You remember all that stuff, don't you? Society? Friends? A purpose in life."

For a time, several of the guards looked at each other and their leader, a few hushed comments being exchanged. Bishop couldn't hear their conversation, but it was clear Terri's statement was of interest to the men.

"Wait right there, and instruct your friends to stay in the car."

A few moments later, a man exited the building and strolled casually toward the gate. Bishop would have identified the fellow as a lawman immediately, even without his Stetson hat adorned with a shiny star on the front.

The ramrod straight gentleman was slender, but not skinny. Probably close to 6'4" in height, his weathered face surrounded eyes that spoke of having seen just about everything and not been troubled by any of it. His walk betrayed confidence with a grace of authority, but showed no indication of abuse. *Here's the guy that's in charge*, thought Bishop. *Here's the man who is holding all of this together.*

The newcomer walked directly to the fence and tipped his hat to Terri. "Ma'am, I'm Sheriff Watts. What can I do for you?"

"Nice to meet you, Sheriff." Terri turned and indicated the car before she continued. "We drove here from Alpha. The town has reorganized and is in the early stages of recovery. We have electrical power and rule of law. We're growing so quickly that we need trained, professional law enforcement. My husband was aware of your location, so we decided to travel here and see if you or some members of your group would be interested in helping us rebuild Alpha and Meraton."

"You have electrical power?"

"Yes, we have restarted the windmill generators south of Alpha. The town has organized schools, medical care, and other essentials. We need policemen who are part of the community. The mayor of Alpha is in that car. I'm sure you would enjoy speaking with her."

"*Her?* I met the mayor of Alpha a few years back. That office was held by a man."

Terri nodded, "Many of the townspeople died in a horrible accident right when the country was falling into the abyss. There's a new group of citizens trying to build something special there."

The sheriff was skeptical. "I've no interest in helping a self-appointed king. When you say mayor, was she elected?"

"Yes, and we intend to have more elections soon. Even the sheriff will be elected in our town," Terri answered.

Sheriff Watts nodded toward the car. "Who else is with you and the mayor?"

"We brought along security. It's far too dangerous for two women to travel alone these days."

The tall lawman considered this new information for a few moments and then waved to one of his men standing by the entry. "Let them in. It won't hurt to talk."

As the deputy moved to unlock the gate, Watts turned back to Terri. "I'm going to allow you inside to talk this over. Your men can come in as well, but no weapons. You have my word that no harm will come to any member of your party."

Nick whispered, "No fucking way," but Bishop reassured his friend.

"I believe him, Nick. Besides, they have so many guns in that place we wouldn't be able to do much anyway."

"I don't like it one bit, but if you say it's cool, then I'll go along."

Terri proceeded to step back to the building with the sheriff while Nick pulled in the car and parked. Bishop left his weapons in the back seat, soon to be keeping company with Nick's rifle and pistol.

Terri turned and indicated Diana, "Sheriff, allow me to introduce you to Deacon Diana Brown, mayor of Alpha, Texas."

"Ma'am," Sheriff Watts responded as he offered his hand and tipped his hat.

Introductions were completed, and then everyone entered the building. It was immediately clear that strangers were extremely rare as the occupants of the facility stared to the point of rudeness. "You'll have to excuse us, folks. There haven't been any outsiders inside this building in almost seven months."

Watts elected to give Diana's group a tour. The huge warehouse was occupied by row after row of floor to ceiling shelving, many of the units full with cardboard boxes and wooden containers.

One wall was lined completely with enormous commercial freezers that had once stored hundreds of pounds of frozen food, including several sides of beef.

"We've now consumed the contents of three freezers. There are five left. After we use up the food inside, we convert the space into a community area of some sort. We have a school, theatre and music room. This place echoes badly, and the freezers allow for the night owls to gather without disturbing everyone else."

During the walkthrough, their guide disclosed that there were 110 people living inside the distribution center. "We had 40 law enforcement officers who brought their family members with them to begin a fresh life here. One of our citizens nicknamed our new home 'Wallyworld.'"

As the group meandered through the cavernous interior, Sheriff Watts pointed out this and that. The tour finally ended at the rear of the facility where a playground had been erected, and a garden had been tilled. "One of the tremendous advantages to settling here has been the availability of critical items stored inside the building. While the warehouse was never designed for long-term occupancy, its stored goods have allowed us to maintain a certain level of civilization. We know our food will eventually run out, and we all crave the flavor only fresh crops provide. Our biggest issue with the garden is that none of us were blessed with a green thumb, and the harvest has been a disappointment."

The tour proceeded to the front of the building where a cluster of offices had been constructed. "There's a conference room up here. I suggest we talk inside."

Bishop and Nick remained quiet for the most part, playing the role of hired security to the hilt. Both men were amazed at the organization and the thought that had been invested in developing the community. At one point when they were alone, Nick whispered to Bishop, "I wouldn't leave here if I were them. They've got it made."

After everyone had taken a seat in the conference room, the sheriff looked at Diana and asked, "So you said someone told you of our location? I'm curious how that individual knew we were here."

Bishop spoke up, deciding honesty was the best policy. "That would have been me, sir. A few days ago, one of your deputies had an encounter with someone in the desert to the west of here - right after a rather large diversion occurred up on the ridge. I was responsible for that. My apologies for any inconvenience, sir."

Anger flashed for just a moment behind the sheriff's eyes, but it passed quickly. For a few seconds, Bishop thought his confession might have been a mistake, but then the leader of Wallyworld snorted and looked down. "You caused me to lose a night's sleep, young man. We thought the entire world was going to roll down that ridge and kill us all."

"I had good reason, sir. I was operating under the direct orders of the President of the United States. Your signage and warnings precluded me from approaching, so I took action on my own. Is the man I encountered in the desert okay?"

Sheriff Watts almost smiled, the corners of his mouth rising just slightly. "Yes, no casualty but his ego and a few bruises. In a way, your little show was a good thing. Up until that point, we were getting lax and complacent."

Diana interjected, "Sheriff, we can offer a community - housing, soon-to-be schools, electrical power, and most importantly, a healthy social environment. You have done a fantastic job here and are maintaining a quality of living higher than anyone else we've encountered, but you have to know it can't last."

The older man nodded. "I know; the subject is something that haunts us daily. We continue to burn fuel and consume food that can't be replaced. My people are comfortable, but this place isn't a home. This lifestyle isn't how anyone wants to live long-term, nor is it a good setting to raise children."

Nick spoke up. "Sheriff, why don't you load up a few carloads of your people and come visit Alpha? Spend the day outside these walls and just walk around the community. See for yourself what we're doing. After that, drive on down to Meraton and visit the market there. Have a seat at Pete's, wet your whistle, and shoot the breeze with the locals."

Diana continued, "Our towns aren't perfect. We welcome refugees and stragglers, but some of those folks are troublemakers or potential problems. We need professional, even-handed police officers. Men and women who are trained on how to deal with situations fairly and competently."

Sheriff Watts nodded his understanding and then looked at Nick. "I'll call a meeting and let everyone know why we allowed strangers in the building today. I'm sure rumors are already making the circuit. We'll take you up on that offer, young man. I'll load up a group of folks and declare a vacation day."

Terri smiled broadly. "We look forward to having you visit, Sheriff. If there's any way you could let us know when you're coming, we might be able to organize a barbecue."

Nodding, an unusual look crossed the lawman's face. "Is there a functional church in either town?"

Deacon Brown glowed at the inquiry. "Why yes, there is. We just had a beautiful Christmas service. You and your people are always welcome – regardless if you take us up on our offer or not."

Watts smiled, "How about we come calling Sunday? My wife and I would welcome hearing a good choir and God's word. I know it would renew this old soul of mine."

Diana stood and offered her hand. "So, we have a date then. Services start at 10 in Alpha. Ask anybody for directions to the church. We look forward to seeing you, Sheriff."

Diana stood at the church's door, shaking hands and greeting everyone as they left the service. It had been another packed house, with extra folding chairs required to house the worshipers. The fact that over 40 law enforcement officers and their families had attended made her Sunday morning even brighter.

While she was hugging babies and grasping hands, Diana noticed all of the visitors from Wal-Mart were huddled in one section of the pews, apparently having a private meeting. Eventually the line of parishioners dwindled, and the elders were almost through cleaning up after the service. Diana decided to let the visitors have their privacy and found Nick on the front steps talking with Terri and Bishop.

“Are they still in there having a meeting?” asked Terri.

“Yes. I thought I’d let them have their privacy. We’ve presented them with quite the dilemma, I’m sure.”

The door behind the deacon opened abruptly, Sheriff Watts and his people exiting quietly and filling the front steps.

“Diana, we would like to take a tour of the town, if that’s all right with you. My deputies are interested in seeing some of the available housing. Some of our folks with young ones would also like discuss what the town’s plans are for a school.”

Smiling, Bishop stepped forward and said, “I’ll be happy to give a tour of the school. It’s not far, so we can just walk over if you wish.”

Nick volunteered to give a tour of the downtown business district, including the courthouse, police department, and jail. Diana added that everyone was welcome to wander around on their own as they wished.

A few minutes later, Bishop left with several moms and a few fathers in tow, the group laughing as they began the short trip to the school building.

Sheriff Watts hung back, waiting until his people had scattered with their tour guides. Diana approached the tall man and asked, “You’re not interested in seeing the town, Sheriff?”

A friendly look filled the man’s eyes, “I saw everything I needed to see this morning during the service, Miss Brown. I’m a professional people-watcher... in a way. No offense, but my eyes were on the town’s people more than the pulpit. I saw what I needed to see in their faces. You’re doing a good thing here, and I personally want to be a part of it.”

The lawman’s statement brought a smile to Diana’s face, “Why thank you, Sheriff. That makes me feel good inside.”

“I’m not a dictator, Miss Brown. I can’t order my people to leave the safety of the distribution center. I won’t do that. You’ve sold me, and I believe most of my people, but I’ve got to let them make up their own minds.”

“I wouldn’t want it any other way, sir.”

Terri cleared her throat and looked down shyly. "Sheriff, when you gave us a tour of the distribution center, I noticed a truck full of deer corn. It was backed up to the dock, but the trailer looked completely full. Are you folks using that feed?"

The lawman shook his head, "No, we've not been able to find any use for it. You can't eat it. We've even tried to make bread out of it, and that experiment failed badly. Right now it's just sitting there taking up space."

"If I were to offer you a trade... say 10 sides of beef for that load of corn, would you consider it?"

Watts thought for a moment before answering, "I don't see why not. As long as you had the truck to haul it off. We haven't started any of those diesel motors in months. I'm not sure they'll run, and we've drained all the fuel out anyway."

Terri stuck her hand out, "We have a deal then, Sheriff. In a few days, you'll be seeing a truck coming up your lane. Please do not shoot at it. *It* will be me coming to deliver the beef in exchange for the corn."

The sheriff nodded, "Okay, I'll let the boys know. That brings up a good point. How should we communicate? I don't want any accidents on either side."

"Do you have HAM radio capability?" Diana interjected.

"No, no we don't. The radios in our patrol cars are short range without the tower. We've found CB radios inside the center, but nothing long range."

Diana rubbed her chin for a bit before brightening. "How about plain old white flags? Will you honor a white flag?"

Again, it took Watts a few moments to consider. "I suppose so. We've not had any trouble for months, with the exception of your husband, ma'am. I'll give orders to honor a white flag."

A few hours later, the lawmen and their families gathered again on the church steps, the general mood upbeat and positive. As soon as everyone was accounted for, Sheriff Watts passed the word to everyone to load up into their cars.

Goodbyes and waves filled the air as the sheriff approached Diana. "We're on our way to Meraton to see the market and talk to the mayor there. Afterwards, we will want to talk things over for a day or two. I'll send word as soon as we've reached a decision."

"Thank you, Sheriff. You and your people are always welcome in Alpha, even if you decide not to join our community. Please come back to our services regardless of what you decide."

Tipping his hat, Sheriff Watts strolled to the lead patrol car and began what was a long convoy of vehicles out of the church's parking lot. Diana, Nick, and Terri stood and waved until the last car was on its way west.

Chapter 8

Midland Station, Texas
February 3, 2016

Lou's earplug sounded with a crack of static followed by a transmission. His gaze dropped to the floor as he listened in silence, his index finger pressing the tiny device tight into his ear. "Hold them there," was his response after the report had finished.

The security man turned to Mr. Lewis and cleared his throat. "Excuse me, sir."

A glance from the nearby desk gave Lou permission to continue. "We have Dr. Prescott with a fully loaded sedan, his wife, and daughter at the west roadblock. They're trying to leave."

Cameron looked up from his stack of papers with a questioning expression. "What exactly does the term 'fully loaded' mean, Lou?"

"All of their personal belongings are packed in the car, sir."

"I see. Inform your men that I request a word with the good doctor. I'll be there in a few minutes."

Lou transmitted the 'request,' and then called for additional men to escort Mr. Lewis for the trip. In a few minutes, a black SUV exited the parking garage at the headquarters building and proceeded on the cross-town excursion.

Cameron rarely traveled through this section of Midland Station, his rapt attention on the surroundings passing by his window. It would be easy for the eye to be drawn to the destruction. Entire blocks of homes burned to the foundation – evidence of a fire department that could no longer respond. Several automobiles were overturned, their rusting frames surrounded by piles of blackened ash and pools of melted plastic – a symptom of rioting that the local police force couldn't contain.

Mr. Lewis had seen all of those sights a hundred times before, and they held little of his attention. His examination focused on the people, and the prognosis wasn't good. Rail thin and grungy looking citizens were visible here and there, most of them shuffling along with stooped shoulders and distant gazes. The images reminded Cameron of the black and white newsreels from WWII - footage of disheveled, defeated refugees fleeing a conquering army.

The comparison pushed Cameron's mind to another analogy from that same war – the citizens of Midland Station bore an uncomfortable resemblance to the films of concentration camp survivors. Dark, sunken eyes that didn't focus, atop skin and bones bodies that ambled about with no vigor or purpose.

Exhaling loudly, Cameron turned away from the SUV's window glass, and concentrated on the back of Lou's head in the front seat. Despite removing the visual, his mind couldn't ignore the image. Most of the problem was hunger. Adequate nourishment would go a long way to improve people's lives. But Cameron knew it was more than that - hope was evaporating in Midland Station.

Calories were critical, but people also needed the chance to progress – to improve their lives. *Hell*, he thought, *I'm sick and tired of the whole ordeal, and I'm eating quite well.*

His analysis was interrupted by the slowing of the SUV, a signal they had reached their destination. Lou and the security team exited the vehicle first, scanning for trouble and doing their job before opening the door for their charge. Cameron stepped out, immediately surprised by the scene.

A line of cars, wagons, bicycles and just about every other method of transportation imaginable was waiting to leave Midland Station. Frowning, Mr. Lewis scanned the exodus, intrigued by the ingenuity of the transportation and the attitude of the travelers. Bundles of clothing were secured to makeshift carts being towed by bicycles. The few automobiles were stuffed to capacity, trunks overflowing with bags and personal items - lids held down by strands of rope or yards of duct tape circling the bumper.

Some people carried their earthly possessions on their backs, enormous hiking packs bulging with content. One couple simply pulled along wheeled suitcases as if they were traveling through an airport.

But there was something else – something beyond the creativity of transportation.

These people carried themselves differently, he realized. While they were still thin, heads were held higher, and eyes were brighter than the people Cameron had just passed by in the town. There was a hint of purpose in their step. *Optimism*, thought Cameron, *The word I would use to describe these people is optimistic. They're looking forward to something – thinking about the future.*

Mr. Lewis' gaze focused on a car that had been pulled out of line, a security man and driver standing by the hood having a conversation. With his ring of security tightly around him, Cameron moved closer, his presence drawing attention from everyone in the area.

"Hello, Danny," Cameron said to the driver, "I was quite surprised to hear you were leaving town."

Dr. Daniel Prescott wasn't embarrassed, but pretended to be. "I'm sorry, Cameron. I should have stopped in and said 'Goodbye.' It seems like you're always so busy, and I didn't want to be a bother."

"A bother? My best friend from high school - the town's most respected physician - a man I've always considered trustworthy, is leaving town and doesn't even send me a note?"

Shaking his head and looking down, Dr. Prescott responded with a quiet voice. "I was concerned you'd try and talk me out of it, Cameron. Or worse yet, forbid me to...."

"To what, Danny?" Cameron snapped. "Forbid you to sneak off in the middle of the night and leave everyone who depends on you behind to fend for themselves?" Cameron waved his hand through the air, clearly dismissing the man in front of him. "It doesn't matter. I won't stop you, but I do have one question. Where are you going to go? What paradise summons you so strongly to make the physician violate his oath?"

Dr. Prescott ignored the bait over his oath, and looked at his former friend through melancholy eyes. "We're heading to Alpha, Cameron. Word is they have electricity and food. People say they're rebuilding, and I want a future for my daughter. Cindy and I want to be a part of that."

Snorting, Cameron's voice became monotone. "You have all of that here, Doctor. *Your* family isn't starving, *your* daughter is in school, and I see lights on in *your* home at night. There's something else, and I'm insulted that *you*, of all people, don't have the courage to say it to my face."

"Okay, *Mister* Lewis," the doctor hissed, "I'll spell it out for you. I want to live in a place where there's a future. I want to live among people who determine their own fortune, choose their own leaders, and live in a free society. You've lost touch with reality, my old friend. Your priorities are protecting a company, not the people you grew up with, and I don't want to be a part of this any longer."

Dismissing the statement with a wave of his hand, Cameron retorted, "All of that bullshit about Alpha is just rumor and fantasy. You're chasing rainbows, Doctor. Regarding your high-minded statement about protecting my company, you're absolutely right. Without Lewis Brothers Oil, there are fewer people left alive in our little berg, sir. Without the corporation, there's nothing."

"You've got that backwards, Cameron. Without the people, there is no Lewis Brothers Oil."

Pointing his finger at Prescott's chest, Cameron's voice filled with rage. "I won't debate this with you. If you want to leave, then leave. But before you go, I need to be assured you're not absconding with any company property, Danny."

"I'm not a thief, Cam. You know that."

"I thought I knew a lot of things before today, Danny. Where did you get the gasoline in your car?"

The question seemed to surprise the physician. "I... I... I earned that gas, Cameron. It was part of my compensation for working at the hospital. If you disagree, then take it back. We'll walk to Alpha."

The response seemed to distress Cameron. He was about to reply when he noticed a considerable crowd of people had gather around – the throng clearly making his security team nervous.

"No," he decided, "take the gas, Danny." Without another word, Cameron pivoted and began a brisk stride toward his SUV. Almost as an afterthought, he stopped and yelled at the men operating the checkpoint. "Let them through."

Once inside the SUV, Cameron told the driver to wait. He watched as the line of people exiting Midland Station began passing through the checkpoint one by one. "How many are leaving?" he asked Lou.

"About 30 per day, give or take."

Grunting, the boss replied, "That's 30 less we have to feed. Let's get going."

Cameron sat in silence the entire trip back. As he and Lou rode the elevator to his office, the headman looked at his trusted aide and inquired, "What do we know about Alpha?"

"Only gossip and speculation. My people hear that they have electricity. Not generators, but electrical power through the grid. There's some woman who runs the town. She has a couple of hotshots that aren't afraid to pull the trigger. There's also been a rumor floating around for a long time about one of her henchmen named Bishop. Story goes he has a large amount of gold, hundreds of pounds of the stuff, hidden away at a ranch. Word is he killed a bunch of bank robbers who had stolen it in the Midwest right before everything went to hell."

"Interesting," replied Cameron. "I wonder if that gold has anything to do with how they're obtaining electricity."

"I don't follow, sir."

"They must be obtaining fuel from somewhere. While I personally don't think gold is worth its weight in cow dung at the moment, other people might find value in it. They might be using the precious metal to buy fuel."

Lou's shrug indicated he had nothing to add.

The elevator opened, and the two men strolled back to Cameron's office, securing the door behind them. "Lou, I think it's prudent we find out a little more about our competition in Alpha."
"Competition, Sir?"

Cameron sighed, "More so than ever before, it's every man for himself now, Lou. Resources, food, personnel, labor, and skills. Losing Dr. Prescott made Alpha stronger and Midland Station weaker. A minor loss in the grand scheme of things, but a loss nonetheless. I consider that competition, and knowledge is power when it comes to a contest."

Lou caught on and offered, "Sir, not long ago we had some ex-soldiers show up at the checkpoint. They claimed to have been recently discharged from Fort Bliss. I've given them menial jobs in our security force because my gut tells me they are deserters, but there's no way to be sure. They wouldn't be missed if they should have an unfortunate incident. Would you like for me to provide transportation and ask these gentlemen to perform a scouting mission to Alpha?"

After a period, Cameron nodded his approval. "That's a good idea, Lou. My primary curiosity is about their electrical system, but any information they can gather might be of value."

"Yes, sir."

Alpha, Texas
February 3, 2016

"I need you to take me on a trip," announced Terri.

"Sure," replied Bishop. "Where are we going? A cruise? Hawaii? Let me get my grass skirt! I know, let's go to Alaska!"

"Silly, not that kind of trip. A business trip."

"Okay, what is our destination?"

"The Beltran Ranch. I want to go feed some cattle."

Bishop shook his head, "I'll say one thing about the new Ms. Terri – there's never a dull moment."

Brushing off her husband's comment, Terri relayed the tale of her conversation with Sheriff Watts and the deer corn. When she finished, Bishop smiled broadly and declared, "Terri, that is one hell of a good idea. Okay, let's go visit the Beltran Ranch. Maybe they'll share their barbecue recipe with me."

After Terri's bidding Nick and Diana farewell, Bishop filled the truck with gas and headed west. The route took the couple through Meraton, and time allowed a brief stop to visit with Pete and Betty.

"Terri, I think you've probably saved the ranch!" was Pete's assessment.

After a quick tour of the market, Bishop headed east from Meraton. "We've not been on this side of Meraton since our bug out from Houston," Bishop noted.

"Sometimes I want to go back and see our house. Sometimes I miss it so very much. Do you think we'll ever get to go back?"

"Maybe," Bishop commented softly. "Maybe."

Eventually the truck came to a well-worn dirt ranch road leading north off the highway. There wasn't any sign announcing the entrance… no fence or gate.

The service road was washboard rough and required a slow pace as it wound through the lower foothills of the eastern-most Glass Mountains. Eventually, Bishop steered over a crest that revealed the ranch's main cluster of buildings in the flat of a valley below.

Negotiating a few easy switchbacks, the couple eventually encountered a fence line and gate blocking the path. Three signs adorned the obstacle, the first stating the reader had indeed arrived at Beltran Ranching, Incorporated. The second warned of trespassing. The third listed instructions on using the phone box to call the main offices.

Bishop exited the truck and walked to the dusty plastic box mounted on a steel pole next to the lane. After opening the shell, he lifted a heavy receiver that looked and felt like it had once served in a payphone booth.

Holding the device to his ear, Bishop dialed zero just like the instructions prescribed. It was almost a full minute before someone answered. "Beltran Ranch."

"Hello, we're here to see Mr. Beltran. We have an urgent matter to discuss concerning his recent trip to Meraton."

"Hold on, please."

Five minutes later an electrical hum sounded from the gate, followed quickly by a solid thunk. Bishop walked to the heavy barrier and pushed it open, drove the truck through, and closed the entryway behind them.

Mr. Beltran was waiting on the couple as they followed the signs to the main house. The tall rancher greeted Terri enthusiastically, while Bishop and Slim eyed each other. Bishop remembered Terri's debriefing on the episode in Meraton and guessed Slim was the fast-handed shooter.

Slim stepped off the porch, his thumbs hooked in his belt, a neutral expression on his face. Bishop realized the approaching bodyguard was probably dying to see inside the cab of the truck, no doubt curious if Bishop harbored any weapons within reach.

Bishop didn't move as the man took a few steps closer, opting out of accommodating the visual search of his vehicle. Terri interrupted the standoff, her voice calling out, "Now where are my manners? Mr. Beltran, this is my husband, Bishop."

Bishop and the tall rancher shook hands, the older man's grip firm, but friendly. "Terri, I believe you've already met Slim. Bishop, this is one of my longtime employees, Slim."

Slim extended his own welcome as he extended his hand, "I've heard about you. You shot it out with those bank robbers down in Meraton."

Bishop replied, "I've heard a story about you as well. Rumor has it you're lightening quick with that Glock you've got in your belt." Deciding not to be such an ass, Bishop opened the truck doors and waved Slim to have a look.

Terri got right down to business. "Mr. Beltran, I'm sorry to drop in unannounced, but I thought it was critical. Would you be willing to trade 20 sides of beef for a semi-trailer full of deer corn?"

Grunting, the rancher didn't need to think it over. "Twenty? Why, young lady, I'd trade 50 sides for that much feed. Where on God's green earth did you find a truck full of deer corn?"

"Technically, Mr. Beltran, the owners of the feed only want 10 sides. The other 10 are my broker's fee. The deal requires my fee be delivered to Alpha."

Terri explained the location and terms to Mr. Beltran, the rancher's smile growing larger as the conversation wore on. "Don't forget the white flag. Those lawmen are a little trigger happy."

"Slim, go get Mack and ask him to come up to the house, while I offer our guests a cold drink."

"Yes, sir."

An hour later Bishop and Terri pulled out of the ranch and headed back toward Meraton. Terri was beaming with the success of their trip, clearly satisfied with her accomplishment.

"You did a good thing today." Bishop said with pride.

Waving him off, she replied. "I just coordinated two parties to fix a problem. No big deal."

"I don't know about that, Terri. Four of us toured the distribution center. All four knew the ranch needed feed. You were the only one that put two and two together."

"Maybe I've got a future in brokering? Do you think?"

Laughing, Bishop nodded. "I am pretty sure you have a head for business, but I think we need to test your instincts further."

Puzzled, Terri replied, "Go on."

"I think we should stop on the way home and get a room at The Manor… for a little *monkey* business."

"Bishop! Is that all you ever think about?"

Her question was answered with a glance, Bishop's eyebrows going up and down.

"Which arm hurts, Bishop?"

The next morning, a semi branded with the Beltran Ranch logo rolled into Alpha, its trailer full of beef. The driver and supporting ranch hands stopped and quickly unloaded the "finder's fee" Terri had negotiated for the town.

As Bishop readied to escort the truck to the distribution center, Diana supervised the unloading and storage of the meat. "That will make up for some of the food that was stolen. Thank you so much, Terri."

Before long, the truck was ready to leave and pulled out behind Bishop's pickup. "Did you remember the white flag?" Bishop asked.

Terri reached down and showed him a white towel, "I hope this is big enough for them to see at a distance."

The trip to the distribution center passed without incident, Bishop leading the two-vehicle convoy through the curvy West Texas highway while listening to vintage Rock 'n Roll on the pickup's sound system. He and Terri were both in high spirits, singing along with the music and teasing each other about their lack of vocal talent.

The white flag procedure went smoothly, Bishop's truck leading the Beltran 18-wheeler to the long row of loading docks that dominated one side of the huge facility.

A few hours later the beef was unloaded, the meat stored in one of the huge commercial freezers. While the Beltran crew began transferring pallet after pallet of deer corn to their truck, Sheriff Watts motioned for Bishop and Terri to follow.

"Can you deliver a message to Diana Brown for me?" he asked Terri.

"Happy to."

The sheriff reached into his pocket and produced a multi-page letter. "These are our terms for joining the communities of Alpha and Meraton. Really, it's more of a plan. It's signed by every single person living here at the center."

Terri hadn't expected anything so formal. With a slight grimace of concern, she glanced up and asked, "Do you care if I read it?"

"Be my guest."

Taking a seat at the conference table, Terri began to scan the pages. "This is fair - you want housing for each family," was her initial remark. "This is reasonable – compensation for duties performed."

After finishing, she beamed at the elder officer. "I don't see anything in here that should be a problem, Sheriff. I think your idea of keeping some men stationed here at the center to protect all of these goods is wise as well."

Nodding at the paper in Terri's hands, Watts remarked, "We argued over the evaluation period mentioned in there. If things don't work out, our people want to keep the option of moving back here to the center. We thought 60 days was an equitable period for both sides to evaluate our job performance and for us to determine that the relationship is working for everyone."

"I'll hand this to Diana immediately. I'm sure she'll respond quickly."

Two days later, the first officers began moving their families to Alpha, Texas.

The miscommunication over the HAM radio and resulting waste of resources didn't sit well with Pete or Diana. For the men who had dropped everything and rushed to the rescue, the false alarm left a bitter taste. It was difficult enough putting food on the table and accomplishing the daily activities needed to survive without wasting an entire day on an unnecessary trip to Meraton.

The fact that a potentially dangerous situation had narrowly been avoided in the market wasn't lost on either of the elected mayors. If Alpha's men had invaded the small town, there was no way to predict the outcome. Meraton's citizens were well armed, and the legacy of bank robbers and rogue gangs was still at the forefront of an edgy populace's mind. A full-fledged firefight could have easily broken out.

The raid on Alpha's courthouse added another level of frustration. Many residents were questioning what would have happened if Nick and the men of Alpha had been present when T-Bone's crew rolled into town. Could the extreme loss of food have been avoided? There was no obvious answer, but human nature kept the topic alive and hotly debated throughout the town.

Adding yet another layer of frustration, the Beltran Ranch

debacle had been narrowly avoided, and everyone knew it. Terri's creativity and sharp eye received due credit for heading that problem off at the pass.

Diana looked at Pete and said, "I just can't keep up. How do you do it?"

"My problems are on a much smaller scale than yours, Diana. We don't have the immigration issues, and our town is a quarter of Alpha's size. That, and my moonshine mellows everyone out quite a bit," Pete added with a grin.

"I'm going to need some of that white lightening if things keep piling up around here. If I could focus on just Alpha's problems, I would be just fine. It's all the outside crap that drives me nuts."

Pete nodded his understanding, adding, "If Terri hadn't figured out how to feed Mr. Beltran's cattle, I would have probably tried any number of crazy schemes. She's got free drinks at Pete's Place for a month."

Diana waved off the silly comment. "She's pregnant Pete; she can't drink."

The bartender chuckled for a bit and then brightened with an idea. "You know what we need is an ambassador. Someone to coordinate our two towns and take care of all the outside stuff."

Diana's expression signaled she found merit in the idea, but then a frown crossed her face. "And who could do that job? You and I both ran unopposed."

Pete thought for a minute before suggesting Nick. "No way," Diana responded, "He's complaining constantly about not having enough time with Kevin. Besides, he'd be like a bull in a china shop. Nick thinks the only thing people respect is blunt force. While he's right far too often these days, we need someone who will try to resolve issues without violence as the first option. "

"Bishop?" Pete suggested.

"Same irk as Nick – a little too quick on the trigger. While I think this last wound has mellowed him a little, we need someone with both a little fire in the belly and a healthy dose of diplomacy as well. What about Terri?"

Pete blurted out, "She's pregnant. Isn't she due in less than four months?"

Diana crossed her arms, a defiant look on her face. "I know lots of women who had multiple children and still had a career. I don't think we should take her off the list just because she's with child."

Pete was skeptical. "I know that used to be the case, but times have changed. You're right, that would be Terri's decision. She handled the Beltran ranch thing like a UN Ambassador. I think she would be perfect if she would take the job."

Diana's gaze wandered off for a moment. "You should have seen her the first time we visited Sheriff Watts. She did a great job there, too. I was scared to death, convinced we were all going to be shot right on the spot. Terri hopped right out of the car and started negotiating."

"Can't hurt to ask her."

"They want you to do what?" Bishop's expression projecting total confusion.

"They want me to be the ambassador for the two towns," answered Terri.

Bishop dropped off the makeshift chin-up bar, the attempt to exercise without utilizing his left arm already causing frustration. He could tell Terri was excited about the offer – she hadn't immediately scolded him for not taking it easy. "What exactly does this job entail?"

"They want me to coordinate between the two towns and take care of any outside business that might crop up. They both said I had done a wonderful job with the Beltran cattle and negotiating with Sheriff Watts."

Nodding, Bishop said, "I can't disagree with that; you did a great service to everyone."

Terri ambled to a nearby chair and relaxed in its seat, clearly lost in thought. "I feel strong most days, Bishop. I feel like I could do the job. So far, being pregnant isn't causing a lot of health issues."

Bishop was skeptical. "That position sounds like there would be a butt-load of stress involved. I'm all for your supporting the family and helping out the communities, but not at the expense of my son."

Terri's face became stern, "You mean our daughter?"

Dismissing the potential banter with his hand, Bishop grinned at his wife. "Twins. Now, back to this diplomatic role, tell me what you're thinking. I can hear the wheels turning all the way over here."

"I want to do it. Ever since those men kidnapped me, I've wanted to get involved and make things better. I think this is a perfect opportunity. In the hospital at Fort Bliss, the Colonel visited me a few times while you were snoozing. He told me that I could run and hide from the political beast, or I could get involved and fight for the American dream. You basically said the same thing when we talked about it. I have decided to get involved – I have decided to fight."

Terri pulled her laptop out of a shoulder bag and began typing.

Not sure the conversation was over or what decision had been made, he asked, "What are you doing, now?"

"I'm making a positive and negative list, and then I'm going to list a set of goals – if I take the position."

"Sounds logical," Bishop observed and then returned to his workout, lifting a single dumbbell with his good arm.

After a few sets with the free weight, Bishop lowered his barbell and observed his wife peck on the laptop computer. In addition to her grunts, whispered protests, and general air of angst, Terri's expression constantly shifted between a troubled grimace and an annoyed scowl. Pretending to return to his exercise, he waited patiently until she spread her arms wide in a gesture of frustration, closed the lid of the PC, and set it on the end table. Terri's mood was clear, as she leaned back on the chair with a heavy sigh of exasperation.

"How's it going?" he cautiously ventured.

"Not well. Too many problems and not enough solutions."

Bishop wiped the sweat from his forehead with a towel and then pulled up a chair close to his wife. "Terri, did I ever tell you about my grandparents?"

Terri's initial reaction to Bishop's changing the subject was a dirty look, but she quickly decided he was trying to take her mind off the critical decision they faced. "Very little, Bishop. You've never talked much about any of your family. Why do you ask?"

Bishop stretched his arm high above his head, the movement eliciting a slight wince. He detected his wife's concern and smiled to reassure her that he was okay and that the pain was insignificant.

"Because I think it pertains to what's going on in the world right now. I believe it relates to some of the problems we are facing. I don't know why it never occurred to me before - it just dawned on me as I was watching you work."

"Okay," Terri replied, adjusting her perch on the chair to face him. "You've got my attention. Tell me about your grandparents."

"I was young when they both died, but I still remember a lot about them. They had survived through the first Great Depression and as a result, had a different perspective on things than their children did. In fact, my dad and his brothers often teased Grandpa about being a cheapskate and a penny pincher. He would just laugh it off, but I used to worry that they were hurting his feelings."

"*Was* he a cheapskate?"

Bishop stared off into space, obviously trying to recall old memories and revive feelings from long ago. "No, he actually was very generous. He wouldn't spend money on himself, but would go all out with other people."

Terri frowned, not quite understanding.

Bishop continued, "He and my grandma lived on a five-acre place in the Midwest. It was like a mini-farm, if you will, and they were very self-reliant there. They had an arbor that was heavy with grapes during late summer, as well as a neatly tended garden filled with everything from watermelons and squash to mustard greens. Beyond the garden was the barn where Grandma's prized laying hens roosted on one side, a hayloft occupied the center of the structure, and the other side provided shelter for the cow during harsh, winter blizzards. There was a root cellar full of canned food preserved from the garden's bounty. The two of them didn't waste anything and detested going to the grocery store."

"Maybe they just liked homegrown food better."

"Maybe. When I was a kid, I used to hoe the weeds and pick the ripe veggies. I'll tell you that I've never tasted food like that since. Pulling a tomato off the vine and taking a bite is a completely different experience than eating one that's from the supermarket. Same goes for beans, strawberries, and corn. There's just no comparison."

Terri grinned. "I'm having trouble picturing a young Bishop in denim overalls, working in the potato patch."

Bishop chuckled at the observation. "Oh, I did my share. Not with overalls mind you, but I sat with my grandparents and shelled peas and snapped beans on many a summer eve. My grandma used to cook 'right off the vine' green beans with fresh onions and bacon. Heaven on earth it was... well-worth the hours of pulling weeds."

Terri rubbed her tummy and protested. "Stop that, Bishop. You're making me hungry!"

Bishop smiled and continued, "I know they didn't choose that lifestyle because of lack of money. My grandfather had actually done well financially. Taking care of a cow and a coop full of chickens is a lot of work for folks with the means to just buy their own eggs and butter. Canning a one-acre garden's worth of food is a serious undertaking, too. And I don't think they did it just for the taste either. No, I am sure they did it because of what they lived through when they were younger. They wanted the security of knowing they would never go hungry again."

Terri crossed her arms, clearly deep in thought. "So you're saying they did all those things because they lived through a depression? I suppose that makes sense, but wouldn't the memory fade and the extra work seem pointless after a while? Wouldn't they quickly figure out it is more convenient to go buy a dozen eggs and get out of the poultry business? I can see gardening as a hobby...maybe it is even fun, but livestock and canning?"

Bishop laughed, remembering his grandmother standing over the pressure cooker, suffering from the steam. "I don't think it was a hobby or amusement. I don't think any of it was based on that or saving money. I think they were driven to do what they did out of fear."

"Fear? What kind of fear leads to storing sweet potatoes in a root cellar? What were they scared of, Bishop?"

"My grandfather said something interesting to me one time. I remember that day because I'd never seen him so serious." Bishop paused for a bit and frowned before lowering his voice to a grumble. "Son," he imitated, "being hungry, truly hungry, exhausts you in a way you cannot imagine. Trying to sleep at night doesn't work. Listening to your children complain about empty bellies strikes a nerve unlike anything else. Wondering where your next meal is going to come from consumes all thought. Once you experience that, you'll do everything in your power to make sure it never happens again."

Terri nodded, her gaze indicating she was digesting the quote. "You're relating how your grandparents lived to what we can expect from the people that are still alive now. They've been through hell, and it's probably changed their lives forever."

Bishop said, "Yes, that's exactly what I am getting at. We were lucky, Terri. We had food and supplies, and a bug out location. Many people weren't prepared for what happened, and they suffered for it. Many paid the ultimate price. As you, Diana, and the others guide us through the coming months, you need to remember that the mindset of the survivors will always be different."

Terri thought about her mother and the childhood lessons that had been passed down from her mom. "I remember her telling me that getting an orange for Christmas was a big deal when she was a little girl. I know that her family lived through some really tough times. I never knew my grandparents; they died before I was born. I wonder if Mom inherited some of their conservative nature."

"No doubt," Bishop responded. "My father wasn't nearly as frugal as his dad. I probably have even less of that quality. There's this phrase "living memory," that people throw around, and I think it's a legitimate phenomenon. Look at Pearl Harbor or 9-11, both of those horrible events faded in the minds of Americans, especially those very young or a generation removed from the event. I've always wondered if 9-11 could have ever happened if the lessons from Pearl had remained at the forefront of the average citizen's daily life. Time may heal, but I'm not sure that's always a good thing. Sometimes I think we'd be better off as a society if we had certain things permanently imbedded in our collective thoughts."

Terri rubbed her chin and shifted position. "I think you're right on track with this, Bishop. How do I use this information, though?"

Bishop grunted and then met Terri's gaze. "That's up to you and the council, if you take the job. They were elected. 'We, the people' have put our trust in their hands. I only brought this up because I see you struggling with defining the role the new government is going to play. I think you need to keep this generation's living memory in mind as you plow forward. The people around us will never be the same. Hell, you and I will never be the same. Look at you – my darling, ex-bank teller now talking about being the ambassador."

Terri grinned and playfully waved her husband off. "I see what you mean, though. We survivors won't have the same issues or priorities as we did before the shit hit the fan, and that can work for us. The council needs to focus on the future and keep in mind the lessons of the past."

Bishop shrugged his shoulders. "A year ago, quality medical care meant prolonging life and keeping people comfortable. Now, it means simple survival... living another day. The same logic could be applied to a good meal. I felt like the peppered bacon you made me on Christmas Day was a feast fit for a king. A year ago, that would have simply been a super-sweet gesture from my loving wife. The priorities are different now, and I'm sure we aren't the only ones who realize that."

Terri nodded her agreement. "Still, it seems like everybody's goal is to get things back to the way they were before the collapse as soon as possible. Diana actually had someone complain about the electricity going off at night and requested the council look into it. Can you believe that?"

"You're going to have some of that, darling. It's unavoidable. I hope reality will set in for those people. For most of us, it has already."

Bishop reached across and touched Terri's shoulder. "Here's the real lesson... what I was really driving at with my long-winded story. You brought up the Colonel and fighting the beast. Do you remember when I told you that the only way to control the 'beast' was to control fear?"

Terri nodded, remembering the conversation on the base's parade grounds.

Bishop continued, "The only way to control that fear is self-reliance – just like my grandparents. It's not some law, or form of government – it's eliminating the need to depend on anyone for anything. That's how you control fear and thus control the Colonel's metaphoric beast."

Terri turned and picked up her laptop and began typing some notes. She paused and looked up. "Thank you, Bishop. I see what you are saying, and I agree wholeheartedly. I am going to give the highest priorities to projects that enable the people to be more like your grandparents. We don't have enough manpower or resources for our fledgling council to rebuild society, so I think we should make sure everyone knows how to provide for themselves and then get out of their way. That will eliminate fear and control how much any beast can eat and grow."

"Now you're talking," agreed Bishop. "There are some things only the community can do as a whole - projects that will be beyond the scope of individuals. That's why governments have always been formed. You can't ignore that reality. There has to be a balance."

"I'll accept under one condition," Terri announced to Diana.

"Okay."

"I get to address the issue at Fort Stockdale first," she said with defiance.

Diana shook her head, surprised at Terri's request. "I know that day at Station #4 shocked you, but I thought you had gotten over that. I'm a little surprised it's still bothering you."

A look of frustration crossed Terri's face, her voice becoming cold. "Please don't underestimate me, Diana. I'm not making that demand based on revenge or some ivory tower concept of righting all the wrongs in our little corner of the world. More than half of the people that are immigrating to Alpha are coming from the Fort Stockdale area. While I would love to set things straight in that little town, my motivation is to take the pressure off Alpha. If we fix things in Fort Stockdale, people will stop migrating here."

Diana's finger found her chin, "I'm sorry; I did underestimate you. You're absolutely right about Fort Stockdale. If we addressed the source rather than bustle around trying to treat the symptoms, the patient would no doubt improve. I'm a little embarrassed I didn't think of that myself."

"When I told Bishop about my plan, he told me a story about Afghanistan that made a very good point. He made me promise to remember that nothing is as it appears, and that I should use that as a rule moving forward."

"Sounds like sage advice. It also sounds like Bishop is completely onboard with your taking the job."

Terri grinned, "I wouldn't go that far. He still has reservations about being married to a politician."

Both women laughed, and then Diana rose up from behind her desk and walked around to take Terri's hand. "Welcome to the jungle, Ambassador. Come on in - the water's fine."

"Liar."

Diana snorted, "You've got the hang of this game already! I'll let Pete know your decision. I look forward to hearing your idea regarding how to fix the problem in Fort Stockdale."

Alpha, Texas
February 7, 2016

Lou deposited the three men four miles outside of Alpha. It had dawned on the security man that he, personally, was one of those people who believed gold would have astronomical value when things settled back down. Since the Mr. Lewis didn't have any interest, Lou felt no disloyalty in asking his team of spies to check out the rumors floating around about this Bishop character.

Each man was issued an AR15 and several magazines of ammunition. Their orders were very specific – find out as much as possible about Alpha's electrical capabilities. If information comes to light about the gold, all the better.

As he watched the three saunter off, a wave of second-guessing gripped the man. He had recommended these guys to the boss, and if the whole thing went south, it might blow up in his face. The men he was sending into Alpha weren't overly mature and definitely not the highest IQs in the county. Far too aggressive, cocky, and unafraid, the trio was bound to run into trouble.

As he turned the SUV around and began the long drive back to Midland Station, his concerns began to fade. *What's the worst that can happen?* he thought. *Alpha's a tiny little shithole, and no one really cares much about what's happening there anyway.*

Sergeant Mitchell hoped this town would be more interesting than the last one. After getting busted for his third drunk and disorderly in the last eight months, he had decided his military career was over. His service record in Iraq and Afghanistan had kept his rank at an E7 after the first incident. They had demoted him one pay grade after the second infringement, and he was surely facing time in the brig after this last little session with a bottle of moonshine smuggled in from El Paso.

Fort Bliss and the Army were deteriorating, anyway. Since Mitchell had been stationed at the desert base, there had been an assassination attempt on the president, tanks firing on civilians outside the front gate, and even a murder mystery involving some dude and his wife. Things were surely going to hell.

Food rationing had begun not long ago, followed shortly after by the base's generators being shut down at night to conserve fuel. Training exercises were canceled, MP patrols minimized, and even the movie theatre was closed. Morale was low and desertions high.

The two privates strolling along with him had been fast acquaintances, all three men drying out in the base's drunk tank. They were far from model soldiers themselves, and it had been a mutual agreement to desert if the opportunity presented itself.

It finally did. Released until a court martial scheduled for the following week, an unattended HUMVEE had been far too tempting. One of the privates swore his family owned a nice country place outside of Katy, Texas where the trio would be welcomed. A land of plenty... plenty of booze, plenty of women, and plenty of food.

So down I-10 they traveled, barreling along in the stolen HUMVEE and heading east for Katy. One little problem occurred a few hours after their departure, however. That diesel engine under the hood of the military vehicle consumed a lot of fuel, and no one had counted on gas stations no longer being an option. They had walked 12 miles to Midland Station, the HUMVEE pushed off the road and hidden until they could find, steal, or earn some fuel.

Nick was helping Kevin clean his rifle when the radio transmission came in. "Nick, this is Corey at the north end roadblock. Are you there?"

Nick unhooked the portable from his belt and acknowledged the call.

"Strangest thing just happened. We had three healthy looking guys walk up to the checkpoint. They were wearing civilian clothes that looked cleaner than mine...accessorized with military-issued packs. They claimed to have walked from a relative's house up by Fort Davidson, but there wasn't any dirt or dust on their boots."

Nick thought about the description for a moment and hit the push-to-talk button. "Maybe they cleaned themselves off before coming into town. Maybe they wanted to make a good impression on someone."

The response was almost immediate. "That could be. As they were walking off, one of them turned around and asked if I knew a guy named Bishop."

Corey had Nick's attention now. "Go on."

"When I told him I did know of a Bishop, the guy asked me if he was in Alpha. Claimed Bishop was an old Army buddy of his and wanted to look him up."

Nick walked away from the workbench, staring into the distance. "Were these guys military?"

"I would say yes. Short hair, the right age range, and in pretty good condition."

Nick's voice sounded strained. "Weapons?"

Corey was now becoming nervous, no doubt wondering if he had done something wrong. "Well, that's just the thing. I noticed the outline of a rifle barrel protruding from one of the packs. I told the guy he didn't have to hide anything – that weapons were allowed in Alpha. I thought he was going to freak for a second when I mentioned the gun."

Nick turned to Kevin who had been listening to every word. "Go warn Bishop… right now… hurry."

Kevin answered "Yes, sir," as he ran out the doorway.

Corey transmitted again, "Nick, did I mess up?"

Nick shook his head even though the man at the other end of the conversation couldn't see it. "No, no you didn't do anything wrong. As a matter of fact, I appreciate your being so observant. We'll let Bishop know to watch his back. You did the right thing by contacting me."

"We sent them to the courthouse. They should be getting there about now to check in."

"Okay, Corey. Thanks for the heads up. Nick out."

Nick hefted his rifle and shoved in a magazine. He grabbed two spares from the workbench and headed for the door. A single bound down the front steps left him beside the golf cart, within seconds speeding toward the courthouse.

A short time later, he arrived, the scene seeming like a typical day. The volunteers were at their usual stations, ready to help the new arrivals. While the inflow had slowed somewhat, Alpha still received 25-35 new refugees a day.

Nick slung his rifle and approached the main reception station. The three ladies looked up and smiled. "What brings you here today, Nick?"

"I was wondering if three young men checked in recently. Say, the last 10-15 minutes?"

The women all looked at each other and then checked the clipboards full of paperwork sitting in front of them. "No," one of the ladies answered, "we had a single older man and a family with a 17-year old boy, but that's been it."

Nick looked to the north, hoping to see the three men walking toward the courthouse. There wasn't any sign of the strangers. "Okay, thanks, ladies. If three younger men do check in, will you ask someone to radio me and let me know they're here?"

"Sure, Nick. Is there a problem?"

"I don't think so, but I just want to be certain."

With that, Nick waved farewell and began walking toward the north, pulling his rifle around to the ready. While Alpha was as free a society as one could imagine, there were a few rules. When the men working the checkpoints instructed a newcomer of the need to check-in at the courthouse, it was expected for people to comply.

If these guys didn't show up soon, Nick had the excuse he needed to become inquisitive. Nick grunted. *And I can be very inquisitive*, he thought. Continuing toward the northern roadblock, he reached the point where he could see the barrier off in the distance. Corey and two other men were sitting in the shade of their golf carts, that approach to Alpha not having any traffic at the moment.

Nick couldn't see anyone walking between him and the outpost. *They've disappeared*, he thought. The big man pivoted and headed back for the church, hoping Kevin had found Bishop and Terri. Retrieving his electric ride on the way back, he soon saw Kevin trekking in the same direction.

"Did you find Bishop and Terri, son?"

"No, I searched the church and didn't find them, but one of the ladies said she thought they were working at one of the schools. Westside Middle School is what she said."

"Hop in. We'll go look together."

Nick floored the golf cart and never let off the accelerator, swerving the small machine around any curve or obstacle, Kevin hanging on to avoid being thrown overboard.

A few minutes later, they came to a stop in front of the school's main building. Hopping up two steps at a time, Nick was relieved to hear Bishop's voice at the top of the stairs.

"Hey, Nick... Kevin... what are you guys doing here?"

"Everything okay over here, Bishop?"

Terri appeared at her husband's side. "Everything's fine, Nick. What's going on?"

Nick explained the incident at the roadblock, watching Bishop's reaction closely. His friend was still handicapped, and Nick wasn't sure how he would handle any sort of threat. Nick had to smile when Bishop subconsciously moved his hand to the .45 pistol on his belt.

"I can't think of any Army buddies who might be looking me up," replied Bishop. "My name's not that common, so it probably is the same Bishop."

"Bishop, did they ever catch the guys who tried to kill you at Fort Bliss?"

Bishop shook his head as Terri moved closer to her husband. "Not that I know of. No one told me if they did."

Terri added, "I didn't hear anything about it while Bishop was in the hospital."

Nick turned and looked outside, his body language indicating he was lost in thought. Finally turning back, he said, "It might all be innocent... and it might not. My biggest worry is that we don't know where they are. They could be hiding anywhere right now. They could have crosshairs on this very doorway waiting for you to come out."

Bishop responded, "Alpha's a big place to search. There's still so much of it that is unoccupied. If I were a shady character, I could hide out for a long time in the shadows, and you'd never find me. If these guys have skills, they'll be difficult to locate until they take action and show themselves."

Nick nodded, "You're absolutely right about that, buddy. Would you two mind hanging out around the church until we can find these guys? There's no way we can protect you until we locate them and find out exactly what's going on."

Terri nodded, looking up at her husband. "He's supposed to be resting anyway. This will give me an excuse to keep him in bed."
"I'm loving this," grinned Bishop. "Maybe I should find those guys myself and pay them to stay quiet for the rest of the week."

"Bishop," Terri sighed, "Which arm hurts?"

Alpha, Texas
February 10, 2016

"Honey, I've got bad news, I'm going to become scruffy."

Diana looked up from her desk and shrugged her shoulders. "That's news?"

Nick snorted, "No, seriously, I'm not going to bathe or shave for a few days."

Mayor Brown frowned, "Is this some sort of protest or hunger strike or something? I'm not going to shave until my mommy buys me a new whatever?"

Nick pretended to be considering Diana's statement, then became serious. "I've been talking things over with Terri and Bishop. We think it's time to address the Midland Station issue, and Bishop came up with a pretty good plan, but it requires me to avoid bathing for a while."

"Where are you going to sleep while you stink? You're not soiling my church."

"I'll find someplace to crash. Kevin didn't seem to be all that concerned about keeping my company."

"Kevin's your son and family. He has to love you no matter what," she teased.

Nick laughed and bent to kiss Diana's cheek. "I just wanted to warn you."

Leaving the deacon's office, he found Bishop in the basement of the church, searching through boxes of clothing gathered for charity.

"You're a problem," he proclaimed as Nick entered the room. "You're too damned big. There weren't that many guys in Alpha who wore a size 58 jacket."

Shrugging, Nick proceeded to help Bishop search.

After an hour, the two men had finally collected an outfit both deemed acceptable for the mission. The pants and shirt could be from Nick's normal wardrobe, but that's where the similarities with his regular appearance would end. The skullcap was easy, as were the fingerless gloves. After digging through countless boxes, they had found a London Fog overcoat that would stretch across Nick's shoulders.

"Not bad," Nick commented as he looked at his reflection in the mirror. "I look 'swab' and 'de-boner.'"

"Now it's time to season your outfit," announced Bishop. Nick immediately became wary, Bishop's tone sounding just a little too happy about the next task.

Nick retrieved his oldest, most worn pain of trousers and a shirt that already sported a few threadbare spots, while Bishop prepared for the 'seasoning.' Exiting the church's front door, Nick found Bishop fiddling with a strand of para-cord at the back of a golf cart, the overcoat, gloves and hat lying on the ground beside him.

Bishop squinted up at his friend, his voice demanding, "Throw your stuff on the ground. I'm almost ready."

"What the hell are you doing, Bishop?"

"I'm going to show you how to accomplish the vagabond look. It's the latest thing in Paris, I hear."

Nick, shaking his head, heaved his pants and shirt onto the pile.

Bishop finished his task and then hopped in the driver's seat. "Come on," he motioned to his friend.

The next thing Nick knew, Bishop had turned the cart around and was speeding toward the pile of clothing. "What are you doing?" he shouted just as the cart ran over the attire. Thump. Thump.

Bishop didn't answer, but spun the wheel sharply and floored the accelerator pedal, clearly lining up for a second pass. Timing it perfectly, he peered at Nick and mouthed the words, "thump thump," precisely as the wheels passed over the now flattened clothing. Bishop's face lit in a smile at his impeccable rhythm. Nick just shook his head.

Spinning the cart around again, Bishop waited until just the right moment, and sang "Shave-and-a-haircut…." thump thump.

Nick couldn't help himself and started laughing at the ridiculousness of his friend's behavior. "You're a child," was his only comment.

"I'm just happy I get to sleep with my wife the next few days. Normally, I'm the one who gets filthy, grimy, and smells to high heaven. It's one of the few benefits I've discovered to getting shot."

Bishop stopped the cart and bent to examine the results of his handiwork. The pile looked like it had seen better days. The next step was to tie the individual items to the para-cord at the back of the cart. "We're going to drag them around for a while… maybe find some mud… maybe a good spot of oil on the parking lot."

By the time the men returned, the drag-along articles were well soiled and actually looked aged. Nick shook his head, "I'm not even going to ask how you thought up this trick. I don't want to know."

Six blocks away, in clear view of the church, Mitchell lowered the binoculars from his eyes and turned to one of his men.

"Well, well," he started. "The mysterious Bishop does indeed tread this earth. He and that big dude are tooling around the parking lot on a golf cart."

"They're doing what?" The bored private asked.

Dismissing the question, Mitchell ordered, "Get your shit in one bag, and instruct your ass-buddy to do the same. I want to put a couple of rounds into this guy and get him to talk. Try to hit his legs if possible. No head shots… at least not 'till we get what we want."

Nodding, the ex-private went to get his friend who was taking a nap at the back of the house.

While he waited, Mitchell thought through his plan. The Army deserter really only wanted to talk to Bishop, but had gathered enough Intel to know his mark was most likely going to be a hard case. They had also heard various details about Bishop being injured – something about a shootout with kidnappers. A couple of people even claimed his left side was paralyzed.

Mitchell thought there was a good chance the rumors were true given their target had been holed up in the church since they had arrived in town.

Once they had discovered his hideout, moving into an empty house with a full view of the church's compound was easy. The three men had taken shifts during the day – two of the intruders talking to a few citizens around town - one man always watching the compound.

Now it was time to move. He only needed to keep Bishop alive for a minute or so, Mitchell's experience being that dying men answer questions truthfully.

Looking up, Mitchell observed his two comrades loading magazines. He checked the church again and saw no activity. "He's gone inside again, but that don't mean anything. We'll just go in and get him. Like I said, no head shots."

Everyone nodded in agreement, and then Mitchell led the three-man team out the front door.

Bishop started to set his rifle in the golf cart and reconsidered. Despite Nick's warning of strangers in Alpha inquiring of his whereabouts, his left arm was still practically useless. He had snatched up the weapon more from habit than anything else.

Looking at his watch confirmed he was late for his date with Ambassador Terri, so he decided to take the long gun along for the ride. Besides, he mused, he couldn't let his best girl think he didn't love her anymore. "Shhhhhhh," he held his finger to his lip while looking at the rifle, "We don't want Terri to know about our feelings for each other."

The .45 ACP on his belt provided a little more confidence.

Zipping along to the courthouse, Bishop was considering Terri's new role when three holes appeared in the Plexiglas windscreen, closely followed by the distant sound of gunshots.

Bishop cranked the wheel hard left, the maneuver pulling his body across the seat just as sparks flew off the cart's roof pillars, the sound of screaming ricochets filling the air.

Slamming on the brake, Bishop grabbed the rifle with his good arm and rolled out of the vehicle, scrambling madly for a nearby elm tree. Cracking rounds passed over and around his body as he made for the protection of the trunk.

Bishop's entire left side was throbbing, the emergency movement and use of that arm generating debilitating waves of pain. With a grimace, he chanced a glance around the trunk, the exposure answered with shards of bark stinging his cheeks. Small eruptions of dirt nearby announced his attackers were trying to keep him pinned down – and they were succeeding.

Setting down the rifle, Bishop pulled the .45 from its holster and flipped off the safety. Faking a peek around the left side of the tree, he quickly rolled right and snapped three shots where he thought the shooters were located, pulling back just as two incoming rounds thwacked into the old elm.

During the brief exposure, he caught a glimpse of one assailant, the man shooting over the hood of a relic car 100 meters away. The pistol shots were worthless at that range – a realization that caused him to glance longingly at the rifle lying beside his leg.

Long ago, the instructors at HBR had made every contractor execute what they termed "wounded shooter" drills. Unpopular with the less-experienced personnel, the exercises encompassed shooting, reloading, and remedial action drills while only using one arm/hand.

Young, strong, and feeling invincible, Bishop had hated the workouts. His poor attitude and lack of effort during the drills had resulted in a scolding from one of the senior men. "You think you're fucking superman. You're walking around with this cocky-shit frame of mind that you'll never get hit. Let me tell you, son, that's a bullshit, short-sighted mindset. Shit happens on the battlefield. If you lose a hand or arm, you become a liability for not only yourself, but the team that has to protect your sorry ass. Learn to use that weapon one-handed, boy, or I won't let you work with my squad."

Invincible or not, Bishop went along. While he found there was no way a one-armed shooter could aim and control a weapon with the same proficiency as with both limbs, with work a man could put rounds down range.

Those lessons all came flooding back, as Bishop reached for the rifle.

Charging the weapon required squeezing it between his knees – not a graceful process, but a round made it into the chamber. Flicking off the safety was easy.

Again rolling right, he managed to raise the rifle to his shoulder one-handed. Sighting through the optic was difficult until he braced the weapon against the tree. He started pulling the trigger.

Decades of training had to be thrown out the window. There was no way he could center the dot on a target, let alone hold it there long enough to squeeze the trigger. Without his left hand providing a fulcrum for the weight of the weapon, the small circle bounced, weaved, and jumped anywhere but on target.

But it didn't matter. He wasn't trying to put down the attackers – he only wanted to keep them away. Bishop concentrated on maintaining the shots on a horizontal plane with his adversaries. Recoil was extremely difficult to manage one handed – barrel travel completely beyond his control. Still, round after round left the M4's muzzle, the 68-grain hollow points booming supersonic at 3600 feet per second.

Spray and pray, went through his mind as he continued to pump hot lead at the three men as fast as he could pull the trigger.

And Bishop could pull a trigger.

Two rounds a second slammed into the junk cars, sidewalks, light poles and tree trunks the hunters used for cover. Sparks flew, metal protested, and the air crackled with snapping death.

The men advancing on his position realized the difference between the pistol and rifle bullets. They all knew their target's sidearm was useless at more than 50 meters. The rifle, even with unsteady aim, was a different story. It didn't matter if the round impacted three feet away. If the lead slammed into the ground where a man was about to step, he hesitated before lifting his boot. It a bullet tore into a car fender and spewed shrapnel right past a man's head, he thought twice before exposing his face.

Even the mere chance of being hit by Bishop's seemingly inaccurate fire slowed their advance. Caution took time, and that's all Bishop was hoping for – buying time until help could arrive.

Firing two rounds a second bought Bishop 15 seconds, and then his bolt locked back – the rifle empty.

Ejecting the vacant magazine wasn't hard. Fishing the full mag from his back pocket was clumsy.

He flipped the weapon upside down, and while holding the hot barrel between his boots, shoved the full box of pain pills home. He turned the weapon right side up and punched the bolt-release, relieved when a round seated in the chamber – he was back in business. "You're a beautiful girl," he whispered to the rifle.

He poked his head around the tree and saw exactly what he expected – the enemy had utilized the time for a reload and was trying to advance.

Up came the barrel and back went the trigger, over and over and over again.

They had only managed to travel two blocks from their hideout when Mitchell noticed movement at the front of the church.

There he was - the man they'd been hunting. Mitchell's relief was short-lived, his stomach flipping when their target climbed aboard the golf cart. *Shit*, the deserter thought, *he's going to get away.*

When Bishop had pulled out and turned directly at them, Mitchell began yelling at his team, hastily ordering them to reposition for an ambush.

Mitchell had fired the warning shots at Bishop's ride, hoping the man would surrender or give up. The guy's reflexes were good, his choice of cover a lucky break.

Shaking his head in disgust at both his team and the luck of the man they were hunting, he had waved his men forward to press their advantage. The three pistol shots had been worthless bullshit.

When the rifle rounds began snapping over their heads, the former sergeant knew it was a different story.

The first half-block wasn't so difficult. Enough cover existed that it didn't take a war hero to move forward. That situation soon changed, however. Suddenly, Mitchell and his men were looking at 75 meters of open ground between them and the target. Even a bad shot like the guy hiding behind the tree could do some damage if they tried to rush.

"Pull back!" he shouted. "Every fucking rifle in this town is probably headed this way by now. Pull back to the rally point."

Nick was helping Diana work on a priority list for the community when their conversation was interrupted by distant popping noises. The obvious gunshots caused both to pause, both hoping it was someone target practicing or scaring off stray dogs.

Nick's eyebrows arched when the random pops became a fusillade of rapid, steady fire. A minute later, the radio squawked with activity. "Nick, Bishop's been ambushed. I can see he's still moving but don't know if he's hurt. We're chasing the three guys that jumped him."

Nick launched down the church steps two at a time and almost ran over Kevin who was standing by the front doors holding his weapon. The father's first inclination was to hold his son back, but he decided the extra pair of eyes might help.

The two hustled into a cart and soon found Bishop's parked buggy, complete with bullet holes. Nick spotted a pair of legs sticking out from behind a nearby tree.

Rushing over, Nick was relieved to find his friend's eyes open. "You okay, man?"

"Yeah… I am hurting from the old wound, but didn't get any new ones. That lady never said she was married, I swear I didn't know…."

Nick laughed, glad Bishop's cornball sense of humor hadn't suffered. "If Terri heard you say that, you'd be hurting a lot worse, buddy. Do you want me to take you back to the church?"

"Naw… just let me rest for a bit. Go find those bushwhacking-fuckwads, and put'em down for me, bro."

Nick's radio sounded again. "Nick, we've chased them to the old Berber house out on West Popular Street. They turned on us and shot Cory."

"On my way."

Nick turned to Kevin and said, "Stay here, and protect Bishop. Help should be coming. If you don't recognize the responders, warn them off first."

Kevin nodded and immediately took a knee beside Bishop, his head scanning right and left.

The route to the old Berber place led past the hotel where the contractors were staying. Deke and two of his men were walking down the sidewalk, all three loaded up with a full kit.

"Need a ride?" Nick asked, pulling up beside them.

"We heard the gunfire and thought we'd better see what was happening. Mind if we tag along?"

Nick said, "We can use all the help we can get."

Deke, Nick, and two contractors arrived, the golf cart riding low in the back from the weight of heavy men and their equipment. Deke's team immediately moved for cover, an old habit developed to stay alive when arriving at a hostile encounter.

Nick found four of his own men huddled in a ditch, two of them working on Cory's bleeding leg while the fourth kept watch on a distant house. Joining them behind the embankment, Nick's first concern was the wounded man. The former Green Beret's practiced eye scanned the injury and immediately ascertained the patient would make a full recovery. After patting Cory on the shoulder, Nick peered over the crest and asked, "What's the situation?"

Cory, grimacing in pain, motioned with his head, "We saw them running out this way. No one has lived in the Berber house since before the explosion. I was behind them on the cart, and they turned around and let loose with a bunch of rounds."

"And…"

"I made it to about 100 yards from the house when they opened fire. I flipped the cart over trying to dodge their shooting. Tony helped me get back."

Nick glanced up the driveway and saw the black wheels of a golf cart sticking into the air. He moved his focus to the home where the shooters were holed up and sighed. Whoever was in the house had picked a good spot. There was no cover for 150 yards in any direction, only open, barren desert, and patches of random weeds sprinkled with low cactus. The home was of block construction with small windows and shingle roof. He couldn't detect any movement.

"Deke, what do you think?"

The contractor had been evaluating the property since arriving and answered quickly. "This one's a bitch. I would go with a standoff if you're not concerned about the occupants. There's no way you get close to that place without somebody getting killed."

"That's exactly what I was thinking. There's no one in there I give a shit about other than having a healthy curiosity why they started shooting for no reason."

Glancing at Deke, Nick pointed to the right. "Any chance your team can make it around and cover the rear? You know once we open up, they're going to make a run for it."

"Got it," was the reply, quickly followed by the three Darkwater men moving out.

Nick turned to his crew and asked how much ammo was on hand. The answer wasn't good. "Tony, take Cory and get him back to the infirmary so they can do a proper job on that leg. Find Bishop at the church, and tell him I need to borrow his .308 and all the ammo he can spare."

A few minutes later Nick's people had their injured man loaded onto the cart and were speeding back into town.

While he waited, Nick watched the progress of Deke and his two men. Staying over 400 meters away from the home, the trio moved as well as any team he'd ever seen. Bounding from cover to cover, no two men ever moved at the same time, and their order was completely random. *No wonder these guys gave Bishop hell at his ranch,* thought Nick.

The sound of an electric hum and crunching gravel signaled the return of the golf cart, Tony parking the vehicle where it couldn't be seen from the distant home. Three more of Alpha's volunteers piled out of the electric ride, the men brandishing weapons and bags of ammunition.

Nick scurried back to meet the newest arrivals, smiling as Tony lifted an AR10 rifle from the seat. "He sent six full magazines, 20 rounds each," the man reported.

Hefting the rifle, Nick grunted, "I've got to hand it to Bishop, the man has excellent taste in firepower."

Pulling a white towel from the cart, Nick stuffed a corner in the barrel of the rifle and tested his white flag. Looking around at the curious men, he said, "Here goes nothing," and began walking toward the Berber homestead.

He hadn't made it 100 yards when a shot rang out from the house, the round puffing the desert sand in front of the big man. Turning immediately and running back to the ditch, he commented, "Fuck those guys."

Nick uncapped the 24-x scope mounted atop the rifle and began scanning the distant holdout. While he still couldn't detect any movement, the magnified optic allowed for a detailed examination of the premises. Making sure the weapon wasn't loaded, he swept right and zoomed in on Deke's team, verifying they were in position. Despite the double-check that no round was in the chamber, Nick didn't center the crosshairs on any friendly, a habit of safety developed long ago when using a weapon's optic to scout.

Tony whispered, "Are we going to rush the house, Nick?"

Shaking his head, the big man answered, "We're all going to stay right here... all safe and sound while I rain down pure hell on those stupid shits inside that trap."

"I don't understand? Won't they just stay in the house?"

"Walls don't stop bullets, Tony. Not even brick walls. As a matter of fact, a medium caliber rifle like this one will turn those walls into shrapnel."

"Really? That bad?"

"Watch. They won't be able to hole up in there forever, taking pot shots at the respectable citizens of Alpha."

Nick inserted a magazine into the big rifle, tugged once to make sure it was secure, and then slapped the bolt release. A round entered the chamber, and the rifle was ready to fire.

At his current distance of 450 meters, Nick made an educated guess at the bullet drop. Speaking quietly to Tony, he narrated his scouting. "So if I'm in that house, I'm trying to peek out the windows and make sure someone is not sneaking up on the place. Only the east-facing window has a view of both the front and side of the house, and that's where I'd put one man. I'd do the same in the back."

Nick paused for a moment to adjust his position and then continued. "So if I'm watching out that window, I would also want to cover the front door – just in case. That means I would be facing the front of the house, or on the north side."

Nick's view through the crosshairs was enlarged to the point where he could see old paint peeling from the window frame's exterior. There were ratty looking, off-white curtains covering the opening, and one pane of glass was cracked.

"Going hot," he said to everyone within earshot.

All eyes were on the distant structure when Nick sent the first round. A puff of dust appeared on the exterior wall a little low of where Nick had predicted a man would be hiding. Nick adjusted his aim and started firing in earnest.

Round after round ate at the blocks as Nick walked the shots around the home. After the first two shots in the vicinity of the window, Nick adjusted his aim and sent high velocity lead slamming into the wall at four to six inches above the floor.

Nick paused to change magazines, Tony taking advantage to ask, "Why are you shooting so low, Nick?"

With a grimace, Nick responded, "If you were in that house, wouldn't your ass be hugging the floor? Why waste the ammo firing above their heads? This way, we might injure one or two of them so they know we are serious, but not so much that we can't figure out what they are after."

After reloading, he paused and looked around at his team. There were a few bolt-action deer rifles, one shotgun, and an AR15 among the group. "Start putting rounds into that window – hit the curtains," he ordered. "We'll see if a little smoke helps those guys decide they've had enough."

"Smoke?" asked one of the shooters.

"That lead coming out of your barrel is hot... damn hot. Just about any cloth, like those curtains, will ignite if enough rounds hit it."

Serious amounts of lead started pummeling the hapless

structure. While the hunting rifles couldn't fire nearly as fast as the semi-automatics, they were chambered in a larger caliber, each shot causing more and more visible damage.

Damn, thought Nick, as he watched his team pummel the structure. *That has to be pure hell inside those walls.*

Sergeant Mitchell had been in a few firefights before, but those encounters were with American units that always held the upper hand. Now he knew what it felt like to be on the receiving end of a hopeless situation. Their attempt to interrogate that Bishop character had been an epic-fucking-fail and now they were pinned down inside this death-trap.

A choking cloud of dust filled the air while splinters and shreds of concrete flew everywhere. The sharp, snapping sounds of lead striking the exterior wall joined the constant rattle of debris striking the floor.

It was practically impossible for Mitchell to breathe or open his eyes. Bits of stinging mortar and shredded plaster were flying everywhere, the larger chucks causing pain as they struck his prone body. As the rounds moved away from his position, he took advantage of the brief pause and yelled for the closest private, "Get to the back of the house – now!"

The man didn't move. As Mitchell crawled past, he noticed a growing pool of purple underneath the body and knew one of the bullets had found its mark.

His other man was pinned down next to the window, frozen motionless by either fear or the swarming, stinging storm of incoming fire and the blizzard of deadly shrapnel it created.

Belly crawling toward the rear of the house, Mitchell found a spot that seemed to afford some protection, at least for the moment. As he adjusted his position, there was a slight give in the floor under his elbow. Curious, he felt around the wooden strips and detected a thin seam.

Mitchell pulled his knife and inserted it into a straight, obvious cut in the wooden planks. Prying with the blade, he was soon looking down into a small root cellar, the area just big enough to hold his body, about three feet deep. *Praise the lord*, he thought. *I don't like close places, but I'll do anything to get out of this death trap.*

A few moments later, Mitchell pulled the trapdoor closed over his head and relaxed.

Nick went back to spreading his shots at floor level, working the impact randomly to deliver maximum terror to the inhabitants. Three minutes later, a curtain began smoking, quickly followed by visible flames. Nick adjusted his aim to the window, waiting on someone to show up and extinguish the burning cloth. No one did. *Come out*, he thought. *Get out of there and surrender. Burning isn't a good way to go.*

He waited until the entire opening filled with a boiling black smoke, licks of red flame filling the now-glassless frame.

"Cease fire," he ordered. "They're dead."

"What?" asked a surprised Tony. "How do you know?"

"If anybody inside that house was alive, they would either be pouring out the doors or trying to put out the fire. I know – I was just inside a burning building. They're dead or unconscious, which is one and the same about now."

"Shouldn't we go try and pull them out?"

"No. I'm not risking a single man on that shit. They could have raised a white flag and surrendered. They had plenty of time."

Nick waved his team forward, and the men began a cautious movement toward the residence. Taking random turns, each would jog 15-20 steps and then go prone. By the time they were close to the structure, the blaze had spread to the roofline and flames showed clearly in three windows.

The team eventually halted their approach, the spreading inferno confirming Nick's prediction of zero survivors. Turning away in disgust, he faced the men and experienced a vision that was dark and troubling - medieval. A ring of men surrounded a burning home... human flesh inside... the reflection of the flames shining off the attackers' eyes, flickering reflections illuminating weapons of war.

Nick's mind visualized the Berber home as a castle, his team the victorious pike men and knights from an age long past. The haunting scene could have been a village in Vietnam, or an earthen hut in the path of a conquering Khan. *How many times has the vanquisher stood and watched a foe's stronghold burn to the ground? We're all thinking the same thing. Wondering what it would be like to be inside of that inferno – what it would feel like to be dying in such a way.* The primitive, raw darkness of the event was disturbing.

Deke moved to Nick's side, his perception and experience giving insight to Nick's thoughts. "Shit like this happens too often," the contractor commented, "but you did it the right way. There wasn't any other option."

Nick shook his head in disgust, "That doesn't make it any less fucked up. My mind is already polluted from seeing this shit too many times. You're probably right there with me." The big operator turned and pointed at his team, "But these guys are family men... civilians who didn't sign up for this bullshit. Peaceful men that shouldn't have to wake up in a damp sweat from the nightmares."

"You know it would feel a lot worse if we were preparing to bury one of your peaceful civilians right now. That would be a worse head-fuck. You did it the right way, man. Those guys in the house committed suicide – no one made them do it."

Nick nodded, appreciating Deke's words and the consideration behind them.

The big man turned to his men and shouted, "Let's get the fuck out of here."

Mitchell couldn't stay in the hole any longer. At one point, the heat from the fire had convinced him he was going to be baked alive in his subterranean oven, but it had faded just as he felt like he couldn't take any more. Then the thirst had started, no doubt the dehydration accelerated by the perspiration pouring from his pores to fight the heat.

Twice he had lifted his arm to push open the trapdoor, but the sound of what could have been human voices thwarted the attempt. Now, he didn't care if the burned-out home was surrounded by riflemen ready to shred his body to bits – he had to get out.

Slowly pushing up on his coffin lid, the rush of cool air entering the root cellar gave him strength. He had sensed darkness had fallen, but was relieved to glimpse a view of the night sky above. Opening the door further, he panicked for a moment when he met resistance. Timbers or part of the roof had collapsed on top of his exit and visions of being trapped forever and dying in the small space filled his mind.

Rearranging his body, a shoulder pushed by thrusting legs dislodged the debris, and he was free. Mitchell stood for two full minutes drinking the cool air, filling and refilling lungs that seemed unable to get enough.

He burned his hand slightly when he reached for a handhold to climb out. Some of the surrounding bits of charred timber still smoldered red beneath their carbon black surface. The second handhold was cool to the touch, and then he was standing in the middle of the ruins.

Walking out of the destroyed structure required caution as well - hotspots, collapsed walls, and still smoldering roof joists creating an obstacle course. When his boots hit dirt, he felt like shouting out in celebration, but held the release. Scanning right and left without seeing any movement, the ex-Sergeant hustled off into the Texas night.

Lou didn't recognize Mitchell at first. When the ex-soldier stepped from behind the wall, his appearance startled the security boss.

The arrangement had been that someone would drive to the rendezvous point every other night for a week. As soon as the spies had done their work, they would sneak out of town and be picked up a few miles outside of Alpha.

Mitchell's face was thick with smeared ash, soot and dirt, the affect making him look like he had risen from the dead, or at best had found employment as a chimney sweep. Lou's memory of a neat, well-kept individual didn't match with the disheveled, vagabond looking man approaching his truck. Torn, filthy clothing almost as dark as the man's complexion indicated that the mission to Alpha hadn't gone as planned.

When Mitchell opened the passenger door, a nauseating wave of odor filled the cab, the offending reek a combination of smoke, body odor, and other foul ingredients Lou could not identify. "Water," was the first scratchy word out of his mouth.

Lou reached and tossed Mitchell a plastic bottle of water and then watched as it was drained in only a few gulps. "More?"

"There's a case in the bed of the truck, help yourself."

After watching Mitchell consume two whole bottles, Lou asked, "What about the other two?"

"They didn't make it. Alpha's security forces are more aggressive than anyone anticipated."

"Did you find out where the juice is coming from?"

Nodding while he sipped another bottle, Mitchell said, "Yes. Their electricity is generated by a windmill farm dozens of miles south of town in the desert. I talked with an old dude who claimed to have worked for the power company before he retired. He was bragging about some dangerous adventure to Fort Stockdale to reroute the electrical power back to Alpha. He went on and on about a gunfight and narrow escape. I think most of it was bullshit, but that's what he said."

Lou rubbed his chin, "Windmills, eh? Now that makes sense. I'm not sure how Mr. Lewis will react to that news, but it answers a whole ton of questions. Any information about the gold?"

Shaking his head, Mitchell replied, "No. That's what I was angling for when we were discovered."

"Let's get going. You need to ride back with the window down, pal."

Nick tested the floor with his boot, unsure if the charred wood could support his weight. Stepping gingerly into the Berber home, he began cautiously poking around the ruins. Tony and a few others had joined the big man; Nick wanted to verify three bodies had been cremated in the fire, the others having a morbid curiosity to return to the scene of the crime.

"I've got one back here," announced Tony, his grim expression indicating he had found a body.

Nick stepped over and around debris until he was at his man's side. Looking down at the grisly remains, Nick noticed the barrel of a weapon lying beside what was left of the body. Reaching down, he tapped the barrel to test its temperature and then pulled what had been an AR15 from the ashes.

The plastic components of the weapon were disfigured, the stock transformed into thin, sticky strings of black goo. The rounds in the magazine had cooked off, mangling the thin steel case almost beyond recognition. Unsure if there was even a single salvageable part left, Nick went to toss the junk to the yard when something unusual caught his eye.

Right beneath the magazine release was an oddly shaped bulge. Having held a weapon similar to this for most of his adult life, Nick had never seen any modification, aftermarket part, or feature that would account for the disfiguration.

Nick removed his glove and tried to wipe the black carbon off the rifle. A mouth full of spit and more rubbing eventually resulted in the mystery being solved. Someone had attached an inventory tag to the weapon, which was atypical of most government organizations and even private security firms.

Rubbing more grime from the small steel label, Nick shifted and held the weapon in the air to catch better light. "Property of Lewis Brothers Oil, Midland Station, Texas," he mumbled as he deciphered the tag. Lowering the rifle, Nick glanced at Tony and asked, "Ever heard of them?"

"Yeah, they're a big outfit over that way. Why would an oil company have its own inventory of rifles?"

Nick pondered the question for a moment before answering. "More importantly, why would guys with company rifles be shooting at us?"

Before Tony could reply, one of the other men called. "Nick, you better come back here."

Stepping around more rubble, Nick found two of the searchers staring at a root cellar, the trapdoor wide open. It occurred to him instantly that someone had ridden out the fire down in the hole. "Fuck! That is the oldest trick in the damned book," was the big man's response. "I can't believe I didn't think of that."

Tony stepped over and glanced at the hole. "Only one of them got away. I found the other body over there. His weapon had the same inventory label."

Nick scanned the desert surrounding the burned out residence, hoping to detect the survivor scampering away or hiding nearby. Realizing it was a waste of time, he looked at his men and said, "I'm out of this pop stand – let's head back to town."

Fort Stockdale, Texas
February 14, 2016

The man limping along the sidewalk looked like hundreds of others the guards had seen since the collapse. Stooped shoulders, an uneven gait, filthy clothes, and an unshaven face were all indicators of a man down on his luck – a guy who had been wandering around aimlessly for a long time.

The pull-along suitcase being towed by the hobo appeared to have seen better days as well. The dusty, black canvas shell sported patches here and there, lengths of duck-tape securing the torn exterior. The zipper was clearly broken, random lengths of cloth sticking out of a partial opening along one side. A ragged looking strand of rope secured a wad of newspaper and additional rags to the handle.

One of the enforcers elbowed his partner, nodding in the direction of the vagabond. "Another bag person – it's been a while since we've seen any new arrivals."

"I'll go make sure he finds his way to the camps. They can deal with him down there."

“Hurry, the DA will be coming out in a little bit. You know she gets upset when we have homeless people wandering around.”

“No problem,” and with that, the former deputy ambled toward the new arrival.

Nick saw the guard approaching out of the corner of his eye. He started singing an off-key verse of “Onward, Christian Soldiers,” as the man came within earshot.

The enforcer stopped cold when he detected Nick’s body odor. Deciding to keep his distance, he said, “Hey – you can’t hang around here, buddy. We’ve got a special place for people like you. You need to turn around and head down to the river.”

Nick ignored the fellow, singing his song and shuffling along.

“Are you deaf?” the man challenged.

I can hear you just fine, thought Nick. *Just keep following me a few more steps until your friends can’t see us.*

The enforcer had never been completely ignored before and wasn’t sure how to react. His first instinct was to call over one of the other guys for help, but the teasing he’d receive wasn’t worth it. This bum was tall, but looked old and worn down. Deciding instead to get in front of the man, he trotted a few steps and then stood directly in Nick’s path.

Nick sidestepped the guy, hardly missing a beat of his scuffing gait.

“Fuck,” muttered the enforcer. Pausing for a moment, he became angry, caught up to Nick, and grabbed his shoulder. “Hey I’m talking to....”

Nick reached across his body, grabbing the wrist on his shoulder and pulling hard. The attack caught the guard completely by surprise, his off-balance body surging forward. Before he could regain his equilibrium, Nick was behind him. The last place on earth any man wanted to be was in front of an ex-Green Beret with his back turned. In one fluid motion, Nick’s left boot kicked out, the blow landing squarely in the back of the enforcer’s knee. As the leg collapsed, Nick’s left arm circled the unfortunate fellow’s neck, a ring of steel-hard muscle applying enormous pressure to the helpless man's throat. Turning slightly to the side while tightening the hold, Nick braced his victim's weight on his hip and lifted.

Kicking didn't do any good - twisting didn't help. There was no air in his lungs to yell, not that the crushing pressure on his windpipe would have allowed such an act. Less than two minutes passed before the man in Nick's arms choked out, the limp body lifted effortlessly over the hobo's shoulder and carried quickly behind a nearby building. Checking the guard's pulse, Nick found he pulled the hold just in time – the guy was breathing, but wouldn't swallow anything but liquids for a few days.

Two hundred meters away, Deke watched the activity through a pair of binoculars. Grunting, he said "One down."

"He was too slow applying the hold," commented one of the other operators, also watching through his optic.

"I'll let you take that up with him when we get back," chided Deke.

The second sentry looked up to see the same bum shuffling down the sidewalk, this time going the opposite direction. Glancing around for his buddy, the guard shook his head wondering where his friend had wandered to. *Maybe this dude smells so bad he had to puke*, he thought.

Trotting across the street, the second approach played out much like the first. After Nick ignored the guard's verbal challenge, the anxious sentry stepped in front of Nick and shoved his rifle barrel into the hobo's chest.

Allowing a potential threat to be within reaching distance of your weapon is never a good idea. Doing so when the rifle is attached to your body by a sling is an additional error. Poking a potential adversary in the chest with a slung weapon that clearly has its safety engaged can be fatal.

With the AR15's flash suppresser against his sternum, Nick did the exact opposite of what his foe expected. He stepped forward, shoving the weapon and its owner backwards. As fast as a striking snake, Nick's right hand slapped the barrel away from his torso while the sentry was still off-balance. Stepping nose-close to the shocked fellow, Nick grabbed the sling with both hands and pulled forward at the same time as he reared back and then slammed his forehead into the opponent's nose. The sound of crunching cartilage was audible for several feet.

Nick caught the guard's unconscious body as it fell, pulling the man into a fireman's carry and scurrying off, blood for his victim's face dripping on the sidewalk with every step.

Deke pulled away from his optic and ordered, "Two down. Let's get moving." Simultaneously, the nine contractors rose from their positions and began moving toward the courthouse. Nick's removal of the two sentries exposed one whole side of the structure for their approach. Like a chair with four legs, remove one support, and the seat will fall over - Fort Stockdale's security had just lost a leg.

"Could you guys slow down just a little," complained Terri, desperately trying to keep up with the squad. "I'm going on six months pregnant back here."

Grinning, Deke waved the rest of his team forward and then hung back to escort the lady. Doing her best to keep up, Terri was winded by the time they arrived at the corner. Panting, she whispered, "No one mentioned marathon running. Wait until I complain to my travel agent. This was not in the brochure."

Deke rolled his eyes and whispered back, "You've been hanging around your husband too long."

Deke's team of contractors split up. Two of the men rushed to join Nick, the big man busy assembling the rifle and chest rig stashed inside his hobo suitcase. Three members split right, their mission to subdue the sentries stationed on the east side of their target. The remaining operators made for the north, their task to secure that side of the courthouse square.

Deke, keeping his solemn word to Bishop, stayed back to protect Terri.

Fort Stockdale's enforcers were no match for Deke's contractors. The skills, aggression, and experience of the assaulters overwhelmed the remaining security without a single shot fired - but that had been the plan all along.

DA Gibson finished her morning routine with a flurry, having burned the first two slices of homemade pita bread she was warming. In addition to being disgusted with wasting the food, she was feeling the first touches of a winter cold in her sinuses.

Rising from her desk, she opened her door and surveyed the weather – a cloudy day for a change.

"Hello."

While the sound of a female voice startled her, focusing on the scene outside her office made her heart truly race. Instead of the expected group of enforcers, a dozen armed strangers stood with weapons.

The first question that flashed through her mind was, "Where are my people?" The answer became obvious when her attention was drawn by a low moan. Her focus zeroed on a man lying on the ground nearby, his face a bloody mess. The rest of her security detail was all there as well, on their knees with their hands behind their heads. A pile of weapons was stacked a few yards away.

"You must be the boss lady around here," said the woman standing at the front of the strangers.

Pat straightened, her chest expanding with air. "I am. I am District Attorney Patricia Gibson, acting mayor of Fort Stockdale. Why have you attacked my men and my city?"

Terri smiled, crossing her arms. "I don't think you're in much of a position to be asking questions, District Attorney Patricia Gibson. As a matter of fact, I don't believe this town is yours any longer."

Taking a step closer to the other woman, Terri's voice became low and mean. "You don't have much longer to live, madam. If it were up to me, I would've shot you on sight. But, lucky for you, I gave my word that I would at least give you the chance to be heard. That's probably more of a courtesy than you extended to those people we saw crucified on the way into town."

"We didn't crucify anyone. Those people were already dead. The town was being overwhelmed by refuges from the interstate, and we hung those bodies up there to deter strangers."

Terri shook her head in disgust. "And why, pray tell, do you brand the bodies of small children?"

"We don't have a jail, jailers or any way to separate criminals from the general population. There's no database of felons... no way to protect the honest citizens of Fort Stockdale from the predators. If you are caught stealing, you are branded. If you are caught stealing again, or worse, you're exiled into the desert. It's the only justice system we could come up with, given the circumstances."

"I've seen small girls branded by your *system of justice*. Only a ruthless, heartless person would mutilate a child like that."

It was Pat's turn to get aggressive. "You're damned right I'm ruthless and heartless. What other choice do I have? We lost half the town in the first three months due to starvation and diseases. Citizens were stealing from each other, strangers were invading our town and taking food from elderly residents. Friends of mine were murdered for a slice of bread and a hunk of moldy meat. I'd like to know how you or anyone else could have saved the people we did without being ruthless and heartless."

"And the slave labor camps? How do you explain that Miss Gibson? I've interviewed numerous people who toiled at hard labor for nothing more than starvation rations. What convenient excuse do you have for that?"

Pat's smile was genuine, "Before I answer that, where did you interview these 'slaves?'"

"In Alpha. They are showing up in significant numbers – seeking freedom and a better life."

"And how did they get there? Do they claim to have escaped? Did they sneak off in the middle of the night? I'm not a very good slave master if I'm letting my property run free. No one is forced to stay in those camps. The inhabitants can leave anytime they want. They receive the same rations of food as everyone else, which isn't much, but it is all we have."

Terri paused her interrogation, the conversation not going the direction she had anticipated. While she was considering the woman's answers, Deke spoke up from behind her. "Miss Terri, we're drawing a lot of attention."

Looking around, Terri could see several people had gathered

nearby, the throng appeared to be comprised of ordinary folks that just discovered a celebrity in their town square. She started to step toward the crowd, her instincts wanting to hear what they had to say, but she paused and looked at the DA, trying to judge her reaction.

"Go on," motioned the woman on trial. "Go on, and talk to them. Talk to as many as you want. If I'm the horrible monster you make me out to be, they'll tell you."

"Come with me," answered Terri.

The two women made for the crowd, their first stop an elderly couple. Smiling, DA Gibson said, "Mr. and Mrs. Reynolds, did we get that leak fixed?"

The wife took Gibson's hand warmly, patting it with affection. "Yes, and thank you Pat for sending those men over."

Mr. Reynolds looked over Pat's shoulder at the armed men, and then suspiciously at Terri. "Is everything all right, Pat?"

Terri extended her hand, "My name is Terri, and I brought these men with me from Alpha. We heard that things weren't going very well here, and we thought we might be able to help."

"Why are the enforcers on their knees?"

"We thought they might be part of the problem," Terri said honestly.

The old man nodded, finally understanding. "They get a little rough now and then. I've watched them out my window. If they do, I let Pat know, and she tones them down. The world's a dangerous place now, Terri. Sometimes it takes rough men to keep peace and order."

Terri and Pat spent the next 15 minutes talking to random strangers in the crowd. After several interviews, Terri motioned for the DA to walk with her.

"I've made a horrible mistake," admitted Terri. "I let rumors, incomplete information, and circumstances cloud my judgment. Please accept my apology."

Pat nodded, relaxing just a bit. "Apology accepted."

Terri turned to Deke and said, “Let DA Gibson’s men go. Give them their weapons back.”

Deke started to question the wisdom of Terri’s instructions, but shrugged his shoulders and nodded to his men.

“Terri, tell me about Alpha. I’ve heard rumors and stories myself, but haven’t really believed any of it.”

The two women continued their stroll, exchanging information and becoming fast friends. An hour later, they returned to the courthouse, smiling and laughing together. Deke couldn’t believe his eyes, but was in fact relieved that there wasn’t going to be any large-scale confrontation.

Lou and his team approached the substation on foot, their pickup trucks parked behind a slight rise a few hundred yards away.

It had been easy to follow the high-voltage power lines to the small, concrete-block building – just as Mr. Cameron Lewis had predicted. They had scouted the area with binoculars for 15 minutes, and not seeing any sign of people, were advancing carefully toward the structure.

Watching the LBO team deploy and surround the station, Cameron’s words echoed in Lou’s head. “If we cut off the electricity, Alpha won’t be such an attractive place. We can then approach their leaders with our gasoline and get a better exchange rate of food for our fuel. If we can reroute the power here to Midland Station, it’s a double bonus for us.”

An LBO engineer stood next to Lou, the man clearly nervous about their mission. “What if they start shooting at us?” the man asked, wiping the sweat from his brow.

“Don’t worry, I brought 25 of my best men. There’s more than enough of us to handle the locals. We’ve heard from stragglers that there’s only about 15 guys with guns in the whole town.”

“Sure seems like a bigger place than that,” responded the engineer.

"We'll be fine. You just do your job when we get that building secured – leave the security to me."

Right on cue, one of Lou's lieutenants signaled the coast was clear.

It took two of Lou's men working a long crowbar to open the steel door. Once the portal was clear, the engineer entered the building and began to study the equipment inside.

Terri was still engaged with Pat, the two women discussing everything from health care to gardens. The ambassador, realizing the meeting was going to last a while, stuck her head outside and said, "Deke, you and the guys can tour the town or just hang out if you feel like it, we are going to be a while."

Deke nodded, his response interrupted by shouting from across the street. All eyes turned to see a man wearing a suit and carrying a Bible come running into the square, yelling for one of the enforcers.

"There are dozens of armed men down by my church," the breathless man declared. "They're all standing around that power-building-thing. Lots of them!"

"Settle down now, padre," the enforcer soothed. "Tell me again what you saw."

"There are bunches of armed men I've never seen before.... I was walking out of the church to visit Mrs. Hutchinson, and they were all over the place."

Pat appeared at Terri's side, a questioning look on her face. "There's nothing down at that end of town but a church, some empty houses, and that utility building. Yet, this is the second time something weird has been going on. A few weeks ago, someone started shooting at a funeral."

Terri flushed red, looking down she commented, "That was my husband... sorry...." Terri realized now wasn't the time for a confession. She continued, "That's the power grid substation for the windmill farm I was telling you about. That building controls the entire gird."

A puzzled look crossed Pat's face, but before she could ask another question, Terri was giving Deke instructions.

"Deke, if the equipment in that building gets hurt, or someone switches things around, Alpha could lose its electricity. We can't let that happen – do you understand?"

The Darkwater contractor nodded.

Terri's voice went low. "Keep that building under our control and use any means necessary." The ambassador then turned to Pat and said, "I don't know who's messing around down there, but if your people could help, it would benefit everyone."

DA Gibson didn't waste any time. "Go help these men," she ordered the closest enforcer.

Terri ducked inside Gibson's office, returning a moment later with her rifle.

"Where are you going?" Pat asked.

"They might need help," was Terri's reply.

Lou's earpiece sounded, "I've got armed men moving this direction – lots of them. It looks like the welcoming committee knows we're here."

"Shit! So much for a quick in and out," Lou said to himself.

Pulling out a white handkerchief and wrapping it around the end of his rifle, Lou began walking toward the advancing force, praying they would honor a white flag. He had zero intent of negotiating much of anything, the entire effort a ruse to buy his engineer more time.

He walked 100 yards past his lookout's position and waited, watching with mild interest as the men of Fort Stockdale approached.

Nick stayed with Terri and Pat, the big man very uncomfortable with the 50-yard gap between the women and the advancing line of men ahead. The distance had been a hastily negotiated compromise with Terri – the woman in his charge insistent on keeping close to the men.

A runner appeared, the breathless man reporting, "There's some dude with a white flag standing in the road like he's waiting on us."

Looking back at the ambassador, Nick asked, "How do you want to play it?"

"Sounds too easy to me," replied Terri while glancing at Pat. "I want Deke to take his guys and quietly work their way around to their back. Pat and I will go see what this guy wants, but if I take off my hat, I want Deke and his crew to knock the shit out of those guys. We'll let Pat's enforcers be visible – maybe hold their attention."

Nick smirked, "I love it," and turned to the runner, snapping out instructions for the Alpha contractors. He then turned and said, "I'm staying with you two. Let's go see what this guy wants."

The trio approached to within ten feet. Pat spoke first, "Who are you, and why have you brought armed men into my town?"

The question had been anticipated, Lou's response immediate. "My name is Lou, and I'm from Midland Station. I'm here because someone has hijacked our electrical power. It is controlled from that building behind me, and our city leaders sent me to get it back."

"You're a liar," Terri announced. "That electrical power had been turned off for months before we fixed the controls and routed it back to Alpha. We solved the problem, we own the juice."

Lou grinned at the pregnant woman's tenacity. "Claim what you want, lady. From my point-of-view, possession is nine-tenths of the law, and right now, I'm in possession of the control station."

Terri didn't like Lou's attitude, but that wasn't her primary focus. Alpha had to keep its electrical power – there was no other option. "I'm going to give you one chance to back down, mister. Round up your people and head on back to Midland Station. If you don't, a lot of folks are going to get hurt."

Lou shrugged. "The men I have with me are professionals. I outnumber your forces. We are going to reroute the power back to where it belongs and then sabotage the equipment so it can't be switched back. From where I'm standing, I don't think there's shit you can do about it."

Terri reached for her hat and paused, trying to think of any other way around the situation. She wondered how many times this same scene had been played out in the old American West. She had read the history of range wars – many of those long, bloody fights lasting years and killing dozens of people. Were the next range wars going to be fought over electricity? Was this going to be an ongoing problem?

Refocusing on the problem at hand, Terri lowered her hand and said, "I guess we don't have anything else to talk about. This powwow is over. We're coming in to take our property back in two minutes. I suggest you return to your men, or this big guy next to me is going to shoot your ass."

Lou shrugged and turned away, walking nonchalantly back toward the substation and his team.

Nick cleared his throat and looked at his watch, "I suggest you ladies take cover in that ditch. I don't think our new friend is going to wait two minutes."

"Neither am I," replied Terri and after three steps toward the ditch, she took off her hat.

Deke had been watching the exchange through his scope and knew from the body language that the meeting hadn't gone well. He and his men were perfectly positioned to hit the flank of the 20 or so men he could see spread around the substation.

He had ordered his team to use a tactic they called "concentrated ordnance," a method where all of the contractors engaged a single target rather than each man selecting an individual foe. All rifles would pour lead onto a single man and then move on after that enemy was down.

When Terri took off her hat, Deke turned to his group and simply ordered, "Fire."

Eight rifles exploded in unison, all of them focused on one man 100 meters directly in front of the contractors. When the first salvo impacted the unfortunate fellow, his body began dancing like it had been exposed to high voltage current.

The next three men suffered similar fates within seconds.

After eliminating those four, Deke's people began to receive haphazard, light, incoming fire. Compared to what the contractors were accustomed to, it was nothing more than a mild annoyance.

Deke's team split into three, three-man groups and began their advance. The men from Midland Station had never seen anything like it.

It wasn't a fair fight. Bullying the cowed, starving citizens of Midland Station was one thing, taking on well-armed, professional warriors completely another. Like a pro football team would roll over a squad from a junior high school, the Darkwater men cut the opposition to ribbons in a mere minutes.

Pat's enforcers didn't stand idly by and watch. As soon as Deke's fire attracted the attention of the defenders to their front, the men from Fort Stockdale began their advance, squeezing Lou's team from two different directions.

Nick led the group, the ex-Special Forces operator leveling devastating fire while shouting orders and pushing the attackers forward. While no cowards, the enforcers had never seen a man fight like Nick, his leadership skills taking control without anyone having declared him to be in command. The Fort Stockdale shooters just naturally fell into following his lead.

Nick moved, laid down fire and shouted commands in a whirlwind of efficiency and control. The results were obvious – the defenders to their front were completely ineffective, soon falling into absolute chaos.

Lou was surprised when the gunfire erupted to the north. He had 25 of his best men spread around the substation, but the majority were facing the known foes approaching from town. He tried to adjust his forces, but communication was next to impossible with weapons discharging all around. The screams of dying men, combined with the panicked shouting of the living, didn't help facilitate Lou's wishes.

It became all too clear that the threat from the north was the more serious. Every man he did manage to move to that side of the compound was cut down before he could take more than a few steps. When his last two remaining shooters suddenly stood up and turned to retreat, he watched in horror as their bodies jerked wildly from the impact of dozens of bullets, then fell lifeless to the ground.

Glancing around the corner of the control station, he was stunned to see what appeared to be combat troops at the edge of the grounds. Lou started shouting, "Fall back! Fall back!"

The leader of the Midland Station invaders began running.

The men facing the enforcers faired only marginally better. Nick's people driving them back, yard by yard – the onslaught relentless and brutal. It was too late when the Midland men realized they had been flanked. Deke's team was behind them before they could pull back. Most of the LBO men threw down their weapons and raised their hands – a foolhardy few tried to fight their way out. They fell quickly.

One of Deke's teams entered the substation and found a single man inside. Unarmed and standing in a pool of urine, the terrified man kept pleading, "I'm an engineer… I'm an engineer."

Lou made it back to the trucks, shocked when he realized only four of his force had made it out alive. Worried they would be pursued, each man jumped into a truck and began spinning the wheels to escape across the desert.

Terri and Pat rushed up as soon as the shooting ended. Both women ignored the carnage and made for the substation where a man was on his knees, one of the enforcers keeping guard.

"Did you turn off the power to Alpha?" Terri asked.

"No, I didn't have time. The circuit is still routed west."

Exhaling, Terri turned to Pat and said, "That was close."

Nick walked up carrying an extra rifle. Showing the weapon to

Terri, he pointed to the Lewis Brothers Oil inventory tag. “This is just like the ones we found in Alpha – the guys who tried to ambush Bishop carried identical weapons. This asshole in Midland Station is becoming a real pain in the backside.”

Terri nodded, “He sent men to steal our food, tried to kill my husband, and now they tried to take the electricity. I’m beginning to dislike whoever is calling the shots over there.”

The man on his knees spoke up, “You would be referring to one Mr. Cameron Lewis. He’s the one in charge of things over in Midland Station.”

Nick sighed, “I’ve heard that name before,” and then the big man stepped menacingly close to the prisoner. “Are you sure he’s the only guy causing all this bullshit?”

Pushing his glasses up his nose, the engineer nodded rapidly, his frightened eyes never leaving Nick. “Oh, yes. There’s no doubt – he’s the man who runs the whole town.”

Nick looked at Terri, “Well, Madam Ambassador, what next?”

Terri’s finger found her chin. After thinking for a bit, she looked down at the man on his knees and motioned for him to stand up. Ignoring the smell of urine, she calmly asked, “Is there any way you can go back inside that little building and route some of that precious electricity to Fort Stockdale?”

The engineer didn’t hesitate long. “Sure, this town is a sub-relay off the main grid. All you would have to do is reset that equipment, and it should come on.”

Pat smiled, “Oh my gawd, Terri – that would be a miracle.”

“Let’s see if we can reroute some juice to Fort Stockdale right away.” Terri further advised the engineer to prepare DA Gibson’s people for the potential complications of restarting the electricity in hopes of avoiding the fires that plagued the other towns when current began to flow again.

“I have just one request, Pat, before we head back to Alpha,” the ambassador-negotiator postulated. “Do you think you can spare a little bath water for my friend Nick here? I need to return him to Alpha with a better scent than that ‘Eau de Lack of Personal Hygiene’ he is sporting right now. I can guarantee you will have the mayor of Alpha in your debt for that small act of kindness. It *is* Valentine's Day, after all."

Two of Deke's men were assigned to retrieve their transport, the pickups hidden on the outskirts of town before their infiltration that morning.

Terri finally exited the courthouse, a look of satisfaction beaming from her face. On the way out of town, she glanced at Deke and announced, "We've just added another city to our little coalition. DA Gibson is going to hold an election and then tour Meraton to see the market. Fort Stockdale has agreed to work with Alpha and Meraton on defense, food production, energy and several other projects. They want to join our alliance."

"Really? That's great news," replied Deke. "What do you call your alliance?"

"What do you mean?"

"It seems like to me you're building up a little country… a small state at least. A phoenix rising from the ashes."

Terri smiled at her driver. "You know, you're right. Maybe we should call it the Alliance of West Texas, or something like that."

Deke laughed, "I love it!"

Chapter 9

Not all of the Alliance's expansion was initiated from within. With word of a better life spreading rapidly throughout the region, the council was occasionally solicited by other outlying islands of humanity. Rule of law, electrical power, trade, education, and the opportunity of a better life resulted in the coalition being approached by a few towns for membership or an association at minimum.

The first was the minute village of Preston, Texas. Nothing more than an intersection with a single store, gas station, and a smattering of residences, two representatives of the community arrived at Alpha's south welcoming center one morning and asked to see whoever was in charge.

"We want to be conquered," announced the ad-hoc mayor of the berg. "There are 31 people still alive in our little settlement, and we conducted a vote of the entire population last Tuesday. The ballot consisted of a single question, 'Should we ask to join your new country or not?'"

"Go on," managed Terri, barely keeping a straight face.

"All 31 citizens voted, with 30 wanting to join. One person abstained."

Diana cleared her throat, "I don't understand what you mean by, 'You want to be conquered.' We don't have folks stroll in here every day with a request like that. What are you looking for, exactly?"

The gentleman interrupted Diana's question with a chuckle. "Preston isn't the issue. It's the farms and ranches just south of us who really need organization and help. Their crops are rotting in their fields. They don't have electricity, fuel or the capability to store next year's seed. Preston isn't much value to anyone, but the farmers along the Rio Grande are. That's why we want to be conquered."

Terri leaned back in her chair and responded. "Sir, we don't invade towns. We don't even have an army. Even if I did send some men to the town, having a 'war' would result in people being hurt or killed. There has to be a better way."

The man nodded, "No one in Preston is going to fight you, ma'am. We don't have the energy or the time. The farmers along the border are scared - trying to walk a tightrope. They are Americans, but in their minds, there's no America anymore. Right across the river, there are remnants of the old Mexican army, drug cartels, and even some officials of the now overthrown régime. Those people need to know there *is* an America, or at least an organized government to their north, resembling America."

Diana asked, "Why do you think joining our merry band will help?"

"The population on the other side of the border is larger than on our side, at least in the immediate region. There are more and more sporadic rumors of rogue groups crossing the river. Reports of rustling, looting, and attempts at intimidation are on the rise. If your government shows up in Preston with a show of force and takes over, word will spread all along the river. We firmly believe it will give the farmers backbone and cause the troublemakers on the other side to think twice before crossing into our territory."

Terri nodded, having heard similar stories. It seemed that humanity had divided into two groups, those who produced and those who survived by preying on the producers. *It's probably always been that way*, she mused. *It probably will never change.*

Diana surprised Terri with the bluntness of her next question. "What's in it for the Alliance?"

The expression on the visitor's face showed that he had anticipated the question. "Food... lots of food. Right now, the fields along the river are full of crops. If the Alliance can deliver diesel and gasoline, the harvest would fill several warehouses to the brim."

Terri looked at Diana, the two women exchanging nods. Diana spoke next, "I can offer you accommodations for the night. The council will meet in the morning, and I'll make sure your request is on the agenda. Attend the assembly because I'm sure there will be additional questions. You'll have our answer by the time you leave here tomorrow."

'Thank you," replied both guests. "That's all we can ask."

An assistant escorted the two visitors to nearby lodging. Terri and

Diana sat and pondered their situation.

"I wonder if I'll ever get used to hearing these stories?" began Diana.

"We have to bring them in under our wing. They're no different than any other group of folks that have joined us so far, and if what they're saying about the crops is accurate, that could mean survival for us all."

Diana rose and pointed to the map of Texas hanging on the wall. "But this is growth in the wrong direction. We need to be expanding toward the east, not the southwest."

Terri sighed, understanding Diana's logic. The subject had been discussed over and over again, the facts undeniable. With the exception of El Paso, everything was to the east. Oil and gas fields, refining, population… all in the eastern part of the state.

Diana continued, "We are spreading our resources thin as it is right now. Who knows what predators those people are facing? There's no telling how many criminals are orbiting around those ranches and farms. Our security people are already stretched thin, and adding another big slice of mostly unoccupied territory is going to make the situation worse."

"Diana, our system is working, and we can't lose faith in it. We're helping more and more people every single day, and it's paying off. Who knows what skills those people have in that little town? Not to mention, we could sorely use our own 'breadbasket.' The more citizens that join our effort, the more experience, knowledge, and momentum our society inherits."

The deacon nodded and then laughed aloud. "Do you know what this reminds me of? You and I sound just like the federal government when they were debating immigration issues. How many immigrants should we allow in? Do they help? Do they hurt? We're beginning to sound like Washington politicians."

Terri covered her mouth in mock terror. "Say it isn't so! Oh my goodness, Diana, if it's come to that, we should retire right now and let Bishop and Nick put us out to pasture."

Both of the women laughed, but Diana's point wasn't lost on either. Terri rose to leave the office, pausing at the door. "I know neither of us want to follow in the footsteps of the previous government, but we can't assume everything they did was a mistake. We would be foolish to dismiss something just because Washington did it. They weren't wrong all of the time."

Deacon Brown grinned at Terri and replied, "You're right again, old wise one with the baby bump. We need to keep that in mind going forward."

The Coalition Council consisted of an elected mayor from each town within the Alliance. The normally scheduled meeting was each Monday morning at 8am, but special powwows could be called with two days' notice by any member, the HAM radio operators always giving the council's messages priority.

The location of the meeting rotated from major town to major town. Despite Alpha being the unofficial capital of the newly formed government, Terri thought it important not to establish a "seat of power." Bishop's words were a constant companion in her ear, "Know the people. Work, live, walk and talk with them. How can any government be 'by the people, for the people,' if it doesn't *know* the people?"

Terri thought her husband's words were sage advice and thus she tried to spend as much time visiting the other population centers as possible.

It was Alpha's turn to host this week's meeting. Diana, Pete, Pat and the other representatives used the old city council's chambers on the second floor of the courthouse. The public was welcome to attend, and the seats were typically full. Firearms were checked at the entrance to the courthouse.

Every meeting included an open forum where the public was allowed to speak, raise issues, and comment to the council. Some discussions were heated, others intellectual. Terri had always made it clear that the council meetings weren't the place to settle disputes or identify new issues. There were representatives and processes for both situations.

On this day, the council decided to accept Preston's application for annex. The assembly agreed it would raise the security forces necessary from the usual sources, including the contractors, volunteer security, and law enforcement.

Terri had made plans to have lunch with Bishop, the couple deciding to splurge at Alpha's newest café. The original restaurant's kitchen and dining room had been thoroughly ransacked after the collapse, a state common to any building that was thought to possess food. The resulting damage required outside seating, each table protected by a dark blue umbrella.

A young Latino woman seated them, producing a single page, handwritten menu. The bill of fare had obviously been copied on a machine, but to Bishop and Terri it was as fancy as any. There were three dishes available, all prepared on the barbecue grill residing just a few feet from the patio. Water was the only offered beverage offered by the establishment. The experience was a true luxury, and after ordering, the two sat and gazed as if they were on a Paris boulevard primed to visit the shops.

Bishop sipped his drink and smiled at Terri. "How did the council meeting go?"

"Fine. We decided to integrate another small community. I've got a job for you."

"Oh? Do tell."

"The town is called Preston, and they've got the potential to become the area's breadbasket. There's a catch though – it seems their friends across the Rio Grande are becoming emboldened. It's not a serious problem just yet, but they're concerned. I've got a small job for you and Nick – we need to make a show of force to discourage cross-border incursions."

Bishop snorted, almost spitting his water. "Hmm? That's all?" he responded sarcastically. "Now tell me about the *small* job."

Terri tilted her head, obviously wanting Bishop to expand.

Her husband shook his head and continued to press his point. "Preston, as I recall, is just a crossroads sitting out in the middle of the desert. It's not the end of the world, but you can see the edge of civilization from there for sure. How are we supposed to send a message to our friends on the other side of the border? There are hundreds of square miles of absolutely nothing on both sides of the river."

Terri shrugged, "I don't know. I handle the decisions, and you implement them. I like our new roles."

"Very funny. I don't see anything 'new' in our roles at all. Seems to me it's been this way since we've been married." Bishop flashed a knowing grin at his wife.

Terri leaned across the table and covered Bishop's hand with hers. "You always come through for me too. There has to be a way to send a message."

"That task has historically been extremely difficult in this terrain. Every president for the last 25 years failed to secure that border. Too many canyons, too few fences and way, way too much unpopulated turf. Let me think about it though – I'll talk to Deke and Nick and see what ideas they might have."

Terri smiled and said, "Seriously though, it's probably worth the effort. I'm afraid we're going to see more and more of this sort of thing."

After their meal, Bishop convinced Terri to steer her golf cart to what once had been a 3-star motel on the town's main drag, and now served as temporary housing for visitors. Pulling into the parking lot, Bishop found Deke easy enough – the contractor was doing pull-ups using the building's second story rail.

"Trying to work off lunch?" Bishop hailed.

The panting man turned and smiled, extending his hand. "It's all conditioning and discipline – that's what makes the world go around."

"The council has blessed me with an old problem that needs a new solution. I thought I might stop by and see if the local high-tech bad asses had any ideas."

Deke laughed, "Well, this high-tech bad ass is at your service, sir. Do we have to overthrow a third-world government or something?"

Bishop grinned, "Naw... that would be simple enough. This is a tough problem… we need to display a show of force, visible over an expansive, lightly populated stretch of territory."

Bishop went on to explain the situation, Deke absorbing every detail. When Bishop finished, Deke whistled. "You're right, that is a difficult mission. Too bad we don't have air assets. That's the way to do it… a big ass parachute deployment."

Bishop snorted, "That's no shit. I was with the 82nd Airborne. We would do an annual exercise where an entire combat brigade would jump. People would come from miles around to watch the sky filled with paratroopers. It was impressive as hell."

Terri rubbed her brow, "How about a sky writer? We could paint a message in the clouds that read, 'Leave us the hell alone.'"

Both men laughed, Deke adding, "I would make the message a little stronger than that, but I might offend some of our more religious citizens and small children."

The idea sparked another thought. "Deke, didn't the allies drop hundreds of fake soldiers during D-Day in WWII? Seems like I remember seeing that in one of the Duke's movies."

"Yeah! I remember that. They were like little dolls and had firecrackers that started exploding when they got close to the ground. The plan was to make the Germans waste ammo shooting at fake paratroopers. Is there a doll store in Alpha?"

Bishop grinned at the concept, but then shook his head. "We've only got one pilot that I know of. There is a sign at the Alpha Airport advertising a sky diving school, but it didn't look like a big place."

Terri piped up, "Wasn't Diana a pilot in the Navy?"

"Even so, I don't think there's a big enough plane around to haul up a bunch of fake paratroopers."

Deke scratched his head, "You wouldn't need hundreds. If you got everyone's attention with some low flying planes… like fighters making a strafing run, and then dropped in 20 parachutes, it would make a good show."

"Some large explosions on the ground after the fakes had landed would make a lot of people think a battle was going on," Terri added.

Bishop snapped his fingers, "I know. We just send in the cops. We have one heck of a police force and a parking lot full of squad cars with pretty strobe lights. We'll just ask Sheriff Watts to provide a prominently visible presence in the area. Maybe even send our plane up to zoom over the region now and then."

"Folks, this is Deputy Ramirez, he used to patrol the area along the Rio Grande, including Preston. I'm sure his expertise will add value," Sheriff Watts began.

The mayor's office was full, the Coalition Council members all in attendance as well as Bishop and Nick. Once introductions were completed, Terri addressed the topic.

"The gentlemen from Preston said that the farmers along the river were in a state of uncertainty over a lack of fuel and a lack of security. We can provide the fuel necessary to harvest crops and for ongoing operations, but the security aspect is critical as well."

Diana continued, "We were hoping that a strong law enforcement presence would deter any cross-border incursions and help spread the word on both sides of the river that the people of Texas are well protected."

Both Watts and Ramirez nodded their understanding. The young deputy cleared his throat. "That area is sparsely populated on both sides of the river. Many of the farmers are isolated, several miles from the nearest neighbor. Sheriff Watts and I have estimated it will take 16 officers in order to establish a visible presence. Knowing the people in the region, I would guess we could cut that back by 50 – 80% after two weeks. Word spreads quickly along the river. Many of the families on both sides are related to each other."

Sheriff Watts added, "There may also be an opportunity to establish trade with the Mexican side. Their agriculture zone along the river is almost as large and productive. I think it is a safe guess that the farmers on the south side are suffering from many of the same issues as their neighbors to the north. If we offered fuel, transportation and other services, they might be happy to barter their harvest."

"Twice the breadbasket, perhaps," observed Diana.

Pete made a motion to dedicate the necessary resources to support Sheriff Watts with the establishment of security along the river. The item passed unanimously.

Preston, Texas
February 20, 2016

The small town of Preston had never seen such an event, at least as far as anyone could remember. The first indication that it wasn't going to be the typical day was the low buzzing of an airplane. Air traffic hadn't been common in the area before the collapse, none of the gathering citizens could remember a single flyover since.

At Terri's urging, officials from Preston had been visiting the local farmers for days, begging and even bribing the busy men and their families to come and witness what they promised was going to be a grand celebration. The public relations campaign had worked, the town's population nearly tripling in size due to the number of visitors.

The next eyebrow-raising event was a long line of police cars, complete with flashing lights, rolling down the highway and into the sleepy town. The convoy comprised ten vehicles in total, the sheriff even deciding to include his SWAT team and their menacing-looking armored van.

The law enforcement officers entered town with friendly smiles and warm handshakes, Sheriff Watts instructing everyone that the days' activities were intended to be a public relations event, not an invasion.

As the officers were mingling with the town's population, the plane reappeared overhead. Terri's script had included specific instructions for the policemen on the ground to make sure everyone's attention was focused on the air show.

Mr. Mills had worked for two days on the old Cessna 210, the aircraft originally used by Alpha's small skydiving business. The plane was designed to carry six passengers, but with Hugh's supervision, five of the seats were removed – the modification providing room for six fully equipped contractors and the pilot.

As everyone in Preston watched the small craft fly overhead, men began jumping out of the tiny plane. Most of Deke's contractors were airborne qualified, and soon the spectacle of colorful chutes drifting down toward the berg held everyone's attention. The event drew more than its share of "oohs" from the crowd – not something one witnessed in Preston every day. The fact that the skydivers were fully armed with battle rifles and load vests wasn't lost on any of the spectators.

The final phase of Terri's well-choreographed plan involved one last convoy rolling into town. Led by a police car escorting an 18-wheel semi pulling a flatbed trailer, a Class-A motorhome with shiny chrome wheels rounded out the last arrival.

The flatbed was loaded with 50-gallon barrels, stenciled with yellow labels identifying "gasoline," and "diesel." There were also a few smaller containers secured with rope ties, courtesy of Pete's bar in Meraton. Word quickly spread that the unlabeled, plastic gallon jugs contained moonshine and homemade beer. While loading the truck, Bishop had teased Meraton's mayor about the danger of storing his contributions so close to the petrol – the potential for fire or explosion being the gist of the humor. Pete had beamed with pride over Bishop's concerns.

While the cargo of fuel was obvious, the motorhome was not. The unit parked in the center of town and immediately began to discharge smiling and waving council members, while one of the policemen unfurled a large banner hanging on the side of the huge camper. It read, "The Alliance of West Texas Welcomes the Citizens of Preston." The council members immediately began shaking hands and congratulating the throng of residents, their intent of making each and every citizen of the tiny berg feel like they were important.

Terri paid special attention to the area farmers and ranchers. She and Deputy Ramirez were sure to visit and talk with each agricultural operation, inviting most to come inside the air conditioned RV and sit, take a load off.

"This is Miguel Hernandez, Ms. Terri. He operates the biggest spread in the area. I've known his family since I was a toddler," introduced the deputy.

After shaking hands and offering refreshments, Terri got right down to business.

"The towns and cities to the north need produce. We need every bushel of food we can lay our hands on. In exchange, we can offer security and fuel."

Mr. Hernandez smiled, his wrinkled, weathered face expressing the wisdom of a successful businessman. "We'll need access to more than just fuel to keep production levels high. We'll need fertilizer, insecticides, and other necessities. While my operation and many of my neighbors have some supply of these items, that inventory won't last more than a year at best."

Terri had anticipated the issue and chose her words carefully. "I can't guarantee anything other than fuel right now. We're expanding rapidly, so there's no way of knowing what resources we'll encounter during our growth. I wish I could give you a more optimistic answer, but I can't."

Hernandez seemed to appreciate Terri's honesty, accepting her response with a simple nod and smile. "What the most critical need at the moment is the irrigation system. We allocate water from the Rio Grande via a system of pumps and levies. That equipment requires constant maintenance and is beginning to fail."

"We have a potential source that may be able to help with this issue. Let me be clear about one thing, Mr. Hernandez, the council doesn't order or command people to do anything. My role is as a rainmaker – someone who connects private citizens together so they can prosper and improve their lives. Our government doesn't want to control or direct business, we want to get out of the way once the introductions are made. After we leave here, I'm going to meet with a businessman who may be able to fix or even expand your irrigation system."

"Expand? This would be an excellent possibility. My ranch was in the process of building an irrigation system to increase our tillable land by another 1,000 acres when the depression hit the economy. We never finished. Growing rice on this unused acreage would benefit everyone."

A few hours later, Bishop sat with Terri in the RV's lounge on the trip back to Alpha. "You look tired," he observed.

"I'm beat. I wish I could sleep while this thing's moving, but I can't."

"Don't overdo it, Terri. You're only human, and a pregnant human at that. Building a baby is a lot of work."

Terri nodded, leaning back and stretching out on the sofa. "We made a tremendous impression on these people today, Bishop. I received commitments of more food than I think we can consume in a year."

Her husband agreed, but then had a question. "I heard you talking to a couple of the ranchers about irrigation systems. I didn't want to ask in front of our new friends, but now I'm curious. Who did you have in mind to fix and expand their systems?"

Smiling coyly, Terri wagged her index finger at her husband. "You'll find out soon enough. No more business today, though. Would you be a good hubby and rub my feet?"

"Well, Terri, I would . . . but my arm hurts," Bishop smirked as Terri shot him a playfully intimidating expression.

Chapter 10

Alpha Texas
April 25, 2016

The man standing before the council was known to all of the mayors. Physicians were in high demand, an important asset to the community.

When Dr. Prescott had arrived at the eastern outpost, word spread quickly that a new sawbones was in town, the uplifting news raising morale even higher. The welcoming committee at the courthouse had made sure the arriving family felt at home.

Now, over a month later, Dr. Daniel Prescott had requested a hearing.

"Ladies and gentlemen, let me start by saying I appreciate every courtesy that has been extended to my family as well as all of the others who have relocated here from Midland Station. The kindness shown by the people of Alpha and Meraton should make all of you proud."

The doctor paused to clear his throat and then continued. "As you are all aware, those of us who once lived in Midland Station have formed our own social circles here in Alpha. It is comforting to see familiar faces when living in a new place, a natural desire to interact with people who share your history and experiences. We also share news from home, bits of rumor and gossip about the state of the friends and family we left behind."

Shifting his feet, the doctor continued, his voice now low and serious. "The news from home isn't good. Thousands of people are starving while a select few eat well. Personal freedoms are non-existent, the rule of an elite class enforced with an iron fist. The problems that motivated me and hundreds of others are deepening in their severity. I, and the others from Midland Station, feel the need to intervene, and that is why I stand before you today."

Making eye contact with each council member before continuing, the doctor proceeded to shock everyone in attendance. "We want to form an army... an armed force, and take back our city."

Terri flashed Diana a look while Pete grunted. DA Gibson's only reaction was a slight nod of her head.

"Obviously, we don't wield the resources to accomplish this action on our own. We would require the assets of the entire community to pull this off - weapons, training, and transportation to name a few. Now, I know this may sound selfish. I know my request presents an extreme risk to the people of the Alliance, but I believe the potential reward far outstrips the investment. Midland Station has oil refining, loads of engineering talent, and thousands of citizens that could contribute to our efforts to establish a new society here in West Texas."

Nick, sitting in the audience, leaned over and whispered to Bishop, "Here we go again, brother. Who said the plow was mightier than the sword?"

"Wasn't that the pen that was mightier than the sword?"

"It changed after the apocalypse, bro."

West Texas
April 28, 2016

Bishop stopped the truck outside T-Bone's hacienda, his attention distracted by the seemingly endless expanse of equipment, pipe, and discarded vehicles stretching off into the desert. While he had seen the boneyard from the air at night, it was his first visit up close, and the scope of the place was amazing.

Terri opened the passenger door and climbed down, her eyes amazed at the volume of equipment as well. Nick and Deke were in the back seat, both men having visited Mr. T-Bone before. A second truck full of Deke's contractors pulled up behind Bishop, the show of force deemed necessary in case T-Bone had a short memory of his prior commitments.

Zeus and Hercules were both on the front porch, neither animal apparently concerned with the new arrivals. Deke decided to avoid the gnarly beasts, just in case they didn't appreciate being shocked into submission.

T-Bone showed himself in the modest entryway, a wry smile on his face. "When you said I owe you one, you weren't kidding. I didn't expect you to call the debt so quickly."

Introductions were made, the team from Alpha relaxing after T-Bone's demeanor proved he indeed wanted to cooperate. The junkman invited the group into his home and offered refreshments as a sign of good will. Lyndon and a few of the other men were soon invited to the meeting, their attitude friendly and open as well.

Terri began, "Sir, we've discovered a potential new line of business for you and your group. The farmers and ranchers along the Rio Grande have need of someone who can fix and expand their irrigation systems. After what Nick and Deke told me of your operation, I thought it might be something you were interested in."

T-Bone took the carrot, his eyes brightening as Terri expanded on the needs down by the river. An hour later Terri had arranged to escort T-Bone and some of his workers to the river and facilitate introductions. Despite Terri's non-technical description, Lyndon was excited, sure that the boneyard and his crew had the necessary equipment and knowhow to improve the rancher's lot.

"I thought you were coming here to collect your debt," T-Bone commented to Nick, "Not to give us a golden egg."

"We're coming to the part about the debt, T-Bone," interjected Terri. "Is your crew capable of making some delicate modifications to a refrigerator trailer? Welding, sheet metal work – that sort of thing?"

Lyndon snorted, "I've got two of the best welders this side of the Pecos living here. Dad's not so bad with working metal either. What do you have in mind?"

It was Bishop's turn to speak, "We're going to address the situation in Midland Station, and we're going to do so using a very old trick."

"Trick?" asked T-Bone. "Would, by any chance, this trick allow me to keep Eva in their hospital *and* make an honest living again?"

Terri laughed, "It might… it just might."

"I'm in," replied T-Bone.

Midland Station, Texas
April 30, 2016

T-Bone and Lyndon stopped at the west side roadblock leading into Midland Station. An armed guard approached the semi cautiously until he recognized the driver. "Not seen you pass through here in a while," he greeted.

Smiling, T-Bone's voice was cocky. "I've got a trailer load of beef and veggies back there. I assume a man can still barter food for fuel hereabouts."

"Let's take a peek," replied the guard.

Lyndon climbed out of the cab and proceeded to the back of the trailer. Climbing up, he pushed up the latch and then opened the heavy door.

A slight mist formed when the outside warmth mixed with the cooler, refrigerated air from the trailer. The fog cleared quickly, revealing several hanging sides of beef, crates of melons, and other green vegetables.

Whistling, the guard asked, "Now where did you guys manage to get all that?"

"We've got a new source," replied Lyndon.

Nodding, the sentry stepped back to the concrete barriers and picked up a radio. A few minutes later, he received clearance to proceed downtown.

Obviously excited about the potential exchange of goods, Lyndon motioned for the guard to follow him back to the rear of the trailer. "Hey, I forgot I brought something special along. I don't have enough for everybody, so keep it quiet."

Intrigued, the man followed Lyndon. Opening the trailer's door again, the guard watched as Lyndon climbed inside and then waved for the man to follow. "Come on up and take a look. Maybe you can tell me what this is worth."

The sentry glanced around to see if any of his comrades were paying attention. They were not, so he climbed aboard and entered. Lyndon was almost to the front, pushing past the cold slabs of beef swinging with his passage. Following a few steps behind, the guard watched as Lyndon bent down and pulled a bottle of whiskey from a small crate. Reaching for the ultra-rare item was the man's last act.

Lyndon watched as a shadow appeared over the guard's shoulder and then a solid thud echoed through the confines of the trailer. The man facing Lyndon jerked slightly, and then his eyes went wide with disbelief before rolling to the back of his head. Nick appeared behind the collapsing man, and a moment later, he and Lyndon were stripping the clothing and weapon from the body.

Lyndon didn't really look all that much like the fallen sentry, but the baseball cap, shirt and weapon would pass a quick glance. Sticking his head around the corner of the trailer, he shouted at another guard, "Hey! You're not going to believe what these guys have back here," and motioned for the fellow to hurry and have a look.

When the second sentry rounded the corner of the trailer, Nick and Lyndon shoved their weapons in his face, and then two were down.

At Nick's signal, the car in line behind the semi started honking its horn, the woman driver sticking her head out the window and yelling, "What's taking so long? What are you guys drinking up there?"

Her shouting brought a third sentry to check on the commotion, and he was disabled within seconds. The remaining three security men working the roadblock didn't put up a fight when several gun barrels appeared in their faces.

Bishop and Deke survivede the situation with cautious smiles. Nick, reaching for his radio, transmitted, "The west side roadblock is now open."

After the semi and Terri's car pulled through the concrete barriers, four school busses arrived, each full of men. Nick waved them through and then jumped in the back of the trailing pickup.

The convoy used an abandoned strip mall as a staging area. Men poured out of the school busses, weapons pointed skyward and grim expressions on their faces. After 15 minutes of organization, one last briefing of orders, objectives and well wishing, groups of men began trekking toward downtown Midland Station. The refrigerated semi pulled out, rolling slowly to the center of the business district.

Lou looked out the high-rise window on the western side of Mr. Lewis's office, anticipating the arrival of what his men at the roadblock had described as a big-ass trailer full of food. Such a shipment arriving unexpectedly would surely improve the boss' mood, and perhaps ease the tensions of the day.

There were three company warehouses used to store consumables, the largest of which was two blocks away from the headquarters and well within the inner ring of security he'd established for his principal.

Lou smiled when he spotted the oncoming 18-wheeler, the elevated perch providing a clear view of the over-sized grocery cart as it rolled up to another checkpoint. A wave of pride passed through his mind as he watched the sentries open the trailer for an inspection, despite everyone with a radio knowing "that junk dealer dude," was delivering a truck full of calories.

The contents of the trailer must have been as advertised. A few moments later, the semi was waved through and began its slow progress toward the warehouse.

T-Bone wasn't the most experienced over-the-road truck driver and required three attempts to back the trailer properly to the loading dock's ramp. Normally, the Midland security personnel would have been harassing the driver to death, but the contents of this load provided a free pass to the unskilled teamster. The armed men were standing on both sides his rig, waving their arms in an attempt to guide him in.

Finally, T-Bone got it right, cheers erupting from the handful of men loitering inside the warehouse, waiting to unload. T-Bone and Lyndon climbed out of the cab, both men carrying paper bags that immediately piqued the interest of the security guards.

Motioning for the armed guards to follow, Lyndon lead the men on his side of the trailer like a mother duck trailing a line of her offspring. T-Bones' side of the big-rig was more of a gaggle, the excited sentries eager to see what was in the sack.

Inside the trailer, wedged in a three-foot wide welded compartment, Nick, Deke and the Darkwater operators sat in silence, cramped in the tiny space by their number and the heavy assault packs full of equipment. The hidden section at the very front of the trailer was Bishop's idea, his concept of using the "ol' Trojan Horse routine," initially drawing laughs and chuckles. The deft touch of T-Bones' welding and manipulation of sheet metal had changed everyone's opinion, the boneyard owner creating a nearly invisible hidden compartment, which included peepholes and slots in the roof for circulation.

As the driver and his son occupied the guards with their bags of liquor, Nick and Deke observed the situation through the tiny, cleverly disguised opening on each side of the trailer. "I'm good over here," whispered Deke.

"Let's do this," came Nick's hushed response.

The man who was squeezed into the middle reached down and twisted a latch and then shoved against the wall. A section opened, and the contractors began pouring out of their hide.

The first dockworker they encountered was hefting a side of beef onto his shoulder, the man's eyes opening wide when he looked up into the barrel of an M4 carbine, the owner of the rifle whispering, "Make a sound and die."

The remaining workers were subdued without a peep, the group of frightened men locked inside a large freezer. "We probably should remember to come back and get those guys," one of Deke's men noted.

The comment was met with a shrug from his buddy, "Let's hope there are enough of us alive to come back and let them out."

Nick and Deke watched T-Bone and Lyndon outside, each man joking with the huddled security men. T-Bone handed the remains of his bottle to a guard and announced, "We've got to get going. You guys finish that off," as he turned to walk back to the cab. "Lyndon! Let's get moving."

"Okay, dad. Let me see if they've finished unloading."

T-Bone climbed into the cab, revving the truck's diesel engine and reaching for the horn.

Nick nodded to Deke, both men pulling canisters from their vests, readying to spring on the distracted guards. In unison with T-Bone's noisy manipulation from the cab, the two flash-bang grenades arched through the air, their metallic impact the last noise the surprised guards would hear for several minutes.

Two brilliant strobes flashed, the white light accompanied by a thunderous wave of sound pressure that completely overwhelmed the nervous systems of the huddled sentries. Some of the victims fell over while others maintained statuesque poses, unable to command their bodies to move.

The assaulters fell upon them, kicking away weapons and shoving the stunned men to the ground. Nylon ties bounded legs and hands in a flurry of activity, and they soon joined their co-workers in the walk-in.

Lou had moved away from the window, his view of the semi blocked by the outline of the warehouse's facade. The sounds of the diesel racing its motor caused him to glance up for a moment, the big truck's loud horn blasts even more noteworthy. He had just taken a step toward the window when the muffled reports from the grenades reached his ears. Unable to identify the source of what seemed like small explosions, he hurried to the window, but couldn't see anything but small puffs of black smoke rising over the warehouse roofline, evidence of the diesel's exhaust.

Keying his radio, Lou requested a status report and waited for a response. He repeated the transmission after a minute, his heart rate increasing when no one answered the inquiry. The rattle of distant gunfire brought home the realization that something was terribly wrong.

Bishop, with Terri at his side, stayed at the back of the formation approaching downtown Midland Station. His emotions had been on a rollercoaster ride all day. A strong desire to be in the thick of the entire affair, an almost uncontrollable urge to lead the assault had been squelched by Terri's rather clever manipulation.

"You can do anything you want," she had stated, "Just keep in mind that the baby and I are going to be right at your side. You can charge in like a one-armed tornado of death and destruction for all I care – but I'm going to be standing right beside you. Your risk will be shared by your child and wife. Your call."

"That's bullshit," had been his response. "I'm feeling much better and getting stronger every day. I can do this. Those guys going into Midland Station need me… we need every man we can get."

Terri had crossed her arms, the look in her eyes making it clear her decision was granite reinforced with steel – unyielding and immovable. "I'm not telling you what you can or can't do. I'm simply stating that I'll be right at your side. Right where a good, loving spouse should be. So whatever role you take, include me in the deal. I'm not letting you out of my sight."

Bishop had rumbled around pissed the rest of the day, his disposition ranging from pouting to outright anger. He eventually settled on taking charge of the reserve unit, which unless something went horribly wrong, wouldn't be in danger.

The busloads of fighters from Alpha had split into three groups. Team A was comprised of 35 shooters and assigned to assault the headquarters building from the south.

Team B, also 35 marksmen, would strike from the west. Nick, Deke and the Darkwater operators had the job of creating a diversion, hopefully tying down a large number of Midland's security forces.

Bishop led the final group of 15 rifles - the reserves. If A or B got into trouble, were flanked, or about to be overrun, Bishop's team would come to their aid.

All of the Alpha planners with combat experience had demanded a simple approach. Complex plans always failed in the fog of battle. Simple, flexible schemes worked. Every single person carrying a rifle knew not only his job, but the objectives and position of the other teams. Nick had drilled everyone on the operation repeatedly, the rehearsals taking place at an abandoned building in Alpha for three days prior.

The reserve forces stayed back from Team A and B, those groups rushing forward to their jump-off positions. In addition to riflemen, three medics accompanied Bishop's team.

As the last man in Team B's column disappeared around a corner, Bishop's radio announced, "A is staged," followed a minute later by "B is staged." Less than 30 seconds after that, all hell broke loose in Midland Station.

Nick's earpiece buzzed with the reports that the two primary teams were in position, he and Deke making momentary eye contact and nodding. *Here we go,* thought the big man. *Let the party begin.*

The men with Nick had a very simple job – keep the enemy tied down.

Despite being a full block away from the headquarters building, the storage warehouse had been chosen as Nick's Alamo for several reasons. The first was the obvious utility associated with Bishop's idea of using a Trojan horse. Secondly, the walls were constructed of poured concrete, an excellent barrier against light weapons. Finally, there were very few windows or doors built into the facility. All of those factors made it a solid base for defense.

Most of the indigenous security presence in downtown Midland Station was concentrated around the Lewis Brothers Oil high-rise office building. Sandbagged outposts were staged at many street corners, with mobile patrols randomly moving around the downtown streets. Whoever had designed the defense was clearly willing to give up everything but the actual HQ building - the scouting reports indicating a 30-member quick reaction force barracked within the main structure.

Once A and B were in place, Deke wasted no time signaling his men, two of whom promptly aimed their rifles at the outpost on the next block and opened fire.

There were six Lewis Oil guards stationed at each intersection around the HQ building. Each post had built "V" shaped, sandbag fortifications, primarily designed to protect against projectiles thrown by rioters.

The defenders had no clue of Nick's presence in the warehouse. Some of them were leaning on the waist-high wall of sandbags, while others huddled in a small group, waiting for the next vehicle to approach their position. Less than 100 yards away, four of the guards went down with the first burst from Deke's shooters, the other two falling into the pit, more from being startled than any reaction to take cover.

Gunfire erupted from the opposite end of the warehouse at the same time, the target being another checkpoint one street over. The defenders' causalities began mounting quickly.

Lou pulled the earphone from his head, thoroughly frustrated by the device. The two-way radios being used by his men weren't designed for military operations, and the channel quickly became overwhelmed by the garbled cries of frightened, confused men.

From his top floor window, Lou could see his people scrambling for cover at several different locations. One intersection, only a block away, told a different story – the pavement littered with unmoving men lying in pools of blood.

By the time he re-inserted the earpiece, the radio chatter had died down somewhat, and he seized the opportunity to transmit. "If you aren't being shot at, stay off the fucking air. I repeat, stay off the air unless you're under fire."

Five seconds later, a very high-pitched voice sounded through the earpiece. "This is Ma... Ma... Martin on 3rd Avenue. We're under attack! Everyone's dead!"

That report was quickly followed by another, a panicked man yelling, "They're in the warehouse! They're in the warehouse!

There must be a hundred of them!"

The warehouse? Lou's gaze focused on the structure, his view mostly obstructed by a block of restaurants, shops and other retail stores that resided between him and the storage facility in question. Glancing back at the bodies lying in the street, he realized the angle was right, the two muffled explosions now making sense.

Broadcasting over the static filled channel, Lou began to issue orders. "We've got intruders in the Elm Street warehouse. I want all LBO security personnel from all facilities to converge on downtown. Leave only a skeleton crew at your facilities and immediately send everyone else here."

One of Deke's men waved his hand in the air, the signal-based communication necessary, given the incredible level of noise being generated by gunshot reports bouncing off the hard, interior walls. Deke watched as his operator flashed five fingers twice, and then pointed toward the distant hills.

We've got ten hostiles approaching from the east.

Deke dispatched two additional operators to that corner and watched as the four men identified individual targets among themselves. Were it not for the end result, the team's activity bordered on art, a choreographed dance with exquisite, balanced timing.

Rising together, the four operators fired at once and then quickly acquired secondary targets. *An exquisite move in an foul business*, thought Deke. After breaking the back of the eastern assault, the two shooters returned to the center of the warehouse, waiting for a different corner to require reinforcement.

Over the next few minutes, the defenders of Midland Station mustered three different efforts to oust the men occupying the warehouse, all three assaults resulting in significant carnage among the attackers. Bodies littered the streets, the cries of begging wounded drowned out by the constant discharge of weapons.

Nick scurried to Deke's central position and took a knee. "There're going to catch onto this pretty soon. I can see trucks arriving with more and more of their men. Somebody with half a brain is going to stop these suicide charges and try something clever. Do you think it's time to go up top?"

Deke pondered the question for only a moment before nodding. "Sure, why not? So far, they've not even pressured us. We can handle this level of bullshit with two less people. Have fun."

Nick and another man jogged to a nearby wall and pulled down an access ladder. The rusted steel rungs led to a trapdoor high in the ceiling above. Each operator pulled on a different pack and extra rifle case and began climbing.

Pushing open the hinged door, Nick bobbed his head out the opening and then quickly ducked back down – just in case someone had beat them to the spot. Seeing nothing but air conditioner units, exhaust fans, and a couple of electrical boxes, Nick climbed out and made for the nearest HVAC condenser. The contractor soon joined him, both men scouting the area with intense scrutiny.

"That tall building one block over is the only structure I can see that we've got to be careful of," the man reported. "If they get a sniper on that roof, he'll have his way with us. Other than that, I think we're in good shape."

Nick agreed with the report. "You take the east corner, I'll take the west. Let's get off this roof after five minutes. We'll do as much damage as possible and then skedaddle back down."

The contractor nodded and then added, "Good hunting," as he scrambled for the east side.

Nick pulled the .308 out of the case and slammed home a full magazine. *I'm going to talk to Bishop about this rifle when we're done. I wonder if he'll trade something for it.* Dismissing the clearly insane thought, Nick bent low and ran for the west corner.

The extra height exposed far more of the surrounding urban area than was visible from the first floor below. Without even needing the optic, Nick could see clusters of men gathering in the street four blocks away, their leaders pointing, shouting and performing other animated movements.

Nick uncapped the scope, deployed the bipod, and calculated the distance to the largest group of men. He judged the range at 450 meters, an easy reach for the .308 caliber weapon. Glancing at his counterpart, both men signaled with a thumbs-up that they were ready to engage.

An auto-loading, magazine fed, semi-automatic rifle like the one in Nick's hands was a significant game-changer on the modern battlefield. With a well-trained operator, the weapon was capable of projecting terminal force at over 900 meters. While bolt-action sniper rifles had possessed that same range for over 100 years, the modern replacement could deliver accurate rounds at three times the rate of fire, and that could be devastating.

Only 20 years prior, a sniper in Nick's position would select a single target, normally whoever appeared to be in command. While that one man was killed more often than not, the time to work the bolt and reacquire another target afforded all other combatants the time to take cover. The tactic was effective – critical - but did not result in large numbers of the enemy being taken out of the fight.

Weapons like the one now being aimed by the two rooftop-operators changed all of that. They could deliver red-hot slugs of death as fast as a man's finger could pull the trigger. The .308 round used by both shooters fired super-sonic bullets, which translated into the lead arriving on target before the sound of the shot could be heard by the victim. There was no warning, no time to duck.

Nick picked his three targets, judging he could fire that many rounds before the men below could react. One last glance at his co-sniper signaled both were going hot at the same time. Long-distance death began pouring from the warehouse rooftop.

The optic, click-adjusted for a drop of several inches, was ready. Nick centered on a man standing in the bed of a pickup, clearly issuing orders to a large group of armed men.

Nick whispered, "Cry havoc… and let slip the dogs of war."

The former Green Beret pulled the trigger, the weapon's recoil aligning the crosshairs instantly on another foe – that lead on its way before the empty case of the first shot rolled to a stop on the nearby tarpaper surface.

It was a slaughter. The defenders of Midland Station weren't combat soldiers with finely honed reflexes and nerves accustomed to incoming fire. It took the gathered throng far too long to realize they were under attack, longer still to seek cover. Even then, there wasn't any place of protection. Several of the faster reacting men dove for the various vehicles parked in the street, and Nick ignored them. He also ignored those who stood dazed by the carnage around them, instead focusing his shots on the men running for cover. Few made it off the street.

Round after round poured in, the withering fire quickly exhausting the targets in the open. With the street littered with bodies, Nick began focusing on the easy marks – the men hiding around the vehicles. One after another, 168-grain balls of jacketed lead punched the sheet metal originally made in Detroit. Car doors and fenders only made the impact of Nick's shots worse for the victims. The bullet would enter one side, expand and fracture, exploding out the other in dozens of lethal fragments that shredded flesh and ended life. There was no place to hide, nowhere to escape the death raining from the muzzle of Nick's rifle.

And then it was over. Nick watched his rooftop partner take two more shots, and then his weapon fell silent as well. Time to go.

As Nick started to disappear through the trapdoor, he stopped, something catching his eye. The sun glinted on the piles of shiny brass casings lying on the black tarpaper background of the roof. The glitter of the brass catching his eye for a moment, and then he was distracted by movement in the window of the tall office building beyond. The outline of a man was visible on the top floor, the sun positioned perfectly to penetrate the tinted glass. The man was pointing at Nick while talking into a radio.

Nick disappeared, stepping two rungs down the ladder. Looking past his boots, he said, "I just spotted something important, I'll be down in just a second. See ya at the bottom."

His partner acknowledged the statement with a nod and proceeded to climb down.

Nick's precarious perch made unslinging the AR10 a difficult balancing act. Inserting another magazine was even more difficult. A few moments later, with a round chambered, his boots firmly locked around a rung. Nick popped out of the trapdoor opening and began firing at the top floor of the Lewis Brothers Oil headquarters building.

Lou was reversing his orders. For five minutes, he had been screaming into the radio, first trying to warn his people of the snipers he had spotted on the warehouse roof. After the two shooters had begun slaughtering his men, his next set of commands had been for someone to get on the LBO building's roof and kill the two men that were decimating his security staff.

After finally receiving a transmission that acknowledged an ex-police sniper was on his way to the top of the LBO building, Lou watched in frustration as the two men below retreated back inside their stronghold.

Red-faced mad and pacing back and forth in front of the floor to ceiling windows, his vision went to slow motion as the glass beside him exploded inward, the glistening shards resembling snowflakes floating through the air. Lou's brain couldn't command his legs to move, the mental signals out of sync with his nervous system screaming at his muscles. Another window became a geyser of glass, the impact causing an instinctive twist to avoid the projectiles flying at his face.

The third round slammed into Lou's back just below his rib cage, the expanding lead exiting an inch below his sternum. Collapsing to his knees, the dying man looked down at a golf ball-sized hole in the middle of his chest. He was dead before his face came to rest on the glass-littered carpeting.

Nick had no way of knowing if he had hit anything or not. He did speculate that top floor was where the headman would reside and decided it wouldn't hurt to deliver a strong message to the enemy leader. After splattering 20 rounds into the top floor, he ducked down into the interior and began his descent to the waiting contractors below.

"It's time to fire the signal," he shouted to Deke over the sporadic gunfire. "We just broke their back."

Reaching into the pack at his feet, Deke pulled out a plastic, large barreled pistol and hustled for a door. Pointing the odd gun skyward, he pulled the trigger. The flare popped out of the muzzle and rose several hundred feet into the air before a small parachute opened, slowing the pulsating red light's descent. It was time for Teams A and B to begin their assault.

Bishop watched the signal rocketing skyward and exhaled with relief. Nick wouldn't have sent the flare if things weren't going their way. He was also a little surprised at how soon the contractors had determined it was time to begin the final phase. Things must be going well, indeed.

Like the pinchers of a giant vise, the two main teams rose from their positions and began moving for the objective - the headquarters of Lewis Brothers Oil. After waiting for both groups to advance, Bishop waved his small force forward to keep the reserves in a prime position to react if their help was needed.

While Nick's team had inflicted significant damage to the defenders, the advancing teams began to meet resistance. The defense wasn't spirited. Random pockets of desperate men fired at the approaching Alpha teams, their efforts answered with overwhelming fire. Many died, most surrendering quickly.

One group of LBO men managed to hole up inside of a limestone bank building, the thick, stone walls providing better cover than most structures. The Alpha teams bypassed the barricaded men, making their position irrelevant.

Block after block fell, the defenders pushing back at a steady pace. One group of Midland personnel, retreating in a near panic, made the mistake of exposing themselves to the contractors positioned in the warehouse. They paid dearly for the blunder.

Disarmed men with their hands on the back of their heads began arriving at Bishop's location. At first, it was a trickle, but as the teams advanced, more and more of the defenders decided they were done fighting. Unhappy with the drain of manpower required to keep an eye on the prisoners, Bishop decided it was a better job than his people entering the fray.

Terri appeared at his side. "Bishop, why don't you let them go home?"

"Huh?"

"Just use that real stern grumble of yours, and tell them to go home. Look at all of them - they're beaten... whipped and disarmed. I don't think they'll rejoin the battle."

Bishop began studying the group of men sitting nearby. She was right. He walked over and shouted, "Listen up! Every man who gives his word he won't reenter the fight can go home. Go home and hug your wife and kids... go home and keep your ass out of sight until this is all over."

At first, the prisoners didn't know how to react. Several of the disheveled men just looked at one another with blank stares and shrugging shoulders. Finally, one man stood and approached Bishop. "I'm done. I won't shoot at anybody. Can I go home?"

Bishop nodded and the man hurried away. The example motivated several others, and soon all the prisoners were shuffling toward their homes.

Cameron, at Lou's insistence, had been sheltering in an interior office on the top floor. The sounds of Nick's raking the windows had stopped some time ago, the ongoing silence following the attack raising the boss' confidence and curiosity. Crawling to his office's entrance, the destruction caused him to inhale sharply and pause.

Summoning all of his courage, the businessman crawled toward the open air that had once been a wall of windows. The remains of the glass panes were scattered throughout the workplace, the razor-like shards forcing Cameron to hug the wall, carefully plotting a path to avoid being sliced. He ignored his security chief's lifeless body.

Peering over the edge, his attention was drawn to crackling gunfire. It took a bit to decipher what was going on, but after a few moments, it became painfully obvious that his security forces were falling back.

After watching the ensuing gunfights below, Cameron reached the conclusion that the barbarians would soon be at the door. His heart raced at the prospect of capture, morbid visions of being at the mercy of unknown assailants filling his mind with terror.

Crawling backwards through the glass, he made it to the threshold and them rose and ran for Linda's desk. There was a special radio there, the device sitting in a recharging mount so it would always be ready. Picking it up, he quickly turned it on and selected the predetermined channel.

"This is Cameron Lewis," he broadcasted. "I am ordering Plan-B implemented immediately."

His hands shaking, Cameron listened intently to the static, a prayer forming on his lips. Just as he decided to reissue the command, a voice sounded through the static. "Yes, sir, Mr. Lewis. We'll be there in five minutes."

Exhaling from relief, Cameron dropped the radio and made for the stairwell.

Bishop watched the teams closing in on the office building, their final objective in clear view. The remaining defenders were being pushed into an ever-tightening space, those choosing to continue the fight becoming more desperate.

Causalities were now flowing back to the medics in Bishop's group, the wounded being carried or limping in on their own. Terri had taken to helping with the treatment, some of the gunshot wounds extremely serious.

"We need to get some of these people out of here, Bishop," his wife announced. "We need to get them back to the doctors, or they're not going to make it."

Bishop agreed. Raising his radio, he read the street signs into the microphone and called for the ambulance to come forward.

A short time later, the sound of an engine drew Bishop's attention, the pickup truck designated as the ambulance racing up to haul off the wounded. As men were being triaged for transport, Terri pointed to an injured man and asked the medic, "Why isn't this man in the first load? He seems to be in the worse shape."

The medic grunted, answering with a low, "He's one of theirs."

Bishop heard the exchange and nudged the care provider. "That doesn't make any difference here. The worse go first, no matter which side they're on."

"If you say so," grumbled the man as he moved on to help with a bandage.

Bishop was about to pull the guy aside and give him a good lecture when the loud whirr of a helicopter reached his ears. His first instinct was to grab Terri and head for cover, but he quickly determined that the craft wasn't headed in their direction.

Scanning the horizon, he found the approaching bird, watching fascinated as it flared its nose and hovered slowly over the LBO office's rooftop. Gradually the chopper descended, eventually landing on top of their primary objective. Only the top of the spinning blades was visible from below, but after only a minute, it became clear they were increasing their revolutions.

The helo lifted off and banked sharply toward the north. It took a moment before Bishop realized everyone had stopped shooting. *That was it*, he thought. *The king is routed and running from the field - his army will collapse.*

It began as a murmur in the distance, slowly building volume until it became a loud roar. Terri appeared at Bishop's side, her eyes staring toward downtown with wonder. "Bishop, what's going on? What's that noise?"

"They are all shouting at the top of their lungs, babe. They're shouting because we've won."

Looking down at his wife, Bishop smiled and then pulled her tight in an embrace. After enjoying the moment, he said, "Oh, shit. I almost forgot Hugh."

Reaching for his radio, Bishop transmitted, "Mr. Mills, Mr. Mills – time for the drop."

The reply came quickly, "On my way."

As the celebration began to lose steam, a small airplane appeared on the horizon. The craft began making slow, low circles over the Midland Station area, the buzzing engine causing everyone to look up. A trail of white snow appeared behind the plane as two passengers began empting bags of papers out the side door.

Eventually, the sheets drifted to the ground, curious residents all over the city venturing out to see what was going on. Some of the papers fell close to Bishop and Terri, one of the men gathering a handful from the ground and bringing them over.

Terri held up the sheet. At the top was a picture of Dr. Daniel Prescott. The boldface type below the photograph declaring:

My fellow citizens of Midland Station. Today is a great day for our city. The unelected leadership of Mr. Cameron Lewis has ended, the result of your fellow citizens and our neighbors from surrounding towns banding together to force a change. For a short period, I have agreed to lead our community, my selection voted upon by residents of Midland who left our city seeking a better life, but who could not abandon those of you left behind. We have organized and returned to make a change – a change for the better.

I will make one promise to every citizen of Midland Station: We will hold elections within 30 days. Democracy will return to our great city.

For those of you in the employ of Lewis Brothers Oil, fear not. Petty retribution will not be tolerated. Drop your weapons. Prepare to return to your jobs, prepare for a better life as free men. My heart is full of amnesty, and my head excited about the future. Work with us for a better future. Participate in the rebuilding of Midland Station.

Bishop looked up to see Nick and the contractors walking his way. He exhaled as a headcount proved no casualties. While the group looked tired, the random laughter made it clear their spirits were high. As Nick came within earshot, he yelled to Bishop, "I need to talk to you about this rifle, brother. I think it considers me its new master and wants to follow me home."

Camp David, Maryland

May 1, 2016

President Moreland looked across the conference table at the Colonel, his eyes tired and bloodshot. He gently positioned the report on the polished surface, neatly aligning the edges of the paper to create a neat stack. It was a nervous habit everyone in the room had grown accustomed to.

"Our progress is painfully slow, gentlemen," the chief executive began, "while other regions of the nation appear to be making headway on their own."

Pushing back his chair, the Commander in Chief nodded at the report and continued. "Every week, I read reports of our failures, setbacks and schedule delays while at the same time I see small, regional groups making great strides. I am frustrated to say the least – almost embarrassed at our apparent ineptitude."

The president stood and began pacing around the table. "I've heard all of the excuses. I've been a patient, understanding man. But this," he said, pointing at the report, "This is unacceptable. How is it that the finest minds in the nation, with all of the resources of our federal government, can't pull ourselves out of the mud – while a bunch of small towns in West Texas have managed to accomplish... no, exceed every goal we've set for ourselves?"

Moreland glanced around the room, not really expecting any answer to his rhetorical question. "How is it that a few clusters of people, without any appreciable resources, have accomplished what our entire array of military, government, and civilian assets appear to be incapable of? How can this be?"

Again, no answer to the executive's question was offered, and he hadn't expected one. Moreland moved back to the report, picked up the stack and thumbed through the pages. A look of disgust crossed his face as he held the paper for everyone to see. "These people are in the desert, for heaven's sake! They don't have water or nuclear power – they live on some of the worst scrub land I've ever seen. I know some of the key players – I've met them personally. They are not Harvard graduates! They are not MIT scientists! How is it they can accomplish what seems to elude us?"

Pointing to the Colonel, the president prodded, "Colonel, you've had more recent experience in the region than any of us. What's their secret? What are they doing that we are not?"

"Sir, comparing the progress of that isolated region to the rest of the country defies logic. The population density, resources and infrastructure pre-collapse was on a much smaller scale than the eastern corridor or other major population centers we are dealing with on a daily basis. They didn't suffer nearly the percentage of population losses that the rest of the nation incurred."

"That may be true, Colonel, but the fact remains that they have electricity, agricultural production, basic health care, and rule of law. The vast majority of the rest of the nation does not."

The president moved again to the assessment and flipped through several pages until he found what he was looking for. Holding the sheet high in the air, he continued. "This is a report from the commanding officer of the Houston garrison. He is now processing requests for key individuals to leave his jurisdiction and relocate to West Texas. According to this report, doctors, engineers, and nurses... all wanting to leave... all wanting to pack up and head off to a better place. This commander even refers to the situation as a 'brain drain.'"

Moreland paced the room for a few moments until his posture indicated he had reached a decision. "We can't tolerate this, ladies and gentlemen. We can't have individual kingdoms sprouting up all over our nation. In addition to West Texas, we know of several other examples. We have independent groups in North and South Dakota, Utah, Wyoming and parts of Idaho, Northeast Georgia... all have staked out their own little domains while we are struggling to jumpstart the entire country. They are all Americans, and they all need to contribute toward the greater cause, not create their own little city-states. This is not an acceptable model for governing all the people. We're not living in the Middle Ages for heaven's sake."

The president stared at an older man at the end of the table. "Dr. Harris has warned me that if this trend continues, the United States will look like continental Europe during medieval times – trifling, independent organizations that preclude the amalgamation of the population into a broader, regional government. We can't let this happen – recovery is proving difficult enough without our focus being divided by competing governments."

"In addition," the chief executive continued, "Dr. Harris recommends that these area organizations be compelled to contribute their excess in order to enhance the greater good of the country as a whole. His view is that allowing the people of West Texas to eat well while their neighbors in Eastern Texas are starving will eventually lead to a series of conflicts, or small civil wars. These regional disputes, according to Dr. Harris' analysis, will slow down the recovery - even more so than what we've experienced to date."

"Sir," the Colonel spoke up, "I don't believe that is a wise strategy. I think that these regional governments have formed solely to fill a void, and for no other reason. If anyone tries to 'take' what they're producing, it will increase tensions, not eliminate them."

"You may be right, Colonel. That's why I'm going to send you on a little fact finding mission. I want you to travel to West Texas and see what's going on firsthand. I've arranged transport and expect to see you back here at Camp David within ten days."

The meeting adjourned with the Colonel in a foul mood. Taking his time while gathering the documents and papers spread out on the table, he sensed a presence over his shoulder. Turning, he saw the smiling face of General Marcus.

"General."

"I want you to know I'm on your side with this one. I think it's not only morally wrong, but also bad policy to even consider what Dr. Harris is proposing. I'm not sure my voice is enough to persuade the president, but I'm with you."

"Thank you, General. That means a lot."

"Let's wait and see what your trip uncovers. I'll volunteer to be a sounding board for whatever you want to talk about. I'll see you when you get back."

Alpha Texas
May 3, 2016

Bishop strained with pushup number 47, sweat running into his eyes while his arms were screaming for mercy. He lowered his weight, determined to make it to 50. Sucking in another lung full of air, he opened his eyes and discovered two pairs of boots standing directly in front of him.

He looked up to see Kevin was the owner of the smaller pair, his ex-boss, the Colonel occupying the larger.

"Life is obviously too easy here, son. You're getting soft," the older man hailed.

Standing, wiping the sweat on his pants, Bishop extended his hand for a vigorous greeting with the man who had been his mentor for years. "It's good to see you, sir. What a pleasant surprise."

The Colonel got right down to business, "Sorry to drop in unannounced, Bishop. I was ordered by our new Commander in Chief to come and see what was going on out here. Your little social experiment has drawn the attention of the higher-ups in Washington."

Turning to Kevin, the Colonel said, "Thank you young man," a clear message that Kevin's services were no longer needed. As Kevin left, Bishop wiped his face with a towel, trying to gather his wits after the surprise.

"Colonel," Bishop said, "I'm not the person you need to see regarding our success. Terri, Diana, Pete, and a host of others are primarily responsible for the gains we've made. I've been convalescing mostly, since I saw you last."

"I know, son. The feds have been watching what's going on around the country more than what you're aware of, I'm sure. I wanted to stop by and speak with you first because we know each other – we worked together for years. We speak the same language."

"Go on, sir."

A look of disgust crossed the older man's face. "My current task is to not only evaluate your success, Bishop, but also to determine what level of assets your organization can contribute to the rest of the nation. I don't like, nor agree with my assignment, but as you're no doubt aware, we don't always get assigned to tasks we like while serving others."

"I'm not sure what you mean by 'assets your organization can contribute.'"

Shaking his head, the Colonel replied, "President Moreland and his staff think that all of the country should pool resources. You may not realize it, but your little civilization here in West Texas is doing far better than the majority of the country. Some people back east believe your wealth should be redistributed for the good of everyone."

Bishop smirked, "That will fly like a lead balloon, Colonel. We've earned what we have with blood and sweat. No one has helped us one single bit."

Nodding, the Colonel continued, "I agree. I agree 100 percent, son. Like I said, I don't like my assignment, but I do what I'm ordered."

"Well, sir, I'm not in charge around here. You should probably talk with Diana and Terri. I'll be happy to help you find them."

The Colonel agreed. Bishop poured his guest a cup of coffee and then hustled through a quick shower and change of clothes.

The two men left the church, the Colonel deciding he'd prefer to walk instead of riding in the standby golf cart. "It was a long flight out here, son. I need to stretch these old legs."

As the duo made for the courthouse, one of T-Bone's trucks honked as it approached, the bed of the pickup and long trailer full of old pipe sections, valves and other miscellaneous parts. T-Bone was riding shotgun, his son Lyndon behind the wheel.

"Hello, Bishop!" the junkman greeted.

"Hey, T-Bone. How's the irrigation project going?"

"This load of pipe should finish another hundred-acre section. I'm hoping to turn on the water by dusk," the man answered, a smile brightening his face.

"That's great news, sir. I'll pass it along to Terri."

"I'll be bringing up a trailer full of melons on the return trip. The work crews from Midland Station have been picking some beauties. They're perfectly ripe, and the juice just runs down your chin."

"Save me one, would ya? Nick and Diana are having us over for a cookout tonight, and I'd love to surprise them with some fresh fruit," Bishop responded.

"You got it! See ya later, Bishop."

Watching the truck pull away, the Colonel grunted. "Irrigation? Work crews? Melons? Do you know what 90% of the country's population would give to hear those words?"

The two men continued their walk. "Sir, that man owned a junkyard full of old oil field pipe and equipment. Terri came up with the idea to recycle it. We do a lot of recycling. Look, over there," Bishop said pointing to a nearby home.

They paused, watching a woman carry a bucket to her garden. She tossed what appeared to be table scraps onto an unplanted section and then started covering the organic material with a hoe. Bishop continued, "We don't waste anything. See those goats over in the park. They keep the grass down. They are milked daily and someone gathers the manure twice a week to be used as fertilizer."

Shaking his head, the Colonel responded, "Amazing. I can hear the pride in your voice, Bishop, and I don't blame you."

A few minutes later, the two men arrived at the courthouse and found Diana and Terri inside working with a group of people who wanted to reopen Alpha State University next summer. The meeting was just breaking up when Terri noticed the Colonel and immediately rushed to hug the embarrassed man.

"Colonel, oh my goodness! How long... when... I am so surprised to see you."

"I'm sorry to just drop in, Terri. I was just explaining to Bishop that my visit was mostly business, not pleasure."

A serious look crossed Terri's face at the man's words. "Well, let's go to my office and you can explain to me what's going on."

"In summary, the federal government is looking at your activity and growth with an eye toward skimming food, energy, personnel, and other assets. Words like 'society equality' and 'redistribution' are being used again. My mission is to find the facts and report back," the Colonel finished.

Bishop was in shock, the audacity of the entire affair overwhelming his sense of right and wrong. Diana seemed to be in a similar state. Nick was difficult to read.

Terri was no-holds-barred angry, the pressure rising higher and higher as the Colonel divulged more and more details. Bishop was glad she wasn't wearing her pistol.

When it was clear the Colonel had finished, Terri meandered to the window, apparently in deep thought. Turning, her voice was calm and smooth.

"Colonel, are we talking about trade? Do you foresee the federal government offering to purchase our excess resources?"

Smiling, the visitor said, "Perhaps, but that's not how I would see it going down. My guess is some smart cookie would figure out a way to tax your economy."

Terri shook her head, "Pfffffft – and what would they do with the money? Seriously, Colonel, we have bank vaults in our towns that are stuffed full of US dollars. We limit the supply to keep the value steady, but the West Texas Alliance is sitting on piles of cash. I can send you back to Washington with suitcases full of the stuff, but what good would that do?"

The Colonel smirked, "Not all taxes are paid with cash, Terri. Let me give you an example; men from Washington could visit your refinery and calculate that your population only needs a gallon of the output per day. The rest could be shipped to other parts of the country as a tax. The same could be done with your food."

Bishop couldn't help himself, spitting out, "Bullshit!"

Diana added, "That's a load of crap, Colonel."

Terri cleared her throat, her voice remaining calm and collected. "Colonel, when you and I visited in Bishop's hospital room, we discussed what you termed, 'the beast.' Do you remember those conversations?"

Nodding, the visitor answered, "I do."

"During that discourse, you said to me that the only way to control the beast was to limit its size."

"I did."

"What I'm sensing here, Colonel, is the beast has lost some of its girth with the collapse, and now it's hungry. It wants to begin consuming the juicy morsels it sees growing around it. Would you agree with that assessment?"

"I would."

Terri stepped closer, her voice going low. "Over my dead body, Colonel. You can take that message back to Washington – over my dead body. We welcome trade and barter. Value given for value earned is acceptable. Seizure, taxation or confiscation is not. We started one revolution in this country over taxation without representation, I'm sure the current president doesn't want to start another."

The Colonel wasn't intimidated, "Terri, be careful. You're not dealing with rational men. The beast is cornered, wounded, and irrational. It can strike without warning. You will lose in any conflict. A platoon of tanks, a few air strikes and four attack helicopters would wipe out everything you've worked so hard to build. This beast is dangerous, unpredictable, and desperate."

Bishop spoke for them all, "I'd rather see what we've built destroyed than give it away, Colonel. I'm confident 99 percent of our citizens feel the same way. There's too much of what caused our country to fail in Washington's message. Too much of the old school."

Smiling, the Colonel nodded his understanding. "I'm glad to hear you say that, Bishop. I'm going to return and try to talk the president into working with you, not trying to take over. I'm not sure of my chances. I hope you all know that I'm with you, but that doesn't mean my reasoning will carry the day."

Terri was back to staring out the window again. After a long moment of silence, she turned and declared, "We need an army. We need a military that will make anyone think twice about pulling the type of bullshit the Colonel is speaking of."

Epilogue

Fort Bliss, Texas
May 20, 2016

"Sir, you'd better come to the front gate. We have some, ummm, unusual activity going on."

"What kind of activity, Lieutenant?"

"There is a woman down here claiming to know General Westfield. She has several large trucks with her and is asking for a meeting with the base commander."

"Trucks?"

"Yes, sir. Semi-trucks... like you'd see on the interstate or something."

"Who is this woman, Lieutenant?"

"She said to tell the general that 'Terri is here to see him'... and sir, she has about 300 armed men with her."

"What?"

"Yes, sir... that's my estimate."

"Stand by, Lieutenant."

The major set the phone down on his desk and promptly made for the general's door. Knocking loudly on the frame, he waited until the base commander looked up and acknowledged his presence. "Yes, Major?"

"Sir, I hate to disturb you, but I just received a very odd call from the guard post at the front gate. It seems a woman by the name of Terri is requesting an appointment with you by name. In addition, sir, the LT on duty claims she has 300 armed men and several semi-trailers with her."

The general tilted his head, finally responding. "Terri? As in Terri and Bishop?"

"No idea, sir."

"Well, let's go see what all this is about, Major."

The HUMVEE braked to a halt in the midst of a bustle of activity. The lieutenant had decided that the armed force so close to his post was a potential threat, and requested reinforcements. Two rifle squads answered the call, and there was a tank on the way.

General Westfield exited his transport with his usual air of authority, returning salutes and striding briskly to the iron bars and concrete barricades that blocked the entrance to his base. Peering through, he immediately shook his head and chuckled aloud.

Sitting in a lawn chair 75 feet in front of his base was a single woman wearing a bright pink maternity outfit and sipping what appeared to be an iced beverage of some sort. She was adorned with oversized sunglasses, a floppy beach hat resting on her head.

"Did you stop by to invite me to the beach?" the general shouted out.

Terri rose from her perch and set the glass down on the pavement beside her chair. Despite the large baby-bump, she swayed gracefully toward the gate, her smile warm and genuine. "I thought you military types were gentlemen, General, yet your men kept me cooling my heels out in that hot sun."

The general squeezed through the small walkway and approached the brightly colored young lady. He started to extend his hand, but Terri canceled the gesture by opening her arms for a hug. Embarrassed but unable to resist, he returned the embrace.

"Where's Bishop?"

"Oh, he's over there with all those men. He was concerned there was still a warrant out for his arrest. I told him he was overreacting, but he decided to be shy for a bit."

The general's gaze followed Terri's pointing finger to where three large semi-trucks were parked about 300 meters from the gate.

The base commander could see dozens of men in the vicinity and no shortage of rifle barrels pointing in the air.

"Please, invite your husband to join us. I give you my word as an officer and gentlemen - I won't have him arrested."

"General, I'll be happy to arrange a reunion, but I didn't travel all this way just so you men could exchange war stories. I came here to talk business."

The general's senses were on high alert. Terri was acting strangely, her attitude bordering on cocky. He had a million questions regarding the trucks and the armed men. His curiosity overrode his concerns, mostly because of Terri's projection of self-confidence and partly because the whole scene was just plain weird.

"Business? What kind of business?"

"Why don't we get out of this hot sun, General? Why don't we go over to my office where we can discuss things in comfort?"

"Your office?" the general replied, thinking Terri was joking.

Terri pointed back toward the idling semi-trailers. "I have an air conditioned Class A motorhome with cold drinks in the fridge. It *is* a little extravagant, but it makes a good place to conduct business and allows this pregnant girl to travel comfortably."

The general was still trying to digest it all, his mind reeling from the peculiarity of the scene before him. "Terri, what's this all about? I've not seen you or Bishop for months, and all of a sudden you show up at my base with a head full of attitude and a parade full of weird."

"General, I have a proposition for you. The trucks are a sample and to prove I can deliver what I would like to propose."

"Okay, fair enough. Why don't you come on into *my* office, and we can talk."

Smiling at the uncomfortable man, Terri responded, "General, you have *my* word as the Ambassador of the Alliance of West Texas that I won't have *you* arrested. Besides, I have brought along a few key players that I'm sure will add value to our meeting."

"The Ambassador... of what? What the hell are you talking about, Terri?"

"Just come along and hear me out, General. No harm can come from listening. Can it?"

It took a while for the base commander to sort it all out. His gaze moved from the gate to the convoy and back to Terri as he processed it all. Finally, he shrugged his shoulders and muttered, "Very well."

Terri took off her floppy hat and waved it above her head. Turning to the general, she explained. "I'm due in two weeks and walking long distances isn't part of the equation. You'll forgive me, sir, but I'd prefer to ride."

A golf cart raced from behind the convoy of trucks, the driver stopping while the general and Terri seated themselves. As soon as the passengers were ready, the man zipped the electric car around and headed back to the waiting line of trucks and men.

"Pull up behind the first truck, please." Terri asked the driver.

After stopping beside the first trailer, Terri and her guest exited the small vehicle while another man opened one of the trailer's rear doors. Inside, along one wall were pallets full of burlap-colored bags, each one stamped with the bright red label "BEANS." Along the other wall, sides of beef hung from two rows of hooks, the frosty air of the truck's refrigeration unit misting around the meat. "All three trucks are full of food, General. We are now producing more than we consume. We can provide more than enough to feed your entire base and a significant portion of El Paso."

Stunned, the base commander seemed to have difficulty turning away from the cargo. "Where... how... what the hell is this Alliance of West Texas, Terri?"

Hooking the hesitant officer by the arm, Terri gently guided him back toward the waiting cart. "I'll explain everything, General. Let's get inside some more comfortable accommodations."

The humming ride deposited its passengers at a large motorhome idling at the rear of the convoy. Despite the shock of the moment, the general remembered his manners and opened the door for Terri while helping her up the steps.

Inside sat Bishop, Nick, Diana, and DA Gibson, all of them rising when the general entered the camper. After introductions and handshakes had been completed, Terri asked everyone to be seated, some of the attendees opting for the dinette chairs while others found the couch and loveseat that dominated the space.

Terri began, "General, some four months ago, the small Texas towns of Meraton and Alpha held elections. Electrical power had been restored, and a full recovery was in process. Before long, Fort Stockdale joined in and then finally Midland Station, and Odyssey. The small farming communities along the Rio Grande came to the party as well. During this process, it was decided someone was needed to coordinate the commerce and trade activity among the different towns as well as facilitate sharing of resources for municipal projects. A sort of state government, if you will."

While Terri paused to take a sip of her lemonade, DA Gibson took over. "General, Terri was appointed Ambassador by the leadership of these multiple municipalities. According to the Constitution of the great state of Texas, we are now the only legitimate government in the area. Additionally, Terri is being courted as our first governor."

The general looked around from face to face, not sure that he understood what he was hearing. "So, what's this have to do with me? Are you offering to supply Fort Bliss? I'm sure the United States could arrange a supplier agreement with your... whatever you want to call this organization of yours."

Nick took his turn. "And how would you compensate us, General?"

"Why we would pay you like any other military supplier... with checks from the Department of the Treasury."

Everyone around the table laughed at the remark, the attitude troubling the Army officer. "Checks?" asked Terri. "And where might we cash these checks, sir?"

Flustered, General Westfield threw up his hands. "I don't know. It's not my responsibility to negotiate supply deals. That's handled out of the Pentagon."

Terri cleared her throat and the room became silent. After toying with her glass, she raised her head and stared intently at the military man across the table. "Sir, we want Fort Bliss. We want the forces and facilities under your command."

"What!" the General exploded. "That's preposterous! I already took an oath to the United States of America, and I don't intend on breaking it. If that's what this is all about, I'm afraid you're wasting your time."

Bishop let the man's words settle and then gestured in the direction of the front gate. "When was the last time you received any resupply, General? When was the last time you heard from the Commander in Chief?"

"That's got nothing to do with this, Bishop, and you know it. You, of all people, should understand that I can't just go around joining whatever rebel cause comes knocking at my door. Your little band of misfits isn't any different than the Independents and their harebrained scheme."

"That's not entirely accurate, General," chimed in DA Gibson. "Our government is constitutionally elected and completely legitimate. The previous governor's term expired in November. By rule of law, the state was in violation of our founding document. This administration is entirely within the law."

Bishop didn't give the general a chance to respond, "Besides, General, we're not asking you to swear any allegiance. We're asking you to surrender and avoid causalities."

"What! What in God's name are you talking about, Bishop? Are you mad? Why, just one of my tanks could roll right out that front gate and wipe your forces from the face of the earth. I have over 200 of the most potent war machines on the planet, son. I've got 24,000 fighting men to back them up."

"Yes, that's correct… you could. We wouldn't stand a chance against your forces. But how long can you last, General? We know you're running low on food, fuel… just about everything. If it comes to a fight, *you* know we're not going to let any trucks in. There's no way you can be resupplied from the air – so how long can your current situation last?"

The General's face turned red, and he threw his hands into the air. "This is ridiculous!" Pointing his finger around the table, he pushed back. "You know what I should do? I should roll right out here and confiscate this food. I should then send men into your towns and liberate both the people and the supplies that are found. That's what I should do. The Alliance of West Texas - my ass."

Nick grunted, his voice cool and calm. "We anticipated that might be your reaction, sir. Let me advise against that course of action. We are over 100,000 people strong. Every last man and woman will fight you to the death. We will burn our food and fuel before we let you take it. You can't win that fight. Our forces will fade into the desert and hide, waiting until your tanks run out of go-juice and ammo. We'll scorch the earth in front of you and harass your lines of supply. You'll accomplish nothing but extreme loss of life on both sides."

"You're bluffing, and son, I don't bluff."

"I'm sorry you feel that way, General. We know your men are deserting at a rapid pace. Many of them have already joined us. They tell us of rationing, canceled training exercises due to a fuel shortage and zero supply trucks entering the gate. Morale is already low, General. Ordering your men to kill their fellow Americans isn't going to improve that fact. On the other side, our people are strong, happy, and moving forward. Our survivors are tough-minded people who see a chance at a better life. We're organized and prepared to make any invader pay. We'll make what the Russians experienced in Afghanistan look like a trip to Disney World if you deploy against us."

Terri stood, her expression demanding the floor. "I don't like all this talk of fighting and killing. General, I gave my word no harm would come to you, and we've said all we have to say. You've heard our proposal. Please take a few days and think it over. If you wish to surrender, you can send a message to our HAM radio operators. In the meantime, as a gesture of our sincere appreciation for all you've done for Bishop and me, and as a sign of our goodwill, please accept those trailers of food. My driver will return you to the gate."

Shaking his head, the General stood and looked from face to face one last time. Without another word, he strode to the camper's door and exited.

As he drove off, Nick exited behind him and issued orders for the semis to be unhooked from the trailers and for everyone to prepare to move out.

A few minutes later, General Westfield exited the golf cart and marched toward the front gate. Two majors and a colonel had joined the waiting crowd, more curious than anything.

“What was that all about, sir?” asked the base commander’s aide.

“Major, when was the last time a general in the United States Army surrendered without firing a shot?”

Made in the USA
San Bernardino, CA
22 August 2013